BLOOD LIKE MAGIC

LISELLE SAMBURY

Margaret K. McElderry Books

NEW YORK • LONDON • TORONTO • SYDNEY • NEW DELHI

MARGARET K. McELDERRY BOOKS
An imprint of Simon & Schuster Children's Publishing Division
1230 Avenue of the Americas, New York, New York 10020
MARGARET K. McELDERRY BOOKS
is a trademark of Simon & Schuster, Inc.
For information about special discounts for bulk purchases, please contact
Simon & Schuster Special Sales at 1-866-506-1949 or business@simonandschuster.com.
The Simon & Schuster Speakers Bureau can bring authors to your live event.
For more information or to book an event, contact the Simon & Schuster Speakers Bureau
at 1-866-248-3049 or visit our website at www.simonspeakers.com.
Interior design by Hilary Zarycky
The text for this book was set in Athelas.
Manufactured in the United States of America
First Edition
2 4 6 8 10 9 7 5 3 1
Library of Congress Cataloging-in-Publication Data
Names: Sambury, Liselle, author.
Title: Blood like magic / Liselle Sambury.
Description: First edition. | New York : Margaret K. McElderry Books, [2021] |
Summary: After failing to come into her powers, sixteen-year-old Voya—a Black witch
living in near-future Toronto—is forced to choose between losing her family's magic
forever, a heritage steeped in centuries of blood and survival, or murdering her first love,
a boy who is supposedly her genetic match.
Identifiers: LCCN 2020027953 (print) | LCCN 2020027954 (ebook) | ISBN 9781534465282
(hardcover) | ISBN 9781534465305 (ebook)
Subjects: CYAC: Witches—Fiction. | Magic—Fiction. | Families—Fiction. | Love—Fiction. |
Coming of age—Fiction. | Blacks—Canada—Fiction. | Science fiction.
Classification: LCC PZ7.1.S2545 Bl 2021 (print) | LCC PZ7.1.S2545 (ebook) | DDC [Fic]—dc23
LC record available at https://lccn.loc.gov/2020027953
LC ebook record available at https://lccn.loc.gov/2020027954

To Black girls everywhere:
You can be more than a slave or a lesson for someone else.
You deserve to be a witch or a dragon tamer.
To fall in love with a vampire or lead your friends against a villain.
You are more than the best friend or sassy comedic relief.
You are the hero.

AUTHOR'S NOTE

As much as this novel is set in the future, it also discusses the past and is still affected by topics that permeate our present. Some of these discussions, while important, can be triggering, and as such, it's vital to me that you're aware of these topics before reading.

Content warnings: whipping scene within the context of slavery, gun/police violence, discussion of and character with an eating disorder, blood/gore/violence, death, substance abuse/addiction, mentions of child neglect

CHAPTER ONE

There's something about lounging in a bath of blood that makes me want to stay until my fingers shrivel enough to show the outlines of my bones.

My toes peek out of thick ruby ripples. Slick drops slide off my fingers and splash with an echo in the tub like spicy pone batter dripping off a mixing spoon.

"Sorry to stop you waxing poetic, but you need to get out of the tub." My cousin Keis slouches against the doorframe of our bathroom. The toilet is so close to the bathtub that you have to prop your feet on the ledge when you pee.

She blows a breath out of her nose and crosses her arms. The powder-blue robe she's wearing is embroidered with a *K* for Keisha. Our oldest cousin, Alex, made one for everyone in the family last Christmas. My canary-yellow robe with a *V* for Voya is hanging up in my room.

"Don't call me Keisha, even in your head," she says, casually reading the thought off the top of my mind.

Sorry. Even a year after Keis got her mind-reading gift, I still sometimes forget that she has it.

Granny used to say that Keishas were bad. To fry Granny's battery, Auntie Maise gave the name to *both* her twin girls. Keis, as she insists on being called, is pronounced "KAY-ss," like something you put glasses into instead of the more natural "KEY-shh," which sounds like a delicious egg-and-spinach tart. I figure this is a way for my cousin to differentiate herself even more from her sister, who she's clashed with since birth on account of their shared name.

My cousin clenches her jaw. "Keisha is annoying and obsessed with her feed and dating. *That's* why we clash. Taking those pictures with her ass stuck out like she's some sort of NuMoney tagalong. For what? So some stranger can give her a five-star rating?"

I like Keisha's feed. She makes living outside the downtown core look glamorous, and I find her open sexuality kind of rebel feminist. It is a lot of boobs and butt, but at least she's proud of it?

Keis pulls off her headscarf, and curly ringlets bounce out of its hold. The roots are a black 1B and the ends blond 14/88A. I bought the sew-in wig online for her birthday. "Yolanda," it's called. It looks real for fake.

Keis opens her mouth.

Not fake, sorry. It's real hair, but it's not yours.

Having someone inside your head constantly is an experience. By now, I'm used to it. Sometimes it makes things easier because I have a best friend who can comfort me about something I feel shitty about before I even tell her. And sometimes it makes things harder, like when I feel shitty because I know I'll never be as smart or strong or talented as Keis, and I have to see her face shift as she pretends she hasn't heard the thought.

I press the small button on the bath keypad. It's embedded, crooked (thanks, Uncle Cathius), in the white tiles lining the tub. The steam icon lights up neon green, and the installed jets feed heat into the blood bath. I shiver as the warmth hits me.

Every minute I spend here is another I don't have to pass downstairs. I should be enjoying this time, not spending it dreading what comes next.

Keis's lip curls. "Don't tell me you turned the heat on."

Okay, I won't. I hug my legs to my chest. "Why do I need to get out right now?"

My cousin sags against the door. "I checked on your food, as you bossily messaged me to, an hour ago. It's been ready. We want to eat, but Granny won't let us touch anything until you come down. It's a special dinner to celebrate *your* Bleeding, after all."

I don't know if non-magic girls get excited about puberty, but it's a big deal in the witch community. At fourteen and fifteen, I was disappointed when nothing happened, but not everyone can be an early bloomer. Or an early-late bloomer, given that witches tend to get their periods later. But I always felt like sixteen would be my time. Every day since my sixteenth birthday a couple of weeks ago, I've been in a constant state of anticipation, waiting for the moment that finally happened a few hours ago.

I was in the living room, packaging our beauty supplies with Mom and Granny. It started as a sort of uncomfortable wetness in my underwear. Which, let's be honest, happens sometimes. I already had two weeks of getting my hopes up over false alarms, so I wasn't going to be quick to jump to conclusions. Until that feeling expanded to the point where I thought I, a sixteen-year-old girl with a typically functioning bladder, had wet myself. Which, in hindsight, is so embarrassing a thought that I'm glad I didn't say it aloud. And I'm doubly glad that Keis wasn't around to hear it. But when I stood up to go to the bathroom and check things out, there was a single trickle of blood that dripped down my loose pajama shorts.

Sometimes, the things that change your life are physically small and mentally enormous. Like that little crimson droplet sliding down my bare leg.

I screamed with excitement.

Mom screamed with pride.

Granny screamed for me to get off the rug before I stained it.

I borrowed a pad from Mom so I could slow the bleeding while I rushed around the kitchen trying to get my own Calling dinner in the oven before finally getting into the bath more than an hour later to properly celebrate. I hadn't moved for another couple of hours since.

My Bleeding isn't just a witch's typical massive overproduction of body fluids brought on by the perfect unexplainable mix of genetic predispositions, hormones, and magic, meant to represent the blood of our ancestors. It's also the first step in my Coming-of-Age, of the challenge of becoming a witch.

Which was really hacking amazing until I remembered that I could fail and not inherit magic at all. Now my Bleeding is the only bright spot in this situation. An irony that I haven't missed.

The more Keis pushes, the more I want to stay in the tub. Once I step out, the rest of my Coming-of-Age will start. There won't be any turning back or slowing down.

"I'm naked," I whine.

"Wow! I didn't notice."

Keis is kind of mean. No, not kind of. She is. The closer you are to her, the worse she gets. I've known her since birth and therefore get an equal amount of love and vitriol.

I'm sure it's because Uncle Vacu did her birthing, and he's got a strong negative energy. Not because of the Mod-H addiction. He's just an asshole. Maybe because he's the oldest. But technically, he did all our births. It's a miracle someone like him could have a daughter as caring and loyal as our cousin Alex. If proper genetic sequencing had been around when Uncle was born, it would have shown a vulnerability to addiction and low impulse control. Employers wouldn't have been able to stop him from being a doctor, and they shouldn't—I mean, the human rights concerns would be all over the place—but for his own safety, none would have given him clearance to handle addictive drugs.

Not that we could ever afford detailed medical data like that. Applying for a job would be the only way he could have found out. Even if they did have the technology for it then, they wouldn't have given him the sequence data. They give you enough genetic info to keep you alive. Why offer more for free when NuGene can charge you a premium instead?

I sink deeper into the bath so only my eyes are visible—two dark, almost-black irises peeking out. The blood glides against my lips like our Thomas Brand lip butter.

I look up at Keis's unamused expression and say, "Remember when NuGene was a dinky start-up white people used to find out how many different types of white they were?"

She cracks a smile and lifts her chin to the ceiling. "I'm six percent British, two percent Irish, and ninety-two percent Canadian."

I snort.

"And that sequencing is yours for a budget price," Keis drawls.

The "budget price" works out to a month's mortgage for a fancy downtown condo. And that's just for basic DNA data. What they charge for genetic manipulation makes my stomach clench.

"Is she still in the tub?" Mom screeches from down the hall.

Hack me.

Mom rips the door open and barrels past Keis into the room. She's got her hair cornrowed and tucked away under a wig cap. The braids peek through the skin-color nylon. Not the ebony of our skin, but a light, almost-pink beige. Wig caps our skin color exist but somehow never come for free in the package.

I don't get any privacy here. According to Granny, our ancestors are always listening. Meaning that my family has a long history of being nosy. It's hard to imagine Mama Orimo, who died sneaking fellow slaves from the scorching sugarcane fields of Louisiana to chilled freedom in Ontario, would spend her afterlife spying on us.

Our family lives in secret among people who don't believe in anything without genetic proof, much less magic. Watching us would bore the hell out of her.

Mom tightens the drawstring on her pale green nightgown and stares down at me with a weary smile. "Congratulations on your Bleeding. This is a beautiful moment. You're transforming into a fledgling witch. But I'll be damned if I let you spend the entire night soaking in blood."

"Isn't that part of it?" I ask. For a girl, Bleedings mean you have a long, luxurious bath, and the blood strangely makes your skin extra soft, and then everyone in your family has a special dinner together to celebrate you. Like an extra birthday.

The male equivalent is a lot less exciting. When I asked Dad about his, he shrugged it off as more of an inconvenience. He got the same inexplicable volume of blood everyone does, but if you don't have a period, it has to come from everywhere else: eyes, nose, mouth, and he said with a cough, "private areas." He just showered it off without bothering to make the moment special like most guys do.

Showered, like it's nothing!

Everyone else picks whatever sort of celebration, if any, feels right to them.

"Yes, your bath is a part of it," Mom says, plopping a hand on her hip. "And no, you can't stay in there forever just because. It's time to move on and get ready for tomorrow."

My chest tightens, and I tug my arms around my knees, tucking my whole body into something smaller as if that'll help me avoid Mom's attention. The Bleeding is just the first step of a witch's Coming-of-Age. Tomorrow I'll have to face my Calling. One of my ancestors will appear before me and give me a task that I need to complete to come into my magic and get my gift. Any witch can shed blood and do a little spell. A gift is different.

It's unique to each of us, written in the way our genetic code shifts after passing the Calling.

Mom narrows her eyes. "I'm not asking again. Get out of the tub." She doesn't raise her voice, but she does use a mini utility blade to slice her thumb, then casts a quick spell with the blood dripping from her cut. Suddenly, the blood I'm sitting in turns frigid. My bath thickens and clumps in a way that makes the homemade Dutch fries and curry sauce I had at lunch rush up my throat.

She points at the tub and swirls her index finger. In response, the bath liquid imitates the motion, and clots the size of tennis balls graze against my legs. I slap my hands over my mouth as previomit churns in my stomach.

Mom throws her whole arm forward, and the blood and clots get sucked down the drain in one massive wave. The aftereffects of her magic pull against the hair on my body like static cling.

What's left is me sitting naked in an empty bathtub so dried up inside that I'm sure I'll never have another period again.

Keis rolls her eyes at me.

Mom's chest heaves as she lets out a few short, panting breaths. Only she would overstretch her magic bandwidth for drama.

My cousin grabs my towel from the chrome rack on the back of the door and throws it at me. Not that there's any point in using it since Mom's spell cleaned the blood off my body.

As I stand and wrap the towel around myself, Mom stabs a finger at me. "You need to get out of your head. This isn't just a celebration of your menses! It's the first part of your Coming-of-Age. Your Amplifying ceremony to trigger your Calling is tomorrow night! Get serious."

Mom is bringing up the exact thoughts that I want to avoid. Now that I've had my Bleeding, the ancestors could theoretically Call on me anywhere they want at any time—on the toilet, while I'm doing a product delivery, in the middle of cooking dinner—to have me perform a task of worthiness so they can decide whether or not to bless me with magic.

Which is exactly why everyone is going to be doing an Amplifying ceremony tomorrow. It's supposed to force my Calling to happen when we decide so I can do my task in a more ideal environment and have a better chance of passing. Plus, having my whole family around will give me a bit of a boost from their magic, which might impress whatever ancestor is conducting my Calling enough for them to give me a stronger gift. If we didn't do it, I would still have a Calling, but at least this way I wouldn't have to look my ancestor in the eye and do a task while I'm reaching for toilet paper or something equally mortifying.

Most ancestors won't Call the same day as your Bleeding, but either way, the countdown to tomorrow has started. In twenty-four hours, I'll know whether I'll get to be a witch or . . . not.

I wish I could shrink back into the bathwater.

"Bath *blood*. Just because it's in your head, doesn't mean you can't at least try to get things right," Keis says.

I said she was mean. Didn't I say that?

The mirror flickers when I step in front of it before coming on fully—it's an older model Mom got on sale. My skin has the smoothness the blood bath promised, but it's still dry. I pump our Thomas Brand All-in-One Face Serum and Moisturizer into my hands and slather it over my hickory-brown skin.

The reflective surface of the mirror shifts to show the top stories from my feed once my hijacker chip connects. An alert of a new rating comes up. I tap on it and get a small image of a guy who looks Dad's age, and the rating he gave me at the streetcar stop near our house.

Four stars from Bernard Holbrook.

Beautiful young girl. Could smile more.

Mom stabs her finger on his profile picture. It smudges

the mirror. "I'm gonna report this guy. Look at how old he is! What's he doing sending creepy ratings?" She selects the report button next to his profile. Her eyes continue to rove over his photo, likely looking for a witch mark—the telltale dot within an almond-shaped oval inside a round circle that our kind hide in online profiles, résumés, storefronts, and more so we can recognize our people.

There's no mark on this guy's page.

Mom crosses her arms and shakes her head at the mirror as if it'll relay her disgust to Bernard and fluffs a bit of my hair. "I know this is scary, and you have trouble with choices sometimes, but your Calling is happening tomorrow whether you're ready or not. It's important you pass. And I know you will. But just . . ."

Try harder? Do better? Be *better?*

"Get dressed," Mom commands, giving up on whatever she planned to say before. "I pulled the dinner you made out of the oven. You're welcome."

"Thanks." It starts as a mumble, but I know Mom hates mumbling, so I force my voice into something normal.

She points at Keis. "Please help her pick out a white dress for dinner. Cathius loves that virginal trash, and he'll be difficult about participating in the Amplifying ceremony if he doesn't feel catered to."

Keis quirks a smile. "Yes, Auntie."

With that, Mom leaves the room. I slather on a leave-in before grabbing a jar of coconut oil from under the sink and scooping up the white cream. It melts from the warmth as I rub my hands together and massage it under my thick curls into my now desert-dry scalp.

Usually when I wash my hair, there's a routine of pre-conditioners, natural shampoos, leave-in conditioners, Thomas Curling Custard, gels, and heatless curling rods, but I've spent too much time in the bath to do all that. I'll just have to live with undefined but moisturized curls for now. With magic, everyone else can do their hair at four times the speed I can. Eden and I are the only ones who can't. Not until after we pass our Calling.

I twist my lips into a scowl. "I guess I have to find an uncle-approved white dress." Or rather, Keis is supposed to help me find one, since according to my mom, I "have trouble with choices," which apparently also includes decisions at the monumental level of clothing options.

"She didn't mean it like that," Keis says. "You know Dad won't like anything you pick. It would be an annoying choice for anyone."

Uncle is a frequent stain on the apron that is my life, but there's no way to leave anyone out of this ceremony. More blood means more power, and everyone is hoping I have a strong gift. The adults use their gifts for income, and pooling our money is how we can all stay together in this house. When Granny and Grandad were young and less established, they got loans against the value of the house to help support our family, but the payments and interest grew until managing it was just as expensive as creating a mortgage for our technically mortgage-free home.

Living in Toronto isn't cheap, and we're only managing to break even while other witch families thrive. Our homemade beauty products appeal to the types who want non-modded handmade products, but modded beauty supplies are more popular by far, and we sure as hell can't afford genetically modified ingredients. That's the thing about modded stuff. Some of it is cheap and costs much less than something non-modded, and some of it is so hacking expensive you could never hope to afford it. Which means that most of our customers are witches and a small amount of non-magic families who know our powers are real and our products are the best, even without mods.

If we had money, real money, we could rub elbows with the

sorts of people who hire for the exclusive and frequently elusive internships or can afford the expensive university education reserved for company-funded and rich kids.

Sure, we all went through the government-mandated minimums. Got our elementary school credits with Johan, whose witch school was accredited and able to give them. And then we got our minimum high school credits, which was really only two years of work, half online and half in person. I just finished mine a little while ago.

Keis is the only one of us who takes classes beyond the minimum, and that's solely in defiance of being pigeonholed into using her gift to make a living. She still goes to high school to get extra credits, mostly online but sometimes in person, with the same stubbornness that drives her refusal to use or hone what should be a strong gift to get ahead in life.

She scowls at that thought.

"You're doing amazing for someone fueled by spite. Your grades are higher than any of us have ever gotten." For real. She does at least a dozen courses every year and aces them. Sometimes, I'm sure she has a bigger ambition, something she's trying to achieve, but she pretends like it's 100 percent to piss off the family.

"It's not spite, it's a protest of this family's insistence that your worth is determined by your gift." She gnaws on her lip. "Not that it matters if I can't do anything with my education. I have no connections for the sort of internships that send you to university and no money to go on my own."

She's echoing everything her parents and the rest of the adults have said before. High school credits are well and good, but if you can't get an internship at a good company, the amount of high-paying jobs available drops way down. Not to mention, the chance to go to university is basically zero. We could never afford it. Keis would need to find a company willing to pay for her to go.

The barrier between having and not having a legitimate internship has always been too huge for the rest of us to bother. It's why we rely on magic. But Keis is different.

"You need to put yourself out there." I don't get why someone with the potential of a gift like she has wouldn't want to use it, but I support her. "There are a ton of internship Q&As out there. I'll help you find stuff." I scroll through my phone and sign up for notifications from places I know have great placements.

My cousin raises her eyebrows. "Why can't you do that for you?"

"Do what?"

"Find courses and internships. Create a backup. Stop being so worried about your gift and focus on something you can choose."

"Because I'm *so* fantastic at choosing." Mom wasn't wrong. I'll do anything to help my family, but I've always been terrible at making decisions for myself.

"Vo."

"And do what? Fight with hundreds of applicants to get a minimum-wage internship that goes nowhere? I could never land something with a good company." I don't know why she hits me with spam like that. If you're not good enough to get into a major corporation, you're wasting your time.

A strong gift is all I have to hope for. It's the special sauce we witches have to turn plain potatoes into gourmet mash. And right now, mine aren't anything more than dirt-covered russet.

I glance at Keis. "Nothing to say about that?"

She crosses her arms. "You don't need me to pump you up. Your Calling will be fine, and you'll end up with a great gift."

Doubtful.

I stare at myself in the mirror, finger curling the odd piece of hair into a springy twist.

When I asked my cousins what the ancestors who Called

them gave as a choice for tasks, they were all different. Papa Ulwe had Keisha watch two identical ancestors he brought along from beyond the grave named Sara and Sue for five minutes. She closed her eyes while they mixed themselves up, and she had to choose which one was Sue. Keisha's always been unnervingly intuitive, so it worked out for her. And she ended up with a gift along the same lines, specific and uncomfortable intuition.

Mama Deirdre laid out a dozen outfits and demanded that Alex choose the perfect one for her. My cousin, in a move that is so her, decided that none of the clothes were good enough and sewed something brand-new for Mama Deirdre, who, of course, adored it.

Mama Nora bombarded Keis with the memories of ten ancestors and told her to choose the single false one or be forever trapped in their minds until her body died. Her Calling didn't follow the rules and had higher stakes than it should have. It was unpredictable in a way that's terrifying.

Because that's the thing about a Calling: it depends on what ancestor you get. Whoever Calls me will not only set my task, they'll also decide what gift to give me at the Pass ceremony once my Calling is complete. One ancestor will choose me based on whatever secret system they use, though some people say they pick descendants who are similar to them or who they feel prepared to help in some way. However they decide to pick me, I'll be thrown into a Calling inside my head that I'll need to pass. Sometimes the transition from real life into your Calling is so seamless that witches don't even realize it's happening. I'm not sure if that would make things better or worse for me. On one hand, I wouldn't have to think about it so much, but on the other, I could fail with almost no effort.

No matter what ancestor I get, no matter how they choose to do my Calling, it's supposed to be a simple choice between two options. If I pick right, I get magic, and if I don't, then I'll never get to be a witch.

But what if I get an ancestor who changes the rules like Mama Nora did for Keis? One who wants to up the stakes. The tasks they give are meant to help us become the best version of ourselves. Though sometimes I think they just like messing with us.

The afterlife must be boring.

"Maybe I'll be lucky and get Mama Lizzie for my Calling," I say. She was a baker from Alabama who gathered a bunch of other women in the area to help feed people in the march from Selma to Montgomery for voting rights. Her Callings usually involve spending hours baking something and deciding who to give it away to—the answer always being someone in need. A task so easy that it would be impossible to fail.

Keis shakes her head. "Mama Lizzie has the easiest Callings in the world. You don't want her. Harder Callings mean better gifts."

"I feel like that's a myth."

"It's not!"

I scowl and tuck my towel tighter. "Let's go find a suitable dress that Uncle won't like."

My Bleeding is officially over. There's no more stalling now.

No one in our family has failed a Calling in almost a hundred years.

A Thomas not getting magic has become something so rare it seems impossible to do.

But then again, I don't think the ancestors have ever seen someone as apt at failure as I am.

CHAPTER TWO

I keep my towel tucked around me as I walk along the hardwood floor to my room. They're original. My several times Great-Granny was particular about their upkeep. Her name was Mama Bess, though she wasn't made a Mama until she died. She was a slave in this house in 1811 during the revolts in what was then called the US Territory of Orleans. She was also the one who organized its mysterious disappearance from Louisiana. The ground where it once stood was considered both blessed and cursed.

It took twenty-five of our ancestors to transport the house from the bayous of New Orleans to the plot of land off Lake Ontario in Toronto where we live now. Only, it was called Upper Canada back then. Led by Matriarch Mama Bess to what was supposed to be the promised land. Except when they got here, they saw slaves in houses, on farms, and in shops. Brought over by masters alongside those allowed to call themselves free. Mama Bess learned to read and write, and in her very first journal entry she wrote, "It was better, but it was not good."

It wasn't the freedom the family wanted, but our power had freed them all the same.

Blood and intent.

Two simple ingredients that make up the recipe for magic.

If only passing my Calling were that simple.

Keis trails behind me as I walk down the hall where she, Keisha, Dad and his new wife, Priya, my half sister, Eden, and I all have our rooms in a straight line.

I know it's weird if your parents are divorced and still cohabit, but when you live in a place as big as ours, it's uncharitable not to share. Plus, we needed the extra numbers to help pay for the taxes, utilities, and general upkeep of the house on top of Granny and Grandad's loan.

My room is between Keis's and Keisha's to avoid conflict. Keisha's room is closest to the bathroom we just left because she huffed up a big stink about it and no one in the family wanted to deal, so she got her way.

Mom and Granny have their rooms just around the two corners of the hallway. Granny, as Matriarch, has her own little bathroom that no one else is allowed to use. Alex and Auntie Maise have their rooms on the first floor with a bathroom they share plus the guest bathroom next to the kitchen. Uncle is in a micro-living shed in the backyard, since Auntie kicked him out there five years ago.

Granny always says they got together too early. They were eighteen when they had the twins. "Both babies of their families, and both eager to prove they were grown," is one of her favorite mutterings about it. Auntie usually snaps back that Granny was eighteen when she had Uncle Vacu. That usually leads to Granny detailing the ways in which she and Grandad were more mature, independent, and responsible at that age than Auntie and Uncle Cathius. Then it turns into a big blowup.

I look back at my cousin. "You can go downstairs if you want. You don't have to help me."

"You think I want to hang out down there with everyone's hunger thoughts while they wait for you? Nah."

Keis says that the more emotional a thought is, the louder it becomes until the soft irritating buzz of voices turns into a painful shouting match inside her head. If she didn't refuse to practice, she could learn to block out any unwanted ones. Instead, she focuses on *my* thoughts to help with the noise.

I can't say I was delighted when she decided to spend extra time probing in my head instead of just learning how to control her gift, but I guess I'm used to it now. Sometimes I even forget that she's in there, but I remember pretty quickly when she pulls something out that I hadn't planned to say to anyone.

I shuffle into my room and make a beeline for my closet, whose screen doors light up as I tap my fingers against them and select some underwear. While I change into them, Keis swipes through my clothes.

"What do you think my gift will be? If I get one, I mean." My mind circles around the subject like the way my family hovers when I bake brownies and say they can't eat any until they've cooled for ten minutes. "I've been able to compare my DNA to a few online feeds and DIY sequence it. It said I have a high aptitude for gardening."

"You'll get a gift. And you've never gardened in your life. Those things are from second-rate genetics companies, and your genes will shift after your Calling anyway. There's not much point in guessing now."

"Not everyone gets a gift," I mutter. "You can fail the Calling." The last Thomas to fail was Wimberley, who by her name alone seemed destined to have her shit sparked up. Mama Jova gave the task. Wimberley was supposed to walk across this huge canyon on a thin bridge. Not a normal task at all. There was no choice between two items, just a terrifying action. She refused to do it. Her diary entries in the almanac where we store our family history say, "Because magic isn't worth my life," though everyone else said she was too scared.

They kicked her out of the family home, and she disappeared somewhere, never to be heard from again.

"Get those trash thoughts out of your head. No one's going to kick you out of the house if you fail," Keis groans. "And you're not going to."

Everyone keeps pretending like me failing my Calling is something impossible, but it's not. I might never become a witch, never have magic or a gift. Fade from history until I'm just a footnote in the almanac. I cross my arms over my stomach and cringe.

Keis narrows her eyes at the closet screen and presses her finger harder than necessary. She points at a strapless one that looks like a tube. "This isn't yours. You would never wear this."

"Keisha gave it to me."

Keis lets out a rough grunt and keeps swiping.

Sometimes, I forget that Keis and her sister are twins because they're so separate. Not just different people, but they never actually spend time together outside of things we do as a whole family. Keis is more like *my* twin.

"Oh, wait!" I stop Keis from swiping past a white cotton dress with a blue seahorse pattern. "I love that. But it's not pure white . . ."

Keis groans. "Voya, stop."

"He's going to get annoyed. Maybe let's look through more?"

"No." She selects the dress, grabs it from the drawer at the bottom of the closet, and thrusts it into my arms. "Sometimes you just need to pick something and go with it. You always get so wrapped up in being afraid to be wrong that you don't do anything at all."

I scowl. "Sorry that I'm such a loser who doesn't do anything."

"That's not what I meant." Keis rubs her palms against her eyes. "Just go with this dress, okay? You like it, right?"

I grip the dress in my hands. Alex made it for me. That's her gift. She can stare at a swath of fabric and find the perfect way to put it all together, her seams always straight, impeccable almost without effort. Sure, there are probably non-magic people out there with the same "gift," but Alex has always seemed extra special.

"Uncle's not gonna like it."

"Good!"

Sometimes I feel the tiniest bit bad for Uncle Cathius when Keis says things like that, but he brings it on himself. He's forever trying to tell his daughters how they should live their lives. His way, of course, being the correct one.

I pull the dress over my head, and Keis zips it up in the back.

She looks me up and down. "Not bad."

I bump her out of the way to look at myself in the mirror. The dress hugs my waist and flairs out in an A-line that's a fantastic complement to my wide Thomas hips and butt. It's a great length, not too long or short. Which at five feet is hard to get right. Alex made a beautiful dress, but I make it look good.

"Dinnertime?" I ask Keis.

"Yes! Finally!"

Now we can sit with the family, who will, no doubt, spend the whole meal discussing my Calling. We could be talking about other things, like where Keis should intern.

"Don't you dare try and deflect to me," she says.

"It's a more interesting topic."

"No one is going to think my internship is more stimulating than your Calling. If Granny had the magic to force me to use my gift to make money instead of going to school, she would. Mentioning interning would give her a damn heart attack." The skin around Keis's eyes goes tight. I can't tell if her doing that is going to cause or prevent wrinkles later on.

"She thinks you're making it harder for yourself," I say with a shrug. "The companies that pay interns a livable wage have huge competition, and they're the only ones with the money to send you to university."

"Encouraging."

I turn toward Keis, but she won't meet my eyes. "I'll help you find something. You're amazing enough to do what the rest of us can't. You can be something without magic."

"That's the attitude that makes me worry for this family. For this community."

I'm not going to see eye to eye with Keis on this, so I don't try.

The second we hit the first-floor landing, the perfect spicy aroma from the food I was making hits us. It's my Bleeding, and I'm still the one cooking. Though if I'm honest, I wouldn't have it any other way.

At the foot of the stairs, I spot a sheet of paper lying in front of the door, as if someone poked it under on their way past. I squat, pick it up, and turn the sheet over. The face that smiles up at me from the page is dark brown–skinned and hazel-eyed, and wears a custom lilac wig.

Lauren.

The back of my throat goes dry, and I struggle to swallow. When I think of Lauren, I picture long, swinging curls, a high-pitched laugh that makes you warm inside, and that indescribable rush of being pulled on an adventure. Where I try to plan everything, to struggle over what to do and where to go, Lauren lives without any maps, going wherever she feels like whenever. She was like that even when we were kids. Her poor mom always came by to ask if we'd seen her, and she would never be in the last place we'd played together—she'd already be halfway across the neighborhood, doing ancestors know what.

We were at a party to celebrate her successful Coming-of-Age what felt like barely a week ago, though it was much longer by now. It was a big deal since she's set to be her family's next Matriarch. Though Granny gave me and Keis hard side-eye for going. The Carters aren't a pure family like us, whose magic comes only from our own blood. The strength of impure magic comes from the pain and suffering of others—stealing people in the night, carving them up, and fueling your magic with their blood, then wiping their memories, healing their wounds, and tossing them back out onto the streets like you haven't spent the last few hours listening to their screams.

Lauren's parents always keep her uninvolved, but she told me once that she could hear the screams sometimes and was glad that they weren't the sort of impure family who actually killed people like the Davises are.

The fact that every dark ritual needs to have a pure intent is the sort of thing she takes pride in. The greater good, she says. Like the time her parents did a ritual to help a group of foster kids get placed in good homes instead of the abusive homes they had been in.

She doesn't like to talk about the kickback magic. That's the *real* reason witches choose impurity. Sure, all rituals have to have "pure" intents, but dark rituals also have the convenient side effect of increasing a witch's magical bandwidth and strength far beyond pure magic users. They still have to shed blood for every spell like the rest of us, but they have a much higher ceiling when it comes to how much they can do. Even when they do magic that seems pure, when they cast spells from nothing but their own blood, that magic still got its power from pain.

Lauren hasn't had to participate in a dark ritual yet, but she'll have to someday. She's still my friend. I can't just lump every impure witch into the same category. Lauren isn't some heartless monster. And the day of her Coming-of-Age party, she was just a girl celebrating becoming a witch. Glowing with pride and full of joy.

"I'm going to be someone special," she whispered to me, giddy off a bottle of champagne her parents let us have.

Lauren wants to be remembered. Important. To have her name spoken by Carters for generations.

Now she's gone. She left her house the morning after the party and hasn't been back for a month. And this time, no one can find her.

Keis nudges me with her shoulder, avoiding Lauren's smiling face. "Come on, dinner." Her voice is soft and quiet.

I tuck the paper under my arm and follow her into the kitchen.

Mom is sitting on one of the wooden stools around the laminate counter–topped island. We, the kids, wanted to get a touchscreen island. Granny shot it down, snapping, "Does everything need to be a frying touch screen? Use your damn phone."

Somewhere between leaving Keis and me in the bathroom and coming down here, Mom put on a black bob wig. I'm pretty sure it's called "Eva."

I laid the paper faceup on the island. "Someone slipped this under the door." I push my thoughts at her like she's Keis, urging her to do something.

Mom glances up from scrolling through her phone and heaves a sigh. "We know she's missing. The Carters know we know. I don't know why they're dropping us flyers, wasting paper and time."

"Maybe they're hoping we can help." Mom's gift is reading objects. With a touch she can search through the history of jewelry, clothes, pretty much anything. The set of her face tells me she isn't planning on volunteering.

Because it's one thing to help find a missing girl and another to help an impure family.

It's hacked. We weren't always this squeaky-clean either. Before Granny was Matriarch, the Thomases were just as impure, but now we act like we're above it all.

Witch politics. I gnaw on my lips. That's what's stopping her from helping Lauren.

Today of all days, I don't have the energy to push it. I glance at the door that leads to the dining room and then back at Mom. "Is everyone waiting?"

"Yup. Mom sent me to help you guys take everything in." She points to the oven. "Dang thing shut off twice."

Hack it. Our near-ancient oven has developed a habit of shutting off on its own, and there's no spare cash to fix it right now. Probably not for a while. Auntie offered to use magic, but the last time she did that for the broken microwave, her fire-conjuring gift got in the way, and she sent the whole thing up in flames. She's kind of the worst person to have the power to spontaneously produce fire, but apparently, the ancestor who Called her thought it was appropriate.

Fixing our oven would require either a specific gift for electronics or a strong enough bandwidth of spell-casting power—and increased power has a cost our family isn't willing to cash in: a price called "purity." We could try casting at the same time, but with our family, we're more likely to blow the thing up.

I jerk my head at the open archway leading to the dining room. "Granny's in a good mood?"

Mom laughs. "Oh no. She's pissed, but she'll be happier after eating."

Not bad. Once I get Granny's favorites onto her plate, she'll be pleasant enough that I can maybe avoid any lectures or prodding about my Calling. Years of anticipating my own Bleeding meant that I actually had my dinner menu picked out for tonight. Usually, deciding what to make for dinner takes . . . longer. An amount of time that I'd rather not think about because it reminds me of Mom saying she knows I "have trouble with choices sometimes."

If I really get Granny into a good mood, maybe she'll have a hint about which ancestor I'll get. Every Matriarch has the power to speak and consult with them, though it doesn't necessarily mean the Matriarch will say who's going to Call me. But she must be able to get *some* info. All of my cousins have at least attempted to pester her into saying something before, and I'm no different.

Why give Matriarchs these special powers if they're not going to be used to help the family? And Matriarchs can do more than just commune with the ancestors. They can pull on the magic of those in their family to increase their bandwidth, usually for more difficult casts that require a single focused intention. Or they can do the opposite and suppress the magic of others—though to my knowledge, Granny hasn't ever exercised that power, even on Uncle Vacu. A Matriarch's mental state can even affect the magic of other people, like how on the day Grandad died, every cast the adults made had the scent of cloves and nutmeg, just like his favorite deodorant.

I hand one tray each to Keis and Mom before bringing in the last two myself. We walk through the archway into the dining room.

The ceiling is sky-high, and the plantation shutter windows give you a view that overlooks Lake Ontario, which runs behind our house and flows along the downtown waterfront all the way to the East End. It's a million-dollar sight. When people see us and our house, they must think we're loaded. It's an expectation we've never lived up to.

In 2030, they renamed our area of Etobicoke "Historic Long Branch." What makes rows of mismatched houses, identical low-rise condos, and a main street with restaurants, bars, and bakeries that were all built in the last thirty years "historic," only the city planners know.

The table set in the middle of the dining room is solid, non-modded wood and made to fit at least twelve people, which leaves us just enough room for one more if we wanted.

Granny raps her knuckles on the tabletop. "About time."

Yeah. That's Granny.

Matriarch of the family with a gift she's never shared with any of us. Even Mom and Auntie Maise don't know what it is.

Her hair is kept in the same neat afro she's rocked for as long as I can remember, and she wears the same fluffy red robe with some combination of casual home wear underneath that she's always worn around the house.

We set down the food in front of everyone. Glistening oxtail falling off the bone and smothered in brown sauce. Pelau fresh enough that you can see the bits of pumpkin and squash in the rice alongside the pieces of pork and pigeon peas. Macaroni pie with a golden-brown cheese crust and gooey yet solid inside. And to top it off, a big batch of sweet bread that has Granny sitting straighter in her seat to get a better look at it.

I am a culinary queen.

"And so humble," Keis mutters.

If my Calling task is picking out the perfect dinner menu for my family, I might pass.

Granny gives Uncle a smack. "Get me some of that macaroni pie." He's sitting on her right side, where he always does. As a man, he can never be Matriarch, but he hangs around Granny like he has a chance.

He takes her plate, reaches across the table, and scoops a hefty portion onto it. It stays solid and upright the way I know she likes it.

Uncle gives me a quick once-over as he serves her. His eyebrows are like two half-buzzed caterpillars, and his bald head shines under the lights. "This is a lot of food. Might go bad."

He nitpicks just to nitpick. None of us kids know what his gift is either, but sometimes I think it's just pissing people off. If I make Trinidadian food, he wants to poke at how we should eat more African dishes to honor our roots. If I make something Canadian, I'm turning away from our culture. Everything I do, anything *anyone* except for Granny does, needs to have some sort of mistake he can prod at.

Not to mention, I don't even know much about these so-called African roots. Granny and Grandad's ancestors were taken away from there as slaves, with Granny's, the Thomases, being brought to the United States, and Grandad's, the Harrises, taken to Trinidad. Granny's ancestors transported our house to Canada from the States, and Grandad's immigrated over to Canada from the island. Eventually they came together in Toronto.

We only know where in Africa they're from because we have access to our ancestors. It's a privilege not many other Black descendants of slaves have, even now with advances in genetics.

Grandad's Trini heritage is what ended up sticking with our family, but at the end of the day, Granny's ancestors were the more powerful witches, and that's what matters. It's why we're Thomases instead of Harrises. It's a stronger name to carry.

Keis thumps into the chair next to Alex. I walk over and sit across from her, which puts me next to Keisha.

"Did you make any salad?" Keisha doesn't look up at me. Her long dark hair lies over her shoulder, and she looks casual despite wearing a glittering sequined dress.

So much for my perfect family dinner menu choices. "Granny doesn't like salad."

I thought I said it under my breath, but from the other end of the table Granny harrumphs. "You could eat a bowl of salad the size of your head, and you'll be hungry again in ten minutes. Eat some real food."

I don't think any of us miss the significant glance she throws at Dad and Priya.

Dad shifts in his seat and lets his short dreads drop over his eyes. He doesn't say anything. Just stirs around the spinach, chickpea, and feta-looking cheese substitute on his plate.

Priya follows suit with her own salad, but her jaw is stiff enough that I know she's not happy about the slight. She has her long hair in a single plait that falls down her back and stops above her ankles. She makes separate meals for her and Dad because they're vegan.

"Do you two have any extra Keisha can eat?" I ask Priya.

She bobs her head. "Lots."

I sag in my chair and wave my hand at Keisha. "There you go, problem solved."

She perks up and saunters into the kitchen to search for their leftovers.

I throw a grateful look at Priya, who smiles back at me. It's strange to think I've known her and Dad as a couple almost as long as I knew him and Mom as one. Maybe he and Priya are a better fit. They even both have touch-based gifts. With a single hand on your skin, he can make your muscles unwind and your worries go away, and she can measure romantic compatibility. Matching gifts aren't a prerequisite for successful couples, but Priya and Dad don't fight the way he and Mom used to, so maybe it means something.

Meanwhile, little Eden is waiting while Mom scoops her a serving of oxtail on top of some pelau. I made sure to pick Granny's favorites that I know Eden loves too. I can't not spoil my baby sister. Her hair is cut short to her chin and is run-a-fine-tooth-comb-through-it straight, as if Dad's genes couldn't touch Priya's to make a single curl. Though Eden did get Dad's skin tone, a lighter brown than the rest of us with a warm golden undertone.

To be real, Mom can't stand Dad and is fried about Priya, but she loves Eden. Everyone does. She's the most adorable six-year-old you'll ever meet.

Eden grins at me. "Thank you for dinner."

Polite *and* adorable. "You're welcome."

"You spent a long time upstairs celebrating your Bleeding," Uncle says. "I hope you used some of that time to prepare for your Calling."

He would be the one to start this conversation. Biting my tongue is the only way I can stop myself from snapping at him. "We're still celebrating my Bleeding, aren't we?" I nudge Alex's foot under the table and will her to help me derail this conversation. "Alex, why don't you tell us about your Bleeding? Uncle wasn't in the room, so I'm sure he'd like to hear the story."

Alex looks up with a mouthful of food and raises an intricately drawn eyebrow. For as long as I can remember, she's always had false lashes and glittery eye shadows and lip colors. Every look perfectly complementing her deep, rich brown skin. Her out-there makeup combined with being a big girl catches her a lot of attention. Not just big as in plus-size. Tall too. And always with her hair shaved close to her head. She's striking, knows it, and flaunts it.

Alex swallows, but doesn't put down her fork. "I'm sure Auntie gave him a rundown when it happened."

When her Bleeding started, she hadn't told us she was transitioning yet. We were supposed to go to the store together until she stopped in the middle of the hall, crimson slipping down her face from her eyes and ears. We stood in the hall for a moment, just staring at each other. As the oldest cousin, she was the first person whose Bleeding I had ever seen.

Alex looked at me and said, "I think I want to have a bath. Not a shower."

I made her wait there while I ran and rallied the rest of the women in the house. Auntie Maise, Mom, Granny, Keisha, Keis, and me found any and every candle we had and stuck it in the bathroom along with perfumes and incense. Keisha even threw a wad of glitter in the tub.

By the time Alex got in, the hallway was a sliding mess of blood, but she was in a bath that sparkled like her lashes with a beaming smile on her face, and we were all there. We didn't ask why she wanted a bath, and we didn't need to know.

Alex was happy, and that was what we cared about. She asked that we call her "she" and "her" from then on.

I say, "You don't want to retell it? You always say it's one of your favorite memories." And I would really appreciate if the attention could be shifted off me.

"It is, but"—Alex points a manicured nail around the table— "you all are a bad audience when it comes to a story you've already heard. You interrupt, you wanna add things that didn't happen or dispute things that were said or done. Nah. Too much work."

"I think Uncle would enjoy hearing your version of events." I widen my eyes at her so she gets the hint.

"Are we talking about the same Uncle?"

Uncle Cathius crosses his arms. "Not talking about the Calling isn't going to make it go away. Your choices are what define you. And how you choose to complete your task is a lot more important than deciding what to cook for dinner."

I raise my voice and ignore him. "How about all the women share their Bleeding experiences to celebrate my transition into one?" My eyes flick around for someone to keep the conversation going. "Granny—"

"If you think I want to sit here and talk about the time where I bled at least three quarts of blood from my privates, you need to reassess." She chews her last bit of sweet bread with measured bites, swallows, and stares at me. "Your Calling is *your* challenge to overcome. Try and prepare for it or ignore it. Either way, it's coming tomorrow." She stands from the table and brushes crumbs off her pants. "Sweet bread could use more coconut."

Before she can leave, I blurt out, "Someone left Lauren's missing poster at the door." If Granny says that we should help, then everyone will have to. She's the Matriarch.

"They'll find the girl." Granny's voice is gruff and short.

My shoulders slump. I should have known. At the end of the day, Lauren is from an impure family, and not one like the Davises, who we're linked to with stronger bonds. Uncle Cathius was a Davis once, so they're family. But if we wanted, we could have nothing to do with the Carters.

Granny says that impurity gives you more power but asks for a cost that she never wants any of us to pay. When, newly crowned as Matriarch, she announced that to her family, they left. Moved out somewhere in Quebec or Nova Scotia. She never talks about them. It's part of what she sacrificed.

Purity isn't supposed to be about one family being better than the other. Pure or impure, we're part of the same community. But somewhere along the line, that seemed to change, with pure sticking to pure, and impure keeping with impure. And we've chosen our side.

I remember times when the Black witch community was tight. A moment in my childhood where pure and impure didn't seem to matter as much as Granny made it out to. When I was little, I used to call Lauren's mom "Auntie," and no one seemed to care the way they do now, where we all only gather for Caribana—the annual Caribbean carnival—and the odd backyard party, and otherwise stick to our own kind.

I lick my lips and say, "I think they need help."

"They have help. It's called the Toronto Police Service." She presses her mouth into a line. "They didn't need our help before, and they don't need it now."

I should stop. I should leave it alone. "Maybe Johan can't help this time."

Granny shakes her head and turns away. "If he can't, then we definitely can't. Stop worrying about missing girls and concentrate on your Calling." With that, she walks away. Uncle rises from his seat and follows after her.

Mom sags against the table. I risk a glance at Dad. He's focused on watching his plate.

Keis throws me a tight smile. "Food was great."

That starts a chorus of everyone around the table giving me compliments about the meal.

I clench and unclench my fingers around my fork.

A message from my phone pops in front of my eyes. It uses the microchip behind my ear to hijack my optic nerves into seeing the projection. It's an event alert from the internship opportunities I signed up for before we came down to dinner. There's a pop-up Q&A tomorrow morning at NuGene headquarters for their program.

I don't hesitate to dig out my phone and confirm me and Keis for the session. The Q&A is completely booked seconds after. It's the only good thing that's happened today. When I look up, Keis is staring at me with narrowed eyes.

"We're going," I say.

"Fine," she mutters. After years of having me push her to do one thing or another, mostly endless visits to new restaurants, she's used to going along with my ideas.

I shovel a too-big forkful of macaroni pie into my mouth and slouch in my chair. Keis's problem is on its way toward being solved, but I can't say the same about mine. Or Lauren's.

Granny and I have different opinions about missing girls, but she's right about my Calling. With everything, I never even got to pick her brain about what ancestor I'll get. And even if I don't want to think about it, once the Amplifying ceremony starts tomorrow, my ancestor will be summoned, and I'll be Called.

I have no choice but to be ready.

Unlike Lauren, I don't want to be remembered.

I'm never going to be great. I know that.

I crave the anonymity of a life that was good enough.

Because if I am remembered, it'll be as the only Thomas in a hundred years to fail her Calling.

CHAPTER THREE

The next morning, Keis and I step off the GO train at Union Station at nine thirty a.m. with a flurry of morning commuters. The signature green-and-white transportation costs more since it runs faster and doesn't have the same suffocating sweat smell of the more widely used TTC. For us, being under eighteen, the Toronto subways, buses, and streetcars—the TTC—are free and therefore more crowded and slower.

I lead the way down the gray concrete stairs with Keis sticking close. A woman in mauve athletic gear knocks into her, mumbles a hurried apology, and keeps moving.

"Did you see that?" Keis grumbles.

"She said sorry."

"She said it, but she didn't mean it." As much as she hates being cooped up in the house, Keis isn't a huge fan of downtown, either.

As we pass a group of paper signs tacked up, I pause. The image is of Lauren with a tiny witch symbol in the corner. From the way it catches Keis's eye, I guess that it's probably enchanted to draw the attention of other witches. To non-magical eyes it would appear like the same static photo that was slid under our door yesterday, which is how it looks to me since I'm not officially a witch yet. A voice in the back of my head whispers that I may never be, and I don't have any argument against it.

A month since Lauren's been gone.

It's like a memory that I keep forgetting. I'll pick up my phone to message her, forgetting that she won't message back. I'll walk down the street and think about going to her house, forgetting that she won't be there. I'll tap over to her feed to see what she's up to, forgetting that she's not posting anymore.

Remembering each time is like a realization that never quite sinks in. Is she gone for now, or gone forever?

Keis pokes me with her nail. "She'll show up soon."

"What if she's in trouble?"

"She must have run away with someone. She's done it before, and she's a wanderer by nature."

Lauren once took the train with a boy to Montreal without saying anything about going. Three days into her trip, she sent me a video message complaining about how he hadn't turned out to be that great, and she was staying with a friend now.

It took us three days to hear from her that time, but now it had been thirty.

I try to make Keis's words stick in my head without managing to shake the chill over my shoulders, and focus on weaving through the crowds to the subway.

It's so normal. Like I won't be going home to a task that could mean the end of my life as a witch before it even begins. If I pass, if I have a strong gift, maybe I can find a way to help Lauren. Except helping Lauren feels like the finishing touch on the twenty-layer-cake effort that is my Calling.

We manage to squeeze onto the packed subway. Most people on the train are slumped half-asleep from their commute, and they haven't even started work yet. Despite the AC pumping through the cars, it smells overwhelmingly of BO. I lean away from a man gripping the handhold on the ceiling whose armpit is level with my eyes.

"Okay," I say, turning to Keis. "What's your game plan?"

"Shouldn't I be asking you that?" With a pinched expression, she leans against the doors you're not supposed to lean on.

I grab the subway pole harder. How am I supposed to come up with a game plan for my Calling? No matter what the adults say, I can't prep for it. There are no practice tests or exercises.

Keis groans. "No, not that. I meant you're the one who found this internship opportunity and insisted it would be perfect. I figured you had a game plan for the day."

Oh.

"Yeah, oh."

I lean toward my cousin. "Right. A plan. NuGene is always talking on their feed about looking for new perspectives, like the model who got the internship because she figured out how to make the NuSap robots more aesthetically pleasing."

"The NuSaps that are now defunct."

"Yes, but that's its own thing."

Keis twists her lips. "'Its own thing' of a unit suffocating its user while trying to tuck them into bed is kind of a big thing."

"Not the point! I'm saying those political science courses you take mean you have a new and fresh perspective." Keis wanted to take a host of random classes to piss the family off, and I made her pick ones she actually liked that could also lead to something after graduation. She agreed only because it strengthened the validity of her protest. Really, I think she just didn't know what she wanted to do. Keis has ambition but lacks direction and focus.

She doesn't have any reaction to those thoughts, though she must hear them. I lean in closer. "I'll ask a question that pushes the discussion in your favor, and you answer with your political genius."

"And that's not going to seem suspicious with us sitting next to each other?"

I shake my head. "You go in first, and I'll go in on my own, and we have to sit way far away from each other."

"Fine." Keis blows out a breath.

I tangle my fingers in the edge of my shirt. "And if you want to do a bit of listening in on the presenter's thoughts for an added edge..."

"First of all, no," she says. "Second of all, in a room full of that many people? I'll be lucky if I can concentrate enough to spout out an answer."

Right. A big part of Keis's hatred for downtown is the sheer mass of people. She's used to focusing on my thoughts. Trying to jump into a new brain would mean swapping into an unfamiliar mind; in that time the surrounding voices would get louder, and she may not be able to find the one she's looking for.

Sometimes I wonder if her motivation for not improving her gift is less about protesting and more that she hates the power our ancestors gave her.

Keis doesn't respond to that thought either. "What are you going to ask me?"

"I can't tell you! You need to have a spontaneous answer. They'll know if it's rehearsed."

Arriving at Osgoode. Osgoode Station.

The doors slide open, and Keis and I step out of the subway car. We follow the stairs to the surface, where we're hit by a sharp sewer smell and purposefully retro storefronts. Their signs are flat, unmoving letters instead of the more common digital signs in an attempt to either preserve old traditions or hop on the trend of being retro. It's hard to tell.

"It stinks," Keis groans.

I speed-walk west down Queen Street. "It's just this one place." Once you get down the block, the stench is obliterated by mobile hot dog stalls.

We pass a homeless man with his legs folded underneath him, and a dirt-streaked donation pad. His sign asks for money for food, and in the corner, there's a scrawled drawing of three circles, the middle one almond-shaped. A witch mark. I fumble with my phone and tap it against the pad. Keis does the same.

We're not rich, no, but we're doing all right. Enough that both our moms give us a small weekly allowance. The man thanks us as we leave. Does he have a gift, or did he fail his Calling? I know Keis said the family wouldn't actually kick me out if I failed, but it happens. Or sometimes people just leave, tired of living in homes filled with magic when they have none. Sometimes the families fall out of favor from the shame of having a failure witch. They lose respect, and their businesses lose customers, and everything tumbles down around them.

But that's *not* going to happen to the Thomases. I can't let it.

The whole way to NuGene, I fiddle with my purse strap, tangling and untangling my fingers in the cheap modded leather.

NuGene headquarters is beside the Art Gallery of Ontario, where there used to be an arts school. They closed it down in the STEM boom of '31 where if you weren't learning about sciences or tech in school, you weren't going to get a job that paid enough to make the cost of school worth it.

Mom was a teenager back then. She said that being an entrepreneur was the big thing. Be your own boss without paying for school. It's why Granny started up our beauty supply business. Even during her time, education was pricey. And Uncle Vacu was already a baby. By the time Mom was old enough to go, unless your family was rich or you could get a company to pay for you, which almost never happened when she was a kid, you couldn't afford to go to university. I asked her about scholarships once, and she rolled her eyes.

It wasn't until Keis started looking into schools that I realized what a joke those were. Most only paid for 5 percent of a single year at a school. Like the world's most hacked discount. It was no wonder most normal people didn't do more than high school.

"University," Auntie Maise said, staring at Keis over her tablet when my cousin announced that she was going to continue high school beyond the minimum credits, "is for rich people and special people. Either you have money, or someone decides you're worth spending money on. Sure, you can be special, who doesn't want to be? But these days, special means being locked into a contract with a company you can't leave for half a decade hoping that the perks make it worth it." She scoffed while Granny agreeably *mm-hmm*ed next to her. "You don't know about the real world yet, so I'm trying to tell you. Study if you want to study. But being special doesn't mean survival. Not anymore."

Keis lets out a puff of air and shifts beside me.

My cousin *is* special. I know it. And no matter what her mom or the other adults think, she can do more than survive. She can thrive.

The highlight of NuGene HQ is the giant white amphitheater suspended in the air by towering metal supports bent on an angle. It's tall enough that you could walk for four or five blocks and still see it in the distance, and the sunlight glints off the metal in a way that makes it look powerful and intimidating.

"Stop gawking. We have like two minutes." Keis nudges me forward.

"You go in first so people don't know we're together." I shoo her off, and with a dramatic sigh, she heads inside.

Using my phone, I check the balance on my account and see the couple of dollars I donated to the man. For his safety, there's no name attached, reading only "charitable donation."

It's lacking.

We call ourselves a community, but I wonder if that's truly what we are.

An alert flashes in front of my eyes that declares the seminar is starting now.

Hack me!

I dart into the building and am hit with a wave of cool, but not freezing, AC. The lobby is white with dramatic silver accents and smooth marblelike walls.

There are holo signs to direct people to where the Q&A is being held, and a countdown timer to when the session will start. It states that I have five seconds to get to the Q&A.

I pump my short legs in the most publicly acceptable speed walk I can manage while staring at the clock, my purse thumping against my side.

The timer switches to four sets of zeros, and my stomach clenches.

At the end of the hall is the open door to the Q&A room. Someone's fingers reach around the edge of the door with clear intent to shut it.

I abandon all public decorum and sprint forward. Hack the speed walk. Managing to get to the door before it shuts, I slam my palm against it and shove back against the person standing on the other side.

They increase the pressure, fighting to close the door, but I slip my foot into the open space and slink into the room, trying to smother the pants escaping my lips.

The boy who was attempting to shut the door is finally able to close it since I'm inside and not wrestling with him over it.

I stare into the guy's face and then stare some more.

Beautiful. Curated and crafted.

His hair is strands of blue and gray like rain clouds and crashing waves in a storm, tucked under a white beanie. Retro wires weave through the cartilage of his left ear—a tech-flavored fashion statement. The boy crosses warm tawny brown arms over a narrow chest where the NuGene teal DNA symbol gleams on his lab coat along with a thin white name tag that declares "Luc Rodriguez," and below it in slightly smaller letters, "intern, he/him." Just under the cuff of his sleeve, a Fade Ink tattoo pokes out with little ATGC letters that curve into a design I can't fully see.

"Are you coming in? Or are you here to stare at people?" His words are terse and sharp.

He may be gorgeous, but he's also kind of an asshole.

There are muffled snickers from the crowd. I shuffle up the stairs to a seat in the back corner of the room. My wide hips knock against one of the other desks as I make my way up, the space in between overly narrow to fit more seats. My body is forever smacking against things I was sure that I cleared. When I was fourteen, my hips appearing seemingly overnight, it would embarrass me. I would stutter out a "sorry" and duck my head, face hot. Until it happened when Mom was around. She said, "Don't feel bad for taking up space with your body. People are always going to want to force you to be smaller to fit what they want. You've got our Thomas hips and butt, good, more space for you." And she delightedly knocked her hips into a display that wobbled dangerously, and grinned at me.

My body has never been small, excluding my height, and probably won't ever be. What she said made me feel like I didn't have to keep living like that was a bad thing. Alex didn't. Granny didn't. Mom didn't. So why should I? I still apologize when I bump into things because I'm Canadian and physically cannot help it, but I don't feel bad about it anymore.

I settle into my seat and look around the room. It's built like the university lecture halls I've seen on feeds. Rows of cushy seats with small, attached touch screens that connect to your phone so you don't need to bring tablets from class to class.

I glance around at the other people, who all seem to have

multicolored hair and unnatural eye colors and look like they were born that way. Modded. And those are just the ones I could pick out. There are limits to what you can do. NuGene doesn't dabble in things like animal feature splices or any strange science. The wildest they get are random hair and eye colors. Most people get subtle internal mods for things like medical vulnerabilities and better predispositions for emotional stability.

Keis and I spotted someone with cat ears just last week. Those mods you can only get from trashy illegal modifiers. The government couldn't charge the girl for having the ears, but they could go after the people offering the service. Except it's not that easy to catch those people. But no one in this crowd seems rebellious enough to risk those sorts of mods. They have high-class NuGene-brand ones. These are the sorts of people with connections Keis and I don't have, and they're also her direct competition.

On the lecture floor there are now three people around my and Keis's age. Luc, the beautiful asshole, an Asian-looking girl with short dark hair and sun-kissed skin, and a Black boy with dark skin like Alex and an angular jaw who looks like he's drowning in his oversize lab coat. I'm too far to see the pronouns on their name tags, but hopefully Luc will say them so I can adjust. Otherwise, I can look up their feeds and make sure I'm using the right ones, which, like most people, is usually what I end up doing for strangers.

I search the room for Keis and spot her in the first row with her back straight and eyes forward. Once she's in front of the right people, I know she can show them how special she is. Even before her Coming-of-Age, everyone knew she would have a strong gift. DNA is the most accurate predictor, but Keis has always had an air about her.

Not like me.

Luc steps forward and adjusts the wireless mic pad near his

mouth. "Welcome to the NuGene internship question and answer session. This is your chance to learn more about how interns fit into the company and ask any questions to determine if it's the right fit for you." He gestures to himself and the two people behind him. "My name is Luc. I use 'he/him.' Behind me is Jasmine, who uses 'she/her,' and Juras, who uses 'he/him.' I've been an intern with NuGene for three years, as have my fellow interns."

My eyes bug out. *Three years?* He doesn't look older than I am. Most internships start at seventeen or eighteen unless you're some sort of genius.

"We'll give you a couple of minutes to submit a question on the touch pad, and we'll answer as many as we can."

I type out the first coherent sociopolitical question that pops into my head and send it. Chances are they randomize the submissions and speed isn't a factor, but just in case, at least I was quick.

While everyone else is typing their questions out, I sneak a look at the boy with the blue-gray hair. I lift up my phone and zoom in on his face. The AI rushes to compare his features to any matching feeds and comes up with a result in seconds.

Luc Rodriguez, he/him, age sixteen, two-star rating.

Two stars?! What is he, a serial killer? I mean, since his profile says he's sixteen, that confirms he's been a NuGene intern since he was thirteen, so maybe he is. High intelligence goes hand in hand with mass murder.

I pull up the ratings and scroll through the comments.

Doesn't try to get to know anyone. Thinks he's better than us because he's one of Justin Tremblay's sponsor kids. No point trying to get to know this guy. If he's named CEO after Justin, I'm never using a NuGene product or service AGAIN! —Dorian Munichz

Wait, what? I scroll further through Luc's feed. There's zero about the fact that he's Justin CEO-of-the-entire-hacking-NuGene-company Tremblay's sponsor kid. You would think that would be the sort of thing to mention on your feed?

I go back to the reviews section and stop at another one.

Asked him for a statement about NuGene changing misgendering policies. Instead he said, "Do I look like a feed? Check the company status updates." SO RUDE. Hack him! —Keliah Morgan

I check them all to see if there's a single positive rating and find a couple at the bottom from Jasmine and Juras, the other two interns. They've given him five stars without commenting.

Everyone knows high scores without comments are pity ratings.

Most other people have rated either one star, for pure hate, or two stars for people who don't like him but feel bad rating people one star unless they're actual criminals. Or that's how I do my ratings, anyway.

On his profile, all he has written are his age, pronouns, and that he's a NuGene intern. Alongside those are a sparse amount of feed posts, mostly reposting NuGene news, but there are a couple of posts from Pride last month about supporting LGBTQIA+ people in STEM, where Luc talks a bit about being trans and what it means to him to be in the field.

If he's a NuGene intern, he's probably got access to getting his KO/I done if he wants to. Not everyone does. Alex brought it up as an option to Granny when she started transitioning. There's a special gene where removing it (knockout) or adding it (knock-in) creates the sort of gender-affirming physical changes that used to require surgery. KO/I, for short. But like everything at NuGene, it's not cheap.

Granny put Alex on a waiting list so the government could cover it, but just like every other gene therapy covered by OHIP, you stay on the waiting list for a few years. If you've got money, you can get yours done right at sixteen, the minimum eligible age, and be fully medically transitioned by seventeen. If you don't, you stay on government-covered hormones. Everyone who wants to do a KO/I is on those at least until they hit sixteen anyway, until you either get to the top of the waiting list or save enough money to skip it altogether.

But someone like Luc who has Justin Tremblay as a sponsor dad would never have to wait on a list for a treatment.

In Luc's reviews, people are calling him stuck-up, but it's not easy to be a sponsor kid. Rich people go to so-called "disadvantaged" countries, pluck kids out, and raise them to lead companies. Only, if the child fails, they send them right back. There was a boy, Eddy, on our block. His sponsor brought him from Guatemala to be a feed musician, but he could never get his ratings high enough. Two years later, he was gone.

Luc claps his hands. "Let's get the first question up."

We look at the giant screen behind them, and the first question appears: *Can a person without a STEM specialization be considered a valuable contribution to the company and gain an internship?*

I would be happy that my question came up first if it wasn't accompanied by a gigantic photo of me with my face smushed against Eden's. The room bursts into laughter, and I sink in my seat.

Scramble my feed. The desks must pull data from the phone connection.

Luc looks straight at me and smiles.

Normal grins should make you feel good.

His expression makes me want to slide to the floor and curl up in the fetal position.

"Here's the twist to this Q&A: whoever asks the question gets to pose an answer first before we give the official response." There's a lift in Luc's voice like he's announcing a pizza party instead of a nerve-racking and unexpected surprise.

I'm going to rate him the second I get a chance. I'll write: *Takes an unnecessary amount of joy in humiliating others. Two stars.*

Luc looks back at the screen. "So, Voya Thomas, does a person who didn't specialize in STEM belong in this company?"

My eyes dart around the room and spot Keis chewing on the inside of her cheek. This was supposed to be her time to shine. "I feel there's an oversaturation of people with science and tech specializations in the company. There are others who could benefit NuGene in a different way."

Put up your hand and add something! I shout the thought at Keis and hope she hears.

Luc walks to the podium and brings up my feed. It's filled with photos of food. "You seem to have a lot of culinary interest and background. No high school specialization in anything at all. Since your interest in food is apparently as close to a specialization as you've got, how would that help?"

It wouldn't. If I were one of these people vying to get an internship, I would be ready with some spam-worthy answer. But I came here for Keis. My cooking isn't a skill that creates my career. That's for my gift to decide. It's the reason I didn't bother specializing in anything. How could I pick one without knowing? Assuming I pass and get a gift at all. And if I don't . . . where does that leave me?

I don't belong here, and it's like Luc can smell it. Could sniff it out the instant I walked in. And now he's pouncing on it with a wide-open jaw full of sharp teeth.

I swallow. "It wouldn't, probably."

"You don't believe in your own statement?" he asks, eyebrows quirked in mock surprise.

"I do, I just don't think cooking is it."

"Then why are you here? Why are you taking up a spot in a session meant for people who are serious about considering

NuGene and furthering the future of this company?"

My nostrils flare, and heat forces its way through my body.

"Why are you wasting time with this interrogation?" Keis's voice booms loud and clear from the front row. She narrows her eyes at Luc. "I'll give you an answer."

I sit up straight in my seat. This is Keis's chance to make her impression. It isn't how I pictured it, but it'll work.

"Cooking is a skill that would benefit the company because people who care about creating joy for others through a culinary experience have more empathy than someone with a STEM specialization who's more concerned about humiliating one person than educating a room full of people." Keis pushes out a hard breath when she finishes.

Hack me. The room is silent enough to hear the slight buzzing of Luc's mic.

Keis lifts her butt off the seat in a motion to leave.

NO!

She catches on my thought and shoots me a wide-mouthed stare.

If we leave. He wins. Sit down.

She lets out an audible grunt and parks her butt back in the seat.

Even from the back, I can see Luc's hands clench and unclench.

So much for this internship opportunity.

Juras clears his throat and activates his mic. "Let's go to the next question, shall we?" As he flips to another submission, the screen lights up with a video feed and a bright red LIVE button in the corner.

On-screen is the NuGene CEO Justin Tremblay himself behind a desk that looks like it's made of real non-modded wood. And not old passed-down wood like our dining room table. Shiny new they-grew-and-cut-down-a-tree-for-him wood. His blond hair is fluffy and coiffed with a perfect side part, and though he's Mom's age, there's an extra exuberance that makes him look more like he's in his early twenties than in his midthirties. And there's no missing his signature crimson bionic lenses from a project he started for fun. Today they're the same price as a luxury electric convertible and can pull up data in a blink on anyone or anything you can see that would normally take hours to search for, including genetic information that a person may have purposely or accidentally given public access to. And for someone like the NuGene CEO, he'd also have any company-stored gene data at his fingertips with a glance.

Justin's father was the founder of NuGene, but back then the company was just famous for genetic heritage programs—you know, the sort where you swab the inside of your mouth and send it in for testing. He was focused on the past and history. Justin was the one who propelled the company into the future by developing genetic manipulation and turning the small Canadian company into a worldwide billion-dollar superpower. As much as my entire family makes in a year, Justin Tremblay makes in an hour.

Justin opens his palms toward the screen. "Welcome to this surprise live. At NuGene, we believe in using the power of genetics to shape the future. And the future is now. I'm overjoyed to announce our newest project: NuGene Match. This matching program is a genetically supported means of finding compatible matches from friends to lovers. Discover certainty when it comes to knowing who you're most compatible with in a variety of locations."

Whispers break out in the room. Hack me, this is amazing. Even if you get your DNA sequenced, you don't have access to other people's records to check out their genomes. NuGene isn't supposed to have access either. They're only meant to get data from their clients. But even if you could get that info, how would you know which genes show compatibility between people? Other companies have tried before, usually with questionable science to back it up. But other companies aren't NuGene.

Justin continues, "We were able to work with a variety of governments to organize an algorithm that matches compatibility without giving us access to your private genetic info."

I shout a thought at Keis: *Are you hearing this???*

She doesn't look back, transfixed by the screen.

"This will be a paid program, but right now we are in a testing phase and are offering a free beta version. Participants will have access to their match data and be given monetary compensation in exchange for wearing a tracker." Justin looks around as if he can see us with our mouths hanging open instead of just his screen. "We've released the beta invitations now, so check your feed to see if you've been selected."

He's saying something else about the monitor, but I can't hear it over the explosive noise of everyone digging through their bags and pockets to get at their phones.

I stare at my screen in shock as a white box with the NuGene logo declares: *Congratulations! You've been selected as a beta user for NuGene Match. Please read the following terms and conditions and click accept if you agree to join. Parental permission required if you are younger than 18 years old. In order to receive the full $200 for participation, you will need to visit NuGene once the trackers are available and wear it until the end of the trial.*

I don't bother reading the terms and tap the agree button. It sends off a permission ask to Mom, who accepts it almost instantaneously since she's used to screening parental terms for apps. Under my feed profile are two buttons, one for platonic matches and another for romantic ones. I tap the romantic button and choose Toronto as my location. As I do, I think of Lauren, who always prodded me to "get in the dating game," but it was hard to have time for it between finishing up my school credits and helping with the family beauty business. Even now, I'm concentrated on my Calling and helping Keis, not chasing boys. Romance has never been a focus for me, but even I'm curious about my perfect genetic match.

The screen blurs as it loads before a blue-gray-haired and gray-eyed boy's feed pops up with a 92 percent match.

Luc.

There's no way.

I expand the location to Ontario. The page loads, and at the top it shows . . . Luc with a 92 percent match.

I expand to Canada. To North America. To the world.

And every single time, I get him.

I sag in my seat and turn the screen off. I risk a look at Luc. He's got his arms crossed and is glaring out at the room.

He doesn't care about the new program or that we've been matched, if he even knows about it. Which he likely doesn't because he's not looking at his phone.

What a garbage program. Hack it and hack him.

Keis. Let's go.

He's managed to ruin the most exciting scientific advance of the decade without lifting a finger. Why force ourselves to stay when he's already won?

We leave the room without excusing ourselves.

CHAPTER FOUR

At my insistence, Keis and I take the longer streetcar ride back from NuGene instead of the GO train since I'm not exactly eager to get home. Except the normally lengthy trip passes as fast as Papa Dalton's Calling, which according to the almanac of our family's history, was a record ten seconds. He wasn't a Papa then, obviously, since he was still alive and all. He mistook Papa Yewei for a stranger in the library, and when offered a book recommendation, took it without thinking. The task, he later figured out, was to read the title—a tricky foreign word he got right by fluke. He didn't realize until Papa Yewei showed up to announce his gift.

It's basically some of the most sparked shit that I've ever heard. It came up again when some guy at his work was presenting something that used the book as a reference, and he said the title wrong. Papa Dalton corrected him, and it turns out his boss was a huge fan of the book and was impressed, because Papa got better opportunities after that and ended up with some fancy high-paying gig. No matter the task, or how much of a joke it seems, it's supposed to serve a purpose. Either way, while I stand in Alex's room getting fitted that evening, I'd rather think about Papa Dalton than about my Calling.

Hack it, I'd rather think about being matched up with that asshole Luc than my task.

Alex's walls are a kaleidoscope of retro paper magazine cutouts and sketches of her designs brought to life on yellowing biodegradable paper. Usually, her sewing desk is a neat arrangement of precut fabric patterns, but today it looks like a warehouse explosion of shimmering fabric and thread.

"Your room is a mess," I say.

Alex holds up the custom Calling dress that she made and tugs it over my head. "Thanks, Vo. Great to hear praise after I spent time making this for you."

"What's going on?" I pop my head through and blow hair out of my face.

Alex grimaces, smooths the white patterned fabric, and fluffs the back that billows open in soft waves. I didn't think the clinging gown, long enough to graze my toes, would be flattering, but it flows over my curves like hot white chocolate into a mug. "You know the show I have coming up? It got pushed forward a month. I have to scramble to get an entire hacking collection together in a couple weeks."

"But you have everything planned out, don't you?" I admire myself in the reflective screen of the closet.

Alex hooks a gold beaded belt around my waist as her eyes dart over my body. Straight seams. Sleek design. Impeccable fit. Alex was a whiz at making clothes when we were younger, but after she got her gift, that innate talent became something else. Her designs are an extension of her mind. And when she makes a garment, it's her love for you woven in thread and cloth.

"Don't you?" I press.

"I'm one person, and on top of my collection, I have a bunch of beading to do for the Caribana outfits. Johan wants them earlier this year for a final fitting since last year people had changed shape so much over time that we had to adjust too many of their costumes last minute."

The Caribana carnival happens in Toronto on the first Saturday in August. It's to celebrate Caribbean heritage, but even the Black witch families without that connection participate. It's become an event that brings our entire community together, regardless of our origins or ancestors.

Since Alex could sew even before her gift, she's always helped the Davises—Uncle's, and by extension Keis and Keisha's, family—make their mas camp outfits.

The Davises are the only impure family we interact with on a regular basis because they're technically part of ours too, not like Lauren's family, the Carters. But the Davises, unlike the Carters, are one of the few families who regularly leaves bodies in their wake. At least one every couple of years. It's what's made them one of the most powerful Black witch families in not only the province, but the entire country.

If a Davis was missing, we would be doing everything within our power to help. Family first. But because it's Lauren, because we don't have blood ties, everyone is fine leaving her out in the cold. Even though she's never hurt anyone in her life.

But she would, a little voice in the back of my mind whispers. One day, she would find someone in the streets, a person no one would miss, and torture them while she got stronger.

I push the thoughts away and focus on Alex. "I can help with the costumes so you can concentrate on your collection."

She lowers her eyes to the ground. "You don't have to do that."

"I'm not busy with anything except helping Granny distribute product like usual."

"You may be once your gift comes. Depending on what it is, if you can use it to help out with money, you'll be plenty busy."

"If I pass."

"Girl, you need to go to a self-esteem tutorial or something. You're ridiculous." Alex grasps my shoulders and spins me toward the door. "I know . . . stuff like this, some choices aren't easy, but a Calling is different than doing something like picking a specialization in school. Magic is in your blood. Just trust your instincts."

Alex has always been the kindest of my cousins. She would never say "some choices aren't easy *for you*," but the words unsaid still ring in my ears.

My Calling won't be like choosing what to eat for dinner, or what dress to wear, or what to specialize in at school. This is the only decision in my life that has ever mattered. And I seem to be the only one who's examining the possibility that I may not pass.

I turn over my shoulder to peer at Alex. "I'm helping. You already spent extra time making this dress for me. Consider it payment."

Her lips spread into a small smile.

Everything is ready. I have my dress, and the whole family is waiting downstairs.

It's time.

We walk out of her room and down the staircase together, me stuttering on each step, and her walking with sure-footed strides. I grip the banister between my fingers until they crack. I need to pass. I can't be the first one to fail in almost a hundred years. I can't *not* be a witch.

When we get to the bottom, Dad is there holding my little sister's hand. Unbidden, my mind goes back to the time when he and I stood there. I was the same age Eden is now, and my fingers were as small in his big hand as hers. He'd held packed bags while I'd blubbered through tears and snot to beg him to stay.

"Do you want to come with me, Voya?"

"Are we going?" Eden says, likely confused about why we're just standing around.

I come to stand in front of her. "Of course." My hand reaches out, and Eden breaks away from Dad to slip her little fingers into mine. When she was a baby, she used to grip my one finger between her tiny ones and smile at me with a gummy mouth. I didn't know I could love someone the moment I met them, but it happened with her.

Eden, Alex, Dad, and I head for the dining room. Focusing on the gentle swinging of my arm in time with my sister's is the only thing keeping me rooted to the ground.

"The Calling seems scarier than it is," Dad murmurs from behind me. "The choice you need to make to pass is often natural. If you trust in yourself, you'll do fine."

I practically have to strain to hear him. It's as if sometime between leaving us and meeting Priya, he lost his voice. When I was growing up, he knew how to be loud. He and Mom would scream at each other in the bedroom while I huddled in the family room with my cousins and pretended not to hear.

"Yeah." I push the word out to acknowledge him. Part of me wants to snap, "I get it, I'm shit at making decisions. I don't need everyone to keep reminding me." But talking back is the sort of thing Mom would dock my allowance over, so I bite my tongue.

We walk into the dining room, where everyone else is sitting. Uncle gives me a firm nod, which I'm sure means he approves of this 100 percent white dress.

"Took long enough," Keisha drawls.

"Sorry." I don't want to say anything, but if you don't respond to everything she says, then she pokes you with her nails. And it hurts. I drop into my chair beside Keisha and try not to miss Eden's hand when it breaks away from mine.

Keis sits across from me with her tablet out for self-study. There are few times when she isn't outside, escaping the adults' disapproval for a quiet alcove elsewhere. But like everyone else in the family, she's here for my Amplifying ceremony. The NuGene internship may be a bust, but I'm going to find something else amazing for her. When she sees me, she tucks the tablet away and smiles.

Keis isn't a smiley girl. That's how bad she thinks this is going to be. My legs cross and uncross under the table.

All of us are here except for Priya. Blood calls to blood, and we don't share any. Uncle is linked because the Davises have always had blood ties to ours—a side effect of procreating within a small community. A strong gift means that if you have kids with someone with no magic, you can still produce heirs with strong gifts. But weak gifts beget weaker gifts until the magic dies. If you want your legacy to survive, you need to stick with whoever has power.

And Eden, she's a special case. Normally, we wouldn't bring kids into an Amplifying ceremony, but she's always needed to be in ours. Not that anyone will talk about why that is. I hadn't seen Dad in years, until there he was at our back door on one of the coldest nights in January, screaming for Granny with a pregnant woman I had never seen before. The first time I saw Priya, she had blood flowing between her legs and pooling on the hardwood floor. I was ten.

What Dad needed was Uncle Vacu and his gift of safe births, but by that time, Uncle was too far into Mod-H to be any help.

I don't know what Granny did. Only that whatever it was makes her insist on Eden participating in our Coming-of-Age ceremonies even though she's technically related only to me by blood.

Granny shakes her head. "Late to your own Amplifying ceremony."

"Sorry, we were finishing up with the dress." That, and I wasn't exactly eager to get here.

Dad laces his fingers together atop the table. "She's here now."

"It's about respect," Granny snaps.

I shrink in on myself. "I'm sorry," I say again.

The corners of her lips quirk the slightest bit, and her eyes soften. I'm sure I'm her favorite. We spend the most time together since I'm always helping her pack up products for deliveries and she's always helping me try out recipes. The only other candidate for her favorite might be Eden. Except Granny is Mom's mom, so I don't think she means to show how much she loves the child Dad made with another woman.

I grip the edge of the table and stare at the deep grooves carved into the wood. In the middle is a witch mark with a center circle big enough for someone to sit in.

This is it.

"Anytime now. Get your butt in the circle." Alex waves her hand at me. I swiftly take back what I thought about her being the kind cousin.

Keisha flips her hair over her shoulder. "Yes, please. Let's get this over with."

That's my typical supportive family. My knees scrape on the wood as I climb onto the table and crawl toward the middle.

"We can see your panties!" Eden exclaims in complete horror.

"Ancestors give me strength," Granny groans.

I blink at Alex.

"Transparency is in, and it's only a bit," she says.

Keis barks out a laugh. "Only a bit? I can see the lace edging on her underwear."

I pull my legs together so that I don't have my butt so high in the air, but that makes it harder to crawl on the table.

Keisha threads her fingers together in front of her eyes and shakes her head. "You're making everyone uncomfortable." Her gift of sensing discomfort is as shitty as it sounds, for her *and* us.

Knowing *why* a person is uncomfortable isn't part of her

power, but she's nosy as hell, and intuitive on top of it, so she usually figures it out and likes to publicly air it for the world. Once, she sensed her mom's discomfort at dinner and loudly asked if she had been dumped by the guy she was seeing. Which she had. Auntie Maise cut off her hijacker chip privileges for a month, which Keisha moaned and complained about for the entire four weeks.

Sometimes I wish she didn't have a gift that's both useless and annoying. I know she can't choose what she gets, but damn.

"I cannot do another Amplifying ceremony. There are too many damn children in this house." Auntie rests her head on her interlaced fingers. "When I'm Matriarch, we're just gonna let the Callings come as they will. If you gotta do it while you're taking a shit, so be it."

"When *you're* Matriarch?" Mom says with raised eyebrows. "When is that happening?"

"Neither of you is going to be if you piss me off," Granny snaps, and they both fall silent but throw heated looks at each other.

"Sorry," I mumble as I reach the center of the circle and sit with my legs tucked underneath me in a way that seems decent.

"You're doing good, V." Dad's hands are clasped together so tight the knuckles are starting to look pale.

I force a smile onto my face. I don't like being called "V."

Granny glares at him. "Don't compliment the child for sitting on a table. That's why there are so many overconfident kids these days. You'd praise her for taking a breath if you were present for them all."

"I'm trying to help her feel comfortable."

"The Calling is not a comfortable experience, William."

Uncle nods in agreement, and Granny throws him a grateful smile.

Keis's eyes stay stuck on me. I'm sure she's mentally rolling them at her dad.

Sometimes I can't tell if he married Auntie Maise because he loved her or because he was desperate to be a Thomas. Mom said that he was a huge suck-up even when he and Auntie were dating. That he was always telling Granny how much he admired her converting our family to purity. Uncle never fit in with the Davises, even now. *Middle child syndrome*, Mom muttered under her breath once. But Granny treats him like the son she never had. Or the son she wished Uncle Vacu had been.

Granny opens a black cloth bundle and pulls out a slate rock with a sharpened tip. She passes the bundle around the table, and everyone takes a rock. Each one was carved by our ancestors and infused with a bit of their magic. Once you've gone through the Pass, you get your gift carved on your stone, kept by the Matriarch for these ceremonies.

Keis pulls hers out of the bundle with a slight scowl. After Mom or Auntie Maise, who nip at each other constantly over who will be the next Matriarch, Keis is the most obvious choice. Her gift, so far, has the strongest potential of us kids. Maybe of our entire generation. She has the power and responsibility for the title even if she doesn't want it.

Granny, like all Matriarchs, is supposed to consult with the ancestors on a regular basis about which family members are in the running for Matriarch, just in case something happens to her before she can name her successor. That way, the ancestors can name her true intended person instead of our family arguing over it. I'm 100 percent sure my name has *never* come up—I can't push *myself* in the right direction, much less guide the entire family.

Keis snaps her eyes up at me, and her mouth curves into a frown.

"Private thoughts are private," I say. Even though this isn't one of the times where I actually care that she can hear my thoughts. I don't have room to care about anything other than passing my Calling.

"That's a girl," Auntie says. "Don't let her walk all over your mind. Only uses her damn gift to violate privacy."

Keis crosses her arms and steupses—a teeth-sucking gesture that's the Caribbean equivalent of "get hacked."

She shouldn't have done that.

Auntie explodes in her chair. I'm not being hype. Flames actually burst from her body and lick up the table. I shrink back from them.

"Don't you sass me, Keisha!" She points a heated red finger down the table at Keis.

Keisha groans. "Mom, stop it."

Uncle buries his head in his hands. I don't know why he hopes for a smooth ceremony when our family doesn't do perfect.

"Show some respect!" Auntie screams.

Keis pulls her crossed arms apart with what looks like an effort. She once told me her mom's thoughts feel hot, that it burns to read her mind. "Sorry," she chokes out.

Auntie stares her down. They look so much alike, her and Keis. It's like watching the past and future face off. She deflates, the flames die, and she's left steaming, thudding down in her chair with an audible grunt.

"Are you done now?" Granny hisses.

Auntie doesn't bother looking abashed or ashamed. In fact, I don't know if I've ever even heard her say the word "sorry" to someone. Which, as a Canadian, is basically impossible.

I look to Keis for an answer.

She mouths, "Private thoughts are private."

Fair enough.

Uncle takes his hands away from his face. "Let's keep this going."

Granny clears her throat. "Blood to blood. I won't waste words, intention is everything."

Eden looks at Dad with a rock clutched in her fingers. He reaches out and grips her hands as he helps her draw a cut across the pad of her thumb. I swallow, staring at her as tears streak down her face, and the soft whimpering beginnings of a wail start. No one at this table wants to see her like this, but Granny insists on her being in the ritual.

Dad grips her hands tighter, and the effects of his gift show in the way her shoulders sag and her heaving chest relaxes. The pain isn't gone, but this will calm her enough to not feel it as sharply. Mom hates his gift. Toward the end of their relationship, she wouldn't let him touch her because she said he was manipulating her emotions. But Eden needs it.

I force myself not to think about the times I could have used the support he's giving to my little sister. Times when he wasn't there to give it to me.

Eden is six. I'm sixteen. I shouldn't need his reassurance.

Mom's eyes follow mine. They aren't soft or hard. But they're there, as they've always been.

In unison, everyone slices the tips of their fingers and drips their blood into the grooves carved in the table. Blood begins to flow toward me, the magic of the ritual pulling it closer.

Eden's blood joins with Keisha's, hers with Keis's, Alex's, and mixes with Auntie's and Uncle's, Mom's and Dad's, and Granny's. The stream drops off the edge of the table, where it collects in an egg cup on the floor. It's not ceremonial; it's from Pacific Mall—the gigantic Asian supercenter an hour east of downtown—but it works.

Granny picks up the cup and holds it out to me with stern eyes. As it tilts, the faux gold edging sparkles in the chandelier light.

I take it from her with a trembling hand. The blood inside is dark with a slight sheen to it. It's like my Bleeding bath, though lacking a certain scent. That's something health classes don't mention about periods, the smell.

Keis tosses her head back and rolls her eyes, so I know she's still listening to my thoughts. She can't help it. Or, she could but chooses not to.

I tilt my head back and, staring straight up, I force my right eye open with my left hand and pour from the cup. The blood splashes out, and I will myself not to blink. I inch open my left eye and dump the rest of the blood in. When I squeeze both eyes shut, the thick liquid drips out and slides down my face.

There's shuffling around me, and I don't need to see them to know my family is joining hands.

With witches, *real* witches, there are no Latin phrases or wand waving.

There's only blood and intent.

I press my hands onto the table, tracing the wood grain and the grooves carved into it with my fingertips before closing my eyes and aligning my intention. For my task. The one obstacle I need to overcome to be a witch.

The magic rises, heavy with the tang of our combined blood and suffocating with the sting of a scorching summer afternoon.

Then I hear it.

The sobbing.

I peel my eyes open, and there she is.

Mama Jova faces away from me, her hair pressed with some sort of heat, though not well enough to stamp out her curls that exert themselves as waves, pulled into a bun at the nape of her neck where the wounds begin. Her whipped back still drips with blood in the afterlife.

She's weeping. Mama Jova is always weeping.

Hack me.

Not her.

I've seen her at Caribana, the one day of the year when the ancestors of the Black witch community in Toronto choose to show themselves. Some dance in their ghostly forms down the street and celebrate with their living descendants. Not Mama Jova. She walks with slow, measured steps, crying with a fierce expression as if she were plotting revenge at a funeral instead of celebrating our heritage at a carnival.

And she's notorious for difficult Calling tasks where she changes the rules as she sees fit. The last witch in our family who failed, poor Wimberley, was called by Mama Jova almost a hundred years ago.

And now Mama Jova is here for me.

Her cries cut into silence like hitting mute on a feed show. She turns her head with the slow predatory precision of an owl homing in on its prey. Her sharp gaze bores into mine with a heat more intense than Auntie's flames, tear tracks etched onto her skin.

My eyes roll into the back of my head, and the world goes dark.

CHAPTER FIVE

W hen I peel my eyes open, I'm inside what looks like a small barn. There's enough hay everywhere that I don't know what else to call it. The room isn't much bigger than my bed, which makes me sound a lot more NuMoney chic than I am. But it's just a really small space.

I scramble off the ground and spin around. There's a girl lying on a stiff blanket thrown across the floor, not much older than I am. I inch closer to her.

There's something familiar about her face. I take in the dark inkiness of her hair, the warm hickory of her skin, and the shape of her cheeks. Except they don't look right. They're full in a way that speaks of young beauty. I've only ever seen them sunken.

"Mama Jova?" I whisper.

The door to the room bangs open, and Mama bolts up in bed. Two men barge into the room and grab her by her arms.

"What is this? What's happening?" she screams, voice thick with a New Orleans accent that I only recognize because of feed recordings in the almanac of family who moved back there. I've never heard Mama Jova herself speak before. Only cry.

The tremor in her voice makes a shiver run through my body in a harsh wave. I try to grab onto her, to help, to do something, but my fingers pass through her arm.

The men drag her outside, and I rush out after them.

All around us are Black people. Some are lifting huge bundles of stiff green-and-tan stalks of sugarcane while others help pull wagons full of the crop.

The men keep dragging Mama, and I trip over my feet following them. The people around us look at her and turn away. They pin their eyes to their work.

Her captors slam Mama against a tree and strip her naked. Watching them tear each piece of clothing from her wriggling body makes me hug myself tight. Each scrap of cloth is a fragile bit of glass tossed away to shatter on the ground until nothing is left but broken pieces.

Rough, fraying rope becomes her bonds as they tie her hands to the tree, pushing her face up against the bark. She's screaming in earnest now, so loud that my eardrums feel like they're splitting, and no one is doing anything about her suffering.

I open my mouth to shout for help, but nothing comes out.

There's yelling behind us where two other men are dragging a boy who looks like he's Mama Jova's age. *My* age. He's thrashing like a wild pony, but they manage to hold him steady.

His dark skin glistens in the sun, and sweat sparkles on his face.

When his and Mama's eyes meet, their screams quiet for a moment—before they begin again, louder. His coal-colored eyes are alight with misery.

The men strip him down and tie him to the same tree, slamming his nose on its trunk in the process. His and Mama's hands are almost close enough to touch. They make their best effort at it, reaching their calloused fingers out to each other, and fail, fingertips a hair's breadth from one another. My throat is dry to the point of pain.

"I've got a deal for you two." The man who walks over isn't

the one who held Mama or the boy, but he is the one in charge.

I live in 2049.

I've never been called a slur.

Not to my face.

Or felt ashamed to be Black.

But when that white man comes with his whip, I sink to my knees.

The first lash is so fast that Mama is sobbing into the tree by the time I notice what happened. The whip keeps coming. One strike after the other. They don't touch the boy. The agony in his eyes as he watches makes it feel as if they are. Whispered prayers slip from his lips.

The man stops his whipping, and I cry out.

It's done.

"We're not finished here. Someone's been stealing." He walks over to Mama and brings his face close to hers. "Food is a privilege. So is working in the house. So is your life." He says "life" with enough emphasis that spit flies onto her cheek.

I want to stare at the ground until this is over. But I can't look away. Somehow, it would feel like a betrayal not to witness this moment of my ancestor laid bare. I have the option to look away, but she never can.

The man points at the boy. "Neither of you needs to die today. Someone's getting a whipping, that's for certain. But you can both live. Confess. Tell me who the thief is, because I know it's one of you."

Mama weeps into the bark of the tree but says nothing. I grip my hands into fists.

The man straightens up. "Your choice." The whip comes down and blood flies from her back like sparkling sugar syrup.

I count ten lashes.

Fifteen.

Twenty.

The boy still hasn't been touched. He's sobbing harder than Mama.

On lash thirty, the light goes out of her eyes. Something there snaps like a fresh stalk of celery.

The man pauses his whipping and leans close to her face. "Make a choice, girl. Tell me the truth."

The boy's eyes go wide, pleading. Like he's begging, but for what, I don't know. For her to blame him or take the blame herself?

But Mama says nothing. Only stares.

"Fine, have it your way." The master turns to the man beside him, who hands him a gun. It's long and polished so well it shines in the sun. He backs up and fires a bullet into the boy's head. The gunshot rings in my ear and keeps on ringing. I'm grateful for it. It drowns out my crying.

It's one thing to learn about what happened to Mama Jova in the almanac or from Granny. I know she was a slave and that she died on a sugarcane plantation. That the nakedness of her form and whip marks on her back are all carryovers from her painful death.

But it's a different thing altogether to watch.

The men move to leave, but one pauses for a moment. He squints at the boy's forehead, the bullet hole weeping blood that drips down between his still-open eyes. "What the . . . ?"

For a beat, nothing happens. It's just all of us staring.

In the next moment, a streak of red, solid and sharp, shoots out from the boy's forehead and impales the man. Right through his skull in the same place the boy was shot. The man drops to the ground.

The other men cry out as ropes of red rise high from Mama Jova's and the boy's bodies. Blood from his head and her back fly through the air in stiff, solidified crimson bullets, ripping through the men's bodies like paper.

It only stops when every man is dead.

Mama Jova leans against the tree, breathing heavily, body shuddering. Her plump arms and legs have turned thin and fragile, and the full cheeks of her face have become shallow jowls. She looks like the same Mama I saw in the dining room and at Caribana year after year.

Every witch has a limit, a bandwidth. To cast beyond it takes extreme effort and has a high cost. And something like this, turning blood into a physical weapon—something I didn't even know was possible—seems like it's more expensive than the average cast. But it's a price that Mama was apparently willing to pay.

A Black woman drops the stalk of sugarcane in her hand and stumbles to Mama Jova, hands shaking, unsure.

"Go," Mama whispers, voice hoarse. "Leave me. I won't make it. Go now."

The woman takes one long look at her, staring into her eyes, before she turns and runs. Others in the fields follow after her, dropping their sugarcane stalks and sprinting away as fast as they can. But not all of them go. Some stay, rooted to the ground, unable to move.

All the while, Mama is tied to the tree. I can't be sitting there more than a few minutes, but it's like time is on fast forward. People move around her at a speed I can't comprehend while she stays there, pressed against the tree until, finally, the light leaves her eyes.

"I spent years fighting against what I thought was the right way to be a witch," Mama Jova says, standing behind me.

I swivel around, heart in my throat, and watch her. Still on my knees, legs too weak to stand. Naked and thin, Mama is exactly as she was against the tree. She's still a girl, the same age as me, but the title of "Mama" makes her look older. Technically, she is. Almost two hundred years have passed since she was sixteen.

"I can see you struggle with it. Pure and impure, right and wrong." She gazes over at her body. "I thought it was better to never choose a side, to just float outside it. And it worked for a time. I even loved someone." Tears gather at the edges of her eyes. "If I'd told the master that David stole the food, he would have killed him. Or would he? I didn't know. And if I said it was me, would I die? Would the master kill David just to spite me? Would we both live? Should I try to find a way to use magic to save us? What could I do?" She pauses and swallows. "You know what magic is, don't you?"

My throat is so dry that I have to wet it with saliva before I can speak. Is this my task, answering this question?

"Do you?"

"Blood! And . . . and intent."

"Yes," she says, voice low and melodic. "It's that simple. I spent so much time avoiding choices at a time when it was most important to be decisive. I was too torn to focus my intention on one thing. And he died for it."

My eyes shoot to the boy, David, leaning lifeless against the tree.

"And I only found it when he was already dead."

"I . . . I'm sorry."

"I know." Mama Jova's lips quirk like she might smile, but she doesn't. "Will you accept the task I give you?"

This is it, the moment where I pass or fail. Sixteen years of life spent leading up to this moment.

And it's wrong.

I'm supposed to pick between two options for my task. She's supposed to tell me both, and I pick one. Those are the rules, but like Keis's Calling, they aren't being followed. Mama Jova would never Call with something simple. I stutter out, "What is it? What are my choices?" Desperate for some sort of clue.

Mama Jova's lips go tight. "You can't know this task before you accept it. Reject it, and every Thomas after you will lose their chance to become a witch. Ancestors will Call on them no more. Accept it and fail, and every single witch who is tied to the Thomas blood at this moment will lose their magic."

If I weren't already on my knees, I would drop again.

No. It shouldn't be like this. When you fail your Calling, *you* lose your chance at magic. *You* don't become a witch. No one else in the family should be affected. What she's asking is more than I can give.

I shake my head. "I can't make a decision like that." How can I? It was one thing when this was my choice for my life. But what she's asking is so much bigger than me.

Mama's lip curls. "This is my arrangement and your Calling. That means I Call for you, I set the task, and you answer. Now, what is it?"

I press my hands against my eyes. What will this task be? If I accept it and then fail, I'll lose magic for everyone. We rely on the adults' gifts to support the family. Magic is the only thing that's allowed them to find work with livable pay. Even our beauty products are supported by Granny's magic, though none of us has ever learned how.

We would lose everything.

Where else could we find a place big enough to stay together that we can afford? Sure, we can only just manage this one, but it's still cheaper than any other house we could attempt to buy. None of us has an education to fall back on or the money to try. Starting at the bottom with low- or no-paying internships isn't an option either. By the time anyone worked back up to something livable, we would be overdue on everything.

Dad and Priya will leave with Eden. He'll be gone again, and I'll lose my sister. And Alex has nowhere else to go. She can't be with her Mod-H–addicted dad. Auntie and Uncle will fight over who gets custody of my cousins. I won't wake up to a house full of my family. Me, Mom, and Granny will be packed into some apartment, struggling to keep what's left of us together.

"Mama, please." I hate how pathetic my voice sounds. "Let me talk to my family about this. I can't make this decision without them." This isn't like picking out an internship for Keis. I can't choose everyone's fate.

Mama returns to staring at David. Her hands are fisted at her sides. "I Called, but you won't answer. You have learned *nothing* here today. That's why you fail."

Fail?

Fail.

No!

I scramble to my feet and reach out for her. Midway, my eyes roll back, and I fall.

I wake and my fingers curl into the wood of the dining room table.

I failed.

The family is shifting, speaking, and shouting, but I can't make out the words. My eyes are clenched shut like if I keep them closed, I won't have to see what I've done.

I slam my hands on the table and claw at the wood.

Each generation of Thomases after me will never have a Coming-of-Age. My failure means the magic stops.

I can't let that happen.

I need one more chance to fix this. I can't fail.

"Why should you have another chance? Everyone gets one Calling." I snap my eyes open. Mama Jova appears at the head of the table. Her drawl isn't malicious, and she isn't reveling in her words, just stating fact. She drags a sharp fingernail along the table, and the sound screams in my ears.

If I had one more shot, I would do my best to pass. I messed up, but I can do better.

I just need one more chance.

Please!

My eyelashes flutter, and a thick haze settles in my head. It's like a balloon, filling, and filling, and about ready to pop. My throat burns, and I can't swallow. I struggle for air, shoving my fingers into my throat to try and dislodge what's there. Except I can't grab ahold of anything.

What's happening to me?

The pressure in my head becomes unbearable, and my vision goes black as I wait for my skull to explode.

Instead, I get a punch to the gut.

Again.

And again.

And again.

I cough, and something flies out of my mouth. With my throat suddenly clear, I gasp at the air, ravenous and foaming at the lips like an infected animal—desperate for the caress of oxygen flooding my lungs. Once I have my fill, I sag back into someone's arms. I turn my head around, and there's Keis.

Her face is pale, a sickly-looking washed-out shade, like discarded peanut shells.

Our combined heavy breaths are the only sound in the room.

Uncle slams his hands on the table. "Now you've done it."

"Done what? Saved my baby cousin from dying?" Keis snaps.

"You're only a year older," I mumble. My voice is scratchy and hoarse.

There's a pull around my middle as someone lifts me off the table and into his arms.

Uncle.

For a second, a single second, I thought it might be Dad.

And I hate myself for it.

As much as I shit on Uncle, he's been there for me more often than my dad.

Tears flow from my eyes, and sobs tear from my throat.

Mom is over at my side in an instant, petting my hair and murmuring words I can't make out through my blubbering.

"I'm so sorry." I've ruined everything.

Chairs scrape against the floor as my family gathers around Uncle and me. I bury my face in his shoulder so I don't have to look at anyone's pitying expression. He smells like the musky grass that grows in our backyard.

I've cursed us.

This will be the last generation with magic. Our entire family history, rich and colorful, will run dry.

"If I had another chance, I could do it. I could," I sob.

"Stop crying," Granny commands.

Mom snaps back, "She can cry if she wants!"

"I'm telling her not to cry because there's no reason to! This isn't over."

I choke on my spit and have to take a minute to stop coughing and catch my breath. "What?"

Granny holds up a crumpled piece of paper. I don't know what it's supposed to mean to me.

"It's what you spat out. What you were choking on," Keis says.

I take the paper from Granny with shaking fingers. The whole family presses close to get a better look. Dad has to pick up Eden so she can see.

Auntie lets out a laugh. "Hack me. Mama Jova must love you."

I shake my head. It doesn't make any sense. Mama Jova hates me. I didn't choose.

And yet there it is. Written plain as day.

> Even a trait as deplorable as
> stubbornness can at times breed
> admiration. You wanted another
> chance? Here it is. You have until
> tomorrow's sunset to answer my
> Call.
>
> Don't fail me a second time.
>
> Mama Jova

CHAPTER SIX

Granny eyes a man on the subway until he offers her his seat. She flashes a grin at me and settles into his vacated place. We can't take the GO train to Chinatown, so we're on the TTC.

This has not been my week. I've been humiliated by a boy who is my genetic match and failed the one thing in my life I shouldn't fail. Not to mention, I was given a Calling harder than any I've heard of. Once I managed to stop crying, I updated the family on what had happened, and even Granny hadn't ever heard of consequences like the ones Mama gave.

The paper that came out of my mouth is like a chunk of concrete in my pocket where it sits.

There are three ways this can go: One, I accept Mama Jova's unknown assignment and succeed, everyone keeps their magic, and it continues to flow through our bloodline for generations. Two, I refuse her task, and I will never become a witch, nor will anyone with Thomas blood born after me. Or three, I accept her mystery task, fail again, and not only do future generations lose magic, but everyone in my family will lose theirs as well. The only people in our house that would be spared are Dad, Priya, and Eden, who aren't Thomases. Even though Mom and Dad joined their blood in a ceremony during their wedding, like all witches, they magically cut those ties when they divorced. Auntie and Uncle never officially split their blood when they separated, and Mama Jova even made sure to say every witch who "at this moment" is tied to our blood would lose magic, so trying to cut blood ties now after the fact wouldn't help Uncle anyway.

The only way to win is to put everything on the chopping block and hope I don't let the knife slip and leave us all bleeding out on the counter.

When Granny insisted I come downtown with her to sell some product first thing this morning, I jumped at the distraction. Better than obsessing about the task at home all day.

I clutch at the tote bag of Thomas products we brought with us and shuffle closer to Granny and away from the rest of the people on the subway pressing in on me.

She shifts in her seat. "They can make twenty new subway lines, but these seats are as uncomfortable as when I was young."

The hard plastic seats have the same thin red fabric covers that have never been comfortable. Especially if you have a Thomas butt.

Arriving at Bathurst. Bathurst Station.

The stench of sweat is muggy in the air. I long for the uncrowded and scent-free GO train with its soft, cushy seats.

"Have you made your decision?" Granny asks.

I drop my gaze to the floor and stare at my toenails. Keisha did them for me. Sunshine yellow with little clouds on them. "What do you think I should do?"

"Is this my Calling or your Calling?"

"What I do will affect everyone. I shouldn't be deciding by myself."

"Yes, you should!" she snaps.

I look down at her, and the lady in the seat next to Granny widens her eyes and turns away. Great. Now we're making a scene.

Black people raise their voices for a minute and some folks act like we're seconds away from some intra-racial violence.

No one has ever compared their tan to my skin to see which was darker, or tried to touch my hair, but there are these little reactions that people seem incapable of stopping even after hundreds of years. Longer stares when I first enter a store. Brief surprise when they learn where I live. That we have a house. Tiny moments piled up on top of one another. It doesn't happen often, but each time it does seems to stand out sharply. It's like the better things get, the more people want to pretend that nothing happens at all. But it does. Even if it's not as much as it was, it doesn't take away from the fact that it's not gone. It took centuries to form those ideas, and apparently, it'll take just as long to stop them.

I make an effort to lower my voice, hoping that Granny gets the message. "You *must* have an opinion."

"An opinion!" Granny barks, not getting my mental signals or otherwise ignoring them. "This is . . ." She shakes her head. "I can't believe an ancestor would actually strip us of magic. But the strict rule of a Calling has always been that it's *your* decision. You never know, maybe the real task is that you choose for yourself. So I won't be sharing any *opinions* with you."

Part of me thought she would have this perfect answer. The ancestors speak to her. Shouldn't Mama have said something? But Granny seems just as unsure about it as I am.

Granny's shoulders relax, and she gazes into my eyes. "You can do this. You're a Thomas. We suffer and we survive."

I wiggle my toes in my sandals, wishing I believed in myself half as much as Granny seems to.

Arriving at Spadina. Spadina Station.

I move toward the doors, and Granny stays where she is. "Granny . . . you should get up."

"Are these lightning-speed exits? Are we racing?"

The doors slide open, and people push against me to get out. I step out of the subway car and shift from foot to foot waiting for Granny. She shuffles out just as the doors are closing.

"They have those things going too fast," she huffs.

We follow the flow of the crowd past the ads in English and Chinese characters flashing and trying to grab our attention. One sign features a half-naked man on a horse, who calls out to Granny. "Hey, Ava!"

She stops in her tracks. I grab her hand and pull her along with me. "Ignore him. We have to keep going. We're on a staircase."

Granny blinks and yanks back her hand. "That should be illegal! Ads like that having access to our names."

"It's a feed setting. You can turn it off if you don't want them to pull from your profile."

"How?"

"I can show you later."

"Never mind. I'll Google it."

I almost groan aloud. "You don't need to do that. Use the AI assistant on your phone."

"Why? I've been Googling since I was a kid."

We reach the top of the staircase, where the streetcar, sleek and shiny with a bright red-and-white exterior, is waiting for more sweaty bodies to pack into it. We step inside and manage to grab seats close to the entrance.

Granny pulls out her phone and starts swiping through it. I lean over to see what she's doing, but her privacy screen is on.

A grin slithers onto her face. "Can't see, can you? You know how I figured that out?"

"You Googled it?"

"Damn straight."

I don't tell her that if she used her AI assist, it would have set it up for her in seconds. She's probably just sending a message to the Huangs to let them know we're on our way.

Most of our clientele purchase our goods from the feed store, and it's my job to help package them so Uncle can program the drone shipments. But certain magical families prefer that Granny make the delivery personally.

I've gone to Chinatown with Granny more times than I can count, but I'm particularly glad she asked me along for this delivery. Not just for the pure distraction, but because the Huangs have connections to a few university libraries and may have a lead on an internship for Keis. It's a better option than trying to recover NuGene after dealing with Luc. I'm sure he's already run off to Sponsor Daddy to blacklist us.

The streetcar moves forward, and we pull out of the subway tunnel onto the surface. The glass University of Toronto buildings are as familiar to me as the flashing neon signs and larger-than-life character holos who wave as you go by. The university sprawls over the city with its towering modern buildings while students loiter outside, the scent of flavored vapor smoke milling around them, carefree with their promise of a certain future. Keis deserves to be one of them.

Granny points at a flashing sign advertising the virtual adventure rooms inside. "That used to be a frozen yogurt place."

"Didn't everything used to be a froyo place when you were younger?"

At home, Granny might have hissed at that sass. Chinatown Trip Granny is different. She laughs.

A smile tugs itself onto my face. I can almost forget the conversation we just had about my Calling.

Arriving at Dundas Street West. Dundas Street West.

The intersection of Dundas Street West and Spadina Avenue is marked by the gigantic Dragon City mini mall on the corner made up of green tinted glass and masses of people. I rush out and wait for Granny outside. She steps out of the streetcar as the doors close and mumbles a thank-you.

I force down a laugh. Mom does the same thing when she gets off non-subway public transit. "You know it's automated now, right? There isn't any driver to thank."

Granny shrugs. "Habit."

It strikes me as being painfully Canadian to say thank you to the computer for dropping you off.

We cross the street and head toward one of the dozens of fruit and vegetable stands. There's an intermingling of the scent of fresh fruit and the stink of rotting ones. The stand we pick has a holo sign with Chinese characters on top and below declares "Food Market" with a swipe of red at the end. In the top right corner, so small you might miss it, is a gold embossed witch mark.

The storefront is covered with stands of magenta pitaya and dragon fruit, three-foot-long stalks of sugarcane, overflowing bins of vibrant chocolate-, sepia-, and russet-colored spices, and avocados bigger than my fist.

The windows—what little you can see through the fruits and veggies—are covered with missing posters of Lauren. Her face makes my stomach clench. I could ask Granny again why we don't help find her, but I don't. My Calling has already caused enough drama. I don't want to spark shit by getting into an argument about helping an impure family when she's already made her opinion known. In our family, making five of those posters would exhaust your energy for the entire day. But for an impure one like the Carters, it's no big deal.

Granny will sell to impure families, she'll go to backyard parties and Caribana with them, but she won't do them a favor. Not unless they're like Uncle and willing to convert. Or they're the Davises, and our families are too interconnected to *not* help, no matter what Granny personally wants to do. Though the Davises have always been powerful enough to not need it.

She squeezes through the crowd of people shoving fruits and veggies into their bags. I follow behind, and my eyes linger on an unmarked cardboard box filled with rose-colored lychee. I could eat all of them.

"Voya!"

"Yeah, coming." I tear my eyes away and catch up with her.

The inside of the store has more fresh fruits and vegetables than what's outside. Except these have the benefit of misters that spritz water on them every minute or so. The aisles are packed with imported snacks whose multicolored labels call out to me with promises of red bean–flavored chocolate, green apple chews, and something with a rainbow sticker I'm compelled to eat.

Granny jerks her head toward the East Asian woman behind the counter. "I sent a message twenty minutes ago."

The woman tucks a strand of auburn highlighted hair behind her ear and gestures to the pop fridges at the back. "She's ready for you."

"Thank you," I say on behalf of Granny, who makes a beeline for the door squished between the back fridges and display of carrots without saying anything.

There's a witch mark drawn in off-white on the otherwise eggshell-white door.

She pushes it open, and I come in after her. It swings shut behind us.

The room inside is like a combination retro bar and library. There are floor-to-ceiling shelves packed with thick tomes in jewel-toned ruby and emerald. Smooth jazz yawns through the speakers to fill the room and is punctuated by the low hum of conversation. The bar is populated with a mixture of people, all witches, mostly from Chinese families, and mostly Huangs. The rug in the middle of the room is a mix of scarlet and gold weaved into a large single character that represents their family name. Vapor smoke that smells of strong incense blows in the air and stings my nose.

Rowen Huang sits in a roped-off lounge area on a plush chair that looks like a combination of velvet and leather tanned to a rich mahogany. Not modded leather either. Her dark hair falls in an elegant bob framing her light peachy-colored round face, and thick lashes drape over her ashy eyes. The maroon pantsuit she wears is perfectly tailored to her wide, curved hips and accented with sleek black heels.

Only twenty-five and she's the Matriarch of a family of witches whose lineage goes back as far as our own. Voted into power by everyone of age with her ancestral blood living and practicing in Canada. It's not how every family chooses their Matriarch, but it's how they do it. I suspect that her gift, a honeyed tongue, has something to do with her success. Her words inspire people in a way that ordinary ones don't. It's more than suggestion, it's devotion. People tell her things that they wouldn't say to anyone else. Witches, in general, are notorious gossips, but Rowen's one of the few who actually know real secrets. It makes her a powerful leader.

Her eyes dart to the tote bag in my hands. "What did you bring me?"

Granny and I sink into the couch across from her. I place the bag on the table and take out our Thomas Brand Slicker Than Silk Conditioner, Matter Than Matte Setting Powder, Wrinkle Be Gone Night Cream and Day Cream, and a small, unmarked vial that I swear makes Rowen shiver when she sees it.

Her creamy smooth and soft skin isn't the result of NuGene modding or non-mod plastic surgery. It's from a strict regimen of using our beauty products.

Pure families don't have the magic bandwidth that impure

ones do to clear acne for weeks with a single cast. That's what makes our products useful to them. It does what they can't without sacrificing purity, and with a higher success rate than anything a non-witch could produce.

Rowen picks up the unmarked vial with pointed nails. She holds it up to her eye and shifts the bottle so the blush pink fluid sloshes around.

"A single drop on the tip of your tongue, once a week." Granny eyes the vial. "No more, no less."

She makes this elixir specifically for Rowen. I have no idea what's in it, but Granny keeps a special stash aside for her that she cooks up regularly. Granny's the one who adds that special magic touch to every product we make. I once asked Mom if that was her gift. She grimaced and snapped, "How should I know? She won't tell me, either."

To this day, none of us knows what it is that Granny can do. Not even Keis. She says our grandma's mind is like a brick wall. Hard and unyielding. Granny and Uncle are both the types of witches who keep their gifts hidden. They go alone through the Pass, so there aren't any witnesses when their power is revealed.

Hiding gifts used to keep us safe from people ready to kill or use the knowledge against us. When we decided to come together as a community, it meant we protected each other, and the need to hide them wasn't as necessary. Or that's what it was supposed to be. Not every family decided to be as open as ours. Every Thomas's gift other than Granny's and Uncle's is known. The entire family is there for the ceremony, so when our ancestor announces our gift, there are witnesses to hear it.

That's what the Pass was made for in the first place. Ancestors could have given you your gift as soon as you completed the Calling, but they didn't. They waited for the Pass, when your family members would gather in a circle around you and give their blessing.

Like when we gathered for Alex, Keis, and Keisha, it showed that we believed in their strength as much as the ancestor who Called.

And yet, even without a known gift, Granny expanded our community to pure witches outside the Black witch community, which lets us connect with people like the Huangs, the Martinezes, and Priya's family, the Jayasuriyas.

It was a good thing too, because now there's this constant rift between everyone in the Black witch community that doesn't seem to exist in other racial and cultural witch communities, and it's more than just the divide between pure and impure families. Keisha loudly brought up the discomfort before, but the adults in the family brushed it off. It wasn't always like this. I don't even understand why things changed so much from when I was little.

Granny clears her throat and widens her eyes at Rowen in her signature "pay me" expression.

The Huang Matriarch bobs her head but doesn't take her eyes off the vial. "How you manage to make this and stay pure is a mystery."

Granny's mouth shoves into a frown. "Are you questioning me?"

"No. Impure witches have a scent, like the ashes from the dead victims they burn. Even the ones who don't kill. I'm just expressing my amazement." She sets the vial down and stands. "Wait a moment. I'll get the money. I've been using a secure card instead of my phone. Dad's paranoia is getting to me. He insists that I lock it up." We watch as she opens a door to a second room and disappears inside.

A woman at the bar waves a lazy hand at Granny. I recognize her as one of Rowen's aunties but can't remember her name.

Granny lets out a breath. "I have to go say hi. Tell Rowen I'll be right back. You can collect the payment if she's in a rush." She doesn't wait for my reply and slides over to the woman, pushing out an exuberant greeting she reserves for dealing with potential clients.

Rowen reenters the room with a spring in her step a minute later. She spots Granny at the bar and smiles. "I see my aunt has caught your grandmother."

"It seems like." I pull myself up straight and meet her eyes, glad that Granny is preoccupied. "I wanted to ask, internship application season is coming up, and I wondered if you had heard of any openings in a library? My cousin—you know Keis—is about to finish up a round of courses. She has about twenty-one credits now, and she'll have twenty-eight by the end of the year. She could be a great candidate." I force myself not to check if Granny is watching. She hates us asking other people for favors. I say that if we're supposed to be this happy pure community, why not act like it?

Rowen sinks into her chair and taps her chin. "Is that Maise's daughter? The one who does the modeling or the one who always has a tablet in her hands?"

"The tablet one. She's always studying." I jerk my head as if earnest nodding will make Rowen more likely to help.

"Twenty-eight credits is great—that's eighteen over minimum and fifteen more than my younger brother." She wrinkles her nose. I don't blame her. Yawen isn't known for being studious, more for posting feed pics of himself with sports cars. "I'll send over a few leads for you. My uncle is the chair on the internship board for U of T, and he'd like a couple interns from pure families."

She holds out her phone, and I tap mine against hers to transfer my contact info. I pull my hand back and clasp my fingers together to stop them from shaking. It's a small win, but a necessary one with the way everything else is going.

Part of me hopes our interaction with Luc didn't ruin Keis's chances at NuGene, but that is a long shot. This opportunity is a solid backup. "Thank you. I appreciate it."

Rowen waves her hand. "It's important to stick together. We

came here for a better life. Living secretly can be isolating, after all. It's best to keep close."

This place must be her way of bringing her people together. Johan taught us in our magic community school that witches immigrated here either to escape persecution in their countries or to seek more opportunities than they felt their countries could give. We should be bonded by that, and yet where some communities stick together, ours stays apart. I wish we had a place like this.

The longing must show on my face because Rowen's eyes soften. "It's hard to create a functioning community. Purity and gifts create such divides already without bringing other drama into it." This is not Matriarch Rowen speaking; this is the *other* Rowen. The one who knows things. Feeding you a small crumb and willing you to beg for more.

She's got a secret that she's itching to spill.

I shouldn't get caught in this trap. "I don't think we have any drama. It's just a bit disjointed." I mean, Granny and Johan will always butt heads, but we get along.

"Of course you don't." The smile on Rowen's face is wide and placating, the sort of response you give to a child who doesn't know any better.

What drama could she be talking about? I need to drop this. I have enough on my plate with my Calling without getting drawn into Rowen Huang's gossip. And yet . . . her gossip isn't speculation, it's always facts. "Did something happen?"

"Oh, well, I don't want to spread rumors or anything."

I force myself not to roll my eyes. "Of course."

"It's a shame. Your three Matriarchs worked so hard to build a community, and then that terrible business happened. You can't always trust people. Especially outsiders." Rowen waves over my head. "Here's your grandma."

Hack me. This is why you can't get drawn into Rowen's shit. She dangles something over your head before snatching it back, so you have to agonize and drill to pry the words from her lips.

What is she talking about, "your three Matriarchs"? Does she mean the ones in the Black witch community? She must. She said "your." But we have five Matriarchs in our community, not three—Thomas, Davis, James, Carter, and Bailey. Maybe the three strongest of us? The Davis Matriarch, April-Mae, and Granny are up there for sure, but the others have kind of always floated in the background. Maybe the Carters and their Matriarch? But what drama would those three have stirred up together?

Matriarchs are powerful. If they really got into it, they could create a rift like the one I've noticed between the families. But I've never heard of anything like that happening, and it doesn't seem like the sort of thing they could hide, even if the adults want to pretend there's no tension in the community.

And that's without even getting into this outsider betrayal that Rowen's talking about.

Granny sits down and looks between me and the Huang Matriarch. Rowen is all innocent smiles. I can't get my lips to twist the right way to pretend like everything is fine.

"How was my aunt?" Rowen asks.

Granny's expression is neutral. "Good. I'll have Voya drop off some elixirs for her when they're ready."

"Not my special one, I hope."

"I wouldn't dream of it. That's an exclusive item just for you."

Rowen presents her secure card, and Granny pulls out her phone to arrange the payment.

I can't see the amount but know it's enough to cover our hydro and gas bills for the month. Which, when you have more than ten people living in a house and using every manner of electronics, isn't a small amount.

My glee from finding Keis an internship lead is overshadowed by Rowen's words and the money collected from her. It's like I'm being shown what we'll lose if our magic is gone. If I fail. Granny didn't bring me here as a distraction. She brought me to see this transaction.

I need to take the risk to keep our magic flowing.

Or maybe Granny's telling me that I *shouldn't* take the risk, because if I fail, we'll lose everything.

The sharp ping of the successful money transfer rings in my ears long after we leave the shop.

And as much as I tell myself to ignore Rowen's words, I can't stop wondering about "your three Matriarchs" and the betrayal that split our community.

CHAPTER SEVEN

Later that day, Granny and I walk in the front door just as Mom comes rushing down the stairs. The staircase in our house has the sort of scale and look that make any entry or exit from it grand and dramatic. Like the kind of feed shows that Mom, Auntie, and Granny love. Sometimes I think that's the only reason Mom ever rushes down it at all. For the drama.

"What took you so long?" Her hair is piled high on her head in an elegant twist of braids that she didn't have this morning.

I gesture to it. "Did you get your hair done?"

"It's cute, right?" She strikes a pose to show off the chalk-white and dark strands plaited into braids no wider than my pinkie finger. "I needed a new video for my feed, so I did a quick box-braiding tutorial."

When she's not recording, she can use magic and get a six-hour style done in one. Usually she *does* use magic and just edits the video so it looks sped up.

Mom told me that when she was a teenager, she wanted to do hair, but when her object-reading gift came, she realized using it meant avoiding a competitive and ultimately low-paying intern position. Now the bulk of her money comes from helping private investigators. They don't have access to the kind of genetic data the police do, so they operate more on informed tips, which when given the right object, Mom can provide. None of them know she has magic. They just think she does great detective work.

If I fail, she'll lose that. The only silver lining would be her getting to do what she originally wanted. Financially hacked for personal freedom.

I cut my eyes to Granny, thankful that she doesn't have Keis's gift. I doubt she'd appreciate those thoughts.

She steupses at Mom. "You could have done a reading in the time you did that."

"I would have, but I had a cancellation," Mom snaps back.

"You and Maise love to go back and forth about which of you is going to take over for me, and I've yet to see the responsibility from either of you."

I shift in place. Nothing is more uncomfortable than the way Mom and Auntie argue about being Matriarch. Sometimes I worry that whoever doesn't get the title will be so upset they'll leave the house altogether.

"Are you serious?" Mom gasps. "I'm constantly helping you with the business. And who else are you going to pick besides one of us? The girls are too young. And none of them want to be Matriarch anyway."

"Voya?" Priya calls, and we turn to her. She hovers near the front door of the house, dressed in a long sundress made out of several different types of fabric. Preferring to make her own clothes but disliking purchasing things brand-new, my stepmom collects scraps from whatever Alex has been working on and constructs her own creations. My designer cousin calls them "retro boho chic."

Eden peeks out from around her mom's legs, some sort of juice pouch shoved between her lips. She dislodges it to cry, "We're going to the park!"

"Cool!" I say, using a high-pitched happy voice that comes out exclusively for my baby sister.

Priya makes eye contact with Granny and Mom with a twitching smile. I won't pretend the whole living-with-your-ex-husband's-new-wife thing isn't strange. Mom alternates between complimenting the positive changes that Priya has made with Dad and griping about why he wasn't able to make those changes before. If she's sparked with Priya about anything, it's because Mom's actually pissed at Dad.

"Why don't you come with us, Voya?" Priya asks. Though the way she says it makes it sound less like an ask and more like a tell.

"Right now?" Mom jumps in without letting me respond. "Can't she go to the park later?"

Priya presses her lips into a thin smile. "I think now is best."

"Why don't I come with you? I just need to get rea—"

"I think it's best if only the three of us go."

Mom snaps her head to look at Granny, her expression going from light and happy to a twisted mouth and sharp eyes.

"Um . . ." I look between the three of them, standing in the hall and staring at each other with looks a lot more intense than necessary for a visit to the park.

"Go," Granny says to me. To Mom she says, "I thought you were doing something with your hair?"

Mom gives me a long look and lets out a little sigh. "Yeah. I guess I'll do that." Except she's already done her hair, so I don't know what else she's planning to do. She pushes her lips into a smile for me. "I'll see you when you get back. I have a surprise for you."

I perk up. "What?"

"Didn't I just say it was a surprise?" She gives Priya one last look, nostrils flaring. "I'll see you later." With that, she walks across the entranceway to Auntie's room.

Granny shuffles up the stairs to her room without saying anything to me or Priya.

My stepmom smiles at me as she clutches my sister's hand, the three of us alone in the hallway. "Ready to go?"

"Sure." It's still the early afternoon. Technically, I have more time before I need to make my decision. Not that I feel any closer to knowing what to do than I did this morning.

Outside, the sun is as brilliant and shining as it's been the entire day, with zero regard for the seriousness of my impending future. We make our way down the street on the short block-long walk to Marie Curtis Park.

Eden spends the time alternating between slurping on her juice pouch and chatting about a recent episode of her favorite feed show, *Jaws Journey*. It's this immersive and interactive hybrid cartoon where they follow a shark on his journey through the real world, and kids learn about marine life and that sort of thing. Apparently, the latest episode was scary because the shark went into a deep underwater tunnel, which Eden enthusiastically mimes with waving arms.

Priya hums along and asks questions while her daughter chats, nearly missing getting smacked with Eden's gesturing limbs, and adjusting Eden's sun hat at the same time as she rubs extra sunscreen on her face.

To avoid the horror of SPF protection, Eden runs over and holds my hand instead, streaks of white caked on her brown skin.

Priya watches us with an expression that's half smile and half grimace. The two of us have always gotten along all right. We don't go shopping together or anything, but sometimes we'll cook alongside each other in the kitchen, me making something for the family while she whips up something vegan for her little section of it. On special occasions, like my Bleeding dinner, she'll even let Eden eat some of whatever I have. I like to think of our relationship as comfortable. Easy.

Today is different. Priya's jittery and staring at me a lot more than she ever has. It's making me as twitchy as she's acting. I hope this isn't some weird bonding exercise. If she were anyone else, I would assume this was about my Calling, but it shouldn't affect her in any way.

We arrive at the park, walking down the slope of asphalt that brings us from the road to the main bike and strolling path. The area spreads out in a stretch of short green grass that starts at the rocky shore of the lake and extends northwest toward the different trails around the park. Me and my family have been coming here since I was little. I played in the splash pads with my cousins, went on bike rides that Auntie aggressively led while Granny would sit at a picnic table with Grandad, waiting for us to get back.

There are so many of my childhood memories filled with him. My quiet grandpa, always ready with some sort of candy in his pocket and a magic ability to make Granny less grumpy than usual. He had the power of our Chinatown trips wrapped up in a person. He died when I was seven, but there are still so many moments where I'll think back and see his hard-jawed face full of moles and his chipped-tooth smile.

Eden takes a huge gulp to finish off her drink, and her little eyes roam around the space, looking for a garbage can.

I hold out my hand. "I'll throw it out, go play."

"Thank you!" She gives me the empty pouch and, with a grin, runs off toward the giant play structure to another girl who I've seen her play with a handful of times. The whole colorful mash-up of slides, monkey bars, and interactive feed screens is overrun with kids playing and screaming.

"Shall we walk?" Priya asks with that same pained smile.

"Sure."

If Mom brought me to the park, it was never alone. She would drag out Auntie or Granny and they would sit at a picnic bench with snacks while me and my cousins ran around on our own. Which often meant playing some game that would eventually devolve into Keisha and Keis arguing while Alex and I did our own thing.

But Priya likes to stay busy. Even if we come as a whole family, she'll insist on walking around the playground on a loop, antsy about the idea of sitting still for hours and passionate about staying active. Sometimes I would even walk with her because I was so full of whatever we packed to eat that not walking would just make me sick.

I scramble for something to say. Usually, we could chitchat about whatever Eden's up to. We have Dad in common too, but I don't even know what I would talk to her about when it comes to him. "What's Eden's friend's name again?"

"Lola."

"Ahh."

Our walk continues in an awkward silence. The opposite of our usual settled-in comfort.

Eden squeals as she runs from her friend in a game of tag. She's such a purely happy kid. Maybe because she's the only one. Me and my cousins grew up together, and were running around, screaming, playing, and fighting nearly 24/7 basically from birth. By the time Eden came around, we were almost preteens, and treated her like she was our collective baby sister. Meaning, we were actually nice. Maybe that's why she's so ridiculously pleasant. Or maybe it's the effect of a newly soft-spoken Dad and seemingly always quiet and calm Priya. Mom and Auntie aren't exactly zen, after all.

"Do you know that I have an older sister?" Priya says, staring at Eden as she walks.

I shake my head. "No." I don't know much about the Jayasuriyas in general except that their ancestors emigrated from Sri Lanka to Canada at some point. I think Priya is third- or fourth-generation. That and they've been pure witches back to their first ancestor with magic.

"We were close when I was younger. Did everything together." A little smile tugs at her face, one with a smaller edge of pain. "We would braid each other's hair the same and make lip-syncing videos that we'd posted online. Priya and Rani here for your entertainment."

It's hard to know if she's telling me this to make conversation, or if this is part of the weird bonding exercise.

"She failed her Calling," Priya says. "And I passed mine the next year."

I almost stop walking, but my stepmom keeps going, so I force my legs to move. Is that what this is about? A pity pep talk in case I fail? "She . . . How . . . ?"

Priya shrugs. "She never wanted to explain it, though my parents asked her incessantly. Every conversation revolved around how she could have failed. What did she do? Who Called? What happened? They were forever trying to figure out how they could fix it. My auntie is our Matriarch, but she didn't have any answers either."

My throat is dry. I want to ask every question but also don't. People don't like to talk about family members who fail their tasks. It's as if the failure wipes the person away. Erases them. And bringing them back up just unearths the shame.

"She decided to travel the world," Priya continues. "I was jealous, actually. She stopped listening to my parents and had these cool pictures on her feed of her adventures. When I turned eighteen, I got an opportunity to go to Sri Lanka and do some volunteer work while studying our family history, and we met up."

Eden crashes face-first on the ground, and Priya and I both tense. Her friend comes to help her, and they both laugh, back on their way to running around, and we relax again.

"I made the mistake of telling her how jealous I was about everything she was doing," Priya says. "Of her life."

I swallow, and it hurts going down.

"She was furious. *Jealous?* How could I be jealous? Our parents wouldn't speak to her, wouldn't look at her. No one in the community could interact with her without it reeking of pity. She couldn't see our ancestors at our festivals; they wouldn't show themselves to her. She hadn't had magic before, but she had potential. Now she had none, so even the ancestors didn't want anything to do with her. She wasn't off having a good time, she said, she was trying to find a place to belong."

Priya stops, her feet rooting to the coarse grass. "My sister hasn't talked to me since. She blocked me on feeds too. Blocked the whole family. She doesn't even know Eden's name." Her voice catches on the last sentence. "And I can't blame her, because being in our family just reminds her of everything she doesn't have. She can't belong with us anymore, and it's painful for her, and yet she kept a feed that pretended like everything was okay because the pity is even worse."

Her eyes fill, and she takes a deep inhale. Eden, as if sensing her mom's distress, pauses and looks over at her. Priya forces a smile onto her face. "Are you having fun?" she shouts. Or as much as she can shout. Her outside voice is like Mom's lowest indoor voice.

Eden squints for a moment, but then her own smile comes back. "Yup!" She turns away from us and runs up the jungle gym stairs after Lola.

"I want to be a good mother. I really do." Priya turns to me. "That's why, when my pregnancy went south, I let Will take me to your grandma instead of a hospital, because we both knew that was the best chance we had. And that's why, when she said that she needed to tie my baby to the house, to make her a Thomas for the ancestry in its walls to recognize her as their own and protect her, I said yes."

"What?" The word slips out of my mouth, weak and limp.

None of us kids ever understood how Granny helped, though we speculated. We assumed she used some sort of special Matriarch power to save Eden. Not tying her to the house or making her a Thomas.

Eden is a *Thomas.*

But . . . that means that if I don't accept the task, not only will I be denied magic, but Eden won't get it either. "I don't understand."

Priya adjusts her dress like it's suddenly not fitting properly. "Will and I pledged to choose Ava as our Matriarch, to accept giving her control of our magic without the benefits of her blood or name. Because I have *always* done my best to be a good mom and give my daughter the life she deserves."

Dad and Priya pledged to Granny. Not only did I not know the truth about Eden, I definitely didn't know about that. If Granny wanted, she could pull from or suppress their magic like the rest of us, but they don't get the benefit of taking our powerful family name, and our ancestors wouldn't recognize their blood as belonging to a Thomas. Servitude in exchange for help. Granny probably only did it because she needed to pull from their magic to have the bandwidth to save Eden. Back then, Alex, Keis, and Keisha weren't witches yet. There may not have been as much magic to go around. She doesn't like Dad, so there's no way she would tie him to her and the family if she didn't need to.

Mama Jova said that every single witch *tied* to the Thomas blood would lose magic. That means if I accept the task and fail, if we lose magic, that Dad and Priya's pledge to Granny will leave them without power like the rest of us.

"Does this have something to do with why Eden needs to be in all our Amplifying ceremonies?" It's a painful thing for someone her age, but Granny has always insisted on her participating.

"Yes. Ava said that involving her in them would help solidify her connection to the house and ancestors if she continuously contributes to their blood and they see her with some degree of regularity." Priya swallows and speaks again, her voice even smaller than usual. "Do you know what makes your ancestral home so strong?"

I shake my head. I've never thought of our house as anything but our house.

"Good bones. That's what they say about strong homes, in the magic and non-magic worlds. Strong houses have good bones. And the ones in your house are powered with the magic of every living Thomas. As long as there is a living witch of your blood who resides there, its power will care for anyone who calls on it. That's what's keeping my daughter alive."

"So . . . then Eden will be okay?" The family isn't going anywhere. If we can keep up with our loan payments, we'll still have it, and everything will be fine.

Priya lets out a sharp laugh. "A living *witch*, Voya, a witch."

It hits me then, sharp, cruel, and almost funny because it suddenly seems so obvious. Because of course. As if the choice I had to make wasn't hard enough.

As long as there is a living *witch* of my blood.

If I accept Mama Jova's task and fail, every person tied to our family, present and future, will lose their magic. There will be no more Thomas witches to power our ancestral house. No more magic running through its bones.

And nothing left to keep my sister's heart beating.

"I think . . . I'd like to sit." I drop to the grass, parking myself on it and staring out at nothing.

Priya sits beside me, gathering my limp hands into hers. "We agreed that it was better for you to know everything going into this decision."

"Right." That explains why Mom and Granny were acting so strange when Priya asked me to come to the park. Mom probably wanted to come to support me while this cake splattered on the floor, but Granny wouldn't let her. It's my task, but what I do could mean life or death for my sister, for Priya's child, who I thought was safe from all of this before we went on this walk.

"I want to be a good mom, but even I don't know what's best." She bites her lip. "If you don't do the task, Eden will live as long as someone of your blood stays in the house. Will and I, of course, would stay to help however we could. But then . . . would she have a life like my sister? One filled with feeling like she doesn't belong or that she's missing something? Lost and angry. Dependent on the rest of you, unable to leave to have her own life. Only able to go on so long as one of you does.

"If she had the chance to become a witch, if she passed her Calling, she would become that Thomas with magic in her blood. A witch with her own will and independence, giving life to the house that gives life to her, so long as she stays there. But she would have a full life. And magic is . . . it's so much more than power. Everything I am and ever will be is wrapped in it. The power to know your ancestors as intimately as we do is a privilege, a gift, and to think of her not getting to have that . . ."

Everything she's saying, I know. It's everything I've thought of losing if I fail. How it would feel to be around my family, who, even if they were supportive, couldn't fill the hole that not having magic would leave. Maybe I could find a way to make it through without it, but I would forever be on the fringes of the community where I was born and bred.

And Eden, she's not even old enough to know what she would want. To know what she could be missing. But I also imagine that she would rather be alive than not. "If I fail . . ."

"I know," Priya whispers, gripping my hands tighter. "I have faith. I do. I believe that the ancestors are trying to better our lives, to help us. I mean, maybe Mama Jova doesn't mean it for real.

Maybe she just wants you to make the choice, to trust her. Maybe that's the task."

She takes in another deep breath. "Either way, this is your decision. I promised Will, your mom, and your grandma that I wouldn't try to tell you what to do. But I want a vow from you, too. All I ask is that if you decide to do this task, you commit to it. I know that choices are hard for you. That you struggle with them. But if you make this decision, you need to do whatever it takes to get it right, because failure is not something any of us can afford. Not this time."

I am so hacking tired of everyone telling me how pathetic I am.

My fingers shake within Priya's, Eden's juice pouch that I'm still holding crumpled between our fingers. Even Priya, who's only known me a few years, is familiar with the way I struggle through my decisions. Enough to be afraid of me messing up because of it. To be scared that I would let it stop me from keeping my baby sister alive.

"Promise me!" she cries, staring into my eyes, her whole body trembling. "Promise me that if you choose to do this, if you choose to chase a future where we keep our magic, that you'll succeed. There isn't room to just try. You *need* to do it."

"I promise," I say, my hands clammy in hers.

And I mean it.

If I choose to accept the task, I'll do everything to make sure that I complete it. Because Priya's right—there aren't any chances to take when it comes to Eden's life.

But the truth is that I still don't know if that's what I want to do.

And now making my choice feels more than hard.

It's impossible.

CHAPTER EIGHT

I lie on my bed, alone in my bedroom. I'm thankful that I didn't see anyone when I dragged my feet up the stairs, barely able to say bye to Eden, whose comically furrowed brow suggested that she didn't understand why I wasn't as happy as she was about our park visit.

The sun is low in the sky now, its darkness seeping through my window. Time counting down. It's like there's a ten-ton weight on every limb—pushing me down and making me stick to the yellow banana-print duvet. There's a dress that matches somewhere in my closet.

I flick my finger on my phone screen and get a projection playing on the ceiling. It's some sort of sitcom where every twenty minutes a decision comes up, and you're supposed to choose what they do next. I tap my thumb, and the male lead leaves his current girlfriend for one in Peru.

Contrary to my family's belief, I can make choices. Ones like this are easy. They don't matter.

Other decisions are different. It's like kneading dough that's too sticky. One piece gets stuck to your fingers, and then it builds, until every single one is covered. The harder I try to work it, the more the pieces stick—each one a nagging thought in my brain telling me I'm going to mess it up. I could just throw flour on the dough and everything would be okay. But even that seems wrong. Like I'll add too much and dry it out. And so I end up in this cycle, kneading a too-sticky dough endlessly until someone comes to take it away from me, or I overwork and ruin it.

I can't do that this time. This is one dough that I have to get perfect.

Mom opens the door and lets herself in. She sits down at the foot of my bed and tosses something at me. "Surprise!"

It lands on my chest, and it takes me a couple of seconds to realize it's the brown, crunchy, sugarcoated goodness that is kurma.

I sit up and rip open the plastic package like a girl starved. Mom watches me, her fingers twitching in her lap.

The sweet stick goes soft in my mouth. "Priya told me."

She lets out a long breath. "Guess where I got the kurma."

"At the International Market, where you apparently went without me." She knows that's my absolute favorite place. But this time, talking about it doesn't make me feel better. "Mom, Priya told me about Eden."

"I got it from Jessa, you know her, the woman with the two kids at Toronto French School who's always buying our face masks?"

"You mean the one who can never stop bragging about how her kids go to Toronto French School?"

Mom smirks. "Yes, her. She had gone to the market earlier in the day and gave me a pack as a gift when I dropped off her face masks for the month."

"Oh. Thank you. And thanks to her, too." Now I kind of feel bad for hating on her. I shove another piece of kurma in my mouth and crunch down on it. Sweet sugar floods my taste buds and comforts me in a way only food can. "Mom."

She steals a stick out of my package and sucks on it. Which is gross and the worst way to eat it.

"Mom."

"I know!" she snaps, swallowing the kurma in her mouth with a loud gulp.

"What do you think I should do?"

She presses the palms of her hands against her eyes. We've been here before. Both of us on this bed while she tried to talk her way around telling me that Dad was leaving. "I can't make that decision for you."

I lower my head and my shoulders droop. It's always been easier to have other people make my choices. I could sidestep making a decision without even trying. But this one is too much and no one will help me. "How am I supposed to know what to do?"

"This is your task. All you have to do is complete it."

I scoff. "Oh, that's all?"

Mom narrows her eyes at me. "No sass. I mean, do whatever you think is best."

"I don't know what I think is best."

"At the end of the day, this is a choice between giving up or going for it."

I shake my head and let out a laugh. "No, it's not. It's a choice between Eden dying or staying alive."

"No," Mom says, voice sharp. "That's only the choice if you plan on failing. And I would like to believe in a world where you pass. You can do this."

"Except we're living in a world where I've already failed once."

Mom takes another piece of kurma and twirls it between her fingers. "Do you think you're better off not doing anything?"

I begged for this second chance and told Mama Jova I wouldn't fail if I had one more shot. But now I don't know. Things were different then. No lives were on the line. Maybe it is better if I do nothing. Eden will live as long as one Thomas is alive and stays at home. Me and my cousins are about ten to thirteen years older than her. She can still have a fairly full life.

Only, without magic.

Our family motto is we suffer and we survive. Is it better to survive a life without ancestors or magic, or suffer the possibility of having no life at all? Put like that, the choice should be easy. Except Mom is right. That's only the reality if I fail. If I pass, we can have it all. Is magic worth that risk?

I curl my fingers into fists in my blanket. "We can't afford my failure."

Mom steupses and stands up. "You need to get your mind straight! Stop talking like you've already lost. Take some time and let me know if you want to discuss this more before you decide." She stomps over to the door and yanks it open, only to make a surprised yelp and stumble back.

Keis, Keisha, and Alex are huddled up against the other side. Out of instinct, I shove the kurma packet under my pillow. Alex's eyes narrow at the motion. If there's anyone who loves food as much as I do, it's her.

Mom throws her hands up and leaves the room, and they flood in. It's only once my cousins make it through that I notice Eden sneaking in along with them.

Keisha jumps on the bed beside me, closely followed by Eden, who squishes between the two of us, her sunhat abandoned and her hair flattened from it.

Alex reaches over and snatches my kurma packet from under the pillow.

"No!" I screech.

She takes one out of the packet and shoves it in her mouth before tossing the pack to Keisha, who passes a stick to Eden after taking one for herself and tosses it to her sister. By the time Keis gets her share, it's empty.

I might cry.

Keis collapses onto the bed and crunches on her kurma. "I'll get you another package later."

You'd better.

"I may have found you an internship opportunity, through the Huangs." There are more relevant things I could say, but this is the only one that makes me feel good. My one positive thing for the day.

"I'm not helping you avoid talking about your Calling. I could hear your struggle all the way from my room."

"Because you listen to me constantly," I say, my voice clipped, though I don't mean it to be.

Keis snaps back, "That, and because you're having emotional thoughts. They're loud."

Eden examines my head like my thoughts are projecting in a way she can see.

"If you practiced even the tiniest bit, then you wouldn't have to hear them." I cross my arms over my chest. "Must be nice to pass your Calling, get a strong gift, then hacking *ignore* it just because you feel like it. Must be nice to be too good for magic that some of us may never have."

"Don't get mad at me because you don't know what to do," my cousin says, her voice flat and searing.

It's only once I'm done speaking that I notice my chest heaving, the rage behind my words simmering in the air like an over-spiced curry. I stare down at my lap, not wanting to look around the room at my cousins and sister. At the people whose lives will change forever if I fail.

Keisha pokes me with her sharp nail. "You're uncomfortable."

I wince and fight the urge to scream at her. She's the only one who would be better off if I accepted and failed Mama Jova's task.

"I don't think I'm too good for magic," Keis mutters.

Keisha snorts and Alex's eyebrows shoot up.

"I don't!" Keis shakes her head, curls flying. "I love magic. I do. I love being able to connect with our ancestors. I love casting for fun. I love being part of a magic community, however messed up ours is. I would never want to live without magic if I didn't need to." She looks at me. "I just don't want magic to be the only thing about me that matters. Granny and the adults act like your powers and gifts are the only important things about being a witch. My protest isn't about hating magic. It's about proving that it's not the only thing I can be good at. Witches could be so much more than that if we tried. We could change the world."

I'm too much of a coward to apologize aloud, so I mumble a *sorry* to Keis in my head. She's my best friend, and I never quite understood that's how she felt about magic. I was over here getting sparked, thinking she was taking for granted what Eden and I stood to live without.

"What should I do?" I say for what feels like the hundredth time that day.

Keisha opens her mouth, but Keis cuts her off. "No. This is your decision."

"We don't need magic," Keisha says, ignoring her sister. "We're passing down a bunch of weak gifts, and what we can do with blood spells isn't much to celebrate. There's important shit on the line." She gives Eden a significant glance. Keis must have shared the thoughts in my head, so now they all know. "Why push for more generations of this? Why risk it?"

In some ways, it's easy for Keisha to say we don't need magic. Her gift isn't exactly useful, though it has made her more perceptive than she already was. But she's always just been interested in having fun, whether it's going on her endless dates, or feed modeling, or hanging out with her friends. The complete opposite of her ambitious sister. But she still has a point. Is more magic worth the risk?

Keis glares at her. "This isn't about whether your gift is cool or not. Magic has run in our family for centuries. It's what got us here. When our ancestors were dying of thirst and starvation in slave boats, the magic that runs in our veins kept them alive."

"Yeah. And they were still slaves in the end." Keisha scowls at her sister. "Name a single thing about magic worth risking . . . worth risking you-know-what over."

"What's you-know-what?" Eden interrupts, looking between the sisters.

"Kiddos don't need to know," Keisha says.

My baby sister scowls.

"It's not a risk if you actually hacking believe in Voya." Keis turns to me. "Why can't you just believe in yourself for once? Every single one of us passed. You can too. Passing your Calling is about trusting yourself *and* the ancestors."

"But Papa Dalton's Calling," Alex says, leaning on my pillows. "He didn't even know it was happening. He just picked a book."

"Exactly! He didn't even need to think about it. Believing in them and believing in you should be that automatic." Keis points to Alex. "How did you know you were making the right choice in your Calling?"

Alex shrugs. "I guess . . . I just figured that I was."

"Exactly! Vo, you're making this harder than it needs to be. Some of them may feel impossible, but none are. It's a task an ancestor designed specifically for you because they believe that you can do it."

I curl my knees into my chest. I get what Keis is saying. It's like what Priya mentioned, that maybe the real task is just trusting Mama Jova and accepting it. But I also get what Keisha means. We have magic, but it's never quite saved us from hardship. We have a house, but we're constantly on the edge of losing it to debt collectors. And why risk everything just to keep passing that magic down? Thomases are supposed to be powerful, but we've been on the decline since becoming pure. Rejecting the task would change our futures, but maybe the next generation would do better without. "Maybe we should take a vote?"

"No," Keis snaps. "You need to decide. It's your Calling."

The weight comes back and dumps itself on me. I wish I could sink into the bed and disappear. No Calling. No task. No Mama Jova. Just layers and layers of soft, comforting sheets.

When I was little, I used to have hope for the future. I lost a lot of that when I couldn't stop Dad from leaving. It felt like there should have been a third option other than leaving Mom to go with him, or letting him leave to stay with her. I should have known how to make being with me more important than whatever he expected to find by going. But I didn't. I couldn't choose anything, so I said nothing.

When he came back with a new family, I realized he didn't leave to find himself and come back to me. He left to start over without me.

And just like that, the sticky ball of dough came into my life.

Eden wraps both her arms around one of mine. "Daddy says it's better to try and fail than to never try at all."

I almost laugh and tug her closer, pressing my face into her neck. I'm getting my fatherly advice not from my father but through my baby sister. What would Mom and Dad think knowing they're giving out the same sort of wisdom?

I look at Alex, who's flicking invisible kurma pieces off her fingernails. "What about you?"

Keis makes a huffing sound.

Alex lets out a huge sigh. "I mean, Keis had a point about the whole Papa Dalton thing. I support you and whatever you decide, but I won't pretend my gift doesn't mean something to me." She shrugs and throws an apologetic look at Keis. "I'm sorry, but you all here, right now, are my family. Future generations can figure their own stuff out. I would leave things as they are. There's no risk to that."

Keisha's eyes are sharp as they meet mine. "See? We can keep the powers we have if you do nothing. For anyone who cares about their gifts. I know our history and ancestors are important, but they're just that, *history*. We live right now. The only reason Dad stays in this house is because he has some desperate hope to study under Granny and do ancestors know what. Him being here drives Mom up the wall, but she stays because she wants to be Matriarch, and she's already hot-tempered, so it's a bit hacking much. A future without magic would mean there's no reason for them to keep forcing themselves to stay here."

A shock runs through me. "You want to split up the house?"

"You don't even like Dad."

I rummage in my head for an excuse and fail to find one. I don't adore Uncle, but the idea of any of us not living together makes me feel like I'm breathing through a straw in a sealed box. "We're family. We should live together."

I don't miss Keis shifting on the bed.

Does her vision of the future not include her staying in our ancestral home? Does she want to leave us? To leave *me*?

Keisha throws her hands up. "That's not even the biggest thing." Her gaze burns across my skin. "You know yourself, Vo. Do you think you'll be able to do the task that Mama sets? I know Keis wants you to believe in yourself, but *can* you?"

Her words are like a noose tightening around my neck. A promise of pain. It's the truth in them that stings. If I couldn't manage the standard Calling everyone else in my family before me passed, how can I complete this unnamed task?

Keis jumps up from the bed and waves her hand. "Hack it. Now that everyone's said their piece, let's go. Voya needs to think things over."

Eden pats my hand. That's me. A teenager being comforted by a first grader. "I think you're going to pass," she whispers conspiratorially in my ear. A secret just for us.

My eyes start to water, and I suck them back with a sharp inhale.

My cousins file out of the room except for Keis, who lingers in the doorway.

"Do you not think we should live together?" The words slip out of my mouth like mousse from a well-greased mold.

"Thank you for asking Rowen about the internship." Keis drums her fingers on the doorjamb. "I know you'll do the right thing for the family. You always seem to know what's best for us. But at the end of the day, this task is about you." She leans forward the slightest bit. "Do me a favor, just think about if you could do it. And if you can't believe even for a moment that you would pass, reject the task. But for once, give yourself the benefit of the doubt before you decide." She closes the door behind her without waiting for me to agree, and I listen to her steps get farther and farther away.

Keis is wrong. If this task were just about me, then it wouldn't affect anyone else.

But out of everyone I've asked for advice today, her words will always be the ones I care about the most. My cousin, who has always known me best, even before she could be in my head.

And so I do what she asked and think about if I could do Mama Jova's task.

When Wimberley failed to pass her Calling all those years ago, we were a different sort of family. The kind of Thomases who prized power and survival above everything. Witches who bled people for more magic and competed fiercely to stay on top. Granny changed that. She risked our status to create a sort of Thomas who wasn't willing to hurt others, and she still managed to maintain our reputation. I've never had a lot of friends, only Lauren. But I've always had family.

Just Voya couldn't do this task. She couldn't save Eden and our family's magic.

But Voya Thomas, the girl surrounded by family, I can believe in her. She has a chance to get that perfect ending. To save her sister's life and give her a chance at magic. To make sure that generations after her will have blood that runs full of power. To have a shot at knowing their ancestors until the day they die. To maybe become the witches who Keis dreams of, the ones who change the world.

We suffer and we survive.

I asked Mama for a second chance, and she gave it to me. I'm not going to waste it.

Slipping off the bed, I search in my bedside table until I find the pair of mini scissors I use for cutting my cuticles when Keisha and I have mani-pedi nights.

I try not to cry out as I stab the sharp end into the pad of my thumb, squeezing around the skin to push out a drop of blood.

There's nothing making me do it. No supernatural force is putting this task into motion.

It has to be me. I have to make this choice.

Once I'm standing in the middle of the room, I let my blood drip on the hardwood.

Blood.

And intent.

The words don't come strong out of my mouth. They're a whisper as timid and fragile as my resolve. "Mama Jova."

Heat permeates the room, as hot as the New Orleans sun was in the memory that Mama showed me. Sweat breaks out on the back of my neck and forms a thin sheen on my forehead.

My ancestor curls out of the smoke that appears in the room

as if in the middle of a dance, with her arms curved above her head and her torso twisted. Tendrils of the dark wind sneak into my nostrils and fill them with the harsh vinegar tang of rotting sugarcane.

Johan taught us that slaves used to burn the sugarcane to kill the pests that would try and ruin the crop. Simultaneously, they would burn the dead to save time. The plants would come out of the process for the better, easier to harvest and haul. And the bodies would be tossed away with the unwanted charred leaves and bugs.

Mama Jova lets her hands fall at her sides and observes me.

Her nakedness makes me shift on the spot, but I don't turn away. "Um, hello."

She rolls her eyes.

Off to a great start. I wring my hands. "I've decided to accept the task." I fight the urge to back out on my words, the small bit of me that believes fighting against the bigger doubt.

She doesn't nod. Doesn't move. Doesn't do anything to make me think she's heard me or cares.

After a minute, she holds out her hand.

I stare down at it. I'm not good at making choices, but if there's a chance that I can succeed, save magic and save Eden, I'll take it. And I need to succeed, because I'm not going to lose her.

I reach out my hand and clasp Mama Jova's.

Her lips spread into a thin smile that makes me shudder. She exposes her thumb, the pad of it splits open of its own accord, and she grips my hand, pressing our bleeding thumbs together.

I stare into her eyes. Something moves there. Not satisfaction or sadness. Just something. "Your task is this: you will find your first love and destroy them." Her voice is as empty as her lover's eyes were as he lay dead against the tree. "You have until the Caribana carnival, when your ancestors once again reveal themselves, to complete my task. I look forward to your success. Remember, I chose you for a reason."

She disappears and leaves me standing in the middle of the room with blood leaking from my thumb. The droplets splashing on the hardwood echo in the room.

Destroy.

Reduce to utter ruin. Wipe out. Make void. Vanquish.

It's just a fancy way to say that I need to murder my first love.

We've been pure witches since before I was born, before Mom was born. We promised not to spill any blood other than our own for magic. None of us would ever even want to hurt someone for power. And now I have to do the opposite.

Caribana is a month away.

Thirty days to fall in love and become a murderer.

Mama Jova left me with nothing but this task and the lingering smell of smoke.

There's no explanation that comes along with what I have to do. No rhyme or reason. We have the privilege of meeting our ancestors, but like a ghost in a movie, they don't give you any instructions for how you should please them.

This can't be right.

Mama Jova can't really believe commanding me to take a life will have some sort of benefit to me or the family. And saying she chose me for a reason, how does that help? Do I look like a killer to her?

The knock on my bedroom door shocks me out of my trance. Mom doesn't wait for me to answer before she comes barreling into my room with the rest of the family squeezing in behind her. The strength of the magic must have let them know what I did.

She squishes me in a crushing hug, and Eden joins in. Dad hovers nearby and ends up patting me on the shoulder.

Granny comes over with her arms crossed. "And?"

"I accepted her task." My voice doesn't sound like mine; it's too soft but also too high-pitched. I notice the slightest sag of Granny's shoulders. Priya has the opposite reaction, her shoulders going stiff and hiking up. I continue, "She wants me to kill my first love."

Everyone but Keis looks shocked. She couldn't wait the few seconds not to read it out of my head. She just shrugs in response, though the movement is too sharp. I imagine this isn't the task she expected when she told me to believe in myself.

Mom rubs her hands up and down my arms. She's trying to force her face to be neutral, but her brow keeps furrowing.

Murder isn't our way. Some impure families will split a man from sternum to scrotum to grant a single pure wish. Once, we did too. Our ancestors believed in that sort of blood. It took twenty-five of them to move this house. It also took fifty slaver and slaver-sympathizer bodies, gutted and drained.

But not anymore.

Granny raised us so we would never have to do that.

Never have to stand in a dark basement like the Davis kids and shove blades into someone while they scream and beg.

Just thinking of it makes my throat ache.

Priya clenches her hands into fists. Her family's history is as blood-free as the Huangs. There's no way she would have predicted a task like this. I promised her I would do it, and I have to, but now saving her daughter also means accepting the stain of impurity. One impure soul ruins the whole batch. My deed will mark us all. Everything that Granny worked for will be for nothing. We'll have to start again from the beginning. And after slipping into impurity once, will the pure families even trust our word when we try again? All those carefully cultivated relationships and customers, gone.

Granny pushes forward. "Who are they? Your first love?"

Keisha snorts. "Do you know who your granddaughter is?"

Okay, ouch.

Everyone's eyes swivel to me. "I don't have a first love."

"Shocking," Keisha whispers.

"I could have!"

"You would have to date someone for that, and you don't date." She jerks her thumb at Keis. "She doesn't either. I'm not judging. Maybe you don't even want to fall in love. That's cool too, whatever. But like . . . was I wrong?"

"You'll have to find one," Priya says, her voice quiet. "I just . . . This can't be the task. What were the exact words?"

Keis jumps in for me. "'You will find your first love and destroy them.'"

"Okay . . . That could mean . . . It could be . . ." Priya struggles to come up with an alternative. "They can't actually expect you to *do* this? Our ancestors would never!"

"Meaning?" Granny asks with a scowl.

Priya snaps her mouth shut.

"Say it," Granny says, voice harsh. "Your pure-for-generations family wouldn't set a task like this, is that what you mean? Unlike us. Sorry we don't all have squeaky-clean legacies."

"She didn't mean it like that," Dad cuts in. Even though I'm pretty sure she did. Our family is new to purity. Hers has been doing it from the start.

"I'm sure she didn't. Living in our impure ancestor's house like she is."

Priya shakes her head. "I'm sorry. I appreciate everything you've done for us . . . I'm just shocked, is all."

Granny harrumphs and turns back to me. "You don't have any idea who may be your first love?"

"She's not actually going to do this, right?" Mom says, incredulous. "She's not going to kill someone."

"I'm trying to get more information so we can figure out what this task means."

"More information? You need to have a chat with Mama Jova about what the hell she's doing!"

"Voya," Granny says, voice stern. "You don't know anyone who fits that? Even a crush, for ancestors' sake."

I open my mouth to say no again when Luc pops into my mind. The rude NuGene intern who is *apparently* my highest romantic genetic match in the entire world. At least, the places where genetic data is available, which is pretty much worldwide.

"I think . . . maybe I know a guy," I mumble.

Keis's mouth pulls into a grimace. She says, "Well, genetics don't lie."

"Genetics . . . Hack me! You got into the beta for NuGene Match?" Keisha may not be a mind reader like her sister, but she's quick on the uptake. "I'm so jealous," she whines.

I hit her with a glare.

"Not jealous of the murdering thing, but like, everyone has been waiting for proper genetic matching forever. Now you know who your first love is." She nods at Mom. "And I'm with Auntie, Granny should ask Mama Jova what's up. No one gets tasks to kill people. Not pure families, for sure. There's no way you have to do that."

Granny squints at us. "What's this matching thing? Who is this?"

"NuGene put out a program that gives you a genetic romantic match. I got into the beta test," I say, trying to keep up with her questions while my brain is still processing that I may actually have to do this.

"They do that for teenagers?"

"You have to be at least sixteen is what the package info said— it's age of consent. Mom gave me permission!"

Granny stares at Mom, who shrugs helplessly and says, "I dunno, it didn't seem like it would be an issue. And Voya's already had her sex talk."

I cringe. The sex talk consisted of Mom and Auntie piling me and my cousins into a room when we were twelve and thirteen—sans Alex, who'd gotten her talk three years earlier—and playing an overly detailed feed video, then asking if we had any questions after. Suffice to say, none of us asked them anything and had our AI assists answer anything else we wanted to know.

"Okay," Granny says with a sigh. "You have a potential first love."

Alex gapes at her. "Why are you acting like you're trying to find the target? Voya's not going to kill someone, right?"

"Obviously," Auntie and Uncle say at the same time. They scowl at each other, as if annoyed that they're still in sync after divorce.

Uncle gestures to Granny. "There must be something you can do. You've fought for purity for decades. *We've* fought for it. If she kills someone, it stains the entire family."

Of course that's what he cares about. The stain on the family, not the fact that I would have to murder someone. I stare at Granny along with everyone else in the room, pleading for her to come up with some sort of solution. I know this is the task that Mama Jova set out for me, that I need to pass to save Eden, but *murder* . . . Even thinking of it makes my stomach curdle like butter in a food processor.

"The task is the task," Granny says, her voice strained.

Mom lets out a huff and throws her hands up. "Unbelievable!"

Granny ignores her. "Who is this guy, your match?"

"Granny . . . ," I say. This can't be happening.

"Let's just focus on the falling-in-love part for now, okay? We'll figure out the rest later. Who is he?"

"He hates me, and I'm not jazzed about him." I stare at my bare feet. "His name is Luc Rodriguez. He's a NuGene intern and apparently one of Justin Tremblay's sponsor kids."

Dad's face mutates into a near-teeth-baring expression that he quickly tries to pull back into indifference as Priya grips his arm. Mom's eyes flare wide, and sparks shoot off Auntie's fingers. Uncle crosses his arms and stares anywhere but in my direction. Granny is the only adult who manages to keep her face still. But it's *too* still. Unnatural.

I look around at my cousins, who seem as confused as I do. Except for Keis, who has her eyes squeezed shut and her hands pressed over her ears from what is clearly a surge of emotional thought.

Rowen Huang's words come back to me: *You can't always trust people. Especially outsiders.*

But my family has never reacted this way to non-magic folk. Keisha goes on dates with non-witches all the time. This is something other than them just being upset that Luc and his sponsor father aren't magical. I swallow. "What did I say?"

"I've always said, our ancestors give us the tasks we need." Dad's voice has an undercurrent like a lashing, and he speaks through clenched teeth. "Genetics don't lie. That's the boy, and that's the task."

"You can't be *serious*?" Priya snaps. Having had enough of it all, she picks up Eden and leaves the room, my little sister crying out on missing the drama that I'm sure she hardly understands. Dad hisses out a swear between his teeth and follows after them.

Mom hugs her arms around her chest and keeps shaking her head like that will make everything disappear.

Even if no one wants to tell me why, my task just got that much more complicated.

"How long do you have?" Granny asks.

"Until Caribana."

She crosses her arms and lets out a breath, her face pinched. "Long tasks are not good." She presses her palms to her eyes the way Mom does when she's stressed. "I . . . Just focus on falling in love. We'll figure something out. Don't worry."

Easier said than done.

Whether it takes me two days or thirty doesn't matter. I accepted this task, and my family is putting their trust and belief in me.

I need to get it done, because if I'm honest, I would rather kill someone than let Eden die, no matter how much I hate the idea of it.

Right now, the task is the task.

And I don't plan to fail a second time.

CHAPTER NINE

I'm at the start of my month-long Caribana deadline, and already time is slipping through my fingers. Three days passed with the house cloaked in a suffocating silence where I spent most of my time hidden in my room. Which, granted, isn't super responsible, but I can't just learn that I need to murder someone and jump into courting my victim the next day. The family, meanwhile, has been living on takeout, with Keis bringing fixed plates up to me.

But today I need to bake.

Now the flakes of butter and flour stuck to my fingers are as close to soothing as I can manage.

The kitchen is empty except for Keis, who's sitting at the island doing self-study on her tablet. She usually goes to the café around the corner on Saturday to treat herself to coffee and a cheddar scone. And yet here she is. I get the feeling she's concerned about me.

She scoffs. "I felt like studying at home. I doubt you're going to run out in a panic and stab Luc with a kitchen knife."

"I'm not in love with him, so there's no point in doing that now." I flick a piece of dough off my fingernail. "And you never feel like studying at home because every time Granny or Uncle sees you doing it, they give you some sort of lecture about honing your gift instead."

Keis presses her lips together.

"Do you hate living here?" I haven't forgotten our discussion on the day I accepted the task. How she avoided questions about staying in the house.

She pushes out a groan. "I'm seventeen, and I have no money that doesn't come from my parents. I'm not going anywhere."

"But would you like to?"

"Do you plan to stay in this house until you die?"

"Yes." Why not? I like waking up and coming home to a full space with its normal loud chatter and activity.

Keis stares at her tablet.

Conversation over, apparently.

I was able to hook our family almanac up to my hijacker tech so it can trick my eyes into seeing a hands-free visual of Mama Tolen's recipe for coconut biscuits floating in the air the same way it shows me messages that come through my phone. Well worth the money. A combo of Mom working extra hours and me hustling to push our products.

Keis won her hijacker chip in a feed show called *Quiz Kids* when we were younger. They gave out prizes if you got in the top ten, and one year she managed it. Out of hundreds of thousands of kids all over the world. She has the oldest model of hijacker tech on the market, but she earned it.

My cousin is meant for great things. Even if in her mind, some of those mean living away from us. "Did you get in contact with Rowen about the internship?"

"Yeah, they have a Q&A in a couple of days that I'll be going to. She said her uncle has my feed info, and I can go up to him after the session to introduce myself."

"That's amazing." I beam, folding the biscuit dough over itself a few times to make the layers. "Anything from NuGene? I saw on the feeds that sometimes they do exclusive invites to a group tour."

Keis looks up from her tablet, her mouth slack. "You think they would be inviting *me* to that?"

I wash my hands in the sink and pull out my phone to double-check that I didn't miss an invite. I search "NuGene" in my inbox, but all I get is the odd "You've WON a FREE NuGene procedure" junk message.

When I go to pull out an EcoOven baking tray for the biscuits, the telltale red ON light is a dim black. "Hack me," I mutter.

"We need a new one," Keis says.

"With what money?"

I flip the switch back on the oven and stare at my feed screen. Tapping on the small button that proclaims "romantic match" leads me, once again, to Luc's feed. He's got new ratings. The first one is a two-star.

Went to a Q&A hosted by him, and he wasted the entire session picking on this poor girl who, granted, is never getting into NuGene, but there's a polite way to say it. —[Name Hidden]

My face flushes, and I wrinkle my nose. The person who gave it wasn't even brave enough to have their name linked to it. They probably don't want to ruin their chance at getting an internship.

I move on to the second rating and look at the little avatar of Keis with her curly hair in a pineapple bun that proclaims one star. "You left him a bad rating? You never rate people. Also! Everyone knows one star is, like, for serial killers."

Keis grumbles, "Works for assholes, too."

"You could have hidden your name!"

"Didn't want to."

"'Seems more interested in making others feel small than searching for prospective intern talent, as is his job. It's a sad world when people of a certain privilege have no interest in paying it forward and becoming productive members of society,'" I read and cringe. "You have to take it down!"

"Nope."

"No wonder you didn't get an invite back!"

"If my personal opinion of an employee means I don't get an internship, then I don't want one." She sets her tablet down with an unnecessary clatter. "He has everything given to him. Sure, he had to get the sponsorship, but after that it's smooth sailing. And what does he do with that privilege? Picks on others."

I sag against the counter, squishing one of my biscuits. "You can have your opinion, but you don't have to air it publicly."

"I'm not taking it down."

"Urgh! I'm sending a message to him." It's as good an opportunity as any to reconnect with Luc since I'll have to try and meet him at some point, and I've already wasted three days avoiding it. I can't expect to fall in love with the guy if I never speak with him.

Focus on falling in love. I just need to focus on that and try to think less about the whole murder thing.

Hi, Luc! I feel like we got off to a bad start, and apologies are warranted on both sides. I will go first and say I'm sorry about the rating my cousin left on your profile. I wondered if you would want to meet up and discuss NuGene more? Thanks!

I shoot off the message before I can change my mind and cut out and pile the biscuits on my tray before sliding them into the oven.

His answer comes back faster than expected: *No.*

I resist the urge to throw my phone at the wall.

"Told you." Keis's smugness is palpable. "He's an asshole."

"I know he is! He's also my top genetic match and my only lead for completing this task, so I have to talk with him."

My cousin frowns. "You're really going to do it?"

"I'm not going to let Eden die," I snap.

I type back my answer: *No? I'm not sure what you mean?*

No, I don't have anything to apologize for. And no, I don't want to meet with you to discuss a company you seem to have no interest in.

Okay. What about a non-NuGene-related meeting?

No.

"I actually want to kill him now!" I hiss.

"You have to love him first, remember?"

My fingers shake as I type out my response: *We're a 92% genetic romantic match, and I'm trying to get to know you despite your efforts to be as unpleasant as possible. Do you not care about connecting with your match?*

I don't have time to date right now.

I'm not trying to date you! You think I want to be matched with a garbage person with a two-star rating? I'm working with what I've got!

I type out the last message without hitting send.

Keis's eyes are wide with glee. "Please send it."

"I'm not going to send it." I delete the message and close my feed. When I move to check the biscuits, the oven has shut off again. I flip it back on.

At the very least I'll get the money from NuGene for wearing that monitor. They sent a message that they would be available for pickup tomorrow. That's two hundred dollars. I'll need at least eight hundred more for a new oven. I would have to save up my allowance for almost a year to make that much. Mom giving me twenty dollars a week is already generous. I can't pester her for more.

I flick through contest feeds in the area. Most of them are by chance, which I enter but don't expect much from. It'll be better if it's something skills-based that I can at least be semi-confident about winning.

"Aha!" In one of my usual recipe feeds there's a local Toronto contest for the best heritage recipe with a $1,000 prize. You need a minimum of 2,000 food-interest-identifying feed followers to participate. I have 2,372. Almost all of whom are food-interested people.

"Is that where you should be expending your energy right now?" Keis wrinkles her nose at me.

"I have to fall in love with Luc. It's going to be difficult, and I'll need a break every now and then." And I would rather not have to think about murdering someone 24/7.

She makes a sound in the back of her throat. "There has to be a way around this task. Maybe it's a metaphorical destruction?"

"How do you destroy someone metaphorically?"

"I don't know yet."

"Try and figure it out before time is up. Meanwhile, Luc is being less than cooperative, so I'm going to look into this recipe thing for a bit."

I pull up a stool at the island and grab the tablet, canceling Mama's biscuit recipe holo so I can concentrate. Most of the recipes I find are in our family almanac, which holds the digitized paper records and digital-first records of the Thomases.

It did start out as a real almanac—a yearly catalogue of important dates and information for witches that was passed between families. But at some point, it evolved, and individual families started making their own, just for them. Eventually, we all added our own ancestral histories, diary entries, instructions for future generations, and more. It expanded beyond what an almanac is supposed to be, but the name stuck.

Most of the time I end up tweaking the recipes in there, but this is a great place to start. I do a search and set the results to come up by name, listing the most accessed ones first. Usually, I randomize the results, but I want the best choice this time. The results are filtered, and dozens of entries, all under the name "Mama Elaine," are listed at the top.

"Who is that?" Keis asks.

I shake my head. "Never heard of her."

Mama and Papa, or the gender-neutral Bibi, aren't sentimental names. They're titles given to ancestors who have done something significant to receive the honor of assigning tasks. When Mama Jova died, one of the existing ancestors must have suggested that her time on Earth warranted becoming a Mama. Every one of the honored ancestors voted and deemed her worthy of the title. She would have presented herself to whoever was Matriarch of our family when she died, and that woman would have recorded it in our almanac.

Granny told us stories of each and every one of our fifty-three Thomas-named Mamas, Papas, and Bibis. But I've never heard of Mama Elaine.

I tap on her name, but her profile is blank. No photo, no gift log, no marriage records, not a single piece of information. Just her recipes and another note of what looks like a feed recording. I tap on it, and a red lock icon pops up.

"Try thomasfamily1," Keis says.

Granny is of the generation that uses the exact same password for everything, so we know her code, even when she tries to lock things in the almanac. "There's not even a place to type a password."

Dad slinks into the kitchen, likely lured by the scent of baking biscuits. I try and cook something around lunchtime on weekends for everyone.

"They've got butter in them," I say, as if that matters. Dad isn't as devout with his veganism as Priya. He won't touch meat or fish, but he's hard-pressed to pass up a baked good.

"That's okay." Dad looks at Keis and me, and rocks back on his heels. "What are you girls up to?"

Six years since he's been back, and interacting with him is still strange. It's like talking to a relative you haven't seen for years who tells you stories about the things you did when you were little that you can't remember. Not like someone who I live with and see every day.

He left a hole in my life, then came back as a different shape. He doesn't fit anymore.

Now, with the task, it's even worse. His eyes shift anywhere but on me, and even his breathing looks uncomfortable. If only Keisha were here, she could loudly point it out for us.

I turn the tablet in his direction. "Do you know who Mama Elaine is? Her feed recordings are locked."

His lips recoil like he's bitten into a rotten mango. "Why are you looking into her?"

"I'm going to enter a recipe contest. I went to look at hers, but her profile is blank."

He comes forward and taps on the recipe section. "They're unlocked."

"Okay, but who is she?"

"I don't know."

Keis lets out a laugh, and Dad's eyes widen. "You're not in my head, eh?!" he barks.

We both jump at him using his old loud voice, and Keis crosses her arms. "I'm not trying to listen, but nothing rings louder than a lie."

"If it's locked, it's for a reason." With that, he rushes out of the kitchen, his mission for biscuits forgotten.

I turn to Keis. "What was he thinking?"

"It's all over the place. The reason I concentrate on your thoughts is to block people out. But lies, like high emotional thoughts, are loud. He said 'I don't know,' but what rang back is 'Stop asking me.'"

I slouch on my barstool. "After I mentioned Luc was Justin Tremblay's sponsor, the adults all acted weird. You didn't get anything from any of them then, did you?"

"Not much. It was like everyone was screaming at once. They're not fans of Justin, your dad the least of all of them, that's for sure."

Why would they hate Justin Tremblay? If they knew him somehow, he would be an outsider who came into the community. Could it have anything to do with what Rowen said about one ruining things?

"You know better than to get caught up in Rowen's web of secrets. You wondering about what she said for hours is exactly what she wants. You know that, right?"

"Yeah, yeah. Did you hear anything else?"

Keis squints at the island tabletop. "I don't think I heard it right."

"What was it?"

"I swore there was a thought of Uncle Vacu."

"Uncle Vacu?" We haven't seen Alex's dad in years. He was the only one of our immediate family to get an education through a sponsorship from Mount Sinai Hospital. Uncle was starting his practice when he got into Mod-H, and everything went downhill.

Women from witch communities all over the country used to come to have him do their births. It guaranteed their child would be born healthy. It's why he chose to be an OB/GYN, so none of his patients would ever lose children. He's an asshole, but one with a proper moral compass. Before the drugs, anyway. It's not exactly easy to be righteous when you're controlled by addiction.

He left Alex alone for days in their apartment when she was eight without telling her where he was going or checking in. Somehow Granny figured out what was happening and brought Alex to live with us. Uncle Vacu never came to claim her. When he did come, he stole family artifacts to sell and didn't say a word to his daughter. After that, Granny changed the locks and removed him from the spells allowing access without a key.

"Everything is so weird now," I mutter, turning the now shut-off oven back on.

Keis drawls, "An ancestor telling you that you have to murder someone will do that."

"I also have to fall in love in a month. Is that even a thing?"

"I'm not the person for that."

My cousin isn't disinterested in romance. I've seen her eyes linger on the odd boy passing by in the street. She's just too busy with school to bother.

I tilt my head. "Love at first sight is a thing, isn't it?"

"I think it's a little late for you on that."

Groaning, I retrieve the tablet, scroll through Mama Elaine's recipes, and find a treasure trove of Trinidadian dishes. Homemade pholourie, six different kinds of tamarind sauces, sweet bread towering four layers high, and more.

Cooking wasn't just a hobby for her; she put her heart and soul into her dishes. Why couldn't *she* have been the one to assign my Calling?

I lean my head against the island countertop and let out a strangled whine. Keis pats my head like I'm a sad dog instead of a girl with a hacked task.

"Monday," I say, words muffled from my arms. "Monday, I'll go see Luc. I'll get going on this for real."

"Don't interns there have Mondays off?"

"Get sparked, fine, Tuesday!"

Falling in love in a month. Maybe it's impossible, but I need to try.

And I need to stop thinking about what comes after.

CHAPTER TEN

I walk into the white NuGene building on Tuesday afternoon after helping Granny and Mom bottle our Thomas Brand Curling Custard. The labels have to be stuck on by hand. Trying to do it with magic makes them come out messy. It's usually relaxing. Today it was a silent inquisition. They talked about feed shows and gossip like normal, but their eyes followed me as if the way I flicked on a label would reveal something about my task progress. Meanwhile, the tension between the two of them was as thick as the custard we were labeling. My guess is that Granny either hasn't chatted with Mama Jova, or she did and it didn't go well. As far as we know, my task is going to stay as is.

When they first opened the NuGene building, the receptionist was a NuSap unit. Not anymore. Bad PR isn't worth the money that was saved by using them instead of people. Eerily, the NuSap didn't look much different from the South Asian–looking human receptionist who greets me. It's as if they purposely hired someone who looked like their old android.

"How can I help you today?" she asks.

"I got a notification that my tracker for the matching program was ready." Technically, I got the notification a few days ago, but this was a day when I had a higher chance of running into Luc.

"Wrist on the scanner, please."

I hold out my hand and place it, palm down, on the surface of her desk with a flashing green light. It scans the microchip just under the surface that acts as my identification.

My feed information comes up on the screen. "Perfect," she says. "Let me grab it for you." She turns around and presses something against the wall. Compartments pop out like a filing cabinet, and she looks through them.

I explore the space with my eyes. Stark white walls, white floors, white couches with people waiting to be seen for their high-cost genetic modifications. Maybe an adjustment to weed out an allergy to grass so they can frolic in the sun for the summer. Or something a little more exciting, like unusually strong nails. I know a few witches who have done that to avoid needing to use falsies.

One of the men seated nudges the woman with him and jerks his head forward. I follow his gaze, and none other than Justin Tremblay is walking my way with Luc and the other two interns from the Q&A, Jasmine and Juras.

Maybe the ancestors don't hate me after all. Finally, something has come easy. I hadn't even begun to look for Luc and there he is. I swallow and try not to think of him as my murder victim. He's a potential love interest. Like I'm a girl in a feed show, not a witch meant to destroy him.

Sure, it was easy for Luc to brush me off via messages, but an in-person approach would be harder to push aside. I stride toward him and his sponsor family and paste a smile on my face. It takes two seconds for Luc to spot me and twist his mouth into a frown.

My palms get sweaty the closer I get to the group. I can't back down now. I need to do this. That, and I refuse to give Luc the satisfaction of seeing me intimidated.

I'm a Thomas. We suffer and we survive.

"Fancy seeing you here," I say, voice higher-pitched than normal.

Luc looks somewhere over my shoulder. "Who are you?"

My mouth drops open.

Hack him!

He's seriously going to pretend he has no idea who I am? For real? I grind my teeth together. "You don't know? That's so funny, because you work here, so you must know about the matching program, and yet you have no idea who your match is? Not a big fan of the project, are you?"

Justin's gaze roves over me and Luc, his blond hair as immaculate in person as it is on feeds. "I should hope that's not true. He's the lead on it." He holds out a pale hand to me. "Justin. And you are?"

"Voya." I make a hopefully inconspicuous wipe of my sweaty palm on the bottom of my yellow sundress and shake his hand, avoiding staring into his swirling bionic lenses. With those on, it should pull up my feed and present my info to him in an instant. He could see through my skin and bones to my fast-beating heart if he wanted. Asking for my name is a courtesy.

I expect his hand to be cold, like a cartoon villain's, but it's warm and soft. Granny says you can't trust men with soft hands. But every man in our family except for Grandad has smooth palms. And Grandad's were rough from gardening, not hardship.

Luc splutters before regaining his ground. "I have faith in the program, I just don't feel it has a set timeline. It's fine if I don't immediately connect with my match."

"And yet your focus notes say initial meetings are important and should happen as soon as possible." Juras has a smile on his face he doesn't try to hide.

Luc's shoulders go stiff. "I didn't realize I was meant to be a case study for the program."

"The best way to connect with your project is to participate on a personal level." Justin's voice is as silky as my homemade chocolate mousse. "What do you think of the program so far, Voya?"

I straighten. "I don't quite agree with my match, but I'm willing to invest in getting to know him." I meet Luc's eyes. "He seems content to prove those vicious ratings on his feed right." I widen my lips in a smile at Justin. "People can be so judgmental online. I'd imagine that it would be hard to become the face of a company if you're not well liked."

Luc's jaw twitches, and his eyes dart to Justin. If he doesn't want to participate, fine, but I can bet that Justin wants a successor who people like. He's got no children, so it's likely that one of these three in front of me will lead the company at some point. Luc's got competition, and Juras showed he isn't above undermining him to look better in front of their sponsor dad. I bet Luc would do most things to get on Justin's good side.

At the front desk, the receptionist gawks at us with my tracker grasped in her hands.

"It was wonderful to meet you, sir. I believe my tracker is ready." I force out a heavy sigh and hunch my shoulders. "I don't know if the data will be any good without a participating match partner, but it's a fantastic program, and I hope the beta information is valuable."

"Thank you for saying so," Justin says. "It's a sad day when a participant is more invested than the lead on the program they're participating in." The end of his sentence is clipped and terse, followed by a side look at Luc.

Even as I'm facing Justin, Luc's shaking fists are obvious in my periphery. Sensing an opportunity, I speak again. "It's too bad not everyone can see the best of NuGene. I brought my cousin to the internship Q&A, and she was put off by the attitude of a presenter. I thought she would be a great fit, too."

"What's her name?"

"Keis Thomas."

Justin gestures to Jasmine. "Look her up, please."

I came here to find some way to connect to Luc, but if there's also a chance to get Keis an internship, I can't pass it up. What Rowen's uncle could swing would be nice. But this is NuGene. Keis could get any job she wanted with this on her résumé.

Jasmine pipes up. "Found her."

"Send her an invite to the exclusive tour so we can show her the best of the company. And our friend here too—Voya Thomas?"

My face heats, and I wave my hands. The last thing I need is another chance to humiliate myself in this building. "I'm okay, she's the one you want."

"Nonsense. You have a great passion—you should come on the tour." His eyes bore into mine. "Is that your full name?"

He has my feed data, which means he already knows. The insistence on his part of having me say it is what makes me swallow. "You were right. Voya Thomas." I take a step backward, feeling more seen by his swirling bionic eyes than I want. "Thank you. I'm going to get my tracker now."

"Of course. Lovely to meet you."

"You too."

I should feel triumphant. Keis will get to go to the exclusive tour and be a step closer to a NuGene internship, and I figured out a way to push Luc into at least trying to participate in the matching program so I can increase my chances of falling in love and . . . the other thing that I would rather not think about. At least the sight of his flushed face and shaking fists should have me leaving the building with a skip in my step.

Instead, I shuffle out with a tracker shoved in my purse and Justin's eyes in my mind. I don't know why I'm obsessing over him. The adults hate him for some reason, but that could be about anything.

And then there's that little gnawing in my chest that wonders if I went too far. Justin wouldn't send Luc packing because of what I said, right? I swallow down the guilt and set my face. If he had just agreed to meet me in the first place, it wouldn't have needed to go this far.

Now I'll give him a day before reaching out again.

He's going to give me a chance to love him, whether he likes it or not.

I can't go home after my encounter with Luc and company at NuGene, not while I'm this agitated. Granny will pick up on it and grill me. Instead, I slap the monitor on my wrist and take the streetcar to Gerrard Street East. The neighborhood is considered a smaller version of Chinatown, though it has more than just Chinese businesses. There are at least five pho soup places in a row, and the street smells like a mix of the savory broths and car exhaust. There's one giant mega market that takes up the whole corner block in lieu of multiple blocks of fruit and vegetable stands, and it's busy even though it's a weekday afternoon.

I love the East End. There's a calm here you don't find down-town. It's busy, but not in that way where everyone is rushing and angry. It's just alive with people going about their business.

I hop off the streetcar at the corner of Gerrard Street East and De Grassi Street. The sidewalks alternate between smooth and cracked cement. They keep doing repairs, but with the combi-nation of our cold winters and streetcar traffic, the cracks always come back. I make my way up the street until I reach the entrance of the International Market.

It's as good a time as any to get more ingredients and experi-ment with recipes for the contest. If I win, I can cook without hav-ing to turn the oven back on every twenty minutes.

The holos on the building are in Mandarin, Arabic, French, Urdu, and more. All topped off by a single Canadian flag made up of every single flag in the world. The glass doors are covered with local ads. Lauren's missing posters take up the entirety of one. There's an International Market in every district of the Greater Toronto Area, but this is accepted by most to be the best.

When Eden was four, after a solid week of her begging Dad and Priya, Keis and I took her here. Her face lit up as she pulled us around to look at everything. I bought her way too many packs of kurma. She was bouncing off the walls for hours, to Dad and Priya's dismay. I keep those moments I get with her close to my heart in case Dad leaves again. I'm used to him being gone, but I've been with Eden since the day she was born.

I want her to have those moments and other ones too. Like seeing the ancestors during Caribana. My earliest memory is of clinging to Mom when I was three while Bibi Ulvirae, the ancestor with dark hooded eyes who assigned Mom's Calling, danced over and pressed their ghostly palm to the skin of my cheek. It was cool and comforting.

Eden was so excited the first time she saw the ancestors. She was tucked in a sling around Priya's neck and barely six months old. Her little fists waved with untethered infant enthusiasm, and she's been as excited every year since. I never thought to ask which ancestors she was seeing, assuming they were from Dad and Priya's family. Now I realize that she was seeing Thomases all along.

Experiencing your ancestors is a gift you get by virtue of being born their descendant but lose as soon as you fail them.

There's more to our lineage than casting and gifts. Our magic is our connection to our past, and Eden deserves to experience it all. My sister deserves to *live*.

I slide my eyes away from Lauren's posters and push the doors open. Now I'm just as bad as everyone else. But my baby sister's life is on the line. I don't have time to think about Lauren anymore. After my Calling, after this is all over, I promise, I'll do something to help.

As I enter the market, the air is warm, like folding myself in a blanket of curry and spices.

I make a beeline for the smoothie stand and order myself a small sorrel-and-coconut slush with lychee boba. The lady working there hands me the pink drink, and I stab my straw through the recycled paper lid.

Nothing like comfort food to help ease the ache of needing to murder someone.

"This is what you do after embarrassing people? Come and enjoy a refreshing beverage?"

I nearly choke on a boba pearl as I twist around to where Luc is standing with his arms crossed. "What are you doing here?" I splutter.

"I'm good with computers, and your phone security is lacking."

"You stalked me?"

"Isn't that what you wanted? With your talk to Justin about how unfortunate it is that not everyone believes in the program?"

I roll my eyes. "It's the truth, I just said it out loud."

"You made it look like I don't take my job seriously in front of the CEO! Who also funds my sponsorship and can ship me out of the country any time he feels like it, by the way."

I resist the flush that works its way to my face. I won't be made to feel ashamed because he got caught slacking. Even though I was having the same thought barely an hour ago. "No, *you* didn't take your job seriously and made *yourself* look bad." I shake my head. "I can't believe you're the lead on this project and you aren't taking part in it."

"Just because I'm not pursuing my romantic match doesn't mean I'm not participating."

I snort. "What? So you've met your friendship matches? Your rating is still two. I guess they didn't like you either."

The skin around his eyes bunches, and his expression seems to darken. It slaps right back into a neutral expression a second later.

My cheeks burn. "Would it be so bad to get to know me? I'm not asking you to be in a relationship. I'm asking you to explore the reason why we were paired in the first place."

His expression is flat. Devoid of anything.

"You're already here, right? So just try. Spend thirty minutes with me without being an asshole."

"Now we're name calling?"

I grind my teeth enough to make the sound audible. "Let's make it twenty minutes."

Luc crosses his arms and regards me. He's only a couple of inches taller than I am, and at five feet, it's not like I'm towering over anyone. Our eyes are almost level.

"Think of it this way," I say with a sigh. "Spend twenty minutes with me, and you get that much data you can show to Justin and prove you made an effort."

"Ten."

"Fifteen."

He narrows his eyes at me for a moment more. His shoulders drop. "Fine."

I would cheer except what I've won is time with him. Time with a boy I'm supposed to fall in love with before murdering. If I can even manage to turn feelings of irritation into full-on infatuation in a month. There are people who celebrate one-month anniversaries. That means people can, hypothetically, fall in love during that time. I can do it too. I just need to try.

"What's sorrel?" Luc asks.

I blink and look at my cup. "It's a flower. You can dry it and soak it to make a drink. We brew it for holidays in my family. I get it in a slush here sometimes."

"What does it taste like?"

I thrust the drink out to him. "Try it."

He pulls his mouth into a grimace.

"You're not going to contract anything!"

He leans forward and takes the world's tiniest sip.

"So?"

"It's kind of like hibiscus?"

"Yeah. I guess most flowers taste the same."

There's a moment where we're both not doing anything but standing. I take a good look at him and clue into the fact that this is the first time I'm seeing him out of the NuGene lab coat. He's got ripped jeans and a black short-sleeved hoodie on, with a faded gray beanie pulled over his hair. It's actually a really nice outfit. He is super cute. I remember thinking that when I first met him until he opened his hacking mouth.

"What?" he barks.

I roll my eyes. That mouth ruins everything. "I have to go to a store over this way." I walk ahead without waiting for him.

"What for?"

"Ingredients."

"For?"

"A cooking contest." I glance back at him. "Do you cook?"

"No."

"Personal chefs make your food?" I imagine that Justin's sponsors don't often have to lift a finger.

"You paid attention to those ratings on my profile, eh? Yeah. I have a personal chef, and a servant who wipes my ass when I shit. I live an easy, privileged life." His voice is sharp enough to sting.

I stop and turn to face him. "Okay, what's the deal? If everyone rating you has got you wrong, what is it? You don't have a personal chef, whatever. And maybe your life isn't easy—no one's is—but you've got a lot of privilege. Enough to not invite someone to an exclusive internship tour that could change their life because you're pissed they talked back to you."

"I don't choose who gets invited to the tour. The Human Resources department does."

My mouth goes slack. "Then what's the point in everyone trying to impress you at the Q&A?"

"We can make recommendations, which HR doesn't always listen to. And, not that it matters, I did recommend your cousin. But it's an exclusive tour, and they prioritize people with STEM specializations. That's probably why she wasn't already invited."

My legs feel like they're withering underneath me, and the world is tilting on an angle. "Why would you recommend her?"

"Because she talked back to me." Luc jerks his head forward. "Ten minutes left. Let's go to your store."

We walk down the hall and turn into an alcove. The shop owner's light Trinidadian accent wafts through the air as we enter.

"You came again, eh?" She raises a skeptical eyebrow. "And with a friend, too."

I could curl into a circle and never uncurl. Like a Swiss roll. "I was hoping you had some goat?"

"In the back freezer."

"Thanks." I grab a canvas shopping bag from the front and make my way to the back.

Behind me, Luc walks with his arms crossed, glancing at the shelves.

I let out a sigh. "I'm sorry. Ratings can be complete spam. I shouldn't have judged you by yours."

Luc peeks at me out of the corner of his eye. "Whatever. What's the goat for?"

"Curried goat. The contest is for heritage recipes, so I'm trying out a few."

"And your heritage is?"

"Mostly from Trinidad and the Caribbean, a few from New Orleans and around the US. Africa at some point, but I don't know much about that."

"What is it like there? In Trinidad? I went to New Orleans once with Justin for a conference, and it was interesting. Lively. Lots of history."

I fidget on the spot, though I know I shouldn't be embarrassed. "I've never been to either, actually." We've never had the magic bandwidth for teleportation (even then, it's risky) and definitely not the gifts for it, and the plain non-magic method of flying has always been too expensive. Food and culture recreated in Canada is the closest I've ever gotten to my roots.

He shrugs, nothing to say about not being able to visit my own homeland, which I'm grateful for. "Do you want to go?"

"Someday, yeah." In a future where I can pull together enough cash to afford it, I would love to visit the places my family came from. I glance at him. "You've got a sponsor. Where did you come to Canada from?"

"Mexico."

His voice doesn't hint at pain for leaving the country where he was born, but it must be hard to drop everything and move to a new place. Even at a young age. "Do you miss it?"

"Not really."

"Why not?"

Luc stiffens his shoulders. "I don't get along well with my family. They don't get the whole interest-in-tech-and-science thing. People are more invested in the arts down there. I draw sometimes. My parents wanted me to do that. They have some STEM programs, but nothing near the resources NuGene has. I'm doing my dream job, and I've lived here just as long as I lived there."

He pokes at the eddos in their produce rack. "I went back once, when I was thirteen. I just . . . didn't fit in. People would say they could tell I 'wasn't from there,' except I am. I've never gotten along with people that well growing up anyway. It's not like I left a bunch of friends behind like my sponsor siblings. I never fit in, even when I was supposed to. NuGene feels like home, and Mexico feels like a place I just visit." He gestures to my shopping bag. "What else do you need?"

"Curry powder. So, here is home now. Is your family okay with that? Don't they miss you?"

He shrugs and turns away. "I do video chats with my parents sometimes. They still don't get it. They regret letting me join the sponsor program. Every time I talk to them, it's just a big argument or guilt trip. I'd rather not talk about it."

Sponsorships are complicated. I've heard that when parents let their kids go abroad to be sponsored, they open up a wealth of opportunities, but they also lose a lot of parental rights in the fine print. Like, they can't bring their kid back without probable cause, and to prove that, they would need to go to court. I can't imagine that there's a high success rate in a family going up against lawyers from major corporations.

But if the kids are like Luc and don't want to leave, that's even more complicated. Especially if every moment they do get to spend time with him, it's wasted on arguments. It's not the sort of thing a non-sponsor kid like me is ever going to understand completely.

There are a lot of people, Keis included, who say sponsorships are just modern colonialism. Going into countries you deem less evolved and, instead of forcing your culture on them, you take away members of their society you decide have value and tell them they're better than their peers. You make them adapt to your culture while they lose their own. In the end, they're dependent on their sponsor, who in turn can throw them away without a second thought.

But for people like Luc, this sponsorship is easily the most important thing in his life. I've only known him a few days and I can tell that. Doing some good doesn't make the whole program worth it, but it also makes it harder to say the entire thing should be trashed.

It's a broken system that you can't shut off without breaking it even more.

Not wanting to push about his family, I ask, "How did Justin find you?"

"You know that feed show *Quiz Kids*?"

"Yeah. My cousin got in the top ten once." Proud of Keis, I feel my chest puff out involuntarily.

"I was first five times in a row."

Hack me.

"Justin made a visit down and we talked about robotics. He had sit-downs with my teachers, too, before offering the sponsorship." Luc pulls a tin off the shelf. "Is this the curry powder?"

"Yeah, thanks." I accept the tin from him. There are hundreds of thousands of kids participating in *Quiz Kids*. To get first that many times in a row, he must be a genius. I stare at him for a moment. "And thanks for actually trying to have a normal conversation with me. That's pretty cool how you ended up being sponsored."

He struggles with his words for a moment before snapping out, "Five more minutes left!"

I only slightly hate myself for the smile that slips onto my face. But as quick as it comes, it's gone. It wouldn't have been easy to kill a boy I thought was uppity and rude, but it would probably have been easier than offing a boy with an awkward family situation who left his whole life behind to follow a passion.

Luc clears his throat. "What do you need now?"

"Paratha roti. I can make it from scratch, but I'm feeling lazy about it." There's a bit of bragging in my voice, and I let it slide. I *can* make it from scratch. There's nothing more perfect than that soft flat bread for dipping into curries and sauces.

"And that's an Indian roti, or . . . ?"

I find it on the shelf to my left, still somewhat warm from when they made it in the morning. "I guess so? People eat it all over the Caribbean. That's how I know it. It's a roti without the dried split pea pieces."

I pull some cumin, clove, and garlic off the shelves and shove them into the bag. In the produce section, I grab a few Julie mangoes because I know the family will be all over me for them. The ones they sell in the regular grocery stores are often underripe and flavorless. By the time I pick one for each family member, the bag is heavy enough that I wish I had the extra cash to order a car to get home. Almost everyone uses a self-drive model, but some people like our family insist on keeping old vehicles that need manual drive. I prefer the former. It's a calm, even ride, unlike driving with Auntie Maise, who spends half the time screaming at other cars following the rules that she isn't.

I glance at all the groceries in my hands. When I buy any sort of groceries for meals, I use the joint account Granny set up once it was obvious I was going to be doing both the cooking and the shopping. It's a good thing too, because I don't have the extra money to pay for this.

Luc takes his right hand out of his pocket to gesture to the mangoes. "When I was little, we used to dip mango slices in Tajín. It's like a mix of spices, salt, and lime."

"I've never tried that." I've heard of it before in Mexican cuisine feed videos, but never got around to doing it myself.

"It's good if you like spicy."

"I like spicy." Speaking of, I reach behind him and grab some cayenne pepper off the shelf. "So we've established that you don't cook. What do you eat at home?"

"Instant noodles. Boxed mac and cheese. Takeout. That sort of stuff."

I balk and look him up and down. "How are you not dying? That's not real food."

"It's enough." He shifts under my gaze.

"What about vegetables? Fruits? Meats? Seafood?"

"I eat apples sometimes."

I grimace so hard that my neck strains. "Your shit is so sparked. You need to eat proper food. Maybe I'll drop off some of this curry for you."

He raises an eyebrow. "You would cook something for me?"

My mouth snaps shut. I wasn't thinking about what I was offering. But damn, macaroni and cheese from a box! How did I get looped into going from wanting to smash the guy's face in to offering to cook for him? "I'm not cooking *for* you. I'm giving you the pleasure of eating my leftovers."

He bites on his lips and quirks them up a bit. It takes me a couple of seconds to realize it's a smile. He seems to catch himself and wipes it off his face. "Anything else?"

I go to the front of the store and stuff packages of sweet red mango slices, kurma, tamarind balls, and salt prunes in my bag. I don't come here often enough to practice restraint, and Granny's more likely to be mad I didn't get enough than upset that I got too much.

Luc raises an eyebrow. "That's going in the curry?"

"Nope. Snacks for my family to fight over."

"Who's that? Parents? Your cousin? The little girl in your feed profile?"

"I live with my mom; dad; his new wife, Priya; their daughter, Eden—she's the girl in my feed profile—my aunt and uncle; my cousins, Alex, Keis, and Keisha; and my grandma."

"That's like how it was back in Mexico," Luc says. "I lived with five of my cousins and their parents."

I notice that he doesn't say "back home," the way I've heard other sponsor kids talk about the countries they came from. "Did you like it?"

"When I was there, not really. I always wanted my own space. But now that I have it, sometimes I miss the noise."

There's something about the sounds of family that make a home. The symphony of everyone chatting, shouting, and laughing is what makes our house feel alive. "I get that."

I cash out, and we make our way out of the store. "Time's up. That wasn't so bad, was it?"

He grumbles something and strides away from me without so much as a goodbye.

If he noticed that he stayed five minutes longer than he needed, he chose not to address it.

I think of that brief, awkward smile.

Maybe falling in love with him won't be as impossible as I thought.

CHAPTER ELEVEN

A couple of days after Luc's and my unofficial twenty-minute date, I go to Alex's room, which is more of a wreck than when I was last in it. The decorated walls have adopted the style of a panicked detective relying on a case to save their career. Dozens of sketches are taped to the walls, some with fabric swatches, others with frantic splashes of watercolor, all connected with a dizzying amount of ribbon and thumbtacks.

I stand in her doorway with my mouth open. "You've been busy . . ."

"Spare me."

My cousin, who is usually decked out like a feed model, is sitting at her sewing machine with no lashes or makeup and with deeper dark circles under her eyes than the days before. Even her head lacks its sleek razor shave, covered in a little mini afro that is dangerously close to resembling what Granny has going on.

I'm glad I offered to help.

I close the door behind me and toss Alex a pack of red mango from the International Market that I hid away specifically for her.

"You saved more?" She beams and tears the package open. "I knew you were my favorite cousin."

"I'm always the favorite." I gaze around the room. "Where do you want me?"

"Topaz dropped those off the other day when he brought Eden by on the bus. You need to glue on the beading in the patterns on that sheet." She points to her bed, where four plastic sacks full of sparkling silver short shorts, bikini bottoms, and bathing suit tops are stuffed.

I pick up the pieces of paper lying on the blanket. "Where do you get these printed?"

"Staples."

"I thought they shut the printing center down ages ago."

"They keep one going. Some people do still use paper, you know."

"Yeah, for cute retro notebooks and flyers made in a desperate attempt to stand out from the mess of digital ads. I could have looked at these on a tablet."

Alex scowls. "Are you helping or not? You're making me want to box you upside the head."

Damn, she's on edge. I find the bags of sequins, each separated by color. Shuffling into a comfortable position on her bed, I open the closest bag and get to work lining up and gluing the sequins on the fabric. "I haven't done this since I was like twelve."

Alex keeps her eyes on her sewing but laughs. "You begged me to let you help, and after that year you never asked again."

It was hard not to be attracted to the Caribana outfits with their glitter and glam. Not to mention the enormous feather headpieces. Alex has helped out ever since she was eight—the first year she came to live with us.

We had gone over to the Davises' place for the annual backyard BBQ they throw for the Black witch community before Caribana, and she'd declared to Johan that she could design better costumes. He leaned down in her little child face and said, "Prove it."

And she did. Even before her gift, she was amazing at creating clothes that dazzled. I was in constant awe of my big cousin. But after realizing the work that went into helping with the costumes, I figured I would opt out. Twelve-year-old me was not prepared for the hours of beading.

Now it's kind of nice to have something to occupy my mind that doesn't involve murder or maybe-maybe-not trash boys. "You can't use magic to help this go faster? Isn't that what you usually do?"

Alex furrows her brow. "I tried yesterday, but . . . I think I'm too tired."

"It's not working?" If you reach your bandwidth for the day, you can't cast anymore. But it not working at all isn't normal. How exhausted is she?

"It's fine. You're helping, and there's plenty of time until next Sunday."

"The show is *in a week*?!"

Her answer is a loud sigh.

No wonder she's so stressed. It's Thursday, which technically means she has more than a week, but it's not a ton of time to finish a whole collection. "Don't worry. You focus on your line, and I'll get this stuff done."

"Thank you." She pauses sewing and gazes at me. There's a heaviness to her eyes, and it feels uncomfortably like guilt.

"What?"

"Don't you have . . . other things you should be focusing on?"

"I'm working on it." I press down hard on an aquamarine sequin and decide to cut to the chase. "It's not like I can sit here thinking about Luc until I love him. I may as well be productive."

"Keis said he's a huge asshole."

Dammit, Keis. "He may not be too bad. I hung out with him a bit the other day."

"You *hung out*?"

I give a little shrug without repeating myself.

"Keis said he wouldn't even chat with you online."

I grind my teeth. "Nice to know that Keis is so happy to spread the news of my pending relationships around."

"Just this one."

Just the one where I have to kill the boy in cold blood, she means. My fingers shake as I place a sequin, and I use my other hand to steady it. "I don't understand how the Davises can do what they do."

"Caribana?"

I'm about to cut Alex a glare, but her face is impassive. She knows what I mean.

"All dark rituals have a greater good," she says.

Both my eyebrows shoot to my hairline. "Better not let Granny hear you saying that. She will fry her chip."

Alex rolls her eyes. "Maybe killing someone is easier if you feel like it has a higher purpose."

Is fulfilling my task a higher purpose? Or is it just selfish? Sure, the dark rituals that impure witches cast need pure intent, but the kickback magic they get is the real prize, and that's less selfless. "I guess."

"Did Granny say anything about whether you'll really need to do this? Maybe destruction is symbolic?"

"Symbolic of what exactly?"

"I don't know! Doesn't Mama Jova know we're a pure family?"

"If she does, she doesn't care very much."

Alex runs a hand over her head. "I think that maybe you just need to do the falling-in-love bit, and she'll pass you off that. She can't actually make you kill anyone."

I remember a time not that long ago when some people thought I just had to accept the task and would magically pass. Everyone keeps thinking there's a way out of this, but I don't know that there is. "I'm just trying to focus on the falling-in-love thing, like you said, and less on the other thing."

"Fair enough. At least we'll get to see how accurate this NuGene matching thing is. I mean, if you do fall in love, then the program is gold, right?"

I bob my head in a nod and peek over at Alex. "Have you ever been in . . . ?"

"Yes."

I drop the now-sequined bikini bottoms in my hand. "With who?"

"Fashion."

"Urg! Alex!" I love food, but I doubt that's what Mama Jova had in mind when she set out her task. Besides, I've destroyed, aka devoured, several meals since then and definitely haven't been passed for it. Symbolic my ass.

"For real. It's something that's always in the back of my mind. When I think of my future, I can't imagine it without fashion. To me, that's love."

If I fail and Alex loses her gift, will I be taking that love from her? Sure, she was always good at designs, but trying to make it in the fashion world is something different. It's competitive. Eden's life is the biggest risk here, but my failure will have even more ripples of pain than that. "I don't know if I can apply that to people."

"Why not? If you picture him in your future, and he's part of most things that make you happy, wouldn't that be love?"

I can't see Luc in my future, because in the best version of it, he's gone. Happy doesn't factor either. He's still kind of irritating. Especially now that I know he has the capacity to be decent and instead chooses to be pompous. "I'm not at that point with him."

"Maybe you don't know enough about him. You tend to like people better when you know them more."

"And if that doesn't work?"

"For ancestors' sake. Try one thing and see before you start worrying about failing or not. That was Dad's one piece of good advice."

Every once in a while, Alex will mention Uncle Vacu. Not about how he was at the end, when he left her alone to fend for herself in their apartment, but little mentions of him. Even Uncle Vacu was in love at some point in his life, if he had Alex with her mom. Ideally, anyway.

I try to picture Alex's mom and come up blank. I shift in place. Was her mom ever around? Did I meet her? It seems like I should have, but I can't think of any memories, so maybe I never did.

Either way, how difficult could falling in love really be? A month isn't a great timeline, but I must be able to manage something. Maybe I'll try to think of every nice thing he's done so that when I see him, I don't feel annoyed over the shitty things. Or maybe I should get relationship coaching from Priya.

"You're doing that thing," Alex says.

"What thing?"

"The thing where you get quiet and I know you're going over some decision in your head." She adopts a high-pitched voice. "Should I make curry goat tonight or curry chicken? I planned to make curry goat, and I have the ingredients for it, but now I'm thinking curry chicken. Let me stand here for twenty minutes and decide while my family starves."

I wrinkle my nose. "Someone's circuit is fried about having to wait for a dinner that someone else is kind enough to cook for you. Also! Is that supposed to sound like me?"

"It does sound like you, and that's what you do. Hell, even in your Calling you somehow managed to swing extra time to agonize about a decision."

I smash a sequin onto a pair of booty shorts and grumble, "I helped you decide on the colors for the mas camp fast. I chose a bunch of internship opportunities for Keis. Yesterday, I helped

Keisha pick her outfit for a date, and *you know* how picky she is about that."

Alex shrugs without missing a stitch on her sewing machine. "If it's about helping other people choose, you never have a problem. If it's a decision about something *you're* going to do, forget it."

I gnaw on my lip. "I don't sound like that."

"Fine, then hurry up and make whatever decision it is that you need to make. What are you struggling so hard with anyway?"

"Just trying to figure out the falling-in-love thing. What made your..." I pause, about to ask about her parents but also not wanting to bring up what could be a sore subject.

"What?"

I shift in place.

"Just spit it out, Vo."

"What about your parents? Like, your mom and Uncle Vacu. I wondered if you knew what made them fall in love. But then I realized you don't really talk about your mom at all."

Alex leans back in her chair. "I don't really know what made them click. To be honest, I don't have a lot of memories of my mom at all. I think maybe she left when I was little. At one time Dad must have had pictures of her, but I don't remember them well." My cousin lets out a sharp laugh. "Sometimes it feels like it doesn't matter. She left. And sometimes I really want to know about her anyway. What she was like. That sort of thing."

I don't know what to say to that. Maybe that's why I don't remember her mom, because she left them so early. It makes sense.

"Love is complicated," Alex says with a joyless grin. I shouldn't have asked about her parents. "Now, did you figure out what you're going to do about Luc?"

"Maybe" is what comes out of my mouth. But, of course, I can't actually settle on what I want to do to try and fall in love with him.

Which is usually when I employ my number one tactic for when I can't decide on one thing.

I do them all.

I eye the two steaming trays in front of me. One is a variation of curried goat, and the other is another curry with oxtail I found in the basement deep freezer. Both have a rich, spicy scent and come from Mama Elaine's recipes in the almanac. I got up early to get both cooked and had to turn the oven back on at least four times.

Everyone is buzzing around the kitchen, getting their morning coffees and teas. With the exception of Alex, who is still sewing at all hours. The energy of everyone moving makes the room feel full without being crowded. You wouldn't think that a Saturday morning would be the time for this sort of activity, but none of the adults have any sort of job with normal hours, so our weekends are more likely to be something random like a Tuesday, where we all hang out in the living room, while on Saturday, we're up at the crack of dawn, ready to work a full day. Johan has his kids running special weekend classes to help out with childcare for witches, so even Eden has somewhere to be. Though she'll get to play games instead of sitting at a desk.

Uncle, as usual, is peeling a Honeycrisp apple as big as his fist at the speed of an ancient computer. He regularly sits with a plate and peels, cores, and slices his apple into perfect pieces.

I weave around him and bring the giant peach-colored rice cooker over to the island to pack everyone's lunches with a portion of both curries and rice. In between the two curries I stick a metal divider.

"Everyone needs to try both curries and tell me which one you like better!" I yell into the air. Which is pretty much the best way to address everyone. I need to make progress on this recipe contest. "Dad!"

He jerks to attention with a reusable tumbler of coffee in his hand. He'll be off to the spa, where he's used his gift of relaxing touch to garner a good amount of regular massage therapy clients. "Yeah?"

"I made you and Priya a version with jackfruit instead of the meat, so tell me what you think about the curry sauce."

He bobs his head. "Thanks."

Eden walks over to the island and tries to wiggle onto the stool with a bowl of cereal in her hand. I take the bowl from her so she can get on, then set it down in front of her.

"Thank you!" she chimes with a mouthful of Cheerios.

Keisha hovers over my shoulder. "What did you make me?"

"I gave you a tiny bit of the curries and rice, so please give it a try. I put a salad in too."

"What's on it?"

"Mango dressing on the side. Spinach, strawberries, sliced almonds, and a little bit of avocado."

Keisha takes out her phone and hovers it over the lunch box. It spits out a calculation of the amount of calories, fat, iron, and vitamins included in the lunch. "I'll have a few bites of your stuff." She almost moves away, then recounts the number of lunch boxes. "You have one extra."

"Yeah."

"Why?"

"Don't you have to go do a shoot or help Auntie at the studio or something?" Keisha sometimes does feed modeling for a bit of extra cash. Mostly she goes with her mom to a shared studio space to help with her glass-blowing pieces.

Keisha points at Auntie lounging against the kitchen wall, scrolling through her phone. "She's gotta drive your mom to a client's place, so we're waiting for her." She squints. "Who else are you making lunch for? Wait, is it for . . . him?"

The entire room freezes.

Uncle stops peeling his apple. Dad has his tumbler to his lips but isn't drinking, and Priya is stopped short behind him. Auntie ceases her feed scrolling.

Only Keis and Eden are still moving. My cousin presses the heels of her hands to her eyes, and my sister continues obliviously eating her cereal.

"I can totally feel your discomfort right now," Keisha whispers. Which I'm sure is her version of being sensitive to the situation. "It definitely is."

I hate Keisha's gift more now than I've ever hated anything in my life.

Granny shuffles into the kitchen with an empty mug and pauses in the entryway, reading the room. "Who died?"

Everyone cringes.

"Voya made lunch for her genetic match," Keisha says, voice back to normal like she didn't drop the bomb of the morning.

Granny looks at me for a beat before bringing her mug over to the kettle and fixing herself a cup of tea. "Where are those biscuits you made the other day?"

"In the fridge," I reply.

"Warm one up for me."

Obediently, I head over to the fridge and get one of the coconut biscuits for Granny, slicing it in half and popping it into the toaster. I'm shocked there are any left, except I guess I shouldn't be. The adults seemed to be avoiding me up until this moment, so most probably didn't even realize I made them.

"You're making food for this boy," Granny says, bringing her cup to her lips. Her voice has a pressing edge to it, like the dull end of a chef's knife.

"I thought it might be a nice gesture," I mumble.

Priya is the first to move, continuing to pack her and Dad's lunches in their individual lunch bags. "Food is a powerful thing in relationships. It shows that they matter to you and warms the heart." Her words sound normal, but her voice is even sharper than Granny's. "But does your ancestor care about that? Apparently not." Suddenly, I have a lot less desire to ask Priya for relationship advice.

"Granny, they can't make her do this," Keis says finally. "Mama Jova can't—"

"Mama Jova," Granny says, voice firm, "can do whatever she wants. She is an honored ancestor, and this is the task she has given." She snaps, "We don't have to like it. But it's happening, and pretending otherwise isn't helping anyone, least of all Voya."

I swallow and take Granny's biscuit from the toaster, putting it on a plate and brushing a generous helping of salted butter over it before handing it off to her.

Mom chooses that moment to bluster into the room, her hair loose around her shoulders. She pauses as she steps in, looking around. "Who di—"

"Don't!" we shout in unison, and she shuts her mouth.

Everyone reanimates and goes about their business like they were before Keisha questioned my extra lunch.

Keisha slides up next to me. "Are you going to see him today?"

"Keisha!" Granny snaps. "Stop bothering your cousin."

"I'm not both—"

"No talking back!"

Keisha lets out a combination of a steups and a sigh but leaves me to it. There are few things she loves more than relationship gossip, but she seems to have conveniently forgotten the bit where I have to kill Luc. Or maybe she's like the others and doesn't think I'll actually have to do it.

But Granny was firm with her words.

If even *she* doesn't think there's a way around it, there must not be.

"What are you doing today?" Keis at least has the decency to come close so not everyone can hear our conversation. She has her bag over her shoulder, ready for her usual escape out of the house for the day. Since it's the weekend, she doesn't have class but will probably do self-study at the library for most of the day.

I purposely sidestep her question. Given how things went earlier, I don't want to discuss my plans to seek out Luc while the whole family is still here. "Are you ready for the NuGene tour?"

She rolls her eyes. "That's not happening until next week."

"Yes, but prep is important! I think you would be such a good fit there."

"Why?" Keisha says, eavesdropping without shame. "She doesn't have any sort of science or tech specialization."

"Not everyone who works there has a STEM specialization," Keis snaps back.

Granny claps her hands. "Okay, that's your cue. Maise, Ama is done getting her tea. Take your troublemaker and go."

"Which one?" Auntie Maise grumbles.

Keisha glares at her sister because she can't glare at Granny before grabbing her lunch and following her mom out.

Mom comes over and kisses my forehead. "Have a good day. Happy thoughts. We'll work on a way out of this." She hugs me, which she doesn't usually do in the morning, and it's so tight that I almost have to push her away to breathe. Finally, she lets me go.

"Thanks, Mom." I hand her a lunch, and she heads out with one last long look at me over her shoulder. She missed Granny's big declaration of my task being my task, and I don't look forward to how that goes down when Auntie Maise spills the beans during their drive.

Priya waves to Dad. "We need to get going. I need to get to my client." I'm assuming she means one of the many people who sign up for her matchmaking service, which hopefully won't suffer too bad now that NuGene is doing one. They grab their bags, and Priya takes Eden's empty cereal bowl from her with a scowl on her face that she tries to make into a smile for her daughter.

Eden shuffles off the stool, and I hand her the smaller lunch box I prepared. "This one isn't as spicy. Let Johan heat it up for you, okay?"

"Yup. Thank you."

"You have to tell me which curry you think is yummier."

She screws her face into a serious expression. "I will."

"Thanks. Can I have a hug, or a high five, or a wave?" She barrels into me for a hug before running off to follow her mom. I say to Dad, "I left a few plastic bags at the door—they're for Topaz. Can you give them to him when you put Eden on the bus?" It'll save me some time if Topaz brings the finished beaded costumes home.

"Yup, we'll grab them," he says before he and Priya leave with Eden.

Now, it's just me, Keis, Granny, and of course Uncle, who spends the entire day trailing her, crunching away at his apple.

Granny crosses her arms. "The next time you see that boy, make sure to ask him what that thing is tracking."

"What?" I blurt out.

"The thing on your wrist that NuGene put on. We have neurotransmitter signals that show magic, you know."

I lower my brows. "They look like anomalies to doctors. No one is going to jump from that to magic."

Uncle adopts Granny's crossed-arms pose. "Justin Tremblay isn't no one. If this is his sponsor son, he's going to be looking at that data."

"What am I supposed to do? I need the money for participating. Even if it is tracking neurotransmitters, I'm not going to take it off."

"Girl!" Granny snaps. "Whatever they're giving you isn't worth that man getting data from us. You don't know what he can do."

"Tell me! What can he do?"

"This isn't a democracy. I am your Matriarch, and I'm telling you that if that thing is tracking our neurotransmitters, the, the—"

"Dopamine in the amygdala," Uncle chimes in.

"Yes! That! He's going to figure out what that means."

I throw my hands up. "I'll ask Luc, or one better, I'll go to a store and get it looked at. Then you'll know it's only tracking romantic matching stuff. Okay?"

Granny huffs. "Watch your tone."

"Sorry," I mumble.

"Good!" She finishes her biscuit and smacks her lips. "I like those biscuits."

My frown morphs into a little smile. It's hard to stay mad at Granny. "Thanks."

"Cheddar is good too. You should make some of those." With that, she makes her way out of the kitchen, and Uncle follows behind her.

I sag onto the island as they leave.

"She has a point," Keis says. "About the monitor."

"Never mind her point. Concentrate on how scared they are of Justin. It's weird." I was a bit creeped out by him myself, but not to their level. "I was planning to find Luc today anyway."

"So you do have plans for the day?"

"Yup."

"It's hacked," my cousin spits out. "Mama Jova can't make you do this. Who even thinks of this shit? Fall in love with someone and then kill them?"

I flinch a little. "I don't know. Granny said I have to."

"What does she know?"

"Um, she's the Matriarch, so she knows a lot."

Keis grinds her teeth together. "Sometimes I think you forget I can read your mind. Even you have doubts about if this is real."

"Yeah, because I wish it weren't. But that doesn't change the task." I let out a deep breath. "Now, are you coming with me?"

"To see Luc?!"

"No! Are you a mind reader or not?"

She scowls. "I wasn't paying attention. Why do you need me to come check out the monitor? Just go on your own."

"Pleeeeeease," I beg. I hate going downtown on my own. It's boring being on the train alone, and we could get breakfast snacks together. There's a place that does dollar Danishes before ten a.m.

"Fine. And where are you planning to find your genetic irritation?"

I hold up my phone triumphantly, open to a page on his usually sparse feed. Except a couple of weeks ago he was tagged by someone at the Night Market, which happens on Saturdays, apparently during the whole day, not just at night.

Keis raises an expertly drawn eyebrow. "That exclusive underground art thing?"

"Must be." I shoot a message off to Keisha to see if she knows where it is. If anyone would, it would be her.

"What's your plan?"

"I surprise him with some lunch, hang around the market, get info about this monitor, apparently, and get to know him all in one. Multitasking!"

Keis grabs her lunch. "I still think it's hacked."

"It is, but I can't do anything. This is Eden's life we're talking about."

"I know." She grabs her backpack and shoves the lunch in. "Let's go."

As we leave, a message comes in from Keisha with the address. I check the time. Perfect. It's too early to head over with a lunch for

Luc right now, which means we have lots of time to get the monitor checked and grab Danishes.

Keis rolls her eyes at me, which I ignore.

I refuse to fail anymore. Not at this recipe contest. And not at this task.

No matter how high the cost, the risk is even higher.

CHAPTER TWELVE

The bright summer sun beams down on the Electronics Den, tucked between a Royal Bank and a vegan hot dog takeout. Its storefront is alive with holos, flashy neon signs, and an ancient blue-skinned NuSap woman welcoming customers inside. She's locked and chained to a pole to prevent theft, seemingly programmed to do nothing more than stand and wave. They used to have the ability to program their AI to make actions based on incoming data without commands—like interpreting an owner's lower body temperature as needing more blankets tucked around them. The government made those sorts of settings illegal. Now if anyone is using the androids, they have to program each action and command.

Staring at the machinery reminds me of Luc and makes me hyperaware that I'm a little over a week into my task without much to show for it. I take a rough bite out of my cherry and cream cheese Danish for distraction.

Keis walks along with me, chewing on her spinach and cheese pastry, which honestly seems like a waste of a baked good, just saying.

She rolls her eyes at me. "Can we just go and do this? I have that Q&A at the library with Rowen's uncle on Monday, and I'm supposed to be spending this time prepping for it."

A bit of cherry filling drips onto my chin, and I use my thumb to swipe it off, going in for the lick only to pause. Instead of the thick red filling, on my finger is a swipe of dark crimson that looks a lot more like blood than delicious dessert innards.

"Vo?" Keis says, brow furrowed.

"Yup! Sorry, uh, that'll be exciting to go to that."

"Yeah . . ."

When I examine my thumb again, it's just plain old cherry filling stuck to it. I frown as I stick my thumb into my mouth.

Keis tilts her head and examines me. "Are you okay?"

"Are you excited for the Q&A?" I ask, ignoring her question.

"I think it'll be all right." Her words are tentative, like she's confident about it, but not as excited as she could be.

"But it's not NuGene."

She doesn't deny it. "I don't know for sure if NuGene is the right fit."

"You'll know better after the tour. And it wouldn't hurt if you used your natural gifts to give you a leg up."

Keis narrows both eyes at me. "No."

"You have a gift for a reason! Why not use it to help you get ahead a bit? No one in the family has to know you did, so it won't ruin your protest."

"I'll know! Why does everyone in this family think you can't accomplish anything without magic?"

"I'm not saying you can't. You have the education *and* the magic. Why not use both? Isn't that what you were talking about, being more than just a witch?"

Keis rubs her arms and looks away at the store. "Let's go get this monitor checked out."

We make our way into the Electronics Den, where we're greeted by the smell of burning plastic and four walls covered in phones, tablets, smart watches, self-install hijacker chips, and more.

At the front desk, scrolling through her phone, is a Black girl about Alex's age with ochre brown skin and a forest-green hijab. There's a tap-donation pad with Lauren's face on it. I dig out my phone, select five dollars, and tap it against the white pad. My friend's face disappears, and a green checkmark takes her place, confirming my donation and thanking me. It's the last of what I have until I get my allowance tomorrow. At least I can use the little bit I have to help Lauren since I can't do anything else right now.

"I can't believe they haven't found her yet," Keis murmurs.

The girl smacks the gum in her mouth. "People are saying she ran away. I don't buy it. It's been too long."

I agree with her. Yeah, Lauren would run away every now and then, but never for this long. My stomach aches, the Danish churning in tight circles. "Can you tell us if my monitor has any recording devices installed? And if it does, what sort of NTs it's tracking?" I unclip the monitor from my wrist and hand it to her.

She furrows her brow. "Where did you get this?"

"It's from NuGene. I'm in their matching beta test."

The girl's eyes light up. "I've heard about that. Wish I had gotten in. Anyway, I'll go check it."

As she retreats into the back room, I glance at Keis. "What do we do if it doesn't have any recording tech on it?"

"Then I guess we don't have to worry about that."

I sag against the counter and chew on the end of my nail. If it's clear, that will be one thing off my plate, which gives me more time to contemplate the murder I need to commit. "Sorry to bring you downtown again. The buzz of thoughts must be loud."

Keis makes an odd expression.

"What?"

She shakes her head. "Have you thought about the 'how' of all this?" Her voice is strained.

"The 'how'?"

"As in, how are you going to do this task in a way that doesn't land you with a life sentence?"

I haven't gotten that far. I can't picture the act in my brain, much less how to cover it up. What am I supposed to do? Chop Luc up into pieces and hide his body parts in garbage bags around the city? Or boil his innards down and mix them into the beauty products? They'll call me the Curling Custard Killer.

"For ancestors' sake, Vo," Keis groans.

"Impure witches do it all the time, don't they?"

"Uh, no. Tons of impure witches steal and torture people, but they leave them alive. Not that many are doing the full deed these days." Keis shrugs. "But that's them. This is you. Or do you have some sort of impure witch 'how to hide a body' manual that I've never seen?"

Once I kill Luc, I'll have passed my Calling, and I'll be able to cast. I try and think of a ritual I could use to hide his body—except I can't move past those words. His body. Him lying prone, covered in blood, blue-gray eyes vacant and open.

A shiver crawls up my spine.

"Did Granny even make contact with Mama Jova?" Keis snaps under her breath. "There must be a way to make her change the task. Ask for something different. A deal or something. Murder doesn't fix things. This task is so hacked."

"I don't think she's open to negotiation."

Keis shakes her head again. "You're not even trying to figure out a way around this."

"I'm being realistic about the fact that there is no way around this."

"Really? Because it sounds a lot like you've just given up."

Before I can snap at her, the back door swings open, and the girl passes the monitor to me. "It's clean. No video or audio recording. Nothing that could latch onto your chip and hijack your feed."

"What's it monitoring?" I ask, leaning against the counter, glad to have an excuse to stop arguing about my task with Keis.

She shrugs. "Physiological stuff. It does connect to your chip, but all it does is relay things like your heart rate, neurotransmitter data, stuff like that. It must send a signal when you get any NT activity that indicates attraction."

"NT activity where?"

The girl brings out her tablet and shows me a visual of the brain with some areas lit up. I focus in on the amygdala, but there's nothing there. It's not tracking magic.

The girl grins. "It's a cool NT sequence tracker, though. Data says it's something called the Elaine sequence."

Mama Elaine pops into my mind automatically.

"There are lots of people named Elaine," Keis says.

"Do you mind letting me form my thought fully before you stomp all over it?" I hiss low so the Electronics Den girl doesn't hear.

Sure, maybe there are a lot of people named Elaine, but Justin's face sticks in my brain along with the strange discomfort of being around him. Not to mention the whole family freaking out about Justin in general. Maybe there's no connection at all, but maybe there is.

Hidden things are fragile. Once they start to be revealed, each prod and tap forms a new crack until the whole thing shatters and leaves the truth exposed.

Maybe I'm poking at nothing. Or maybe I'm unearthing something that wasn't supposed to be uncovered.

The girl clears her throat.

"Sorry," I say. "How much?"

"Ten dollars."

Hack me. I gave my last five dollars to the Lauren donation, and even if I kept it, I wouldn't have had enough. I turn pleading eyes to Keis. She's always been better with her allowance, putting it away in a savings account and only using half every week instead of blowing the full thing like I do.

She taps her phone against the pad with a huff.

"Thank you," I chime. "I'll pay you back."

"You'd better."

We walk out of the store together, and I take in a cleansing breath of the summer air. "One problem solved. Granny will be happy."

"I don't think anyone will be happy until this is over."

I wring my hands. Until this is over. Until Luc is dead.

That's the happy ending we're striving for.

I jump on the mention of the Elaine sequence. Whipping out my phone, I have my AI search for any mentions of an Elaine Thomas, an Elaine sequence, or any instance of a Justin Tremblay and an Elaine. The only results I get are the odd feed link for a couple named Justin and Elaine who have nothing to do with my ancestor or the NuGene CEO.

"See?" Keis pushes. "No connection."

"What if this could affect my task? It's Justin who's related to Luc, and Elaine who may be related to us. Maybe it's some sort of mystery or clue from Mama Jova?"

Keis raises a highly skeptical eyebrow.

"It's weird, anyway."

"I don't think it's a thing, Vo."

I nod along with her but resolve to ask Luc about it anyway.

We take the streetcar together since we're both heading in the same direction, though Keis is going a lot farther west than I am. A man begins a loud and furious rant at the front of the streetcar over something vaguely religious and political. I wince, glancing at Keis, who would usually be cringing from the emotion of his thoughts in concert with the buzz of so many people.

But there's no firm set to her mouth, and no screwing up of her eyes. The slight crease between her brows is more indicative of general annoyance from listening to a man blend the devil and liberal agenda together. But she doesn't seem overwhelmed.

It's almost as if she can't hear them.

And I can bet it's not because she's been practicing in secret.

I watch Keis out of the corner of my eye for the rest of the trip. Everyone has secrets, but she and I share ours. Something this big, a dulling of her gift, she would tell me about.

She would.

Wouldn't she?

The Night Market, according to Keisha, is tucked away on Queen Street West and John Street in an underground space that used to be a parking lot. It doesn't happen exclusively at night, though my cousin insists that after dark is the only interesting time to come. I pass the entrance about three times before spotting the black spray-painted door leading to a narrow set of concrete steps. There's no railing, and it's so steep that I have to press my hands against the two walls on either side to keep my balance. When I finally reach the entrance at the bottom, I let out a loud exhale and knock on the door.

It swings open, and I'm face-to-face with a tall Black man with bionic eyes. He's dressed in a charcoal suit, dress shirt, and tie. He looks me up and down. His bionics must be accessing every bit of online data I have. I've only seen them on celebrities, and even then, there's a limited amount. "You're new."

I jerk my head up and down.

"Do you have an invite?"

"I'm a friend of Luc's."

"I'll message him." He digs out his phone and walks out of my sight.

I bounce on my toes, while he contacts Luc. It takes longer than I would expect. I'm waiting about five minutes when the man comes back.

He tucks his hands into his pockets. "Says he has no idea who you are."

That enormous, pompous asshole! I raise myself up as tall as I can make my five-foot frame go. "You tell him that he can go choke on his boxed mac and cheese!"

Luc appears from behind the man at the door. "You go from chill to sparked fast, eh?"

I blink and look at the doorman with my mouth open to the wind.

He raises his hands up. "I'm sorry, I thought it would be funny."

"Are you for real?"

Luc crosses his arms. "Terrance likes jokes. Are you coming in? Or should I stay back here and choke on my boxed mac and cheese?"

My face feels like I stuck it in the oven. "I'm coming."

We walk down the hallway leading away from the entrance.

"For someone so upset about my supposed stalking, you don't seem opposed to doing it yourself," Luc drawls.

"I'm surprised that you let me in."

"I'm interested in getting some qualitative data about your matching experience."

"Now you care about your project?" I say, not hiding my skepticism.

Luc furrows his brow and glares at me. "I always cared about my project. I'm just not interested in getting into it myself." He takes a deep breath. "That being said, I would be remiss in not being open to exploring the data firsthand. We did the fifteen minutes of interaction the other day, and it was a useful exercise."

Technically twenty minutes, but I won't be the one to tell him.

Scramble my feed, he's like a big gray wall. I glance at the color of his hair and eyes and the Fade Ink on his arm. The design is a black double helix made up of tiny ATGC letters. Okay, maybe not that boring after all.

This is the person who I'm supposed to fall in love with. My toes curl in my sandals.

Who I'm supposed to kill.

I push my shoulders back and stand up straighter. "Qualitative data, eh? I'm having not the greatest experience, but I'm willing to improve it. I think if we get to know each other more, we'll understand why we're a genetic match."

"That sounds logical. How do you plan to do that?"

"Ask questions. That's how you tend to get to know people. Like your name, is it short for anything?"

Luc avoids my eyes. "Why does it matter?"

I groan. He makes everything so hacking hard. "I'm trying to get to know you."

"Names are tough." He tucks his hands into his jeans pockets. "You don't choose it. Someone else does, and it ends up defining your whole life. And when the name and who you are don't match, you have to spend time changing what people think when they look at you. Not just people who already know you, but everyone else too. How the whole world sees you. You know?"

I stare at his downturned face. "I don't, honestly. I've always liked my name. My mom made it up out of nothing for me. And I guess no one ever questioned whether it fit me." I pause for a moment. "Is Luc a name you picked?"

He gives a jerky nod.

"That's cool. Like, creating your own definition of yourself."

"Yes. Exactly that." His voice sounds surprised, like he's shocked I could come close to getting what he's saying.

The dark hall breaks out into a huge warehouse space. There are more booths than my eyes can follow as I scan the room. Some are small with cloth and paper signs while others span whole aisles with holos of animated models flashing smiles. There are even some that are projections—showing the artist sitting at the booth as they sketch live.

And the people! Not only are they stylish, but tons of them have the sorts of genetic mods NuGene would never allow. There's a woman whose skin is covered in soft peach-colored fur, and a man who's so tall that he almost reaches the ceiling, and even more subtle but so-called unacceptable mods like a person with two sets of eyelids, falling asleep at their booth with only the first translucent set closing, making their irises look foggy underneath.

The feed videos don't compare to being here myself in this hub for artists and artisans. I'm bouncing on my toes and holding my hands over my mouth so I don't squeal.

"Have you . . . never been here before?" Luc asks, his voice cautious, like he's approaching a wild animal instead of asking a question.

"No! The Night Market is super exclusive, and I'm . . . not that."

"How did you find it, then?"

"I asked my cousin Keisha. She does feed modeling and stuff. She's plugged in."

"First rule to being here, don't call it the Night Market. If you're a person who comes here, you call it the Collective."

"Oooh!" I'm pleased that not even Keisha knew that. Luc looks like he regrets bringing me with him. I'm beyond caring. "What do you do here?"

"Fade Ink," he says.

"And Justin doesn't mind that this is what you do with your time off? He doesn't want you studying or something?"

Luc shrugs. "Justin understands the value of work-life balance. That's why he makes sure interns get three days off in the first place."

It's not the greatest insert, but I can't help it since we're already talking about Justin. I blurt out, "Speaking of, do you know if Justin knew a woman named Elaine Thomas?"

"Sloppy transition. No."

"Nothing?"

"Justin is my boss, not my friend. He doesn't sit down with me to reminisce about the past. Not since I was little, anyway." I don't think I imagine the bitter edge to his voice.

"Could you find out?"

Luc stops in the middle of the aisle. "Are you here about the matching or to grill me about Justin?"

"They're not mutually exclusive. Aren't you curious about this? If our pasts are maybe connected, don't you want to know about that?"

"That's his past, not mine." His words sound like a dismissal, and yet his voice sounds like it's trying to convince himself more than me.

We fall into silence as we walk to a Fade Ink booth. The banner pulled across the top is a squid floating with tentacles that decompose into an explosion of tendrils that look like the night sky. When we get close enough, I realize the tendril explosion is a bunch of ATGC letters, the same as the ones on Luc's arm, and they finally click together in my brain. They're the letters for the four DNA nucleotides. Adenine . . . and the others. I took my basic science credits what seems like ages ago, though it was only a couple of years back. They were the first ones I signed up for so I could get them out of the way.

The booth is separated by a table with a large showcase tablet of the art and a second section with three walls covered by a privacy screen.

"This is yours?" I splutter.

He quirks the corner of his lips and leads us around behind the tables.

"Can I look?" I point to the giant showcase tablet.

He seems to stand up straighter. "If you'd like."

I scoot closer to the tablet and swipe through the pieces. Some of them are simple sketches, others look outlined and perfected, and some are photos of the work on people. All of them in some state of decomposition, and all beautiful. "You drew these?"

"Yes."

The connection between the rude and industrial Luc I've known and the person drawing these beautiful pieces is disjointed. And still, both are a part of him.

Where are these Fade Ink client ratings on his feed? I can't imagine any of those happy customers giving him two-star reviews. Then again, Luc seems like the sort of person who would discourage them from leaving one.

I don't understand why Luc and I were paired at all. He's an intern at NuGene and a talented artist. I cook, and I know that I do it well, except it's not serious. Everything he does has purpose and drive behind it. It reminds me of Keis with her education, Alex with her fashion, and even Keisha with her feed modeling. Everyone is moving toward something, and I'm floundering.

And the only way to guarantee my future is to destroy Luc's.

"How do you decide?" I flip past an ATGC sketch of the CN Tower.

Luc tilts his head. "Decide what?"

"What you're going to do? Are you going to be an artist or do something at NuGene?" Though I guess if he was going to do art like his parents want, he would go back home. Or maybe not, if their relationship is that strained.

"Why not both?"

"My grandma says that when you have two options, and you choose both, you aren't choosing either." Like how I can't help my family and spare you. I clench my fingers against the tablet and shove the thought down.

"How did you decide that your cousin should intern at NuGene?"

I lean my head against my hand. "She doesn't have a science specialization, but she's in tune with the political climate and how people react to it. The problem with NuGene is that it's exclusionary on principle. She would be good at figuring out how to make it more inclusive in a way that's lucrative for the company."

"There, that's a decision. A big one too, choosing the best internship fit among dozens of options. Just do that for yourself."

"It's not that easy."

"Nothing is easy."

I set the tablet down and pull out the lunch box from my bag. "I brought you some lunch so you can avoid boxed mac and cheese."

Luc's eyes go wide at the sight of the container. "You really brought food for me?"

"I was making it anyway, so I figured I would bring you some." The back of my neck is sweaty. "There are two curries. Tell me which one you like better."

"For your recipe contest?"

"You remembered?"

"I have an excellent memory."

I roll my eyes. Right, prodigy NuGene intern. "Speaking of your genius status, do you know anything about the Elaine sequence that this is tracking?" I hold up my wrist.

"Elaine sequence?"

"You're the lead on the project and you don't know?"

Luc scowls. "Being the lead on a project at NuGene doesn't mean having full control. Justin comes in and adds some special aspect to it that only he knows about. I'm not a lead, I'm a glorified data babysitter." His face flushes. "Is this why you're asking about an Elaine Thomas and Justin? 'Cause the sequence is named the same? That's a big stretch."

I force myself not to cringe. "Sorry to hit a sore spot. And yeah, but whatever. If you don't want to look into it, then don't."

He collapses onto a chair and rubs his eyes. "I have a Fade Ink appointment in thirty minutes. You should go."

"So that's it?" The tablet is slack in my hands.

"Yes. The qualitative data thing was a bad idea. I don't have time for this."

I'm not ready to leave. Over a week, and Luc and I can't even manage to interact with each other for more than fifteen minutes at a time. I'm never going to fall in love this way. "What if I'm a customer?"

"What?"

"Maybe I want to get a Fade Ink tattoo." I definitely can't afford it, but I can't leave, either. I can take the payment from the grocery money and deal with Granny being pissed off later. I wouldn't put it past her to chew me out on "wasting money" even if I say it's part of bonding with Luc for my task. Already I can hear her snapping, "You can't get to know the boy without paying him?" and letting out a long steups, shaking her head, with Uncle Cathius copying her to double the guilt.

I'll just owe her and Keis for the next couple of weeks and deal with the annoying follow-up.

"A Fade Ink tattoo of what?" Luc asks.

I balk. The idea of choosing one design out of the hundreds of sketches in that book makes my stomach churn and my palms sweat. "Artist's choice."

"No." His lips pull into a smirk. "Either you choose, or you go."

I look around for some sort of inspiration and catch sight of two guys putting up posters of Lauren. I wring my hands. "Isn't that the sort of thing that would be right up NuGene's alley? Lending help with genetic profiling or something?" A couple years back, Justin helped find a little boy that way. But that boy wasn't Black. Which shouldn't matter, but it does.

"You're changing the subject."

"I'm asking a legitimate question."

His eyebrows push down. "Someone pitched it to Justin, but he said she isn't in the system."

"What?" The question slips out of my mouth before I can shut it. I swear Lauren got a gene mod for a custom curl pattern in her hair. I remember her twirling around and showing it to me. She wouldn't have lied if it were a wig or sew-in or something like that. I don't think she would, anyway. And she didn't mention going to an off-brand modifier either.

"Yeah. She's not in our NuGene files. The police have her government genetic records. They can't give us access without her permission, and her parents are being strange about giving it out."

I clench my jaw. The Carters aren't pure, which means looking too deeply into their DNA could connect them to anyone they've stolen, tortured, and put back in the past. I could see them not welcoming the increased attention.

Luc pushes out a hard breath. "Enough stalling, either you're getting inked or you're leaving me alone."

"I . . ." A bunch of ideas come to mind, and none of them seem cool enough. Not that I need to impress him or anything. I just don't want to pick something bad.

He tousles his hair and sighs. "It's temporary and easy to remove if you don't like it." He waves his arm, exposing the design inked there. "I'll probably change this next week. That's the point of Fades. The fact that it's impermanent is part of what makes it fun. So you don't need to get caught up in it having any special meaning or getting the perfect design."

He's trying to make the decision easier. This is what everyone does for me. When I was seven, Mom gave me a choice between two things for lunch because when she asked what I wanted straight-out, there were so many options, and not being able to choose . . . well . . . it made me feel like crying. Which I did, so she started narrowing it down for me.

Even Luc, who seems like most of the time he can't stand to be around me, feels bad enough to try and make this easier.

My face heats up, and I turn away, suddenly wanting to be anywhere but here. "I'll go." I take only two steps before Luc grabs my hand.

The second his fingers make contact, he lets go. I turn around, and he's staring at his hand like he can't believe what he just did. "Hold on." His eyes meet mine. "What do you think will happen if you make the wrong choice?"

It's not *if* I make the wrong choice. It's *when*.

His arms sag at his sides. "I'm serious."

"Don't you worry about messing up?"

"Of course. I work in a competitive company with people constantly waiting for me to spark shit up so they can take my place."

"Then how do you choose?"

"I just do. I commit to my choice and don't let someone else make the decision for me."

"It's easier if someone else does it." The words slip out of my mouth.

"I know."

As our gazes stay level, something settles into place that wasn't there before. It's like when I understood what he meant about names. He's picked up on what I wanted him to know without me saying it outright.

I could leave now. Try and connect with Luc another time. It's not the most responsible choice, considering my task, but less painful in the short term. Except part of me wants to stay. And not just because I have a task to complete. "Can I get it in red?"

"Whatever color you want." We make our way over to the application area of the booth. "I can freehand it, if you have a good idea."

I pull out my phone and show him a picture so he can get a visual of what I want.

He bites down on his lip as it quirks up at the corners.

I smile back. "Good choice?"

"It's your choice."

I know what he means. It doesn't matter what he thinks about it. It's about me making the decision.

From start to finish, I force myself not to ask him to stop or choose something else for me as he sketches the design onto my exposed shoulder blade. I'm so in my head about the choice that I don't mind the silence while he works.

Fade Ink being applied is like a light brush of hair on my skin.

"I got my first Fade here at the Collective," Luc mumbles.

"What of?" Whatever it was, it would have faded to nothing by now unless he continued to get it touched up.

"My name." He fidgets behind me. "It was when I was thirteen and came here. Terrance, the guy at the door, he was the first person I introduced myself to as Luc."

It hits me then, the real importance of names to him. Alex has always been Alex. But it's possible Luc was given a name at birth meant for a girl, not for him. He had probably spent a good chunk of his life living as someone whose name didn't fit how he felt. I didn't think about how prying about it could be painful for him.

"I like Luc," I say. "It's a good name."

He lets out a half sigh, half laugh. "I think so."

"Thank you for telling me. You didn't owe me that."

"I never make a choice I don't want to make."

I envy his conviction. He holds up a mirror to my back, and I look over my shoulder at the design. I gnash on my bottom lip to hide the quiver. "It's beautiful."

The flower is in full bloom with soft crimson petals bleeding into the small ATGC symbols that mark Luc's style. The leaves curl to envelop the plant like ribs over a heart. For someone who only learned what sorrel was the other day, he's done a great job of drawing it.

He rubs at his face. "I pulled up your genes, if that's all right. I wanted to make sure I had the right DNA coding."

"I don't mind." The words slip out of my mouth. I'm busy admiring the piece. Those are my genes. My lineage boiled down to four letters.

Stamped on my back is a piece that represents my culture and family. Drawn by a boy who I'm supposed to kill in their name.

CHAPTER THIRTEEN

On Monday, while Keis is at her Q&A, I step off the bus and look down an almost empty street in a neighborhood that isn't mine. The air is crisp and breezy, despite the heat, courtesy of a nearby lake—the same one that runs along the back of our place. None of the houses can seem to figure out what they want to be. There are three in a row that are identical, from their matching second-floor faux balconies to their 1.5 car–width driveways. That's where the consistency stops. The next house over is a bright yellow rectangle with floor-to-ceiling glass windows and accented wood paneling. The one over from that is a plain single-story brick house. There's a constant smell of freshly mowed grass.

Port Credit is one of those neighborhoods that was supposed to be a perfect development. Every house looking the same, close to the water, but far enough away from the city to avoid the overcrowding that's leaked into Historic Long Branch. Except someone ran out of money somewhere, and the homes had to be finished by third-party contractors. People chose different companies and went with whatever design they felt like. Not to mention more than half the area is towering condos with unfinished community spaces—huge parks without benches or playgrounds and restaurants with flat plots of "for lease" land between them.

Now it's as much of a mash-up as the rest of Toronto.

I walk to a four-story monster of a house that towers over the others and is built on two lots squished into one. The bricks are a crisp white and are complemented by matching ivory columns that support the wide second-floor balcony.

The Davises don't mess around. Their Matriarch, April-Mae—back when she was here and not traveling around the world with her youngest son, Kane—made sure they had the sort of house that would command the respect they feel they deserve. Her oldest son, Johan, runs the family while she's gone. He also leads the community school where the Black witches in Toronto send their kids to learn about our history on top of the traditional elementary school fare.

He's the one I'm here to see.

This morning Luc sent me a message.

Is this the Elaine you're looking for?

Attached to his message was what looked like a genetic profile without the actual genes noted. There was a photo of a woman with short, curled dark hair and deep rich brown skin. The name listed was "Elaine Thomas," and it noted her maiden name as "James." There was no mention of a husband or an occupation, but under a small tab called "genetic offspring," Alex's full birth name was listed. *My* Alex. And the more I looked at Elaine's photo, the more I could see my cousin in her face.

Before I could do anything else, the message disappeared.

It's a temporary message, as I'm sure you can see. This is technically confidential, but you're related, so I'm being lenient.

I rolled my eyes, my fingers shaking against my phone. Mama Elaine was Alex's mom, and somehow I didn't know anything about her. Alex herself barely had any information. She said she *thinks* her mom left when she was little. Auntie Elaine was a James, too, meaning she was related to Dad. Which explained why he had that reaction to her name. He knew her. She was dead and a Mama. It felt impossible that she was alive during my life-time, given that honor on top of everything, and I had no memo-ries of her.

I sent Luc a thank-you, pleasantly shocked that he had actu-ally bothered.

I had time. Plus, you made me lunch. Consider us even.

I wasted no time in reminding him that he had insisted on not charging me for the Fade Ink in exchange for the lunch.

Fine. You owe me more, then.

But when I asked how I should owe him, he didn't respond. Against my better judgment, reading it settled a little smile on my face. He could be nice when he wanted, even if he seemed to have a problem with admitting it. I sent a message back to ask if he knew about any connection to Justin.

I'm not your personal detective.

With another eye roll, I stopped messaging him, and in the afternoon, I got on a bus to go see Johan. Now I'm here in front of his house.

He's my best bet for finding out about Mama Elaine since Dad has no interest in talking about her, and her locked profile in the almanac suggests that Granny doesn't want anyone to know either. And if Granny is hiding this, then no adult in the family will go against her to tell me. Even if Luc couldn't find a connection to Justin, or could and just won't say, it's suspicious that I couldn't find anything about Mama—now *Auntie*—Elaine online or in our records, but somehow, she's in NuGene's files.

And that's not even getting into the disturbing fact of not being able to remember anything about her. Even trying to dig for the memories brings up nothing but an empty space that makes a rush of goose pimples rise on my arms. Lauren always said if there's something that feels wrong, and you can't put your finger on it, it's probably impure magic. And she was intimately familiar.

Not to mention, Johan may also know about this third witch that Rowen mentioned and the supposed betrayal. Whether he'll share any of that knowledge with me remains unknown. But it can't be a coincidence that all this is coming up at the same time as my task. If even any of it is connected, if there's something I've missed that could change what I have to do, I'll follow that thread. Because even though I won't admit it in my head when Keis is around, she was right. I had just given up and accepted becoming a murderer. I owe it to myself, and to Luc, to investigate anything that may lead to a way around this task. Even if the adults don't think it's related enough to stop hiding it from me.

I stand in front of the wrought-iron gates marking the entrance to the Davis home. Instead of vine designs, there are figures of their ancestors cast in metal. I line myself up in front of the scanner to the side of the gate and let the green light flash over me. It swings open silently—oiled to perfection.

I wind my way around the side of the house toward the small structure in the backyard. When me and my cousins were little, we followed this path to school. The Davises may not be pure witches, but they give their personal time and space to make sure we're educated in our history.

Granny taught us about our Thomas ancestors, but I learned the difference between pure and impure witches, the intricacies of spell casting, the links between genetics and gifts, and everything else I know about magic from Johan.

I turn the corner and come up to the schoolhouse. The glass windows expose a cluster of fifteen desks and kids sitting at them with tablets. I spy Eden with her dark hair in two low pigtails and her eyes trained on Johan. He's at the front of the room, gesturing to the flat screen behind him with his waist-length dreads swaying. His skin always looks like it has the perfect amount of shining dew on it.

Most of the kids will ride home on the bus that Johan's son Topaz drives. Every child of my former teacher is named after the birthstone of the month they were born. All six of them. Luckily, they were all born in different months.

Sometimes parents or siblings will come and pick up kids. Today, there's one other person waiting in the yard with me.

Rena Carter. Lauren's mom.

She has a slick weave so long it touches her ankles, and her neon orange dress fits like a second skin. But her eyes . . . The bags underneath are like smudges drawn in charcoal, and her gaze seems to stare out at something no one but her can see.

The last time I saw her was shortly after Lauren went missing. She showed up at our house as done up as she is now to ask if I knew where her daughter was. Now she turns and pegs me with a stare.

I bend my head and hunch my shoulders. "Hello, Ms. Carter." When I was little, I called her Auntie Rena. But somewhere in between, things had changed.

"How old are you now?"

"Oh. Um, sixteen." Her eyes feel like they're peeling off the layers of my skin and digging underneath.

"Have you had your Calling yet?"

I shift on the spot. It's like I'm in an interrogation instead of a casual conversation. "Sort of . . . I'm working on the task."

"They say a lengthy task makes for a strong gift." She tilts her head to the side. "Still, you shouldn't let it go on for too long."

"Johan said that's a myth. That longer Callings don't mean stronger gifts, only harder Callings. And even that's subjective." I want to shove the words back in my mouth. Her daughter is missing. I should just agree with her.

Rena doesn't seem to care that I talked back. "Used to be a time when everyone was so worried about having the *right* gifts." She puts an emphasis on "right" that isn't quite contempt, but something like it.

My family continues to be worried about the strength of our gifts. But impure ones shouldn't be concerned because they have more power from the kickback magic they get in rituals. I assume Uncle Cathius's hidden gift is something powerful, because he came from an impure family. Lauren's gift was kept secret too. Impure families are more likely to conceal gifts to protect themselves from rivals in the community because their powers are so much stronger. That was what the lore was when that was a real danger, anyway. But that was a long time ago. Families haven't gone around killing others to keep their status in more than a hundred years. And yet, lots of impure families continue to hide their gifts.

I assumed they were still strong like we always thought, but maybe they stay secret because they aren't, and it's better to keep the lie going than admit that.

"They aren't worried about gifts anymore?" I ask.

She lifts her shoulders in the imitation of a shrug. "I don't know."

To be honest, I'm not sure if people still talk to Rena. Their little section of the Carter family has been on the edge of the community since Lauren disappeared, their grief pushing people further away instead of bringing them closer.

Rena turns toward Johan in the classroom. "He's a good teacher, isn't he? Lauren thought so. Not that it matters. He won't help find her." The unnerving calm of her voice breaks, and her teeth flash as if she's baring them, on the edge of a snarl.

My eyes follow Caleb, Lauren's brother, in the classroom. He was sick when he was born. The rumor was that Ms. Carter asked Johan to help him. That she petitioned her Matriarch to make the change to impurity so that Johan could save her son. Switching an entire family's stance on purity isn't a small thing, but neither is a life. But now I wonder if a fear of weak gifts was part of it.

Johan doesn't make a habit of doing multiple favors for the same family, not unless there's something in it for him. The impure have limits too. Especially ones like the Davises who take lives. It's not exactly easy to get away with frequent murders, even when you pick people the authorities are likely to overlook. They usually only practice a death rite once every two years to protect Caribana for the same length of time—the pure intention behind their dark ritual.

Now that the Carters are impure too, they should be able to do their own rites. Maybe they've tried and failed. There are lots of impure families out there, but few command the power the Davises have.

I drop my chin and watch my toes. I would give anything to volunteer our help. We knew Lauren, her mom is suffering, and still no one will lift a finger to help. I don't even know how I *could* help without magic or a gift, even if I wasn't wrapped up in my task. We call ourselves a community, but if we are, we should help each other and do it without a price attached.

The door to the classroom opens, and the kids flood out. They go around the front of the house to get ready for the bus, except Eden and Caleb, who run over to me and Ms. Carter.

She plasters a smile on her face and takes his backpack. He's babbling at a rapid rate about his day. Before leaving, she turns over her shoulder. "Good luck with your Calling."

"Thanks . . ." I think about staying silent but can't. "I hope you find Lauren soon. I miss her." My voice catches on the last words. It's true. I miss our late-night messaging. I miss visiting her house to watch feed shows and bake cookies. I miss the life she brought to a room just by walking into it.

Ms. Carter's eyes are distant. "Thank you."

Eden tugs on my shirt. "I'm supposed to take the bus after school."

"We are going to take the bus," I say. "The TTC bus."

Her eyes get wide, and she scratches her jaw. It's the same thing Dad does when he's thinking. I was raised to listen to whatever adults say. Eden was brought up by Dad and Priya to question everything and be skeptical of everyone. In the grand scheme of things, it's great, but when I'm using her as a cover to do something the adults wouldn't want me doing, it's less helpful.

I squat down and pull out a paper-wrapped biscuit from home. Her eyes get wider, this time accompanied by a grin.

Got her.

"Why don't you sit here and wait? I'm gonna talk to Johan real quick." I hand her the biscuit.

"Thank you." She unwraps the treat, taking care not to rip the paper. "And you're supposed to call him Mr. Davis."

"Right, of course." I haven't called Johan "Mr. Davis" since I was thirteen.

With Eden munching on her coconut biscuit, I leave and walk inside the classroom. The desk where I used to sit next to Keis looks about as big as my hijacker chip. I don't know how Johan with his 6'3" frame can be anything but cramped in the space.

"And what can I do for you, Miss Voya?" He hasn't even looked at me, busying himself with checking over what looks like quizzes on the flat screen.

"I was wondering if you knew about an ancestor of mine."

"Why aren't you asking your granny about *your* ancestor?" He turns and leans against the table, staring me down. Sometimes looking into his eyes, I can see the other side of him that lurks under his skin. The flip side of this doting teacher. The man who murders for magic.

He walks that line better than any other impure witch. After all, even pure families trust him with their children the way they trusted his Matriarch, April-Mae. He may be a man, but he's as close to garnering the respect of a Matriarch as any has ever been. Closer than Uncle. I suspect that's why Uncle stays in the house with us instead of moving back into his ancestral home. It would burn him too much to live under his brother's thumb.

I force myself not to wring my hands. "They don't seem keen to discuss her with me."

"Juicy. Who is she?"

"Mama Elaine."

Johan's face slides into shadow. His eyebrows draw together, and his mouth presses into a line. "Don't you bother yourself with Mama Elaine."

"Why?"

"Because I said so."

I groan and throw my hands up. "You said our history decides our future and that's why we have to know our ancestors. Their lives should be lessons for how we live ours, isn't that right?"

Johan clenches his jaw. "Why you gotta throw my words back at me, girl?"

"I don't understand why she's being hidden! We learned about Papa Joen, and he murdered like ten kids!"

"He *sacrificed* ten children to save the lives of a hundred more. So-called dark rituals must have pure intent. And I didn't teach you about him. Don't you remember that I'm forbidden to corrupt the minds of you pure children?"

"I know you didn't." Part of what lets the pure families feel secure is that Johan's tongue is bound to never mention impure rituals to students. He can teach the difference between the two, but that's it.

Johan says, "What she did is not something you need to know about."

"But it has something to do with Justin Tremblay?" The flash of stiffening shoulders and open mouth is enough to confirm the connection. I can't keep the grin off my face.

I'm about to plow into asking Johan about why I can't remember my aunt, but he cuts me off before I can speak.

"I'm not saying another word. You go home. And don't be bringing up Mama Elaine with me again, or I'll curse her name out of your mouth." He points a straight finger at my lips.

I want to think he wouldn't do that to me, but the hard edge of his gaze says otherwise.

If I learn more about Mama Elaine, it won't be from him.

"Fine," I hiss out between my teeth.

Johan sags against the desk. "Good. You'll forget about her again in time. You can't miss what you don't remember. You should be focusing on your task."

The back of my neck goes cold, and I hold back a swallow. Forget about Mama Elaine *again*? Maybe it's just an offhanded comment, but it doesn't feel like it. Especially not when it comes to an aunt who I thought I had zero recollection of to begin with. But . . . what if I did, and I was already made to forget once? Alex, who should know about her, barely does. And none of the adults want to talk about Auntie Elaine. How far would they go to keep her a secret? As far as erasing memories? No one in our family would have the magic bandwidth for that, but a Davis would. I force my voice to sound normal. "Who said I have a task?"

"I can taste the blood of an Amplifying ceremony across Etobicoke." He pauses. "Sorry, 'Historic Long Branch,' and yet, no follow-up magic from your Pass. It's been more than a week already, and if you failed, ancestors know Keisha would have blown up my messages to say so."

At least Keisha had the sense not to blow up his messages with the dirty details of my task. "I'm fine. I have a task. I'm working on it." I open my mouth again and then close it. After I got his guard up over Justin and Mama Elaine, I can't openly ask about what Rowen said. "Who are the three strongest Black witch families?"

Johan's mouth turns downward. "Yours and mine have always been at the top. The rest are the rest."

"But if you were to say a third . . . who would you say?"

"Have you been hanging around Dixie Mall?" He shakes his head and points at the door. "Get out and take your sister home. Girl looks like she's about to throw a fit."

Outside the window, Eden is clutching the paper wrapper and staring at us with the expression of a child who's done being placated. I pull out my phone and shoot off a message to Priya and Dad that I picked her up after dropping off more Caribana things. The lie will help me get ahead of anything Eden tells them.

I turn back to my former teacher. "Well, thank you, I guess."

As I reach for the door, he says, "You leave Mama Elaine alone. And if you can, stay far away from Justin Tremblay."

Once again, I'm thankful no one else has Keis's gift.

There's no way I'm dropping this now that I know it's related to Justin. I'm not grasping at nothing anymore. There *is* a connection between him and Mama Elaine, and it may even link to me and Luc. And Johan unintentionally gave me a lead on Rowen's rumor too: Dixie Mall may be where I can find my answers.

Ms. Carter was right. Johan is a good teacher. He taught me that our history decides our future, and I plan to know about mine. Especially if it's concerning the sponsor father of the boy I'm supposed to kill.

CHAPTER FOURTEEN

The next day, Keis and I are standing in line at Poutine Factory, where they're releasing a new limited-edition pizza poutine—crisp hand-cut fries, cheese curds, shredded mozzarella, homemade sauce, and thick Brooklyn pepperoni slices. Mom transferred my twenty dollars to me yesterday, and though I tried to pay Keis back, she waved me off. And since Luc didn't charge me for the Fade Ink, I'm working with a full week of money. Which warranted a culinary celebration. That, plus Keis did well at the library Q&A, and Rowen's uncle liked her enough to put her on a short list of candidates.

I hold my phone up in front of Keis and me. "Say cheese curds!" My cousin makes a deadpan face at the camera while I grin, and the AI snaps photos of us where I'm the only one changing my pose.

"AI, post with some sort of caption about living that poutine life," I command.

Keis rolls her eyes. "You're unbelievable."

I shrug and peer at the length of the line stretching down the block. This always happens when they do a limited-edition flavor. People lose their minds to try it and post the pics on their feeds before it's gone. "What do you think about what happened with Johan?" I ask.

Last night, we had to push out a special rush order of products for a beauty store supplier, and I hadn't gotten to talk with Keis about what I learned. Like how our memories of Auntie Elaine may have been erased. Instead, I was rapidly bottling and labeling products to the nonexistent beat of tense silence between Granny and Mom. Mostly from Mom stewing over the fact that Granny couldn't make Mama Jova change my task. Which I knew because she occasionally muttered under her breath about "what good is a Matriarch who can't sway ancestors?" Granny was about two seconds away from kicking her out of the room. I could tell from the way her fingers kept clenching and unclenching. If she didn't need the help, she probably would have.

"I've never even heard anyone think about an Auntie Elaine," Keis laments.

"Yeah," I say. "But you're also always focused on my thoughts because you can't be bothered to use your gift properly."

"I'm pro—"

"You've been protesting for over a year now, and the only thing that's come from it is you knowing too much about my private thoughts and too little of anything that's actually useful."

Keis shakes her head at me. "Wow, you know what, I do want that ten dollars back."

"I'm not trying to be mean!" And I'm not, though I wish she would learn to use her gift well enough to not be so in my head all the time. Ever since his text yesterday, Luc has been popping up in my mind against my will. And every time it happens around Keis, she gives me this sharp, alarmed look that quickly reminds me that at the end of the month, I'm expected to kill him. Which, believe it or not, I don't want to think about all the time when I'm trying to fall in love with someone. "I'm just saying that it would be easy for you to miss thoughts like that."

"Really? Because you said a lot more than just that."

We scowl at each other, and I crack first because I'm soft. "Fine, sorry. There has to be a way to learn more about Auntie Elaine."

Last night, I sent a text to Keisha to ask if she recognized the name, but she hadn't heard of her either. I even gently knocked on Alex's door this morning, fidgeted in the hallway until she finally told me to spit it out, and then asked if she knew an Elaine Thomas. If she recognized the name, I would have told her everything right then and there, but she didn't.

My cousin just blinked at me from her doorway and said, "No. Who's that?"

Keis says, "Are you sure this is the way to go? Wouldn't it be better to just research Mama Jova? That seems like a better bet for finding a way out of this than trying to put together clues that may not even be clues."

"I already know about Mama Jova. Her life was hard. Her tasks are hard. That's it. Either way, doesn't it bother you that we have no memory of Auntie Elaine?"

Keis glares at me. "Obviously. But I know someone who may know more about her, if no one else will tell us and you're this determined."

"*Who?* Also, why didn't you say anything sooner?"

"Because you were lecturing me about my gift!" Keis clenches her jaw. "Keisha has been doing feed diary vlogs since she could hold a phone. If we ever did know Mama Elaine, and if anyone has proof of that, Keisha would on those vlogs. I bet the adults didn't think to scrub them."

"Keisha doesn't show her private vlogs to anyone." I have a vivid memory where I almost stumbled onto one and she pounced on me. No hype. For real. Uncle had to tear us apart, and Mom and Auntie had a huge blowup argument over it. If I recall correctly, Auntie Maise did literally blow something up.

"Guess you'd better find a reason for her to share."

Hack me.

I open my phone and scroll through Keisha's feed posts to see what she's doing today. The most recent one is a selfie of her at Brown Bear, rolling her eyes. The caption is: *save me*. It's logged as private, which means only her close friends and family can see it.

Keis peers over my shoulder. "If she doesn't want to be on the date, she should leave."

She's usually a pro at managing to make her date ditch instead. "If she did, they might give her a bad rating. But if we make up an excuse for her, they may still leave her a good one."

"And why would we make an excuse for her?"

"For the love of the ancestors, so we can have her show us the private feeds!" I shake my head at Keis. "Wow, you're book smart, but you're not very street smart."

"Get sparked."

I ignore Keis and type out a message to her sister: *Bad date?*

She replies right away: *THE WORST. It smells like kids in here.*

Should we rescue you?

OMG. Pleeeeeease.

For sure, but can you do me a little favor?

Why is everyone in this family so opportunistic?

Keis snorts. "*She's* saying that? She's the worst out of everyone."

I type: *I want to know about an ancestor.*

Why would I know that??

You may have mentioned it in your private vlogs and forgot.

URG. Fine! Just come get me.

Keis crosses her arms. "I'm not going."

Keis is pissed. I admit this isn't how I planned to spend my day either, but I need access to Keisha's vlogs. Keis sits in the booth across from me staring at the blank touch screen embedded in our table. We're on the first of three floors of Brown Bear—the city's most popular tabletop gaming café with the worst name.

There are other booths surrounding us, packed with couples and groups stabbing at the screens while they sip on lattes and bite into homemade desserts with bear designs on them.

I look around the space for our waiter with his pale white skin and bouncy blond hair. I've got a hot chocolate with a compost cookie coming. They top the hot cocoa with torched homemade marshmallow fluff.

"I cannot believe you got me to come here," Keis hisses. Her long nails tap hard enough on the table that I check for dents on the screen. Her hair is loose and flowing in thick curls around her head while her eyes cut daggers into the couple a few tables over from our own.

Tucked into a smaller, more intimate booth, is Keisha, with waist-length silver hair thrown over one shoulder, decked out in an aquamarine sequined pencil skirt and a thin and low-cut tank top. She's barely holding back a grimace. The animated girl across from her has huge green eyes and an adorable dotting of freckles over her face and arms. She looks Black, but the lightness of her skin tone suggests that she may be mixed. According to her feed profile, her name is Layla, and like most people Keisha dates, the lack of witch mark means she's not magical. Our community provides too small of a dating pool for my cousin to stick within it.

"We're going to get her out of this date and learn something about Auntie Elaine." I am going to miss that poutine, though. Would we still have time to go back after? Better question: Can I fit in poutine on top of the hot chocolate and cookie here?

Keis glares at me. "Is that seriously what you're thinking about right now?"

You know it's what I'm thinking about.

She grinds her teeth, and I cringe from the sound of it.

I'm about to ask how we're going to help Keisha when a message flashes across my eyes. I choke on air. It's from Luc.

How is the Fade setting? Sometimes people have strange reactions to the ink. Be sure to monitor yours.

I press my hand to my chest as if that will hide the increased thumping there. Two unsolicited messages two days in a row. Keis is too busy trying to burn Keisha with her eyes to pay attention to my rushing thoughts.

It's not an interesting or personable message, but still, this could be a sign of interest. Interest in *me*. I go through the short list of the things that I like about Luc so far: he's a talented artist, he's also basically a genius, he kind-of-sort-of gets my indecision thing, and he helped me with Auntie Elaine without wanting anything in return. And, I mean, he is cute. Attractive. Gorgeous. No, too much credit, he can still be a dick. He's cute.

I pull out my phone to shoot a message back: *The ink is looking fantastic.*

No, too enthusiastic. I delete that and try again.

It's looking great. I haven't noticed any reactions.

I struggle to think of something else to add so the conversation doesn't end after I hit send. Last time, I kept it too businesslike, too eager to learn about my aunt. This time, I could do a real back and forth.

I finally settle on a message.

It's looking great. I haven't noticed any reactions. What are you up to today?

I send it before I can convince myself not to.

"Who are you messaging?" Keis asks.

"No one!" That's me, the Queen of Nonchalance.

"You know what? I don't care enough to read it out of your head. Can we go get this over with?"

I look around for our waiter. I don't want him to think we left because we aren't in our seats.

"Really, Vo? I'll make sure you get your damn cookie, let's go."

"There's hot chocolate, too," I mutter as I slide out of the booth.

We walk over to Keisha and her date. Layla notices us and looks up with a quizzical expression.

Keis raises an eyebrow at me. "I'm not getting involved."

Hack me to death.

"Can we help you?" Layla's eyes shift between Keis and me.

From Keisha's face, I can't get any read on what I'm supposed to say.

Luc's message flashes across my eyes: *I'm on my lunch. Speaking of, I never told you what I thought about the food you gave me the other day. I wouldn't want you to lose the relevant data for your contest. It was good, thanks. It's been a long time since I had something home-cooked.*

He messaged back right away! Does that mean he was eager to talk to me, or is he just a prompt message answerer? He usually is unless he's decided to stop messaging altogether.

Layla waves her hand in front of my face. "Hello?"

"Oh!" I scramble for an excuse. "She needs to come with us. Right now." I stab my finger at Keisha, who exhales and hides her face in her hands.

Layla bites her lip. "What? Why? Who are you?"

I look at Keisha for help. She slouches in the seat and stares at the table. I have no idea what I'm supposed to say. The more time passes, the more Luc waits for me to answer his message. If I don't answer right away like he did, will he get bored and end our conversation?

My mouth starts to do the walking. "We're family, and it's an emergency."

Layla blinks at Keisha with wide eyes. "What's wrong? Do you need me to come? I can order a car or something!"

Hack me, now she wants to help with my imaginary emergency.

Keis lets out a hissing breath. "She doesn't like you."

Keisha drops her hands from her eyes and her jaw comes loose.

Layla's eyes dart between the three of us. "I don't understand."

"I'll simplify it for you." Keis points at Keisha. "She's my sister and is too cowardly to be upfront with you. You can waste your time here, or you can leave and try and reclaim as much of your dignity as possible."

Layla's face shifts from confused to hurt to angry. I guess I should be glad she's not going to cry. She throws a cutting look at Keisha, who becomes interested in staring at the touch screen. Their abandoned game of tennis is there on pause.

Layla forces out a laugh. "Unbelievable." She shuffles out from the booth and glares at Keisha. "I saw those couple of low date reviews and ignored them. But you must be bribing anyone who rates you high. Don't expect a great one from me." She slaps her phone on the touch screen to transfer money for their bill and leaves.

Keisha won't look up.

"Keisha . . . ," I start.

Keis tugs on my arm, and we squish into the seat that Layla left. I suspect it's not meant to fit two people because half my butt is hanging off.

Our waiter comes around the corner, and I flail my arms at him. He walks over and sets down my hot chocolate and a compost cookie the size of my head.

"Thank you!" My drink is topped with marshmallow fluff browned from the torch and white and milk chocolate curls. The cookie is steaming from being warmed and there are pretzels, potato chips, coffee granules, oats, and chocolate chips embedded in it.

"Gimme a piece of your cookie," Keisha barks. Which, knowing how concerningly strict and obsessive she is about monitoring her eating, must mean that she's having a hard time.

I split the cookie in half, split that half, and hand a quarter to Keisha.

"Cheap."

"It's my cookie!"

Keis steals the other quarter, and I snatch up my half to make sure neither of them can try for it. I almost moan when I bite into the warm gooey center.

Another message from Luc flashes across my eyes: *I'll bring the container to the NuGene tour. You can grab it there.*

So much for meaningful messages. I shoot off one: *Which did you like the most? One was goat and the other was oxtail.*

The one on the left was spicier, so I preferred it. Both were much better than boxed mac and cheese.

My chest warms, and I don't think it's from the heated food and drink.

"Messaging your future victim?" Keisha drawls.

Cold slices through my ribs.

"You should talk," Keis snaps. "You leave a trail of broken hearts without a care in the world. That girl—"

"—Layla," I interject.

"Layla is right. Why do you go out with girls you're not interested in?"

Keisha throws up her hands. "I was interested! But she wanted more. She was so pushy. 'Why aren't we official? Why don't you say I'm your girlfriend on your feed? Why won't you kiss me?' I just wanted a hacking second to breathe and figure out if I even like her that way."

"How many dates have you been on?"

"Only four."

"How many do you need to know you like someone? And you go on dates constantly and do this same thing every single time. You can't find a single girl you like?"

"No!" Keisha's voice cracks. The cool-girl facade shatters and leaves her eyes glistening. "Do you know what it's like to go out with person after person, waiting for that spark, that part of you that says 'I want to be with you,' and it never comes? Or it does come, but it's too late, and they've moved on because they kept pushing for you to feel something like you can just hacking turn it on and off at will, and you can't do it fast enough for them."

I've never seen her this raw and shook up. "Keisha..."

"I can't like someone at the drop of a hat. I need time. A lot of time sometimes. But no one ever gets that. No one wants to wait." Her voice softens. "Maybe no one ever will."

I thought Keisha went on lots of dates because it was fun. That she stays single and never has relationships by choice. It didn't cross my mind that she might be struggling.

Keis lets out a sigh absent of the usual annoyance and heat she reserves for her sister. "Sorry, I didn't mean to . . . to judge you. You'll find someone. We're seventeen. Why don't you try being upfront with people about needing time?"

Keisha swipes a finger through my hot chocolate's fluff topping. "I do. They don't listen. Or they think needing time means a week. Or they say they understand, but five dates in, they stop sending messages or say that I 'play games.'"

"Hack those girls," Keis snaps.

I snort, and Keisha cracks a smile.

"But you should keep doing it. For one, because it's plain human decency. And two because one day you'll meet someone who *will* get it. And it'll be worth being honest with them."

"For someone who never dates, you don't have half-bad advice," I muse.

Keis grins at me. "Street smarts."

"Hardly," I say with an eye roll.

Keisha steals more marshmallow fluff from my drink. "She's going to give me the worst rating."

"I thought you had some magic date-ditching method," I say, chomping on my cookie. "It didn't work?"

Keisha frowns. "Most of the time I say random things until I hit on what makes them uncomfortable and push on it until they leave. But this time . . ." She shifts her eyes at her sister, then tugs them away. But this time, her magic isn't working properly. I'm sure that's what she means.

Keis stiffens in her chair.

Keisha jumps to the rescue, pointing at my phone. "Do you like this guy? Luc?"

I know they're trying to change the subject to avoid talking about our weakening magic, but I let it slide.

A few days ago, I could have said with confidence that no, I don't like Luc. Now I don't know. For all his asshole bravado, there are snatches of an intellectual with admirable decisiveness, and an artist who's earnest and passionate that I could love. Maybe.

I picture coming here with Luc and squeezing into one of these intimate booths for two. It would be uncomfortable at first, I'm sure, but it could happen.

As I'm gazing around the restaurant, imagining us on that date, we appear.

Tucked into the booth that Keis and I vacated are carbon copies of Luc and me. My hair is thick and loose, and I'm wearing my sundress with a golden banana print. Luc has his signature beanie on and has abandoned his usual hoodie for a black T-shirt and shorts.

We're leaned over the tabletop, tapping at the screen, him with his awkward smile and me with mine. My hands curl around a butter knife, though we don't have any food. Phantom me swivels her head and looks me in the eye as her grip tightens around the handle and she raises the blade in the air.

"Voya!" Keis shouts.

Her grip on my arm makes me face her. My fingers clench at my chest hard enough to scratch the skin, and there's a throbbing in my ears making me feel faint. I look back at the booth, but it's empty. No Voya and Luc. No butter knife raised menacingly.

Keisha leans over our table toward me. "What happened?"

My throat is too dry to croak anything out. Scramble my feed, what was that? I take a look at Keis to see what she thinks, but her expression is the twisted mouth and eyebrows of confusion.

She didn't see it. It was in my mind, but she couldn't pick up on it. She still can't.

Alex is having trouble using magic to sew her clothes faster. Keis isn't hearing thoughts she should be hearing. And Keisha is missing discomfort cues that she'd usually use to get out of a date.

Their magic is weakening as if I've already failed at my task. And I would be a fool to think it won't get worse the longer this goes on.

I swallow. That thing I saw, the vision, will those keep happening? Most Callings last one or two days max. I've never seen an almanac entry of one for a month like mine.

Granny was worried about my task going on too long. Maybe this was why? Our family's magic weakening, and chilling visions like this and earlier, when my Danish filling looked like blood.

Keis and Keisha are staring at me. I shake my head. "I . . . The Luc thing is stressful. That's all." It's an explanation that falls flat. I can tell by their expressions that they don't buy it. And even if Keis can't see the memory of what I did, she knows I'm not telling the whole truth.

Now we're both keeping secrets.

"You may not have to do it," Keisha whispers.

My hands slam on the tabletop before I can stop them. "I wish everyone would stop saying that! This is happening. It is. And maybe there's a way around it, but what if I can't find it? Then I *do* have to do this." I press my palms against my eyes for a moment before releasing them. "It's not helping. Pretending like this isn't happening, or telling me that maybe I won't have to do it, or thinking Granny can convince Mama otherwise, it doesn't make me feel better."

Keis looks down at the table, and Keisha presses her lacquered lips into a line.

"I'm not giving up. I'm going to try and find a way around this. But if I can't, and I have to do it, I at least want to feel a little prepared. And if I spend the entire time pretending like I won't have to, it'll just be harder." The hot chocolate turns bitter in my mouth. I can't stop seeing the raised knife, almost glittering under the stark white Brown Bear lighting. "I made a choice."

"But . . ." Keisha trails off.

Keis says, "This is our heritage. Magic is weaved into our lives and the lives of those before and after us. Maybe one life isn't worth that. But one life is worth another, especially if that life is Eden's." She nods at me. "I'll stop. Because I know that if you need to, you'll do it to save Eden. It's hard enough already without us making it harder."

Keisha looks unsure but nods. "I can try to help the adults understand too. Do uncomfortable stuff around them until they listen."

"Thank you," I say, my lips pulling into a smile.

"But I'm still gonna be mad at Mama Jova, 'cause hack her. Where does she get off?"

I think of my ancestor, curling in smoke smelling of rotten sugarcane, and her words that she chose me for a reason. Except

I still don't know why. Sure, she was indecisive too, but she got over that. I still don't know what I'm going to do. How I'm going to manage falling in love with Luc by the end of the month, and definitely not how I could kill him. I don't even know how to put these maybe-maybe-not clues about Justin and Auntie Elaine together to find a way out of it.

I look at my plate with a single cookie crumb left on it. I pick up the tiny piece and put it in my mouth. "So, can we see those private vlogs?"

"You didn't even get me out of this right!" Keisha grumbles. "She's gonna give me the worst rating."

"So . . ."

She grunts and flips her shining silver hair over her shoulder. "Fine."

It's a small win. But I need it.

The moment we get home, I rush so close behind Keisha that I'm almost tripping on her heels.

She turns and glares at me. "Can you cool it? You look so suspicious right now."

"Sorry," I mutter.

Keis trails behind us with dragging feet. I'm sure if she had it her way, she would be off at the library doing self-study. Maybe prepping for the NuGene tour on Friday. Speaking of, I say, "Have you done anything to get ready for the NuGene stuff?"

"How am I supposed to prep for a tour?" she says. "Also, it's only Tuesday."

"Think of how to sell yourself. Maybe practice a bit of mind reading for the occasion." The one advantage of what I'm 99 percent sure is her magic weakening is that she won't be as distracted by the buzz of other voices. It would be easy to jump from my head to someone else's.

Her eyes are sharp, but she doesn't deny it.

"Use every advantage! This isn't the time to get caught up in your protest that, frankly, isn't doing you any favors. You want to show the family you can be more than just a witch, sure. But you can be a great witch *and* great in NuGene."

I expect the same snap of refusal, but instead she says, "I'll think about it."

My face lights up with a grin.

Keisha opens the door to her room, and we file in. Unlike Alex's room, her bedroom is in pristine condition because it's where she does a lot of filming for her feed modeling. Her closet screen broadcasts images of women in bikinis posing. If she were someone else, I would think it was attractive women she liked looking at, but for Keisha, I know these are inspiration images. Bodies she wishes were hers, as if her own isn't something to celebrate as is but a work in progress that never reaches completion.

Keisha bounces onto her bed and grabs her tablet. "What am I looking for?"

I sit down beside her. "Mama Elaine."

"That lady you asked me about before? Who is she?"

"It's Alex's mom, but our memories of her are gone, so we need to see if you have footage of her."

Keis steupses. "Stop saying 'we' like I'm involved in this mess. I still think researching Mama Jova would be a better idea."

"Alex's memories are gone too? Does she know you're doing this?" Keisha says.

I shake my head. "Alex doesn't even recognize her mom's name. I think our memories were erased, and that's why none of us remember her. Alex has so much going on with the fashion show and Caribana. I don't want to mention it and then have almost no information to give her." Honestly, knowing that I had almost nothing to share, I probably shouldn't even have brought up Auntie Elaine's name with her in the first place. "I don't want her to get distracted wondering about her mom. Once I know enough, I'll tell her." I stare straight at Keisha. "Don't blab before then."

"Fine," she drawls. "And how am I supposed to know what this lady looks like? Also, this reeks of impure magic."

"We can't remember her either," I say. "That's the whole point of this."

Keis crosses her arms. "Just look for the one woman you don't recognize. You make things so hacking hard."

"Get sparked," Keisha snaps back.

"For real?"

I roll my eyes. Keis and Keisha have been nipping at each other since they were kids. When they were eight, they had an epic battle over an ImagaModel. It was this doll that came blank, and you could customize the gender, face, hair, voice, and more. Auntie got one for them to share. They asked for two, to which Auntie responded by saying, "Am I made of money?"

Keis wanted the doll to be a studious political woman who moonlit as a spy and helped save the free world. Keisha wanted them to be a non-binary pansexual seducer who traveled the world having romantic escapades. Neither of them seemed to care what the doll looked like, which was the whole point of it—they fought over who the toy was meant to be. They had screaming matches that left them both red in the face and crying with rage.

In the end, Auntie burned the doll to a crisp, but that friction between them never seemed to go away.

"Ancestors help me, Voya, you remember that shit?" Keis groans.

"It was traumatic!"

They may have had a sisterly moment at Brown Bear, but it's clearly over now.

"AI Search: entries with the word 'Elaine.'" Keisha looks at us after issuing her command. "I don't even care what you two are talking about." She flips her tablet toward us as the AI speeds through her private feed entries and pulls up a list of precisely one.

"Only one?" I blurt out.

Keisha throws up her hands. "My private feeds when I was little were about random stuff I liked. I didn't talk about other people unless they pissed me off."

"Of course," Keis mutters.

Her sister ignores her and presses play on the video.

A miniature Keisha pops up on the screen with her natural curly hair in two high pigtails. "Today, I was supposed to go with Mommy to get new hair ties, but now Uncle Vacu and Auntie Elaine are visiting with Alex, so I can't. Which is SO unfair."

Keis rolls her eyes. "Typical."

"Shh!" I say. That confirms that we did know her at some point. The genetic profile checks out. And it's clear now that our memories were taken.

Johan was wrong. I *can* miss what I don't remember. There was an entire person in my life wiped out like they never existed. Just pulled from my memories without my permission. My family are the most important people in my life. I can't imagine one of them just taken away from me in mind and body. A shiver crawls along my skin.

Tiny Keisha frowns. "Auntie Elaine wanted Granny, and Auntie April-Mae, and that other lady to talk about some fancy genetics thing at the hospital where she works. And Granny said she shouldn't be telling people our business because Granny is SO bossy. And I said so, and she sent me to my room. That's fine! I like my room!"

Little Keisha goes on at length about what hair ties she wants to get, and if her mom is still going to take her after Granny had to punish her. She doesn't mention Auntie Elaine again.

"Okay." I scrub at my face once the video is over. "The fancy genetics thing *must* have something to do with Justin. That's why she's in those genetic records from NuGene. And now we know Auntie Elaine worked at a hospital and wanted to show something to three people, Granny, April-Mae, and some other woman." Johan said our two families were the strongest, but it seems like Rowen had the more legitimate information. She always does. There were three Matriarchs that Auntie Elaine needed to consult. And the third wasn't someone who Keisha knew well. That means it couldn't be the Carters.

"Why do we care about this?" Keisha collapses onto her bed.

I throw my hands up. "Do you not care that you have a relative who you don't remember because those memories were purposely erased? With *impure magic*?"

"Why are you acting like you weren't, like, best friends with an impure witch?" she claps back.

I force myself to ignore the past tense in her words about Lauren.

"And maybe they were erased for a reason. Impure rituals have pure intent."

I screw my mouth up into a scowl. "I just don't think this coming up as I'm doing my task is a coincidence. Besides, she's our aunt, and whether or not the memories were taken for a good reason, shouldn't we be the judges of that?"

Keisha twirls her hair around her finger. "I don't know. I just can't see Granny making a call like that without good reason. And she must have agreed to it, even if we obviously didn't do the ritual since we're still pure. I'm with Keis for once. Seems smarter to look up Mama Jova."

"I can do both!"

"Classic Voya," Keisha mutters, putting her tablet away to scroll on her phone.

I glare at her. For once, I understand why she pisses Keis off so much.

Fuming, I leave her room with Keis trailing behind me. Why does it matter if I look into both things? This isn't as serious as deciding whether to accept my task or choosing how I'm going to do it.

"What are you going to do after you complete your task?" Keis says suddenly.

"I don't know, why?"

She stops in the hall. "You really can't imagine it."

I stare at my cousin.

"In your head, what your future looks like, you can't even see a hint of it?"

"I'll know once I have my gift."

"Will you?"

I turn on my heel and stalk to my room. It doesn't matter. I'm sure Keis can hear my thoughts ringing loud and clear.

Keis is right. My future, what I want my life to be like beyond my task, is blank. But what I can do is focus on right now. And my next step will have to be making a trip to Dixie Mall and finding out who the third strongest Black witch Matriarch is. And when I track her down, I'm going to get the answers to what went on between Auntie Elaine and Justin Tremblay that no one in my family wants to give.

CHAPTER FIFTEEN

T here are malls like the Eaton Center, huge downtown for-tresses of shopping filled with shiny new stores and brand names everyone knows. Then, there are places like Dixie Mall. Located over the border of Etobicoke in the more western Mississauga, the mall has brand-name stores with dozens of SALE signs slapped over them, and it's peppered with shops named things like Jeans 4 All.

I look longingly at the fresh juice stand. A lychee slush with boba would be amazing, but we have the NuGene tour tomorrow, and I'm going to want to grab something celebratory to eat down-town. Better to save my money for that.

Our family frequents Dixie Mall, partly for the outlet deals and partly for the reason I'm here today—the flea market. I keep my eyes straight ahead as I walk toward the gray entrance door. No one looks my way.

They never do.

Tucked into a small alcove is a foggy glass door with a witch mark printed in peeling vinyl. I go down the stairs into the flea market. I've never come here on my own, but Keis said, "I can't just follow you around. I do actually have my own shit to work on," before she took off to the library, so it'll be a solo mission.

Plus, I think she's still a little fried. Yesterday, a day after

Keisha showed us her vlogs, we researched more about Mama Jova at Keis's request and, as I predicted, didn't find anything we didn't already know. She's one of the ancestors Granny taught us about. She's not a mystery like Auntie Elaine or the third Matriarch. Or rather, in a way she is, but nothing in our family records could explain what would possess her to give me this task. Ancestors exist in a plane where bouncing from past to future to present and back again is normal. And explaining to the living how any of the things they do come together is abnormal. We're the ones who record our history, not them. If they don't tell us, we don't learn. We can only make guesses.

As far as I'm concerned, Mama Jova and I have no special ties beyond being an ancestor and a descendant, no matter what she says. But Auntie Elaine, the third Matriarch, and Justin are three pieces that are at least connected to Luc and me.

What awaits me at the bottom of the stairs is a low-ceiling space that contains Canada's largest witch-exclusive market—the Flea at Dixie. It isn't like the swanky St. Lawrence Market downtown with artisanal cheeses and locally made moccasins, whose fresh bread smell compels you to buy expensive baked goods. And it's definitely not like the Collective with its modded, youthful, artsy crowd.

The Flea at Dixie is an expanse of rickety tables seldom replaced and dust-covered antiques older than Granny. What wafts through the air is a mixture of curry spices from the many ethnic food kiosks and that indistinguishable *old* smell that sticks to objects and people.

There are more than two hundred booths in here, and I have to find this third Matriarch within them.

I walk toward the first booth at the foot of the stairs. It's the length of at least three tables and covered in a shimmering purple cloth. The man there straightens as I approach, probably thinking I'm interested in the array of lighters on his table.

"Hello, sister!" he cries.

I cringe. Why some Black people think calling you a family name when you don't even know each other will make you buy crap, I'll never know. He opens his mouth to do his sales pitch, and I cut him off. "I'm looking for a Matriarch. The strongest one you know."

He raises his bushy gray eyebrows. "You can't say hello?"

"Sorry," I mutter. "Hello."

Now, with my apparent rudeness out of the way, he considers me. His eyes notch up and down my form, not creepy, but assessing. I'm tempted to tell him my name, but Granny and Uncle sell our products down here. I don't need someone telling them I was poking around.

"April-Mae Davis," he says finally.

I want to slam my head onto his plastic table. "She's not here. I mean, the strongest Matriarch at this flea market."

"Oh!" He nods in earnest. "Ava Thomas."

I shuffle back from his table. "Okay, thanks." I'm not going to get anything from this guy.

He gestures to the lighters. "You want one? Promises to never go out."

"I'm good." I walk away before he can redouble his selling efforts. Hack me. There's no way I'll find this woman if I have to question every person here and dodge their sales pitches.

A shock of blue-gray makes me whip around. I know objectively that Luc isn't here. The door is enchanted so that non–magic users can't get inside.

And yet my eyes find a boy who looks suspiciously like Luc, dressed in jeans and a hoodie, who ducks under the black sheet covering the back of a stall.

How is he here . . . ?

Before I lose my nerve, I follow him. Inside the stall, it's dark, and the ceiling is covered with bunches of stinging nettle. Granny uses the root to make a tea to help with urinary tract or yeast infections. Which, in our house, is common enough.

I shift my eyes from the shelves of jars and bottles along the sides of the room to the moving shadows at the back of the room, where another black cloth acts as a wall. With a hard double blink, my hijacker chip manipulates my ocular nerve to activate better visibility, and the once-dim lighting becomes clear.

What I see there almost makes me drop.

In front of the cloth-covered wall, Luc is holding on to a rope that's hung along the stiff iron piping of the low ceiling that runs through the whole flea market. The end of the rope is looped around Keis's neck. Her manicured nails dig into the noose, and her feet with their white tennis sneakers kick out frantically.

Luc can't be here. Keis isn't here. This isn't happening.

But it is. I'm watching my cousin fight for her life. Her eyes bulging unnaturally.

"What are you going to do?" Luc says. It's his voice, but he's like a stranger.

A chill rises over my shoulders and makes me shudder. It's the only movement I can manage. I'm frozen with shock.

Keis tugs the rope away enough to wheeze, "K—k—k—"

I shake my head. I don't know what she's saying.

"K—k—" Every vein in her neck is bulging. She keeps pulling at the rope. Luc holds it steady, not loosening it, but not making it tighter, either.

Finally, Keis gets enough breathing room to scream, spit flying, "KILL HIM!"

The dark space bursts with light as a woman whips aside the cloth behind Luc and Keis. I throw my arm up over my eyes and squeeze them closed, panting hard. When I open them, Luc and my cousin are gone. All I have are her words, so shrill, so unlike Keis, drumming through my head.

KILL HIM!

I did nothing. It doesn't matter that it wasn't real. He was suffocating my cousin, and I stood by and did nothing. I wouldn't even kill him to save her. I failed.

The woman watches me in silence. Her hair is in short, springy coils of gray and black, and her face has a stretched smoothness that speaks of surgical, genetic, or magical intervention. She's Black, but the shape of her eyes seems to suggest some East Asian heritage too, and her skin is a few shades lighter than mine.

"I'm . . ." I struggle for an excuse.

She crosses her arms and examines my face. "You've been looking for me."

"And you are?"

"Everyone calls me Lee."

That's not a family name. "Lee . . . what?"

She smiles in a way that makes me ashamed for asking. "They prefer I don't associate myself with them. Just Lee." She gestures up to the ceiling. "Grab some nettle for me."

She disappears behind the cloth, and I scramble up a nearby stepladder to grab a bunch of nettle. The stingers slide into my skin, and I wince.

I walk under the cloth where Lee disappeared. Out the other side is a set of stalls arranged in a square with the same thick cloth hanging around the perimeter. The air is humid and heavy with the spiced scent of the incense she has burning. Some of the tables are stacked high with books while others house strange artifacts that are scrubbed clean, so different from everyone else's dusty jugs and vases. In the space in the middle, there's a single table with two folding chairs and a small teapot.

"Have you always had a booth here?" I hand the nettle to her.

Lee waves me off, so I set them on a nearby table. She collapses into a chair and adjusts her purple wrap dress over her legs. "I hate chitchat."

Hack me, she's worse than Granny. "You're the strongest Matriarch here?" I ask, making a guess.

"Used to be." Her voice holds no wistfulness or longing. Just statement of fact.

I shift in the chair. "I don't understand . . ."

"I know you don't. Too young to remember, maybe, and it's not like anyone talks about me anymore. But at one time, I was stronger than your granny *and* April-Mae. And I did it without slitting a single throat. I was a big deal until I wasn't."

My shoulders go stiff.

She smiles, mirth dancing in her eyes. "Yes, I know you, girl. Eleven years hasn't been long for me, though I know it's probably a lifetime away in your mind. I remember you tottering around with braids in your hair, forever stuck to Maise's girl. One of them, anyway."

"Keis." Saying her name reminds me of her thrashing against a rope. But Lee's right. Forgetting someone who was a part of my family was far-fetched—that was clearly a magical intervention. But a Matriarch, however powerful, probably wasn't something my child self would have hung on to. She would have been easy enough to forget if, like Lee said, no one wanted to talk about her. I swallow and push on. "Do you remember my aunt? Not Auntie Maise, Elaine."

"Vacu's wife."

I jerk my head up and down and sit straight in my seat. "Do you know what happened to her? How she died? What was she trying to propose to you, April-Mae, and Granny?" The questions spill out of my mouth before I can reel them in.

Lee stands and clicks on a kettle in the corner of the room. She uses a pair of gloves to shred the nettle leaves into a metal bowl.

"Sorry . . . Was that too many questions?" I hover half on and half off the seat before deciding to park my butt.

"The real question is why are you asking me about your own family?"

I swallow again and play with my fingers. "I can't remember her. None of my cousins can. And the adults don't want to talk about her."

Lee pauses. "I see."

"I just . . . wanted to know."

She lays the stems in a separate bowl, movement restored. "She was a kind woman with big ambitions who married a man with a predisposition for addictive behavior who never got help for it. Not that we knew that then. They seemed like a good match, the doctor and the nurse."

Keisha's vlog said Auntie Elaine worked in the hospital, apparently as a nurse. Did her gift guide her career like Uncle Vacu's did his? Maybe she had some sort of medical ability.

Lee turns over her shoulder and waves at a photo frame. In it is a younger version of her with a girl who I assume is her daughter based on the way their faces seem to match, but with much lighter skin, along with a fair-skinned East Asian–looking man. "I had a risky birth with my daughter. When I learned about Vacu's gift, I was so happy. It gave me hope that no one in our community would have the tough time that I did." She sighs and shakes her head. "So much promise ruined with a needle. She just tried harder, of course, to make up for it. She was like that."

"Auntie Elaine?"

Her fingers pause their plucking. "Mama Elaine now."

"What did she do to become a Mama?"

Lee abandons the nettle leaves and swivels toward me. "She protected her family. That's what I would guess, anyway. Only your granny can speak to your ancestors and know for sure."

Her gaze is heavy. As if she knows what I saw in that back room. "Protected us from Justin Tremblay?"

Lee's eyes flicker. "Protected us from the consequences of flying too close to the sun." She pauses and presses her lips together. "For a time, anyway." With an assessing look she asks, "How old are you?"

"Sixteen."

"Your Calling . . . ?"

"I'm working on the task. I have until Caribana."

"Long tasks can be dangerous," she says, voice low and careful. "Plays with your magic and your mind. Best to try and finish them as soon as possible before any hallucinations kick in."

Keis's white tennis shoes kicking in the air come back to me. "I *am* trying."

The more I push myself to fall in love with Luc, the more obvious it becomes that it's not something I can manufacture. I just need more time to fall naturally. In two weeks, I've gone from not particularly liking him to at least being a little excited when he sends a message. We've messaged each other a couple of times since too. Once because he realized he didn't know what oxtail was and I explained the unexpected deliciousness of cow tails. Another because I wanted to know if he watched *Quiz Kids* sometimes, for the nostalgia. He was, of course, too busy to waste time with feed shows.

Lee shoves the nettle leaves into a metal thermos and pours the hot water in along with a couple spoonfuls of sugar.

I lift myself from my seat. She doesn't seem like she's going to tell me any more.

Which family she used to belong to nags at me because I must have known at some point before everyone stopped talking about her. We weren't close with every Black witch family. The Carters we knew, and the Jameses were Dad's family, but the Baileys, they're the only ones I can't remember well.

"Was your name Bailey?" I ask.

"Something like that." Lee claps the lid on the thermos and hands it to me. "Take this upstairs for me, will you? My daughter Hope is working at the Golden Wok."

I bob my head, not sure what her answer is supposed to mean. "All right. Thank you for talking with me."

"The faster you finish your task, the better. Callings weren't meant to be longer than a couple of days."

Resisting the urge to snap back, I just nod.

The walk upstairs is quick. I force myself not to go looking into shadows for fear of seeing a vision of Luc bleeding out or stringing up Keis. I send a message to him, a completely inane *What are you doing?* just so he can respond, and I can be reminded that he's not lying in wait to threaten me.

I recognize Lee's daughter at the Golden Wok. She could be in her twenties or thirties; it's hard to tell with her leaning against the counter, wearing a bright orange visor.

I smile as I approach and hold out the thermos to her. "Lee sent me with this. Nettle tea for . . . you know."

Hope's face turns red, and she takes the thermos from me with a bowed head, her visor blocking her face from view. "I wish she would stop sending people up with this."

"Do you not get a break to go down instead?"

She furrows her brow, and her face turns redder for some reason. "I can't . . ."

I blink at her.

"I don't have any magic, so I can't go down." She shifts on the spot.

"But . . . Lee is your mom. Did you fail your Calling?" I catch myself as I say it and blanch. "Sorry, I shouldn't have asked that."

Hope shrugs. "It's fine. I never had one. Genetic anomaly. It was happening to a few kids born to witches around my time. I don't know why." She lifts up the thermos. "Thanks for this."

It's as polite a dismissal as I'm going to get, but I can't leave it. "Sorry, can I ask one more thing?"

Her body locks up with the same stiffness I saw in her mom. "Yeah, I guess."

"Was your name Bailey, at some point?"

"Kind of. Bailey-Huang, though neither of them want us to use that. We use Anderson now. Very Canadian anonymous. Works for people kicked out of their own families." Her voice has a clipped edge to it that I don't blame her for.

Lee used to be part of not just the Bailey family but the Huangs, too. A double name like that meant she would have been Matriarch of both, easily making her the strongest. More than Granny or April-Mae.

My eyes must be wide because Hope lets out a little laugh.

"You've probably never heard of Bailey-Huang. Both families worked pretty hard to scrub us out of existence. They thought it was contagious and weeded out anyone with a direct connection to the anomaly. And everyone else pretended we never existed. The Baileys never bounced back, but Rowen's running the Huangs like a well-oiled machine. She's my aunt, you know. My dad is her oldest brother. Guess how many times she's ever spoken to me?" Hope's voice is louder now, colored by her anger.

"I don't know," I say softly.

"Zero."

I let out a harsh breath. "But . . . if Lee was Matriarch and isn't anymore, how is she still alive?" A new Matriarch can only be crowned when the old one dies. If you switch prematurely, it would mean the death of the current leader.

Hope gives me a gentle smile. "Loophole. Being Matriarch of two families means you're technically not Matriarch of either on their own. It's the one thing that worked in our favor." A customer slides up to the counter, peering at the offerings there. Hope tips her orange visor to me and walks over to them. "What can I get for you?" Her cheery voice conceals the bitter rage I just saw.

Both families purposely separated to distance themselves from a Matriarch whose child was born without magic because of a genetic anomaly.

But what if you didn't want to let that position go? If you wanted to hold on to being Matriarch and to being part of your heritage and family? Or if you were scared that you would be the next one to have a child without magic and fall from grace?

A genetic anomaly is the sort of thing a talented geneticist could fix if he was let into the community to learn about magic. It's as good a reason as any for why Auntie Elaine would have sought Justin out if this was something witches were worried about, and a solid reason for why Granny, April-Mae, and Lee would have agreed to work with someone like him. To let an outsider in. And it explains why Rowen Huang of all people would know about something that would have been Black witch business, because her family was a part of it too.

But something went wrong between Justin and Auntie Elaine, and she had to protect us from it. Maybe dying in the process. And becoming a Mama in the end.

The image of Keis hanging from the rope that Luc held comes back to me. How much am I willing to do to protect my family? To save us from the fate of being buried and forgotten like Lee and hers? Not even allowed to use their own family name. Forced into a dark corner of the flea market.

Auntie Elaine may have died to protect us.

And I have to kill to do the same.

CHAPTER SIXTEEN

The next day, when Keis and I arrive at ten a.m. for the exclusive tour, we're shuffled into a white room off the waiting area at NuGene HQ. It's strange in a way, to be in the building now that I know Justin may have a less than ideal relationship with Auntie Elaine. But that doesn't change how good of an opportunity a position here would be for Keis. Maybe it's better—keep your enemies close and all that.

"We don't know that he's our enemy," Keis says. My cousin crosses her arms over her chest, stretching the blazer I made her wear.

I say back to her, "We don't know that he's not."

She lets out a sigh and scrolls through her phone.

I keep thinking of her strung up by Luc, legs kicking, neck veins throbbing.

Keis doesn't ask me about it because she can't hear it. Can't see the memory even if she tried to read it out of my head. I know she can't because Keis typically has this no-reaction reaction when she hears something embarrassing or particularly private in my head—her face gets very still as she actively works to pretend like she didn't hear it.

That's not how she's been this time. Her face is calm and unbothered. She's not pretending to not know about the visions.

She truly doesn't. Maybe something about them stops her from hearing them. And aside from that, the way our magic has been waning means she's missing more of my thoughts than usual. Which in one way is a relief. I have privacy again. In another way, it's a chilling reminder of how time is ticking down.

Both of us are in business casual skirts and blouses with jackets. Even Granny gave a nod of approval as we left that morning. It's a nice change from the way her eyes have been following me lately, like she's searching for something but hasn't found it yet.

True to her word, Keisha gave the adults an uncomfortable talking-to on my behalf, and since then, none of them have mentioned the idea of me not having to do the task in the end. Instead, most have opted to say nothing about it at all. If Granny is miffed that it came to that instead of them just listening to her in the first place, she doesn't show it.

There's a good chunk of people in the room with brand names on their lapels or cuffs that mark their outfits as more expensive than our own, not to mention that their little mods are likely triple our monthly loan payments: flecks of gold in one girl's eyes, a boy whose skin is so pale and immaculate that it could only be manufactured, and even more beyond that. None of them seem to exist without some piece of NuGene in them.

I can't imagine having money like that. Able to casually toss several months of a mortgage or rent at your teenage kids for something that doesn't actually do anything except look nice. It makes our allowances look like less than spare change.

And they can tell too. They toss side glances at us as the obvious outliers.

The door at the far side of the room swings open, and a Black boy around Keis and Keisha's age enters dressed in a teal version of the NuGene lab coat. "Welcome to the intern tour. My name is Dennis, I use he/him. I'm an intern myself, and I'll be bringing you around today. You'll get to have a look at the NuGene facilities and the chance to speak to our other interns."

He beckons us out of the room, and we shuffle behind him into what I expect to be another hall with more white walls. Instead, we enter a glass hallway where dozens of offices branch out. The furniture is sleek and colored in the NuGene-brand teal instead of the hospital white. At the back, there's a common area with what looks like a café, where people are chatting and laughing. I thought it would be a cultlike sea of white NuGene uniforms, but the only people decked in white coats are those in the lab. Everyone else is dressed so casually that I'm tempted to untuck my dress shirt.

I look at Keis, whose mouth has fallen open.

I press my hand over mine to cover my smile. "It's pretty nice, eh?"

"It's okay," she mutters.

Dennis gestures toward the space. "These are the first-floor offices. We work in an open floor plan, so our employees have the option to move from floor to floor during work hours as it suits them. There are five floors with a top one that's for employee housing. If you're full-time, you can rent the room at an inexpensive rate, assuming you qualify for financial aid."

Keis's eyes flare wide. I didn't know NuGene would have on-site housing. She would want to take advantage of that if she became a full-time employee. To leave the house and live somewhere else the way she wants. Away from us. The smile drops off my face.

Dennis sweeps his arms around him. "This floor is for people who have direct contact with our audience and clients. It includes teams like customer service and public relations."

I shove down my feelings about Keis living here instead of at home. This could be a life-changing opportunity for her. She

223

would do amazing as a future PR rep, especially with her gift. I nudge her.

"I heard you," she says.

She heard me, but she doesn't mention the living arrangement thoughts.

Dennis moves us forward through the space. "Anyone wearing a teal lab coat today is an intern you can approach. Everyone else is a working employee, and we ask that you leave them alone." He gestures outward. "You have five minutes here. Go ahead."

Keis stays frozen in the middle of the room.

"Let's go." I point to the holo labeled "Public Relations" floating over a workspace. "This is your chance to impress someone."

"Do you really think I could work here?" Her voice is small, and her hands are tucked under her armpits.

I blink at my cousin and put my hands on her shoulders. I could say no. If I want her to stay at home with me, maybe I should. But I can't. Keis belongs here, and I won't let my feelings ruin that for her.

"I do," I say. "The library opportunity is good, but NuGene, this was made for you. You're an innovator. A leader. That's who works here. That's why *you* can work here. You just have to go for it."

She jerks her head in a nod. I let my hands drop from her shoulders as she makes a beeline for the PR section. I scuttle after her.

A white guy with bright red hair and an intern lab coat looks up at us as we get close to him. "Hello! You two interested in PR?"

Keis opens her mouth.

Don't just plow ahead! Introduce yourself. People like small talk!

If I hadn't shouted that thought, she would have jumped straight in with questions. Now is the time to be personable.

"Hi, I'm Keis. This is my cousin Voya." She thrusts her hand out, and I wave.

He springs out of his chair to shake both our hands. "Judas. And before you ask, yes, that Judas."

"My mom named both me and my twin sister Keisha to spite my grandma. I get having an unconventional name," Keis says with a smile.

Judas bursts into a laugh. "Yeah, my mom has an interesting relationship with religion. But going the double name route for double spite, that takes dedication."

"She has that." Keis gestures toward the space behind him. "What sorts of things does the NuGene PR team look for in their interns? Besides interesting names."

Judas grins. "It's a mixed bag. There are a lot of people with science specializations and some specific PR tutorials they took in high school." He scratches the back of his head. "And people like me who did an English specialization."

Keis bobs her head. "Meaning you have a good understanding of human motivations and a better grasp on how to word things to bring out emotion and tell the story of the company."

Judas's mouth hangs open. I'm in awe of how she spun a subject he didn't seem particularly proud of into a positive. Keis goes into a spiel about how she's glad NuGene accepts a diverse suite of skills.

Dennis shouts out from the middle of the room. "We're moving on."

Keis sticks her arm out. "It was great talking to you."

"It was! And I'm not just saying that," he says as they shake hands. "When you do your application, you should address it to Soras Mile. She's the head of PR and loves taking on interns who have a varied background. You can put me as a referral. We had a quick meeting, but it doesn't take long to know when someone can do well here."

I snap my neck toward Keis and force down a squeal of happiness.

My cousin's face glows. "I'll do that. Thank you so much."

"No problem." Judas sits back at his desk as Keis and I rush to rejoin the group.

I grip my cousin's arm. "That was amazing!" I'm so excited I don't even think to push the thought at her instead of chatting out loud.

Keis winces at my voice, and a thin sheen of sweat coats her forehead.

"Are you okay?" I whisper.

"I'm fine."

"What's up? You should be happy—a personal referral is huge!"

"Yeah, and I couldn't get it without magic." She clenches her hands into fists.

Oh. Keis used her gift. She jumped out of my thoughts and focused in on Judas's brain, thoughts she's never been inside, while holding a conversation and shutting out the huge amount of people in the office. She has never done anything that hard with her gift. But now that those intrusive outside voices are dull, it's possible.

"It's not that you couldn't do it *without* magic, it's that you're using your skills together." I wave at the kids milling around the room. "You think those people aren't using every single advantage they have? Calling up aunts and uncles with connections here and getting favors to have their applications pushed up on the list? We don't have money or their kind of status, but we have magic."

For what I'm sure is the very first time, Keis actually looks like she believes me.

"You're still doing it like you wanted. You're more than just a witch."

She lets out a breath, and her lips spread into a little smile. "This place isn't what I thought it would be. It's what *you* thought it would be, so it's better. Thank you for setting this up." She stares into my eyes. "I'm not the only one who can be more than just a witch—you know that, right?"

"I have to be a witch first before I can be more than a witch." I give Keis a gentle push forward to follow the crowd of tour guests. "Now, come on, the group is leaving without us."

Keis is the one who made this happen for herself. I got her here, but it was her decision to use magic that got her the referral. And if she didn't believe this was the right place for her, she wouldn't have broken her personal rule not to use her gift to get ahead. This is the thing that's finally worth taking advantage of everything she has to give. She's carving out what her life, her future, will be.

I can only push her forward and stand in the background.

For a moment, I think of Mama Jova, pressed against the trunk of the tree, watching everyone run to freedom without her. I know it's not the same, not even close, but somehow it feels similar. It's enough that in a small way I can understand what might have made her pick me.

In the elevator, I'm surrounded by a group of people who may one day become employees here. I glance at Keis out of the corner of my eye. With any luck, she will too.

What must it be like to know exactly what you want? Whenever I try to imagine my future, I come up against a block. There's always something in the way, and no matter what route I take, the end is a mystery. I keep thinking that my gift will solve everything, but what if it doesn't? What if I don't have that light bulb moment that helps me decide what it is that I want to do with my life?

I wring my hands.

The elevator door dings and opens into another expansive

space with glass walls and teal furniture. Except here, each person has at least three monitors in front of them.

"This is the second floor," Dennis announces. "You may remember the recently announced matching program that's in beta testing phase. It was developed and is monitored here along with our other ongoing special programs."

It takes me a few seconds to spot Luc at a standing desk surrounded by five screens under a holo that reads "NuGene Match: In Beta." He's an intern, and yet he's not dressed in the teal lab coat that would signify he's available for us to chat with him.

The last time I saw him, he was stringing my cousin up on a rope.

The time before that, I was with him at Brown Bear, fingering a knife in a way that seemed less than friendly.

My hands shake, and I clench them into fists to keep them steady.

"You have another five minutes here to chat with some of our interns," Dennis says.

Keis points to the "Charitable Programs" holo. "I'm going to talk with them."

I glance at Luc, who's staring at his screen. His last string of messages said he would have my container for me.

"Are you coming?"

"Sure," I say. He's so hot and cold. Messages me out of the blue not two but three days in a row, and now wants to go back to pretending I don't exist. Fine. I can play that game too.

I take a couple of steps forward with Keis when a cough rings out across the room. The source of the noise is Luc, who's finally looked away from his screen to stare at me.

"Are you okay?" One of the guys from our tour group has strayed to hover near Luc.

"Fine," Luc snaps.

Typical. I move again to follow Keis, and he makes a hasty cough sound so weak and fake that I roll my eyes. "I'll catch up with you."

"Watch out, sounds like he has a cold." Keis smirks at me and heads off.

I walk to Luc's desk, where he's straightening and alternating between looking at his screen and watching me come over. He doesn't try to murder Keis, so that's positive.

The guy who Luc snapped at gives me a look that says, *Are you sure you want to try and interact with him?*

I stop in front of my match's desk. "You coughed?"

"You didn't seem like you were going to come over."

"You're not wearing a teal coat."

He scowls. "Because I don't want to be bothered."

"Then why am I here?"

"I meant—not you, other people." He jerks his shoulder in what I suspect is meant to be nonchalance. "One person is fine, and it may as well be you."

"Do you have my container?"

Luc coughs into his sleeve. Just as fake as his other one, except I'm not sure why. "No, I forgot it. Sorry."

"You don't sound sorry."

"Never mind that, look here." He comes closer and points at the smallest of his screens. It's a grainy photo of what looks like a laboratory, and a Black woman stands there, curls cut close to her face. I squint and gasp. "That's Auntie Elaine!"

"Keep it down," he hisses.

"Sorry." I shake my head in shock. "Where did you get this?" For all his "That's Justin's past, not mine" spam, he's already done more to help out than I ever expected.

"I asked Justin if he recalled knowing anyone in your family. He said no, which isn't surprising." He stabs at the screen, perhaps a little too viciously. "But I found this in archived files from his private databases."

"Can you send it to me?"

Luc's eyes go wide. "Did you not just hear me say this was in Justin's private files? This data can't leave the building server."

"He wouldn't talk to you about it, but he let you look at his private files?" I tilt my head to the side.

Luc closes the window with a few taps and clears his throat. "Not exactly."

"You *hacked into it*?"

"Shh!"

I glance over at the group, but they're milling around, oblivious. Dennis looks over at us, but a stony glare from Luc makes him turn away. I say, "Do you have to be an ass to everyone?"

"Only annoying people."

"If hacking is your special skill, why are you working on the matching program?"

"My first love is robotics, actually. And I have many skills, including genetic analysis, hence my role in the matching program. I'm very intelligent."

"I'm very intelligent," I mock under my breath, and he scowls. "Wait, why not a robotics program?"

"It's hard to get funding for a program when one of the models suffocates its owner tucking them into bed."

I wince. "Fair enough."

He points to the screen. "What do you think the connection is between your aunt and Justin?"

"That's what I'm trying to figure out. No one else in my family wants to talk about it or thinks it's important."

He props his head up on his chin. "There's a family member who is closely related to you, and you know nothing about them, and no one thinks that's important?"

"Right?" I throw my hands up.

Luc taps on his screen and brings up another photo. It's low-res but unmistakably Auntie Elaine. Justin's there too. They're in a hospital room where she's bent over a patient while he watches her. "He had this, too, and yet he lied to me when I asked if he knew anyone in your family. He never lies about anything, just says that it's classified, but he actively concealed his knowing her."

The twist of Luc's mouth shows me he thinks that's as suspicious as I do. Finally! Someone who understands that this could be important. And it's Luc of all people. "Do you know which hospital that is?"

"No."

"Can you find out?" My eyes meet Luc's. "Please?"

"I'll look into it."

I beam.

His face flushes. "If I have time! Don't get so excited."

I make an effort to press my lips into something closer to a frown. "What about her genetic sequence? Can you access it?"

"NuGene needs permission for that. Justin has a note that he recorded her full sequence, but the file was sent to an outside source. It's some sort of locked local server, so I can't get to it. Justin deleted the original one on file. The only Thomas whose genetics I have access to are yours."

If Justin had Auntie Elaine's genetic sequence done, that means a list of information about what was in her genes. And I can bet that local server is the almanac. There must be some sort of clue in it about what went on between them. Especially if Justin tried to delete it.

"When are you going to kill me?" Luc whispers.

My neck snaps to look into his eyes.

He rubs his arms. "I mean . . . since I have to give you the container."

"What did you say?"

"I have to give you the container?"

"No, before that." I lean toward him, prepared to hear him properly this time.

"When am I going to see you again?"

When is he going to see me again . . . to give me the container. Of course. It's happening again. I'm hearing something that wasn't said, like when I saw blood that wasn't there. Like the visions. "I'll send you a message." My mind is looping on the words I thought I heard.

This can't keep happening.

I need to calm down. This is good. I have another opportunity to see him—another opportunity to try to fall in love.

"Okay, time to move on!" Dennis shouts out.

"I have to go," I say, and stumble backward.

Luc furrows his brow in an expression that looks uncomfortably like concern. But he doesn't ask what's wrong. "When you get to the main floor, you should speak to Abed in the café. I know it just seems like a little spot in the building, but he runs a ton of office-based eateries and does internships."

"I don't need an internship." My foot decides to do a tapping rhythm on the floor.

"Everyone our age needs an internship. And if the curry is any indication, you cook well, so why not look for one?" He tilts his head to the side. "Or can you only pursue internships that aren't for you?"

"I'm not—I don't—" How am I supposed to explain to him that's not how my life works? My future will be decided by my gift. And my gift will depend on whether or not I complete this task. I'm not willing to fight my fate and dive into an unpredictable future like Keis. "I don't have any plans for that. My life is set in stone in a way yours isn't."

"No one's future is set in stone. No one gets that guarantee."

I fold my hands into fists. He's right. His future isn't guaranteed because I'm here to take his life. To put a stop to his bright prospects at this amazing company.

All so I can have a future that I can't imagine.

"I have to go," I mutter, and hustle after the rest of the group.

We move toward the elevator, and Dennis drops back beside me. He leans over and whispers, "How the hell did you get Luc to talk to you?"

"Uh, I met him before."

"Yeah," Dennis says with an eye roll. "We've all met him before. I've met him at least six times, and believe me when I say he doesn't give me the time of day."

I glance back at Luc alone at his desk. He's got almost an entire ring of empty desks around him, as if people who were placed near him vacated their seats to get away. "We have a mutual interest." If not for the connection between Auntie Elaine and Justin, he probably wouldn't have called me over. I'm the one trying to fall in love. He's said from the beginning that he has no interest.

"Whatever you're doing, keep it up. If you get a referral from him, you have a guaranteed spot on his team." Dennis gathers everyone into the elevator.

I stare out at Luc by himself in the back of the room until the elevator doors close.

At the next floor, while everyone makes their way around the space to chat with interns, I shuffle over to sit on one of the couches next to a woman working away on her laptop.

I pull out my phone and bring up Luc's profile with its stream of negative reviews and our matching percentage at the top.

I tap on the rating section.

Talented Fade Ink artist and possible supersleuth hacker. Attitude could use some work. Could be better at returning property also. —Voya Thomas

I give him a four-star rating because giving him five would be a little much and kind of mortifying.

Almost instantly, a comment appears under my review. The only comment Luc has ever made on any of his ratings: *You're ruining my reputation.*

I press my fist against my mouth to hide the smile that blooms there.

The woman beside me leans over. "Who's the lucky person?"

"What?"

She grins. "I always know the look of a girl in love."

Beneath my hand, my smile slides away.

CHAPTER SEVENTEEN

I spend the next day in the kitchen with Auntie Elaine's recipes. My plan was to see if I could find some way to see Luc, but most of his time is monopolized by NuGene, even on weekends like today. His feed shows he hasn't been on it for the past twelve hours, which is basically unheard of for anyone our age but is common for him. I sent him a message about arranging to get my container back that he still hasn't answered, so cooking it is.

It's also a perfect time to try out my recipes for the contest with a bigger audience. In less than an hour, every Black witch family will gather in the Davises' massive backyard for our annual get-together before Caribana. Sometimes it seems ridiculous that we can all fit in someone's—large to be fair, but still—backyard-size property. The community is smaller than it seems. Look at Auntie Elaine, related to me through Uncle Vacu *and* through Dad.

I'm cooking a batch of oxtail curry, the one Luc and my family preferred. Except for Dad, who hasn't gotten back to me about his pick. I make another tin of macaroni pie, too, Auntie Elaine's recipe, and finish off with a rum-soaked black cake that's so moist it's glistening. It's not my taste, if I'm honest, but Auntie Elaine's recipes are popular for a reason, and I'm trying to win.

Granny shuffles into the kitchen around six p.m. I look behind her for Uncle and, thankfully, he's absent.

She scoffs. "Cathius left early to help get ready for the party."

"How did you know that's what I was thinking about?"

She grunts and leans over the black cake. "It smells like a liquor store. Who gave you rum to waste like that?"

"I found it."

Granny's nostrils flare.

"If I win the recipe contest, I'll have lots of money to replace it! And it was the one Auntie complained wasn't good last year. No one was using it."

"Mm-hmm." She makes her way around the island, looking over the dishes I have laid out. "These aren't your recipes."

"How do you know?"

"You never put pepper sauce in your curry before. Only whole scotch bonnets, just enough for flavor. I almost burned my damn throat trying it the other day for lunch."

"You said you liked it!"

"I did. I just wouldn't mind a little warning. It's a cooking contest, so why aren't you using your recipes?" Granny's forehead wrinkles as she studies me. For a granny, her face is sparse when it comes to things like age lines. She looks more like she's in her forties than sixties. Whether that's a benefit of being Matriarch or our beauty products, I have no idea.

I lick my lips. "It's a heritage recipe contest. You're supposed to use ancestor inspiration."

"Did our ancestors not eat curry like you make?"

Hack me to death. I flick my eyes up to the ceiling. "Why am I being interrogated?"

Granny *hmms* under her breath and keeps examining the dishes laid out.

I pull Iron Film (promises to never rip!) over the top of the food in the EcoOven trays. "I just want some more options. My recipes are good, but maybe these are better."

I stack the trays crisscross the way Granny taught me, so they don't sink into each other. Iron Film is strong but not that strong.

"If you say so." Granny leaves the room and screeches up the staircase, "Girls! Come help Voya get this food in the van!"

Keis and Keisha file into the kitchen. Keis has her hair in its signature pineapple bun and casual shorts and T-shirt, while her sister sashays in with a butt-length chocolate-brown wig with pink ends, and a white mini dress that looks like she sewed herself into it.

Granny squints at them. "Where's Alex?"

"She's sewing in her room. Her fashion show is tomorrow." Keisha adjusts her dress that's already ridden up.

Granny squints harder.

"Everything is covered! It's not that short of a dress!"

It takes one more hard stare for Keisha to spin on her heel and stomp out of the room, calling out, "This is some retro sexist bullshit!"

"Yeah, yeah." Granny jerks her head at Keis and me. "Go take those out to the van. Keisha will grab the last one."

Keis and I each grab a tray and head out to "the van," where everyone is packed in. That's what Granny calls it even though it's technically a mini bus. No hype. Shiny, white, and boxy in a way that makes me and my cousins cringe. It's a relic from when Granny and Grandad used to travel around the country when Uncle Vacu was little.

After Great-Granny's death and Granny's crowning as Matriarch, traveling became a thing of the past, and they put the seats back in, and brought the bed inside. It's the same mattress that Granny sleeps on to this day.

We climb in, followed shortly after by Granny, and Keisha in an only slightly longer dress. Auntie pulls out of the driveway, and we make our way to the Davises' house.

Eden kicks her feet in the seat next to me as she hums a tune that I suspect she made up. She's squeezed against my side, playing some sort of racing game.

I dig out my phone and go through my new messages. There's nothing from Luc, and my heart falls a little. I clench my fists in my lap. Was that woman on the bench right? But no, I'm not in love with him. Not already. I think I can at least say that I like him more than I don't. Recently added to the mental list of positives: his help with Auntie Elaine and that somehow being around him has gone from mildly irritating and difficult to pleasant. Which, I admit, isn't great progress for two weeks, but I don't know how to love someone faster.

"Fine line between love and hate," Keis mutters across the narrow aisle where she sits in one of the single seats.

I stammer, trying to blubber something, but end up projecting a thought instead. *Outside opinions are not needed!*

Auntie slams on the brakes, and we lurch forward. "Shit!"

"Language," Priya says from the front seat where she and Dad sit.

Auntie doesn't acknowledge her. She's jabbing at the button to make the window roll down.

Keisha groans. "Oh my God, Mom . . ."

"I'm gonna set this piece of trash on fire," Auntie snarls. "Maybe then he'll learn how to drive without cutting people off."

I doubted that any of the self-drive cars on the road were doing anything they weren't supposed to, but Auntie doesn't tend to take that into account when she gets mad.

Mom gets up and reaches over Auntie to roll up her window. There's a scuffle between them as we swerve to the right.

I grip the edge of my seat and make sure we aren't going to hit anything.

Dad reaches out to press his hand on Auntie's shoulder.

She snaps her head around before he can make contact. "Touch me with that hand, and I'll burn your flesh to the bones. I will *not* be forced to calm down."

Dad slouches back and retracts his hand.

"He's trying to help." Priya doesn't hide the snippiness in her voice.

Auntie steupses, shoves Mom off her, and rolls the window back up. She slams on the gas so we can make the left turn onto the Davises' street even though the light's red.

I shake my head. *Why do we let Auntie drive? She always does this.*

"Because no one wants to deal with arguing with her about who should drive," Keis says. "We're here anyway."

Auntie pulls up in front of the Davises' house and parks on the shoulder. The previously empty front steps are now littered with people hanging out with paper cups. Grandad would have called it "liming." Which is a cooler Trini way of saying "hanging out." We were supposed to be here with food before anyone arrived, but predictably, we are late. It's not easy to wrangle nine people.

Keis, Keisha, and I grab the food trays and make our way toward the backyard. The scanner wafts over Granny, and the gates swing open for us. As we wind our way to the back, it's like everyone's eyes are on me.

And not in the usual "Hey, look, it's the Thomases" type of way; it's a harder stare. Witches love their gossip, and Johan has loose lips when it suits him.

I try not to let it bother me. Mom says that talking is in our blood. That we boil it down to gossip, but in the old days when our ancestors were on plantations, it was all we had. It was how we stayed connected and helped one another. Passing stories from person to person. And before that, it's how we kept our history alive. So sure, we gossip a lot, but in some ways, it's one of the things that brings us together with even our most distant ancestors.

"Don't worry about them." Keis glares at Owen James, one of Dad's cousins our age, whose eyes are near bugging out of his damn head. "Let's get this food down."

We set the dishes on the table decked out with chickpea-filled and pillowy doubles, and freshly fried pholourie. It's the usual fare they make at the Davis family restaurant Roti Roti. Supposedly, they keep it open to stay humble. Every Davis has to work there a minimum of one day a week to build their work ethic. At least, that's the explanation Uncle gave. He also grumbled that his brother just likes to have people under his thumb at all times, which seems equally true.

When we put everything down, one of Johan's daughters, Emerald, comes over with her green-and-black wig swaying, edges done so perfect I almost forget she hasn't had her Calling yet and couldn't have done them with magic. She points a manicured finger at the twins. "Uncle Cathius says you two have to come hand out drinks."

Keisha groans. "Why?"

"Because you're Davises, and you're supposed to help." She glances over at me, or specifically, at my wrist. "Are you in the matching beta too?"

I blink and look down at her wrist, where a white monitor is strapped. "Uh, yeah."

"How is your match?"

"He's . . ." An asshole but not an asshole? Brilliant and artistic but pretentious? Also, I think I like him. But I need to love him, and that's kind of a work in progress. Oh, and I'm going to have to kill him at the end of the month. No big deal. "He's interesting. How's yours?"

She opens her mouth to say something but is cut off by Johan. "Emerald! You and the twins get over here."

She immediately turns and goes to her father. There's no back talking or evasion in the Davises' home. Keis and Keisha drag their feet after their cousin.

I survey the party and find Lauren's family huddled in a corner while the rest of the Carters mill around far away from them. Rena has a bob-length wig and heels, and Mr. Carter is staring into his drink. Caleb is running around with Eden and the rest of the kids.

Caleb was born with a sickness Rena needed Johan to help fix. If Auntie Elaine was around, I think she would have tried to help them for nothing. It's the impression I got from the way Lee described her. She wanted to help people without asking for something in return.

Caleb tags Eden, and she squeals and chases after him. A rare smile graces Ms. Carter's face.

On any other year, Lauren would be here too, talking about her latest dramatic romance or a gene mod she wanted. Back then, her family was on top. Among the Carters, anyway. The rest of their family looking to them for guidance and strength, with Lauren poised to take over once her aunt, the current Matriarch, passed away. It hurts now to see them standing apart and alone.

That could be us.

At one point, Lee was the strongest Matriarch in the community, and as soon as they found out that her daughter didn't have magic, they threw her out.

That's the sort of community that we have. That we've *cultivated*. One that's ready to throw away families who make them uncomfortable. Who don't contribute to their power and status. Who they find sad or embarrassing.

If I fail my task, we'll be no different.

Cut out, like a brown spot in an otherwise perfect mango. Except this mango has already gone rotten, and everyone is still licking the golden flesh like it's sweet.

"They look rough, eh?" Mom comes up beside me with a paper cup filled with bright orange liquid that smells of the rum I put in the black cake. She makes a subtle gesture toward the Carters.

"Have you ever thought about using your gift for more than readings? To help the police find missing people, that sort of thing?"

She lets out a deep sigh. "It's dangerous for us to do things that bring on too much attention. Private investigators are one thing. They have no real authority and don't get press. Being the psychic woman finding everyone's missing loved ones for cops is the sort of reputation we want to avoid. Besides, they use genetic data to find people, and they're good at it. They'll get her soon enough."

I clench and unclench my hands. "But they haven't. There may not be any genetic data to find. And you have something better."

"There are no crimes without genetic data anymore."

"Why don't you want to *help*? Don't you care about Lauren?"

Mom snaps her neck toward me. "Sometimes you try to make something better and you make it worse. Trust that I'm not interfering for a reason." She gestures so wildly, half her drink sloshes out of her cup. "I would love to help people, but I need to focus on the family. Which is going to goddamn shambles because of Mama Jova. And I don't know how to help you . . ." She lets out a little hysterical laugh. "Just . . . focus on your stuff."

I chew on my lip and bob my head like I agree with her. There's a rustling in my stomach reminiscent of Lauren's missing poster whipping away in the wind. Her answer isn't a real reason; it sounds like an excuse. Mom saying that she doesn't know how to help doesn't make it better. I'm truly alone in this task.

Mom nudges me with her shoulder. "Did you hear me? I know it's hard. This task is . . . Keisha said you want us to stop pretending it's not happening, and we—*I*—finally get that. There isn't a way around this. You need to focus on completing it."

"I *am* focusing!" I don't realize how loud my voice is until other guests look over at us. I hunch my shoulders and say, softer now, "I can't fall in love at the drop of a hat."

"Oh, Vo. That's not even the hardest part." Auntie calls for Mom from across the lawn. Mom reaches over and squeezes my shoulder. "If you need me, I'm here, even if I don't have the wisdom for you that I want." She walks toward Auntie and yells, "Get me another drink!"

"Only if you admit I would be the better Matriarch," Auntie calls back.

Mom scowls.

With a cackle, her sister flips a penknife out and slices her finger. She waves her hand to summon a fresh drink. She doesn't need to, but witches are like that. Showing off with unnecessary little casts is part of our culture.

But the spell fails.

A chill settles on the back of my neck.

Auntie's face flashes from confused to understanding to panicked, then smooths over with a smile. "Guess I've drank too much," she proclaims. The people around her laugh because they don't know what's really happening.

Mom doesn't even chuckle.

She knows better.

My cousins aren't the only ones whose magic is dwindling. It's happening to the adults, too. I haven't failed my Calling and yet the consequences of it are surrounding me.

Why does my future have to mean destroying someone else's? Especially someone who seems to have a much brighter one than I do?

Maybe it doesn't have to. There's one person who would know for sure.

My eyes land on Johan entering the house.

．．．

I slip into the house after Johan and follow him as he walks through the hall toward the kitchen.

After a couple of steps, he stops. "Why am I being tailed like a criminal?"

My face glows with warmth. "I wanted to ask you about something."

"Ancestors give me strength," he groans. "No more about Justin or Elaine."

"No! Not about that."

He puts his hands on his hips. "What, then?"

"It's about my task. . . . Has there ever been someone who did a different task than what they were given and passed?"

"Not that I know."

My shoulders sink.

"But that doesn't mean it's not possible." He folds his arms over his chest. "Who Called?"

"Mama Jova."

He whistles low. "Mama Jova is wicked. There will be hell to pay if you fail her task." He leans forward. "It can't be a simple assignment."

"It isn't." I wring my hands. "So? An alternative?"

Johan leans against the wall. "Maybe she wants you to feel what she did. The woman was whipped within an inch of her life, had her lover killed in front of her, and then was left alone, too weak to escape with the slaves she freed. You've been raised in the coddling arms of a huge family. What was the task?"

I shift on the spot.

"You want me to help you, and I don't know the full story?"

"She said to destroy my first love."

He raises his brows. "And you've interpreted that how?"

"Interpreted it? She said 'destroy.' I have . . . I mean, he's, *we're* a romantic genetic match. I have to fall in love with him properly and ... well, you know, right? But if I can avoid that ..."

"Maybe you can. But do you want to gamble on maybe?"

I stare down at my feet. The suns painted on my toes are starting to feel out of place more often than not. I should have Keisha repaint them.

"I heard Keis got a personal referral from NuGene. That's what she's always wanted, isn't it? Some freedom. Her own job, and I hear they do on-site apartments." Johan's voice is casual, but there's a weight to it. Like he's trying to say more than he is.

I don't want to talk about Keis leaving the house. "This isn't about her. I need help with my task."

"I am helping you," Johan says with a shrug. "If you can't see that, that's your problem."

I don't understand how thinking about Keis's future is supposed to help me destroy Luc.

Lately, hers has been falling beautifully into place.

Soon it'll be her graduation, where I know she'll get a ridiculous amount of honors.

After that, an internship position at NuGene, where she'll flourish under mentorship.

Then further on, Keis attending an amazing university on NuGene's dime, dazzling her professors, and graduating to join the company as a valued full-time employee. She'll move into their on-site apartments, and I'll help her do it, even if it hurts.

I see her changing the world, and I plan to be there for everything.

Keis's future is the closest I've ever come to imagining mine.

And it tells me nothing about how to avoid destroying Luc's.

I shake my head. "Thanks. I was wrong to think there was a way around this when I know there isn't." I mumble a goodbye and turn away in shame.

Kill Luc. Or do nothing and lose our already dwindling magic, along with my baby sister.

No matter what I do, this task will break me.

And none of that changes the fact that it has to be done.

CHAPTER EIGHTEEN

⁓⟡⁓

Alex and I pile into a white van with our arms filled with plastic garment bags. The show isn't for another couple of hours, but we have to get there early enough to set up. It'll start basically in the middle of the afternoon, which, according to Alex, is because the day rate at the venue is a lot cheaper than the evening one.

We stack the clothes on the floor and strap ourselves into the seats. As soon as our seat belts are on, the vehicle takes off.

Already, the dark circles under Alex's eyes look lighter. "How was the party yesterday?" she asks.

"All right. I made some oxtail, and macaroni pie, and black cake. Johan brought some doubles and pholourie from the restaurant. Mom and Auntie drank too much, and Dad had to drive us home." I don't mention that Johan basically told me there's no way around my task, and that Mom and Auntie's magic is weakening too.

"Bet everyone liked your food better than his."

"Maybe . . ."

"Maybe?"

"Okay, definitely." I got more than enough compliments through the night on Auntie Elaine's recipes and didn't hear a whisper about the Roti Roti fare. "Are the Davises coming to the show?"

Alex's lips press together. "You know them. They just had the party, and they're finishing off the mas costume headpieces and the float, and then they have that whole thing right before Caribana to get ready."

My stomach clenches like a roast suffocated by twine. "The rite."

"Yeah, that."

Every couple of years, a few days before Caribana, the Davises do a dark ritual. They shed the blood of a sacrifice, and in exchange, we stay safe during the carnival. Not just our families, or witches, but the entire community attending.

Parties, alcohol, and crowds aren't a great mix. Before, bad things happened. There used to be mobs of police waiting for an excuse to use force. Because, of course, we're the ones prone to violence who need controlling. Not anymore. For the price of one soul, we're all safe.

Every impure ritual must have a pure intent.

Like how for the price of Luc's life, my family can keep their magic and my baby sister can grow old.

I wring my hands in my lap and squeeze until my knuckles crack. "Emerald is only a few months younger than me. She's been helping in the rituals since she was twelve."

"Voya . . ."

"She can do hard things for a greater good."

"Granny would disagree. She would say if we came together as a community, we wouldn't need to resort to that for protection."

I steups. The sound slides through my teeth fast. "Since when have we ever done that? It's always the Davises. They're the ones who help people. They bring the community together. Their gifts get stronger every year while ours get weaker. My task isn't a pure one. Maybe the ancestors don't want that from us." Why couldn't this task have gone to one of the Davis kids?

Emerald would probably have no trouble carving up her match to save her family.

But in the same vein, I don't know if that's who I want to be. Someone who can murder without thinking twice.

Alex doesn't say anything, but she also doesn't voice disagreement. She spends more time with the Davises than even the twins do.

"I'm sure they'll come to the show," I say to cut through the silence.

Alex forces a thin smile. "Johan never does anything that doesn't benefit Johan."

"He's our teacher, and he's always answered my questions without asking for anything." He hasn't answered the way I want, and he doesn't answer every question, but technically, he does help for free.

"That's the thing—he never asks, but in the end, you wind up paying for his help."

The fashion show space is a block away from Spadina Avenue and King Street West. It's already hot, and being downtown makes it twice as scorching. The heated sewage smell that sticks to the inner city doesn't help either.

Alex is sweating when we step out of the van with the garment bags. "Hack me, it's hot."

"It's almost August."

"I don't care, there's sweat under my boobs, I'm unhappy."

"Understandable."

The place where the fashion show is hosted is a nondescript brick building that spans about four units across and three floors up, marked only by a glowing "461" holo. Lauren's face is pasted on the lamppost in front of it. Her presence is inescapable. Every poster is a reminder that my friend is gone and may not be coming back.

Alex leads the way up the steps into a cramped lobby with three doors. She pushes on the one marked with a hashtag symbol and walks into a huge open space.

The brick on the wall is exposed along with the beams and pipes on the towering ceiling. They've set up a long, raised platform in the middle that's flanked by gray fabric-covered chairs.

"This is amazing," I breathe.

Alex beams. "Right?"

We make our way to the start of the platform, where an indoor tent has been set up. Inside, it's beautiful chaos. People in various states of dress rush around while bright-colored outfits exchange hands. I spy a veil so long there are two people carrying it.

We find the rack with Alex's name to hang the clothes and help the models into the outfits to check the sizing. The clothes are different shades of purple, blue, and white in a galaxy theme. Her models run the gamut in body types, and they all look gorgeous.

"This is a fantastic collection." I turn to my cousin, who's staring at the models with shining eyes. "You put this all together, and it's going to look beautiful going down the runway."

"Thank you. For everything." Alex pulls me into a hug I melt into. Even when I was little, being close to her always helped me feel calm. Keis and Keisha are more like friends than cousins. Alex is like my big sister.

"I'm happy I could help you," I murmur into her shoulder before pulling away. "Go get changed, because people are coming in, and Keis sent me a message that they're here."

As Alex skitters away to change out of the T-shirt and sweatpants she wore over, I duck out of the tent and search around the room for the family.

Dad, Priya, and Eden are in their seats next to Granny and Uncle. I make my way over to them. "Where is everyone?"

Granny steupses. "You know your mom and aunt never miss an open bar."

"It's twelve p.m. What alcohol could they be serving?"

"Mimosas, apparently."

I search for the bar across the way, and sure enough, Mom and Auntie are in line trying to get one of the orange juice and sparkling champagne drinks. Keis and Keisha are there too. Keisha probably to see if she can also sneak one, and Keis to make sure they don't overdo it.

"I don't know how I raised two lushes like that," Granny grumbles.

She must have blocked out her vodka energy drink days. That or she's bitter her doctor says she can't drink anymore—too much strain on an already damaged liver courtesy of the aforementioned vodka energy drinks. I turn my head around the room. "No Davises?"

"Not a single one of them. That girl kills herself doing their mas costumes and her collection at the same time, and they can't even show their faces. She's lucky she has real family like you to help her out."

"They might come." For Alex's sake, I hope they do. I know them coming is important to her. "Did you have lunch? I left party leftovers in the fridge."

"We ate them." Granny waves her hand at Dad and Priya. "They ate something else."

"There was leftover vegetarian curry. You didn't like it?" I cross my arms over my chest.

Priya shakes her head. "It was great. We just wanted something light for lunch. We know you have a big dinner planned for after the show."

I realize that this is the first time I've talked to Priya in a while. It's like ever since my task was announced, we've been winding our way around each other. Though I haven't forgotten the promise I made her. And if the intensity in her eyes is any indication, neither has she.

I shift my gaze from her to Dad. "You never messaged me which one you liked better. Of the curries."

He clenches his fists in his lap. "You should make your own stuff. You always used to." He's not even pretending he doesn't know whose recipes I've been using.

"Always?" I snap. "Always since when?" He's only been back for six years. I've been cooking my own recipes since I was six. Since he left. Granny would bring me into the kitchen with her and teach me so I wouldn't just stay in my room and cry. Keis would sit on top of the island and watch us.

They were there, and he was gone.

"Whoa, superbad vibe over here. Maximum discomfort." Clearly Keisha's gift hasn't dulled to the point of missing obvious signals.

Keis, Auntie, and Mom come over behind her, the latter two with champagne flutes.

"Let's go see Alex." I lead the way to the white tent with the twins trailing after me.

We duck into the area and sneak over to Alex's section. Her sparkling violet-lined eyes meet mine, and she beams. Her excitement surrounds her in a halo and sails across the room.

She has a sheer black tank top tucked into a high-waisted skirt weaved with silver and violet thread that looks hand-stitched and, knowing Alex, probably is. Over her shoulders lies a transparent amber cape that falls across her back and glitters in the lights.

"You look stunning! Like a queen," I gush. She glams up, but her outfits are for "out there" shock factor. This is the first time I've seen her look curated. Like she thought about every single aspect of her clothes.

"And those heels." Keisha eyes our cousin's feet.

"You like?" Alex holds out a pointed toe to show off the bedazzled stilettos on her feet.

Keisha grins. "I do."

"When does your stuff come out?" Keis asks, looking around the space.

"I'm the closer for the show." The pride is obvious in Alex's voice. "I want people to see themselves. You know? See how beautiful they can be, no matter what."

"They will." Keis watches a few models decked out in shimmering red. "It's unreal that you did this. It got pushed up a month earlier, right?"

"Yeah. At first, I freaked out, but now I'm kind of grateful." She gazes around the tent with a grim smile. "This may be the last time my clothes ever look like this."

"What are you talking about?"

Alex's eyes cut to me, and the guilt in them hits me like a splash of oil from a pan. "I don't mean . . . Hack it, I shouldn't have said anything, it's fine."

"In case I fail, and you lose your gift." I try to focus on a model in the corner getting fastened into a corset. I believe in Alex's skill, in her collection, and I spent this time helping her because of that. And yet . . . she doesn't feel the same way about me. Her magic is running out the longer I take.

Keis grimaces. "You shouldn't worry about that." I don't know if she's talking to me or Alex.

"If you need your gift to make good clothes, maybe you need to get sparked and wake up." Keisha bristles.

The guilt slips from Alex's face and gives way to fury. "Excuse me?"

I tangle my hands into a knot. "You two . . ."

Keisha's voice cuts across mine. "If you need to rely on powers to fuel your talent, you need to face the fact that you don't have any."

Alex's chest swells, and her eyes narrow. "My gift is an extension of my natural ability. It's worth something." She gives Keisha a once-over. "What does yours do? If you're looking for the one born without talent, try a mirror."

"Both of you, shut up," Keis snaps. "Did you forget about Eden?"

Guilt even harsher than before rips across Alex's face. "I know."

"I'm not going to let Eden die," I whisper.

"I know! I just . . ." Alex shakes her head and spins away from us, cape billowing, and rushes farther into the canopy.

I'm sinking into the ground and dragging everyone with me, like a whirlpool that can only destroy and drown.

"Was that necessary?" Keis barks at Keisha.

Keisha's face is contorted with her rage. "When Alex wants to suggest that Voya not killing someone sucks for her? When she wants to conveniently forget that this is about Eden's life and not her hacking gift? Yeah, it's necessary." She jerks her eyes to me. "This is what you chose, Vo."

I keep my eyes on the ground. What am I supposed to say to that?

"There's more to it than that, and keep your voice down," Keis hisses.

"Is there? When Voya came to ask what you thought she should do, you had a big talk about loving magic, and our ancestry, and how she should 'try' and all that shit. Now Eden might die. This is on all of you for pushing that."

"I made my own decision," I say.

Keisha laughs. "That's cute, Vo, that you think you have that sort of autonomy." She glares at her sister. "Everyone acts like magic is a gift. It isn't. It's a curse that lets us pretend we're a connected and functional family when we're actually splitting at the seams." She doesn't wait for us to respond before she stomps away.

I accepted the task because I wanted Eden to have a chance at magic. For Thomases after us to keep that connection to our ancestors. *I* made that choice. Didn't I? I replay that day over in my head, trying to decide if I really was the one who made my decision, or if I let everyone else have so much input that they chose for me, just like I wanted.

I look at Keis for an answer. She's grinding her teeth and staring after her sister.

I nudge her with my elbow. "Let's get to our seats."

We go back to the rest of the family. Keisha is chatting with Auntie, a smile pasted on her face. Keisha must be pissed, but she's pretending everything is fine so she doesn't ruin Alex's show.

Keisha is crass and blunt. And yet she means well. She didn't say those things to spark our wires. She said it because she's worried.

The lights dim and an announcer launches into a spiel about the first designer and their collection. Later, we scream our faces off for Alex when her models grace the runway. We ignore the empty seats the Davises never fill, and no one asks whether Uncle Vacu will be coming. I know Auntie Elaine won't be, even if no one would ever mention her.

I work hard to suppress the sour taste in my mouth, and the voice in my head that wonders if Keisha is right. If magic is a patch that we're using to hide how broken we are.

CHAPTER NINETEEN

F or the entire show Dad sits stiffly in his chair and never
once looks over at me, no matter what glances I throw his
way. I have an aunt who should be here for her daughter's
show, and no one cares to discuss why she isn't. An aunt with as
much of a love for cooking as me and who was connected to someone in NuGene the same way I am. One that he knows about but
refuses to discuss.

I'm tired of being left in the dark about her.

As the show winds down, I shoot off a message to Luc: *I know
a way we can find out more about my aunt and Justin, but you need to
come to my house. Preferably now.*

He responds back immediately: *Address?*

I shoot off the information to him and stand from my chair.

Eden drags Dad and Priya to take a closer look at a model
decked out in slick black feathers that sparkle emerald in the
light. At the rate Mom and Auntie are going, Dad and Priya will be
stuck here to drive everyone home.

I have more than enough time to get back before them.

Keis must have read my thoughts because she says, "I'm
coming."

"You're not."

"Excuse me?"

"I need you to stay here and make sure they don't leave too early." I twist my hands around each other. "And the more time I can spend alone with Luc, the better. I have a task to complete. It's not easy to fall in love with someone when your family is hovering."

Keis crosses her arms. "Fine."

"Thank you!" I head for the exit, where Keisha is swiping through her phone. From the intensity in her eyes, I assume she's setting up a date.

"Where are you going?" she says.

I resist a groan. "Home."

"Why?"

"To get started on dinner."

"Liar. You made everything last night—you just need to heat it up."

Why is everyone in this family so nosy? "I'm going to meet Luc so he can help me find out more about Auntie Elaine."

"Is that it?"

"It's Luc, aka my match, aka the victim of my task. So, no. That's not *it*."

Keisha bobs her head and returns to tapping on her phone, though her lips press together so hard it looks painful.

"Are you done?"

"I've already expressed my opinion a thousand times. Whatever. It's not like we can go back in time and make a better choice. We have to save Eden. Doesn't mean that I have to like it."

"I don't like it either," I snap back, but under my breath so I don't have to argue or get poked with one of her pointy nails.

"Hey, come look at this," Keisha says, her voice softer now. She waves me closer to her.

Tentatively, I take the few steps over, and she shows me her phone. It's her dating feed, which is basically her normal feed plus a bit more information, like how she's looking to date girls. Now there's another word listed: "demiromantic."

"I figured that was as upfront as I could be about not being the sort of person who will know if I like them or not in a week," she says. "I didn't want to be that direct before. But sometimes something comes out of my sister's mouth that isn't complete spam."

"She has her moments," I say with a smile. "That's great, Keisha. Honestly."

She tries to shrug it off, but her chest puffs out and her lips widen into something closer to a smile. "Maybe that won't always be the right word for me, but it's what fits right now." Keisha nudges me. "I know what's right for me. And I'm sure you know what's right for you, no matter what I think. Go do your thing."

It's not quite approval, but it's acceptance. Keisha, like her mom, doesn't always have the most delicate way of saying things, but she always means well. Her being sparked about this is only because she cares, I know that.

"I'll see you later," I say.

I take one last look at my family and find Priya staring back at me, her hold tight on Eden's hand. Her gaze is intense and searching. I swallow and give her a little nod.

I'm working on it.

I step out of the building and make my way home. I'm doing this for the future of the family, and that's good enough for me. Like Keisha said, we can't go back in time and change it.

By the time I make it home, Luc is already there, sitting on the front step of our two-story plantation-style house, looking out of place on our block. But he looks at home among the pristine white columns and shuttered windows, illuminated by the porch lights. "Your neighborhood is a case study in poor city planning."

"Wow. You excel at being an asshole, did you know that? I'm

sorry it's not identical condos or lofts or wherever it is you live."

"Condos." He stands and brushes off the back of his pants. "I'm not saying it looks bad. Your house has a great historical feel to it. It's just a shame it's surrounded by this chaos."

I walk past him to open the door and walk inside. If only he knew how historic this house really is. "We can go to my room."

He shuts the front door behind him. "Doesn't your mom care about you having a boy alone in there?"

My foot freezes on the step going upstairs, and I jerk my head back. In ordinary circumstances, she would, but in this situation, she might prefer it. Especially after what she said at the party yesterday. She wants this task done and dusted. Either way, I hadn't actually considered the implications of being alone in my bedroom with a boy that I kind-of-sort-of like.

I swallow.

Luc does his little smile, a tug and bite on the lips, misinterpreting my discomfort. "You didn't think about that, did you?"

I take my foot back off the step. My face heats, and I rub at it roughly. "Let's do this in the kitchen instead."

We enter the kitchen, where my tablet is sitting on the island from last night when I was trying out some of Auntie Elaine's recipes. I turn on the oven and toss in dinner to heat up. With the amount of times I'll have to turn the thing back on, it'll be ready by the time everyone gets home.

"This situation could have been avoided by doing this somewhere other than your house," Luc drawls.

"Can't. The almanac is on a local server. We can't access it outside the house."

"Almanac?"

"Our family records. We're into history and keeping track of everything."

"And you keep it on a secure local server, which I'm assuming has strong enough security that you need me to hack into it? And I'm also assuming this is the server your aunt's sequence data was sent to?" Luc stares down at the tablet in my hands. "What sort of family history needs that much protecting?"

The magical kind.

I ignore his question, pull up Auntie Elaine's file, and hand the tablet over. "Here."

Luc stretches out his fingers and gets to work on it, pulling up options I didn't know were available. "Someone's tried to access this remotely before."

"The almanac?" That doesn't shock me. I'm sure there are a few people in the community who would want a peek at our secrets. It's mostly tips about how to shape your intention to get better effects with casts but also includes recipes for our beauty products, minus whatever special thing Granny adds to them. Still, they could be valuable to witches from less powerful families.

"Yeah. They tried to send some files over too."

"Do you know who it is?"

"I'm checking the IP address and seeing if I can get a location. Here it is." Luc's fingers go still on the tablet.

I come up behind him and lean over his shoulder. "What?"

"Personal space."

"Get over yourself. What did you find?" Though I do take a step back.

"It's a NuGene satellite office near Yorkville. A private space only Justin and the Tremblays use."

My stomach clenches. "That means Justin was the one trying to send these mystery files?"

"It's so sloppy. I don't know what sort of state he would have been in to take a risk like that." He makes a few more taps on the tablet. "It was around eleven years ago when he made that attempt."

"Okay, did anything happen to him around that time?"

Luc frowns. "Justin made the breakthrough with genetic modification, but that's probably a coincidence." His fingers flick across the tablet screen, and his eyes narrow.

I get as close as I can without violating Luc's personal space.

"It's fine," he says. "You can get closer. I was joking."

"*You* make *jokes*?"

"Sometimes!" he snaps. "Whatever, just look."

I immediately shuffle up so close that I'm basically breathing on his neck. Over his shoulder, a few sequences are pulled up with the plain black dashes that mark our genes. Ava Thomas, William James, Ama Thomas . . . The genetic sequences of everyone in the family. "I don't get it. He wanted our gene data?" If Justin and Auntie Elaine were working together, wouldn't he already have that?

"I assume he wanted the data. It's not in our NuGene files." I can't blame Luc for not knowing any better. He's shared so much with me, but there's no way to explain how I know they were working together and what they were working on without exposing our magic.

"What about the files he tried to send over?"

Luc does some more tapping and frowns at the screen. "I don't get it."

"What?"

"It's the exact same files. Same file names and everything. Why would he be sending files he already knew were there? Or why would he try and access them if he already had them?" Luc shakes his head, then pulls up the two files with Mom's name and scans the code. "Wait . . . They're not the same. Most of the genes are, but there are a few here in Justin's file that are . . ."

"That are . . . ?"

"Let me check the others." Luc goes through each set of files, opening and closing them. "These changes in the code . . . It's

261

shifting the genes to show predispositions for things like tendencies toward extreme violence."

I jerk away from Luc. "I think I would know if my family had those predispositions."

"Not all predispositions end up being expressed."

"I know," I snap. "But that's wrong. Data we keep in the almanac should be originals."

"And where did your family originally get their genome sequenced?"

I bite my lip. We've never had money for full sequencing like that. Justin must have been the one to do it, but he wouldn't have had almanac access. Which means Auntie Elaine must have put the data in there. "Look at the time stamps. Metadata is locked on genomes, right?"

"They are, but if Justin wanted to change them, he could. But let's see." Luc takes a moment to bring up the date for the two files, and it's there, plain as day. The original files in the almanac were created months before, but the files Justin tried to input were made the same day he was trying to send them.

Sloppy, just like Luc said. Whatever was driving him that day, he wasn't in a mental state to be careful.

Luc lets out a sharp breath and stares at the screen.

"Just so we're on the same page," I say, voice low. "The original DNA sequences of my family are stored in the almanac. Eleven years ago, Justin tried to remotely send exact copies of the files, but with the data changed to show, let's say, unwanted genetic predispositions. I assume that he wanted to access the almanac so he could overwrite the original correct files with these fake ones. Meaning that if he succeeded, which he didn't, the only DNA files of the adults in my family in existence would be the fake ones that mark them as potential violent criminals."

Luc shakes his head again. "Yes. That's what it looks like. I just don't understand why Justin would be doing this at all."

The sort of predispositions Luc is talking about would have ruined us. Underlying genetics don't mean they'll become actions, but it would have brought scrutiny down on us from Child Protective Services. Maybe they would be fair. Maybe everything would be okay. But no matter how many people stand and raise their fists in the air with us, there are still people in the system whose prejudice against the color of our skin is too ingrained to give us a fair chance.

Our family would be subjected to constant welfare checks, paying money we don't have for lawyers, maybe even us kids getting taken away for good. Everything amplified by the threat of a predisposition, because that discrimination exists whether people like to admit it or not. Clients would decline to work with or buy from us, cash flow would stop then if the lawyer fees didn't already get us, and creditors would snatch the house as payment within the month.

We never had the money to be sequenced in the first place, much less resequenced to prove innocence. If Justin had succeeded in overwriting the files, we would have had nothing to fight back.

Auntie Elaine needed to protect us from him. This is as good a reason as any. But there's no way Justin would have stopped at not being able to get into the almanac. He would have gone further if he was this desperate. How she managed to make Justin back off is an unknown. Along with why us kids forgot her, and how and why she died.

And the final unknown, like Luc said—why would Justin do that in the first place? It doesn't make sense.

Luc's eyes flicker across the screen, already searching for more, probably as desperate to understand why his sponsor would do this as I am. "I've got video here. Hold on." Luc taps play on a single video file, and we both lean in to watch.

On-screen is a woman who, from her short, curled black hair and dark brown skin, is Auntie Elaine. Her eyes are puffy and strained with wrinkles at the corners too pronounced for someone as young as her. She stares blankly into the camera for the first couple of minutes.

Then, she speaks. "Sometimes, people don't end up being who you thought they were." She wrings her hands. The gesture reminds me too much of my anxious finger wringing. "Maybe that's obvious." The corner of her lip jerks up into a little smile before falling flat.

The video cuts out.

Luc breathes out a sigh and goes back to searching through the tablet. "That wasn't helpful."

I'm not so quick to dismiss it. "What was the date on the video?"

"January 9, 2038."

"And what date were those genetic records sent? The ones Justin tried to put in?"

His fingers flick across the screen, and after a pause, he looks back over his shoulder at me, lips twisted into a grimace. "January 9, 2038."

Justin. That's when he became a person who she didn't think he was, when he tried to mess with our family's genetic records. My stomach clenches. The way she spoke about him, and the expression on her face . . . They weren't just two people working together. It was more than that. It's hard to describe the signs of people in love, but you know it when you see it.

"Justin's dad died that day too," Luc says.

"What?"

"He was in palliative care at Bridgepoint Health Rehabilitation Center. Cancer. Every year Justin takes the day off and disappears."

I sit up straight. "My aunt was a nurse. If that was the hospital she worked at, maybe that's how they met. Were you able to find anything about that?"

"No, or I would have messaged you."

I collapse onto a stool. "That photo we saw of them in the hospital, whichever one it was, maybe they were working together?" The words tumble out of my mouth, and I'm glad I can tell Luc some of what I know without mentioning magic.

"Working on what?"

"I don't know yet," I lie. "Can you find what day she died?"

Luc moves his fingers across the tablet.

I follow with my eyes. It says Auntie Elaine was found stabbed to death in an alley somewhere in Richmond Hill, an hour north of downtown Toronto. I search the screen until I find the date.

January 9, 2038.

That's the day Justin tried to corrupt the family's genes. The day his dad died. The day Auntie Elaine made that video. And, apparently, the day Auntie Elaine was murdered.

I swallow. "You said eleven years ago, Justin discovered genetic modification?"

"Yeah." Luc rubs his hands over his face and sighs. "He built the first machine from scratch. Didn't even have a manufacturer." His voice perks up, suddenly enthusiastic. "They used to have it in the Ontario Science Center on display. He keeps it in his office now along with the first NuSap prototype."

"Your fanboy is fully on display right now."

I get a glare for that.

"I'm surprised he keeps the first NuSap unit—doesn't that remind him of how it went wrong?" Those first units were so basic, like giant expensive versions of the small home units that could turn your house lights on and off. Mostly for rich people with money to burn and lonely people who took out large loans for their robotic companions, desperate for the company.

Luc's eyes are trained on the tablet. "That's why he keeps it. Justin is the sort of man who likes to be reminded of his failures."

I can picture it. Justin staring at the blue-skinned NuSap prototype, fixating on that one failure, ignoring the fact that he's the CEO of a billion-dollar mega power. "And when did Justin make this miraculous discovery?"

Luc's enthusiasm wanes, and his voice gets quiet. "January 8, 2038." He turns to me over his shoulder. "You think they discovered genetic modification together the day before she . . . ?"

The day before everything went sour.

Justin needed Auntie Elaine for something, and she needed him. Together, they were supposed to solve the issue of our genetic anomaly. Maybe they were supposed to be able to help Justin's dad, too.

Instead, Justin made the most important discovery of the century, and then his dad died and my aunt was stabbed to death and dumped in an alley.

I roll my hands into fists. I'm positive now that Justin didn't invent genetic modification on his own.

From January 8 to January 9, something changed.

One day. That's all it took for my smiling, happy aunt to go from helping to discover one of the world's biggest scientific feats to being dead on the street.

It must have been his dad's death that triggered the change, but why would that make Justin go after Auntie Elaine and the family? What was it about their deal to help each other that went wrong?

The door to the kitchen bangs open, and I jump almost fully off the stool. Granny walks into the room and raises an eyebrow at the two of us.

My eyes shift to the tablet, but Luc has cleared everything off the screen.

266

Granny smiles the sort of smile that makes my toes curl. A smile that conveys the opposite of what one should.

I gulp and gesture wildly at Luc. "This is Luc. He works at NuGene as an intern. We were genetically matched."

He's also the boy who I need to murder in cold blood if we want to keep our magic. You might also remember his sponsor father, Justin, who my aunt was somehow helping to make a huge genetic discovery. Who also genetically blackmailed the family and maybe murdered her. You know Auntie Elaine, right? The one none of you will talk about?

"Hello, Luc," she says. "Why don't you two go take a walk or something outside?"

Luc doesn't need to have grown up with my grandma to pick up on the fact that she isn't making a suggestion but a demand. Granny should be thrilled that Luc and I are spending time together. That means I'm doing my task.

But that doesn't mean that she wants to watch it happen. She doesn't want him in her house, near her, visible and present when she's hoping I'll kill him. Like watching the purity that she worked so hard for crumbling in front of her eyes.

She wants me to do that with him away from here.

A flash of irritation goes through me, and I bite down on my lip so I don't say something that I'll regret. I don't even know what the words would be. Only that they would be rude and cutting.

Luc slides off the stool and gives my grandma an insincere smile of his own. "Yes, ma'am."

Granny smiles wider. "Good."

CHAPTER TWENTY

The Thomases aren't a quiet family. Not normally anyway. But the house is silent as I walk with Luc out of the
kitchen, into an empty foyer, and out onto the front steps.
He ruffles his hair and flicks through his phone. The summer air
is soft and warm. There's fading light in the sky and joggers in the
street. It smells like that undefinable sharp and sweet scent of the
season that fills your nostrils and activates allergies in more than
a few people.

"I ordered a ride," Luc says, digging his hands into his
pockets.

So much for that walk Granny told us to take. But I get it.
Today has been a lot. Or maybe he just took her words more as a
complete dismissal than the specific "get out of my house" that it
was. "Container?" I ask.

"What?"

"Did you bring my container?"

He looks away from me. "Sorry, forgot."

I'm about to tell him he may as well keep it at this point when
the front door opens and Alex and Keis step out. My older cousin
is still decked out in her beautiful fashion show outfit, and her
eyes dart over my face and away. Keis shrugs at me.

"What?" I ask.

Alex lets out a breath. "Thought I would come say hi to your match."

I want to shout "Why?" at her. Why would she want to come see the boy I would have to kill for her to keep her gift, to keep Eden alive? I thrust an arm out at him. "This is Luc."

Luc does a little wave before helplessly looking at me, clearly not sure what to make of it all.

"Keis, you've already met. This is Alex, another one of my cousins."

"Ah yes," he says to Keis, "you left that lovely comment for me."

In typical Keis fashion, she doesn't look the least bit embarrassed about being called out for her poor rating. "I stand by it."

"I admire the conviction." He nods to Alex. "Nice to meet you."

"Can I ask something kind of personal?" Alex says. She plays with the fabric of her amber cape as she looks at Luc. My entire body tenses. What is she going to ask him? "I just figured I wasn't ever going to get a chance to ask a real person. I've messaged and gotten copy-and-paste statements, which isn't the same. You're here in the flesh, so why not?"

Luc digs his hands farther into his pockets. "You can ask if you like. I can't promise I'll answer."

Alex twiddles her fingers. "Is NuGene ever going to update the genetic ID-ing convention? It's a government system, but it's you all that set the options. Every time I need to use my ID, I have to see a Y gene pop up and label me something that I'm not."

I remember my cousin mentioning this before. When she was talking with Granny about gene options for transitioning. Getting your knockout/knock-in just affects the special gene that triggers those changes in the body, but it doesn't change your sex chromosomes. They tried that, but it was too unstable. The most you can do is have your gene updated in the system. Something only NuGene can authorize.

Alex continues, "It's not like back in the day. I'm not afraid to be trans and in the world. I feel safe to be myself. People fought for that. But I'm at dinner with my friends, and I go to pay, and my ID comes up with that Y, and the server just looks at me with this little shocked face, and it's just . . ."

". . . Humiliating," Luc says. He's ramrod stiff beside me.

"Yeah," she says. "Being misgendered and outed constantly to people I don't know, even if I'm safe . . . I figure, in your unique position, you might know about the progress of that."

In his unique position. I'm not sure if she's talking about the fact that Luc is Justin's sponsor child, that he's an intern at NuGene, or that he's trans. It might be all three.

I open my mouth, planning to tell him he doesn't need to answer, then close it. This isn't a conversation I should be in. Luc has never had a problem shutting people down. If he's not comfortable, he'll say so.

My stomach clenches. I never knew that Alex was going through any of that. Didn't think twice about it when we went out to eat and she treated me. My cheeks burn. Never once had I considered that things outside our family and home maybe weren't so simple, nor did I think about how she felt about those things.

"It's not ideal." Luc pauses and considers the words. "No, it's hacked." He shakes his head. "People shouldn't have to be misgendered, outed, humiliated, and exposed like that. I've said something about it, believe me. The issue is political. The board of directors at NuGene are reluctant to push options like concealing sex chromosomes because it means they're taking a stance. If they leave things as they are, NuGene can pretend they're just sticking to scientific fact. And Justin . . . He's attached to the science. He doesn't understand why it matters so much." Luc jerks his shoulder in something like a shrug.

Alex pushes a breath out. "I figured it was something like that. Now I know for sure."

I expect Luc to look uncomfortable, but he doesn't. He looks blank. Spitting out a truth I suspect he's known for a long time.

We're silent for a moment after that, each of us sort of shuffling in place, not sure what else to say. Why is Luc's car taking so long to come? I look to Keis for some way out of the awkwardness. She's staring at Luc with more concentration than I'm comfortable with. A small sheen of sweat glistens on her forehead.

Are you reading his mind? Stop! Right now!

She snaps out of concentration and makes a face at me like *Why not?*

It's hard enough trying to fall in love with someone you have to murder. Things can only get more complicated by Keis digging in his head. And it's overly invasive.

She rolls her eyes but relaxes. Alex may have come out here with some sincerity, but clearly my other cousin just came to prod around in my match's mind.

"We'll see you inside," Keis says with zero acknowledgment of my thought.

"Thanks," Alex says, her eyes moving between Luc and me. "I think I understand things a bit better now. I thought I got it, but I really didn't." For a moment, I thought she was talking about NuGene and the misgendering, but she looks at me as she says it. She turns away and waves at Luc. "Not as much of an asshole as Keis made you out to be."

"Thank you?" Luc replies.

My cousins disappear into the house, and I let out a breath. "Hack me, this car is taking forever to come."

Luc clears his throat and points at my wrist. "I couldn't find anything out about that flashing."

"What?"

He points to the monitor on my wrist. "It seems to flash intermittently for some of the users. But I've never seen yours do it. I asked around about it but got nothing."

"Justin didn't tell you anything?"

"No, as usual," Luc huffs. "The monitors are actually his project. We're just using them in the matching program."

I frown at the monitor sitting on my wrist. It's not tracking the same NT sequence that marks magic, but it's weird to know it's flashing without explanation. I shake my head. There's enough going on between the task and now Auntie Elaine and Justin. "I'm gonna head inside if that's okay."

"Yup," Luc says, spinning on his heel toward the street and scrolling through his phone.

"Thanks again."

"It's nothing."

But it isn't nothing. He didn't have to come all the way down here to help me. However he is on the outside, Luc is actually a pretty nice person. He's now done me two favors with Auntie Elaine and didn't pull any corporate BS about Alex's question. He was honest.

I take one last look at him before I walk inside, pressing the door closed behind me and leaning against it with a sigh.

I'm about to head upstairs to my room when a mutter of voices from Auntie Maise's room stops me. With a quick look around the empty foyer, I tiptoe over to the door.

Granny's voice is barely audible. "She won't be able to kill that boy."

My blood feels like it's run out of my body. A Bleeding times one hundred.

"You think she's already in love with him?" Mom's voice sounds urgent.

"Dear Lord, Ama. Voya is a child that needs attention to feel wanted. Look at how she clung to Lauren after the girl gave her a bit of her time," Auntie drawls. "That's just children of divorce for you. *Someone* abandoned her, so I don't blame her for being clingy. But she'd fall in love with any boy who looked at her for ten seconds." The "someone" in her speech is clearly referring to Dad.

I wait for Mom to back me up. She doesn't.

I clench my hands into fists. I'm not like that. Sure, I've always wanted to be around my cousins, and Lauren was my first and only friend outside of them. I was excited to spend time with her and the Carters. Her family felt like an extension of my own. Back then, the entire community felt like my family. Is wanting to be near your family a crime? Since when does that make someone desperate for attention or clingy? And if I was really like that, I wouldn't be struggling to fall in love with Luc the way I am now.

Is that what the adults think of me? That I'm some sort of attention-starved baby? That Dad leaving broke me into something that can never be fixed?

"This boy is a plant. Justin is trying to wriggle his way back into this family." Uncle's trying to whisper. He's not good at it.

"Why?" Mom says. "He got what he wanted. He's a billionaire with a genetic modification process he wouldn't have without Elaine. He's not even supposed to remember any of us."

I frown. What does that mean? He isn't supposed to remember them? The ritual that took our memories must have done the same to Justin. That was how Auntie Elaine protected us, but that makes no sense. If she was the one who did the ritual, we wouldn't be pure anymore, and she wouldn't be dead. I don't get it.

"He'll always want more. That's the sort of person he is," Dad snarls. "I want to know why we're allowing Voya to be near him at all. Even with his memories gone, he's the same Justin. My sister made a sacrifice, and I don't intend to see it wasted."

Sister?! I thought Auntie Elaine was just some relative of Dad's, but it's closer than that. And the sacrifice he mentioned, whatever she did to protect us, must have cost her something.

Mom snaps, "I think you forfeited your right to allow or not allow Voya to do anything a long time ago. It won't be a problem once she completes her task. What Elaine did won't be wasted."

The idea of completing my task makes my hands and stomach clench in tandem.

If Justin had no memories of Auntie Elaine, he couldn't be mad about whatever happened and keep coming after us. And the sacrifice they're talking about, it can't be her purity, or we would all be impure. Even after eleven years, the impure scent wouldn't have faded completely, and one witch's purity affects her entire family. Unless they've cut ties with their leader like Granny's family did. Without a Matriarch, you're guaranteed weaker magic and gifts, not to mention you lose your direct connection to the ancestors, but they must have thought it was worth it to hold on to impure magic. I've heard that a few just pledged to a new Matriarch.

Moreover, why would Auntie Elaine make us kids forget her too? Or was that something Granny had April-Mae tack on? Because when it comes to impurity and Black witches, especially with the way Johan reacted to Auntie Elaine's name, the memory spell must have had something to do with the Davises.

"Completes her task?" Granny says, disbelief evident in her voice. "Voya is not a killer. You said as much yourself. I don't blame her. I raised you to stay away from that sort of impure trash. There are only a couple of weeks left. Maise can't even cast summoning spells! We need to start considering other options."

"We promised we weren't going to keep pretending there were alternatives or ways out of this," Priya's voice cuts in, sharp. "We said we were going to trust in Voya's ability to do this. She promised me that—"

"Voya is a child!" Granny roars, abandoning all attempts to be quiet. "She doesn't know what she can't do. And I'm telling you, she can't do this."

I stumble away from the door, shaking my head. My feet rush out of the house before my mind can catch up, and suddenly I'm racing down the front steps just as Luc is getting into his car.

He spots me as he opens the door. "Voya?"

"I'm glad your ride finally came," I choke out, and rush past him down the street with strides that are so fast I'm basically running.

I don't need to keep being disappointed by my family. I can't believe that I thought Alex was the only one worried about me failing. Somehow, I actually thought everyone else was on board with believing in me. All the doubt and denial in the beginning, I thought it was just because the task felt impossible, but maybe it was just that they never thought I was going to be able to do it. Everyone in that room thinks I'm more likely to let my little sister die.

I wasn't even good enough to become a witch the first time around.

Why would anyone expect me to succeed at this impossible task?

And if I look deep down inside, the last thing I want to do is pass. I don't want to kill anyone, and a tinier voice inside whispers that I especially don't want to murder Luc.

Voya, who can't choose at all, and Voya, who can never make the right choice.

Two halves of a coin worth nothing.

I don't stop until I reach the dock at Marie Curtis Park a couple blocks away, where I stand and look out at the water. It's eerie and quiet. Dusk is falling. I'm used to seeing seagulls and pigeons flapping along the edge.

I let out the sob I've been holding in, and tears fill my eyes.

"Did I miss something?" Luc murmurs.

I jump and spin around. "Why are you still here?"

He tucks his hands into his jeans pockets. "You seemed upset."

"I am! And you can go."

"You've spent how many days stalking me and saying how we should get to know each other because we're matches, and now you want me to go away?"

"You said you didn't want to be in a relationship."

"I didn't." His voice is barely above a whisper, and I blink away tears. "You're clearly upset about something." He shuffles his feet. "And how am I supposed to get you to raise my rating to a five if I don't help out?"

I snort out a watery laugh. "You don't care about your rating."

"I care about yours. Somehow." He comes closer. "The least I can do is keep you company at this shitty dock."

"It's a nice dock!"

"I meant that literally. It's covered in goose shit."

I don't need to look down to know what he means. Marie Curtis is notorious for having a large population of geese that do their business wherever they feel like.

When I wipe my tears away, my fingers are streaked with blood. This time, I'm not shocked by it, used to the visions that seem intent on haunting me as long as Luc is alive. I watch the red stains on my fingers with a detached interest.

Letting my arms fall to my sides, I turn back to the water. "I cried here when my parents split up." I laugh a little. "It was dramatic. My grandma came and sat with me. She said that every time you cry about something, and you think it's the worst thing you've ever been through, remember there's always something worse on the horizon." The blood on my hands increases until it's dripping off my fingers in great sloshes, splashing on the dock with enough force to splatter onto my sandaled feet.

Luc notices nothing. "That's a comforting message for a child."

"Our family motto is 'We suffer and we survive.' I think she meant there would always be something worse, but we would always get through it."

It's one thing for me to think I'll fail. I always mess up.

But I felt like everyone else thought I could do it, even if I didn't know if I could, and I was working hard to live up to their expectations. I thought Granny knew I could suffer and survive.

But maybe a better question is why I have to at all. Why our family motto and the strength of our gifts are so ingrained in pushing through pain, and why we can't seem to break the pattern.

Once upon a time, the whole community was my family. That dropped away, but I could always belong with my first family. People who believed in me when I didn't. Except they don't. Keisha was right. We're just as broken as everyone else.

How did I think I could hold the entire future of the family in my hands?

Auntie Elaine tried. She did her best to make a change, not just in our family but in the entire community.

And she still failed.

I look over at Luc. How could I ever use my hands to steal a life? These hands that bake and knead. Even as blood runs off them, it feels laughable. The idea of me carrying out my task is as unreal as the vision.

I don't know if I'm in love. I could be.

Being in love would mean I'm one step closer to completing my task, but it would also be a step back.

This boy who eats boxed mac and cheese and instant noodles. Who said he didn't want a relationship, but still came out here to check on me. Who was the only one willing to help me learn about my aunt.

"Thank you," I say.

"I benefitted from hacking into your aunt and Justin's thing too, you know? I was curious as well."

"That's not what I'm thanking you for."

"Oh." Luc tucks his hands deeper in his pockets. "Does that mean you'll raise my rating to a five-star?"

I bark out a laugh.

Hack me.

A fresh wave of tears leaks out, and Luc makes a panicked face. "Do you want a hug or something? Would that help?"

My eyes go wide. "You would hug me?"

"If it would make you feel better. But not for long. Five-second maximum. I'll count."

"You don't seem like a hugs person."

"I can be. I'm just particular."

I step close to him, and the panic on his face gets even worse. "Do you actually want to hug me? You look very afraid."

"Okay, yeah, the hug is too much. How about you just lean against my side?"

I let out a tearful laugh and line myself up beside him. Slowly, I tilt my head until I'm leaning against his shoulder. It's bony and awkward, and if I stay there any longer, my neck is going to cramp up. He smells like he uses the same deodorant that Grandad used to. Spicy, like cloves and nutmeg. Which maybe should be creepy, but instead it's comforting. I stay there longer than I mean to, my neck awkwardly bent, spicy scent in my nose, and blood that Luc can't see leaking from my eyes and soaking into his shirt.

For one moment, I let myself forget about the task and its consequences and just lean there.

"Sorry I made you miss your car after it took so long to get there," I mumble.

Luc swallows, and it's so close to me, the sound is louder than it should be. "I hadn't called it yet."

"What?"

"When I said I called it, I hadn't."

"Why?"

He shrugs and my head bobs with the motion. "I don't know. I guess I wanted to stick around a little longer."

My entire body warms, and I have to bite my lip to stop the tremble there. When I finally speak, my voice comes out breathy and quiet. "You could have just asked."

"Yeah, I guess I could have. That would have been more normal." He lets out a soft laugh that makes his body tremble, and it rumbles through my head, leaving the insides fuzzy.

We stay like that for a few more moments until Luc's shoulder starts to stiffen, and I figure he's had enough contact. I lean away. I have to rotate my neck and massage it to work feeling back into it.

"Better?" Luc asks.

"Yeah." I'm not crying at least.

My task comes rushing back.

I have to kill this boy.

What did Auntie Elaine give up to protect us from a man who was more than an acquaintance? Who meant something to her? How did she gather the strength to do what needed to be done for the family?

I don't know. But there's one man who may. The only one in my family who might spill the beans that no one else will.

Because he has nothing left to lose.

And at this point, I need that sort of desperation on my side. And ancestors know, I'm tired of being fed lies by the rest of the adults.

I turn to Luc and let out a breath. "Can I borrow your hacking skills one more time?"

"What do you need?" There's a curious uptick to his eyebrows.

"To find someone."

CHAPTER TWENTY-ONE

U ncle Vacu couldn't stay sober, so he got kicked out of the men's rehab where he's lived on and off for the last few years.

This is an off time.

Luc got his information to me this morning. Uncle lives in one of those apartment buildings that spans more than fifty floors and is packed with low-income people. By law, the city needs to have at least five of these buildings in every neighborhood so that folks can't be completely pushed out like they used to be. But they're never maintained or taken care of like they should be. The front porch has tenants lounging with vaporizers, and there are fresh tags on the outside walls. Not the colorful graffiti in our neighborhood that was made by a hired artist, but black marks with explicit content. The chemical smell of paint floats in the air as I approach the call board.

I was eleven the last time I saw my uncle by blood—Granny's son, and Mom and Auntie's brother. He burst through the back door with a garbage bag, collecting ancestral silverware Granny had in the basement and claiming he had a right to it. I was home alone because I was sick and everyone except Mom had gone to the International Market. Mom had stepped out quick to grab more medicine for me. When I tried to stop Uncle Vacu, he shoved me to the ground and ran out. My already-ill body made the pain of it three times as bad. I sat there and cried until Mom came back.

I thought he would have gone far away after that. Instead, he's been living in Etobicoke, forty minutes away from us.

Sliding into the small glass space before the lobby and ignoring the tenants who look me up and down, I check the call board. Uncle's real name isn't listed. Instead, I recognize Grandad's name, Lowell Harris, and tap out the code.

The call button sounds with a ding to let me know Uncle Vacu hasn't picked up. Luc checked his phone location for me, so I know he's home.

I use the on-screen keyboard to send him a message: *It's Voya. Please let me in.*

It takes a couple of minutes of shuffling in place for me to realize he isn't going to answer my message.

This was a mistake. Uncle is unreliable at best. And who knows how he'll be if I go up.

But still. He's family. I want to think that no matter what he's done or how he is now, that must mean something to him.

I hit the call button again. The rings go on and on. I'm about to type out another message when the screen flickers and an image of my uncle appears.

The thing about Uncle Vacu is he's a functional addict. Desperate often. Mean, almost always, independent of his addiction. But hack me if he isn't put together. His hair is shaved close to his scalp, and his skin shines with evidence of regular moisturizing. Grandad's jaw is mirrored in his own, the strong and square shape of it. Even his eyebrows are trimmed and maintained in a way that Uncle Cathius has never been able to achieve and Dad has never attempted. His eyes are the same mahogany shade as Alex's, but his are flat and cold.

"You've found me. What do you want?" The familiar deep lull

of his voice is shocking. I thought it would sound different for some reason. "Did Mom send you to take back her silverware five years too late?" He smirks a little.

I grind my teeth together. "Can I come up?"

He ends the call. I'm left to stand there in silence for a solid thirty seconds before the door buzzes open. I note his apartment number on the call board and dart into the lobby.

The musk of an unmaintained area permeates the space. I shuffle over to the elevator and make my way to the thirty-sixth floor.

Fingers shaking, I send a message to Keis: *I came to see Uncle Vacu. He lives north of us—that giant purplish building near Islington Station.*

Why the hell are you over there?

The elevator dings, and I step out, sending her another message: *I know you don't care about this Auntie Elaine stuff, but I do. He was married to her.*

I'm trying not to encourage this distraction. And he's not exactly helpful even at the best of times.

I'll be fine. And if I'm not, now you know where to find me.

Keis doesn't answer. Which means she's either so frustrated she'll pretend I never sent her a message, or she'll come here to stop me. If she does the latter, she'll be too late anyway.

Door 3607 swings open as I come close to it. Uncle stands behind it with his arms crossed. "My magic is hacked. I can't even use spells to open the door."

"Sorry, my fault."

"I'm not surprised." He steps back into his apartment without waving me inside.

I invite myself in.

It's a bachelor unit that's sparse but tidy. There's a double bed shoved underneath the single window, and the kitchen has a breakfast bar with a single mug of coffee and one barstool. Not much more than that going on.

Uncle twirls his hand and takes a seat on his bed. "Sit where you like." The tone of his voice suggests he's aware there are not many seating options.

I decide to perch on the barstool. The coffee is fresh, and the scent of it is comforting.

"You failed your Calling, then? Is this some sort of extra punishment?" he asks.

"No!" My nostrils flare. "I'm still doing it. It's lasting longer than usual, and that's why the magic is waning." I decide he doesn't need to know that if I do fail, he'll lose magic for good.

Uncle jerks his chin down once with certainty. "Too much of your dad in you. He's always been lacking."

And you think you're an ideal father? I swallow the words, and he knows I'm holding an insult back. This is what he does. Pushes until you snap so he can snap back at you and unleash the frustration and anger bundled up inside that cool and collected exterior.

I take a breath to calm myself. "I want to know what Auntie Elaine was working on with Justin Tremblay."

Uncle's mouth twists into an ugly sneer. "What she was working on? Spreading her legs maybe?"

I flinch back from his words. "She's a Mama."

"And that means I owe her respect? Did she respect me?!" He doesn't move from the bed, but it feels like he's towering over me. "Was it respect when she got involved with a patient who wasn't hers and started some ridiculous project with his son?"

"Genetic modification," I say, not touching the subject of Auntie's questioned fidelity.

"She wanted to heal the world. In reality, she'd force a gene, and sure, she'd cure someone's mutation, pass it off as a misdiagnosis to hide the magic, but then she'd have to lie in bed the next few days recovering. Even then, she could only do simple stuff. Nothing as complicated as what Mom wanted. Elaine couldn't handle her gift. That rich boy wanted to copy the ability. And now he's making billions off it. And where is she? Where am I? Where is this entire family? She didn't do shit. But I guess any martyr can be a Mama." When he finishes, his fists are tight and shaking. His face is a mix of fury and something like relief.

After being isolated from a family that wouldn't talk about his dead wife, this must have built up. Like he's been waiting a long time for someone like me so he could finally say his piece.

And this means that genetic modification wasn't just something Auntie Elaine helped with. It was her gift. That's why Justin needed her. But she couldn't do anything complicated on her own, which was why she needed him. "She wasn't just *any* martyr; she was your wife," I whisper.

Uncle Vacu says nothing in response.

I stand from the stool, not understanding what he's telling me. "I need to use your bathroom." Without waiting for permission, I shuffle into the tiny room and sit on the closed toilet lid.

I shouldn't have come here. Why did I think Uncle Vacu would be ready to reminisce when I knew there was something more going on between Auntie Elaine and Justin? We act like our ancestors are beyond criticism once they pass on, but that's not true for everyone. He's making it out like being murdered was something she asked for. That she wanted to be stabbed and dumped in an alley by getting involved with Justin in the first place.

Loud bangs on the door make me jump. "Are you touching my things? Get out of there!"

"I'm not touching anything!" What is he talking about? I leap from the seat and go to wash my hands. There's no soap. I wrench open the medicine cabinet and am greeted with the only untidy spot in the apartment. Dozens of needles are stacked on top of each other.

People say Mod-H addicts keep the old needles because sometimes the condensation that builds up makes it possible to reshoot the tiny bit at the bottom they can't get out of the needle.

The door flies open, and I yelp aloud. Uncle slams the medicine cabinet shut and yanks my arm toward him.

There's no more calm in his face. His eyes bulge, and the veins on his forehead and neck pop out enough to see his pulse throbbing there. His grip on my arm is suffocating.

I'm no longer sixteen and inside an apartment I came to of my own free will. I'm eleven and so sick that my head throbs and my throat burns. The taste of garlic and honey coats my tongue from the soothing tea Mom left me with. I'm alone in a huge house, and this man is going to hurt me.

Uncle's face crumples into an expression I've never seen on it. I'm too preoccupied with rubbing the tears off my face with my free hand and trying to hold in my sobs to decode it.

He lets go of my arm.

I press both palms to my eyes as I cry. The sounds coming from my body make my shoulders shake, and I can't stop it.

"I didn't—I wasn't trying to scare you. Just . . . don't touch my things." Uncle's deep voice is quiet in a way I haven't heard since I was little and he was sober.

"I wasn't touching anything!" I cry, shrill and wet. "I wanted to know about my aunt, and I thought you could help."

I pull my hands away from my eyes and watch Uncle curl his shoulders inward. "I wouldn't hurt you," he whispers. "I would never—"

A watery laugh pulls from my throat. My arm will be bruised. After he pushed me that day, there was a mark on my chest in the shape of his hand.

His expression changes, and Grandad's jaw trembles on his face. "I'm trying to get well. I get so sick, Voya. You don't know how sick I get."

"I want to go home." I try to step out of the room, but he blocks me. More tears pour from my eyes. "I'm *going*!"

"Okay." He steps out of the way, and I dash to the apartment door. "Wait!"

I shouldn't stop.

But I do.

It's the panic in his voice. The unhidden desperation that makes me halt. "How . . . How is Alex?"

I snap my neck, and the look I give him makes him turn away. Why should he get to hear about her? If that's a relationship he wants to rebuild, it's up to him to do it, not me. "I'm leaving."

"Wait! Is Alex okay? And how is your sister?"

I blink. Of all the things he could ask about, Eden is not something I was expecting.

He must know about her. How she's really a Thomas and is bound to the house and our magic. The question is, why is he bringing that up? I narrow my eyes.

"They didn't tell you," he says, probably reading my expression as confusion. His eyes flare wide, and a bit of calm returns to his face. "I can tell you, if you tell me how Alex is doing."

He wants me to barter information about the daughter he left for a secret that he knows could mean the life or death of my baby sister. A laugh bubbles out of my throat. I open the door and step into the hallway.

Uncle's hurried footsteps follow me. "Wait! I'm sorry."

"I'm leaving!" I stab the button for the elevator.

"She'll die if we all lose magic! Did they tell you that? Whatever is happening with your task and why our magic is getting weaker, if it stops, Eden will die."

"Oh, I know." I snarl at him, "And if you hadn't been high the night Eden was born, you could have saved her yourself. Her life wouldn't be in danger at all if you had just gotten your shit together!

But I'm glad you were willing to let me go without knowing any of that if I didn't tell you about the daughter that you *chose* to abandon."

I know it's unfair. I know that it's not easy to fight addiction. But I can't help the hateful words that spew from my mouth.

Nausea swirls in my stomach, and I slam my hand on the wall to steady myself. The elevator arrives, and I run into it. Uncle doesn't follow.

I stumble through the lobby on the ground floor and sprint down the steps, ignoring the confused stares of the tenants there.

Keis is waiting at the bottom with her backpack slung over her shoulders and her arms crossed. She strides over once she sees me. "What happen—"

"You were right. It was a bad idea to come."

My cousin blinks. "What?"

"Let's just go, okay."

"You're shaking."

I am. There's a fine tremble running through my body that I hadn't noticed until this moment.

What am I doing? Why did I ever think that learning about Auntie Elaine would magically connect these dots and that I would understand how I could get out of this task? She didn't have a happy ending. She didn't even seem to have a happy life. The excuse seems so flimsy now. I don't think I ever really thought knowing would help. I just wanted to think about something other than killing a boy with blue-gray hair.

"I don't know what I'm doing," I say to Keis.

She reaches out to me, and I don't have the strength to rebuff it. I don't have the energy to deny myself the comfort I'm being offered and desperately need.

And so I stand there and let my best friend hold me while I sob into her shirt.

CHAPTER TWENTY-TWO

We could have taken transit to go home, but I convinced Keis to walk at least to the highway before we hopped on one.

I wish I could go back to before I visited Uncle Vacu. No, back further than that. Before I overheard the adults in Auntie's room. Before Mama assigned this task, and further back than that, too. Before Lauren went missing. Before Auntie Elaine was murdered and forgotten. Before Dad left. To a time where all I can remember is feeling surrounded by love and family. Life was impenetrable and infinite. Everything felt like it was going to be perfect forever.

Until I learned better.

At least I know what Justin was getting out of his and Auntie Elaine's deal. He needed her genetic modification ability to come up with a scientific procedure for it. It won't help with my task, but I still want to know about her.

Maybe because we seem alike.

Or maybe because she tried to help and ended up sparking shit up instead. That could be me. Scrubbed from the history for a severe lapse in judgment. They'll say, "She should have never accepted that task," or, "She should have known she couldn't do it." Branded a failure. A note in the almanac that people could point to as the destroyer of our bloodline.

Except that can't be me because I can't let Eden die.

We reach the front steps of the house, and Keis pauses behind me.

"What?" I say, turning backward.

"I was in Luc's head last night before you got mad at me." She crosses her arms, decides better of it, and uncrosses them.

Her reading Luc's mind seems insignificant now. "Why were you in his head at all?"

"Everyone in the family is on edge about Justin. I figured I would check to see if he had any sketchy thoughts related to his sponsor dad."

I was worried about Luc being violated by having his mind read, and she was thinking about the family. The way I should have. This is why I would make a horrible Matriarch, and she would make a great one. After Auntie and Mom duke it out and finally decide which of them will wear the title, Keis could be next in line. How could I lead the family when I can't think of them first in every situation?

"So?" I press. "Was he?"

"No."

I want to feel relief. Anything other than the vacant hum of emptiness. "That's good."

"He was kicking himself for coming and being confused about why he bothered helping you. And then reminding himself that he came to find out about this mystery with Justin. But I can tell by his thoughts that he felt like it was a flimsy excuse." Keis shakes her head. "He rehearses everything he says about six different ways in his head before he says it and carries on an internal monologue at the same time. It made my head hurt."

"I'm not surprised. Everything comes out of his mouth so precise." Except for when we were in Marie Curtis. And at the NuGene tour. He slipped up. "Why is this important?"

"I think you make him flustered." Keis's eyes look darker from farther away. She stares at me as if I should understand something that I don't. "And maybe you get flustered by him."

I turn back to the door. "Let's go inside."

"There's less than two weeks left."

I don't respond. I push open the door and head for the kitchen because nothing comforts like food.

I rush in and skid to a stop. Everyone is standing around and chatting when they would usually be off in different areas of the house, doing their own thing.

Granny is seated at the island, where she cups a giant mug of tea between her hands. Eden is sitting beside her with a matching mug filled with a dark liquid that must be hot chocolate. The rest of the adults are drinking either tea or coffee, while my cousins forgo any drinks. Uncle is standing at the counter with his usual Honeycrisp apple that he's methodically peeling with a paring knife.

Everyone was chatting at such a low volume. I didn't notice they were in the kitchen. But now that I'm here, the conversation has cut to silence.

A simmering in my belly coils and burns until the heat spreads to my face and fingers. "Talking about me again? Having discussions about how I'm too fragile to do my task and will fall in love with any boy who will have me?" My voice strikes out hot, like popping grease in a pan. Everything that I shoved down from yesterday racing to the surface and mingling with today's self-loathing.

Mom's face flickers with horror—probably realizing that I overheard them last night—but recovers quickly. "You watch your tone!"

"Why? Should I pretend like you aren't talking behind my back?" I look around the room. There are shifts of discomfort as they realize what I've learned. The adults anyway. Keisha and Alex look confused. "As if you aren't trying to hide Auntie Elaine like a dirty secret."

Mom shakes her head. "No one knows who you're talking ab—"

"Stop lying! You want me to kill a boy in cold blood. Everyone is always talking about doing our best for the family. And yet you're trying to bury her memory like it's nothing. Is that what she was to you? *Nothing?*"

There's a massive smashing sound as Dad slams his mug on the kitchen island. It shatters, and the pieces scatter across the surface. Eden screams and bursts into tears.

"Really, Will?" Priya gathers her daughter in her arms and leaves the kitchen.

Dad stares at the shards of porcelain in his now-bleeding hand. He flexes it, willing the pieces to come back together, but they don't. "She wasn't *nothing*. She was my sister."

He looks at me, probably expecting surprise. I have none to give him. "Your sister. Uncle Vacu's wife. Alex's mom. Justin Tremblay's partner in the creation of genetic modification."

Only when I'm looking at Alex's stricken face does the reality of what I just revealed catch up with my brain.

Hack me.

I wasn't supposed to say that. I was supposed to tell Alex everything first. Privately. Not shove everything into the open like this and catch her completely off guard.

Keisha and Keis glare at me, and my cheeks burn. They kept their mouths shut like I asked, but I didn't hold up my end of the bargain.

Granny lets out a loud sigh. "Now we're into it."

"We agreed we wouldn't be talking about this with the children until they were old enough." Uncle's nostrils flare.

"Yes, well, Alex is nineteen. And Voya seems to know more

than enough already." Granny's eyes slide to me. "Don't you?"

I grind my teeth. "No thanks to you." I take a deep breath and turn to Alex. "I'm sorry. I should have told you first."

"Too late now," my cousin says, shaking her head. "I'm very interested to hear what Granny has to say about my mom, who she's always refused to discuss with me."

My eyes go wide and I turn to Granny. I didn't know Alex had ever asked about her mom. "I can't believe you," I say. "If I didn't mention anything, you would have pretended that she never existed."

Granny glares at me. "Don't you put this on me. That was Elaine's choice. She needed Tremblay to forget her, and she didn't want you kids to remember either."

The heat in my stomach extinguishes. "What?"

Alex stands still against the wall.

It never crossed my mind that Auntie Elaine was the one to decide we should forget.

Mom sits down beside Granny. "I can—"

"I'll handle it."

"But I'm her mom, I should—"

"I am the Matriarch."

Mom's mouth snaps shut.

Auntie Maise pulls up a stool and sinks into it. "Let's get into this, then."

"*Now* you're fine with us knowing?" Keis has kept quiet since we arrived. Without looking at her mom, she directs her question at Granny. Keisha and Alex shift their gaze to her too.

For the first time in my life, I watch Granny break eye contact. And it's not with Keis or Keisha.

It's with Alex.

The person who deserves the truth more than any of us. I was so caught up in my task and what learning about my aunt meant to *me* that I lost sight of the fact that this is Alex's mom. How different would my cousin's life look if her mom were alive? Every Mother's Day, she and Granny do something special together. But I always wondered if Alex ever felt sad about not getting to celebrate with her mom like the rest of us.

I can't imagine a life without my mom, but that's how my cousin lives every day.

"Elaine was afraid your lives would be tainted," Granny says. "That you would be scared to try to make change in this community because of her failure."

Dad snorts. "Her *failure*?"

"She said that boy would make the sort of technology that would change genetics for the better, but then he tried to hold our family hostage because he wanted more. Messing around with our genes to hold power over us. Saying he was going to make our lives 'difficult.'"

My lips twist into a frown. "But she didn't fail. They did create genetic modification. Justin just didn't use it the way you, April-Mae, and Lee thought he would. He didn't help you avoid weak gifts or the anomaly that was causing witches to be born without magic."

Granny's eyes flare wide for a second, and Uncle drops his apple, spluttering, "Who have you been talking to?"

"People who will actually tell me the truth!" And relying on Luc's hacking along with my intuition. "People who don't hide things from me, like the fact that our magic is weakening. We're meant to be a family. How are we supposed to stick together with these secrets piled up between us?"

Mom stands from her stool and takes a few steps toward me. "Voya—"

"I don't want to hear whatever excuses you have." I turn away from her, only to have my eyes catch on the doorway to the kitchen.

Luc is there, squatted down behind Eden. I search around them for a sign of Priya. She isn't there. My baby sister smiles at me with her mug of hot chocolate clutched in her little hands.

From behind his back, Luc pulls out a French chef's knife. The knife has notches in the plastic handle from being rested on a hot burner. I've held it in my hand more times than I can count.

He slides it in front of Eden's neck and stares at me with those eyes I've gotten so familiar with. Then, he pulls his smile, teeth biting lips, and moves to slash the knife across her throat.

I scream and grab the first thing I touch, throwing it at Luc's head with as much strength as I can.

It shatters with a thunderous crash, and brown liquid splashes over the wooden floor. There's no more Luc and no Eden.

Only silence and mug pieces sitting on spilled coffee.

My chest heaves, and I shove out a breath with a shudder. Something touches my shoulder, and I jerk away with another scream.

Mom flinches back from me.

I force my lips to move. "Why did Justin turn on Auntie Elaine?" If I focus on this, not what just happened, I can pretend it didn't happen at all. "It was something to do with his dad's death, wasn't it?"

Alex looks between Granny and me. "Wait, pause a minute so I can catch up. Justin? Like Justin Tremblay? That's the Tremblay that Uncle Will was talking about? What does he have to do with my mom?"

Granny tries to meet my eyes, but I won't let her, and she refuses to look at Alex, so she settles on the mug in her hands. "Yes, that Justin Tremblay. Elaine had a gift for manipulating genes, but she couldn't figure out how to use it to fix our issues. It was more complicated than fixing a single mutation like she was used to doing. Justin was supposed to help map how we could alter our genes to produce stronger gifts, avoid the anomaly that caused witches to be born without magic, and save our lineages. In exchange, he could study Elaine's gift and find a way to reproduce it using technology. But what he really wanted was to make this magic cocktail of genetic manipulation to create invulnerable humans. To save his father. But Elaine didn't realize that until much later."

I blink. That is not what I was expecting. "Invulnerable humans . . . Like immortality?"

Granny clenches her fingers.

"Isn't that good?" Keisha's eyes dart to my face, then away. "Who wouldn't want to live longer?"

Uncle steupses, but it's lacking its usual sting. "Did you not learn anything in that school with Johan?"

"The intention is off," Alex says. "People wishing for immortality don't have a pure intention, ever. It's always selfish. No one in our family would support something like that."

"And you can bet that not everyone would have access to it." Keis crosses her arms over her chest and steps closer to me. "Gene manipulation already costs a fortune. Could you imagine the price tag and gatekeeping on that sort of treatment? It would be a bunch of rich people living until five hundred and the rest of us struggling to reach eighty."

"Auntie Elaine didn't want to do it," I say to Granny. "She must have said no to him, and that's when he tried to mess with our genes. That's why Auntie needed him to forget her, because then he would forget us, forget *magic*." I shake my head. "You said she was worried we would be afraid to help the community, but look at us! It didn't matter that we forgot what happened. We've done nothing for our people anyway. Lauren is gone, and we haven't lifted a finger." And she may be gone forever. It's time I start admitting that to myself. The Carters actually have access to impurity and they still can't find her. Realistically, what more could I do? I bite my bottom lip to stop it from trembling.

"We are like this," Auntie Maise snipes, "*because* of what happened. The experiment failed, and Lee ended up kicked out with her magicless daughter. It was easy to pretend the girl just hadn't had her Calling yet while Elaine and Tremblay worked on a cure, but once she turned eighteen, the hacking week after Elaine's death, it got real obvious that it was never going to happen. April-Mae got paranoid about power, and her family moved from one kill every half decade to a ritual every two years. Which puts our community in even more danger, not that they care. The Carters really started to flirt with the idea of impurity even if they didn't actually switch until Rena's boy got sick. The Baileys were a mess after separating from the Huangs, who were always more powerful than them. And the Jameses, well, Elaine came from their stock, so they didn't come out shiny from it either.

"Not to mention we had a man who knew the genetic sequence for magic and could do ancestors know what with that information. We were *this close* to blowing our whole hacking world wide open! The Tremblays not only had immense power, but they had power over us. Meanwhile, we had to hustle to be taken in by other pure families to survive. There was a time when any Black witch family would have bought anything we put down. After this business, though, it was tainted. People were sparked to shit at us. You kids forgetting Elaine gave us a reason to pretend to forget her too, and everyone else did the same. I'm sorry, Alex, but that's the truth."

Auntie Maise has never been one for bedside manner. There it all is, written out plain as day. It's exactly what Rowen alluded to. What Auntie Elaine did to help make the Black witch community stronger was the same thing that broke it apart. They didn't trust us anymore. No one trusted anyone. And a year later, Dad left us. All that time he and Mom spent arguing that year, maybe it would have always happened, or maybe his sister dying made him wonder if we were a family worth staying with. I stare down at my feet and swallow.

Alex lets out a harsh breath. "Why hide my mom for this long? You wanted people to forget, and they did. Why keep it going?"

Dad clenches his hands into fists, outright glaring at Auntie Maise, whose take on his sister he likely didn't appreciate. "It's what she wanted."

My gaze snaps up. "Is it?" I fling my hand at the broken mug on the ground before gesturing at everyone. "Is *this* what she wanted the family to be?"

He doesn't answer.

Alex says, "I don't get it. She made Justin forget, but how did she die?"

Granny's face crumples. Outside of getting teary over feed dramas, I've seen her cry exactly once: when we burned Grandad's body for his funeral.

"She insisted on being the offering in the rite. Was adamant that no one else get hurt for her mistake." Granny puts her mug down on the counter with a clatter that only seems loud because everything is so silent.

I'd already known that an impure ritual would be the only thing with magic strong enough to erase our memories. And it would have been a ritual where shedding blood and torture wouldn't be enough. They would need a life.

But Auntie Elaine was a nurse. Her work with Justin was to help heal people, not hurt them. And if she had killed, we would have lost our claim to purity, but we haven't.

Dad said his sister made a sacrifice, and Uncle Vacu called her a martyr. I thought Justin had had her killed, even if he didn't do it himself.

But I was wrong. It was an impure ritual. Only, she would have never accepted any payment to protect us other than the exchange of her own life.

This is why Granny kept this secret.

Not to honor Auntie's wishes, but to keep Alex from this pain.

To protect us.

The way she always has.

Alex is the only one who speaks. "Who did the ritual?"

"I told him to keep you at arm's length." Granny shakes her head. "You could go to his school, and his yearly BBQ, but nothing more. Did he listen? No. He said, 'She keeps coming to me. What am I going to do? Ignore her?' And I said he should. But he didn't."

"*Him?*" I ask. The Davises would have been the ones to do this. They're family. Even if they didn't trust us, they would have helped. But I expected April-Mae would be the one to strike the blow. She was the Matriarch, after all. But she's not a "him."

It's clear now who Granny's talking about. This was why he refused to speak about Auntie Elaine.

From the watery expression in Alex's eyes as she looks at the adults in the room, I know she knows too. She has no memories of her mom. But she has lots of Johan. Has grown up as basically an honorary Davis. Never knowing that he was the one who killed her mom.

Tears spring to my eyes, and I swallow. "Alex—"

"Save it," Alex says, voice quiet but firm. "I'm not mad at you. I'm glad. You're the only one in this family who's never been afraid to look at the ugly bits of it." She lets out a sigh. "I went to meet Luc yesterday because, yeah, I wanted to ask about NuGene, but I also wanted to understand what this is like for you. Staring into the face of someone you're supposed to kill for this family."

My cousin looks around the room at us. "None of you want to know him. You want to turn away from the ugly things, and yet we're forcing Voya to look at them head-on. Just like you made

298

Mom pay to protect us on her own from someone you agreed to let in as a family. You *wanted* Voya to make this choice to save magic."

Keisha opens her mouth to rebut, and Alex silences her with a look. "*Most* of us wanted Voya to accept the task. To make sure we could have and keep magic. We all want to save Eden, no one's debating that. But you're letting Voya sacrifice herself *alone* the same way Mom did, and it's not fair."

Everyone shifts on the spot except for me. I can only stare at my cousin.

"Sometimes," she says, looking back at me, "I think you're the strongest person in this family, Voya. And the most hacked thing about it is that we have never supported you enough for you to feel that way about yourself."

There's something in Alex's face that matches the mug on the floor.

Shattered.

With that, she turns and leaves the room, her words still churning in my head. Keisha immediately follows after her. No matter what sort of fight they had, she's still always the first to comfort Alex. We're family, so we never fight for long.

But are we a family? Right now, we're just a group of scattered people in a kitchen.

Granny may have protected us from the pain of knowing Auntie Elaine, but at the price of keeping secrets. Alex missed the hurt of losing her mom and yet she was also robbed of the joy of remembering her.

Auntie Elaine put everything on the line for us. Even gave up being in our memories because she worried it might stop us from trying to improve this community. Not agreeing with it doesn't mean I can't respect it. I understand why she's a Mama.

But this is a hurt that even she couldn't heal.

A message from Luc flashes across my eyes: *Are you free for dinner on Wednesday? Justin wants to chat. He must suspect something. I know you don't owe me anything, but I need you to come and pretend you don't know what you do. I can't lose my sponsorship over this.*

I meet Keis's eyes. Her head turns slightly from side to side. *Don't. Not Now.*

I'm not a mind reader, but I know my cousin. It's like I can hear her voice saying, "Stay away from Justin Tremblay."

On the floor, the mug I threw isn't any less broken.

The image of Luc with a knife pressed to my baby sister's neck isn't any less prominent.

And that's the reason why I should do what I'm about to do. Because nothing about my task has changed. I still need to get to know Luc. To spend time with him. To fall in love with him.

Even if I'm throwing myself on the chopping block for the family while they watch.

I send Luc my reply: *When and where?*

CHAPTER TWENTY-THREE

I hop off the streetcar at Dundas Street West and Sumach Street at six p.m. in a banana-print dress that may or may not be appropriate for the occasion. At first it felt brave, wearing the dress from that first vision at Brown Bear. Now I can't stop thinking of the way the other me held that knife.

My purse is stuffed with a folded canvas bag that was recently filled with products I had to drop off for clients on the way. More than a few of them live here: the type of non-magic people who get extracurricular mods for smoother skin or better heart health, and at the same time are adamant about using non-modded beauty products because they're "living a natural life." In my hands is a tin of sweet bread because Granny raised me to bring gifts to dinners, even dinners with the person who ruined our family.

Apparently, a long time ago—we're talking early '00s—the name Regent Park used to make people curl their lips. It was considered a "bad" area, which Mom says meant it had a lot of poor minorities. Nothing makes people more nervous than brown-skinned folks without a lot of money.

Then people started buying out low-income apartment buildings, knocking them down, and building sky-high condos with price tags that even middle-class families balked at. That's why there are laws around every neighborhood needing at least five low-income buildings now, so they can't push people out. Growing up, I've always known this as a rich area filled with tech company geniuses and up-and-comers with money to blow. And about five blocks down, it's more of the same. Lower-income people in the mandatory buildings, but they're not the people who really need the housing. Even people who live in those buildings have half their money thrown in different accounts so they look like they have less than they do and can qualify for cheaper housing.

It's all illegal, of course, but people with money can find their way around anything.

I stop in front of the building. It's approved access only, but Luc must have put my name down for tonight, because the door clicks open when I hold my phone up to it. I flash a smile at the woman working at the front desk before stepping into the elevator.

Destination? The elevator chimes. I hold my phone up again, and it hums to life. The doors close, and it heads to whatever floor Luc lives on.

My foot tries to tap-dance, and I force myself to stop. How in the hell am I supposed to have dinner with the man who single-handedly destroyed a chunk of my family? He didn't put those knives into Auntie Elaine, but he may as well have.

If Justin is suspicious that Luc got into Auntie Elaine's files, does that mean he's remembered her? And what does that mean for us? As much as I'm here to help draw suspicion away from Luc, I also need to get some idea of what Justin is thinking. If he plans on coming after our family again, it'll be my fault. Luc only poked into this because I asked.

Auntie gave her life to protect us, and I may have hacked it to pieces.

No wonder no one in the family thinks I can do this task. That scene yesterday in the kitchen probably didn't inspire confidence either. What Alex said has been ringing through my head since she said it. I keep asking myself if she's right about the family treating me like her mom, making me a sacrifice. Maybe she is, but it doesn't change the fact that I need to do it for Eden.

Now I'm here. Less than two weeks to go, and I've somehow advanced to trying to protect Luc's sponsorship as if I'm not trying to take his *life*.

Hack me.

His eyes staring at me while he held the knife to Eden's neck are fresh in my mind. It may have been a vision, a dramatic version of the truth, but it doesn't make it less true.

If I don't kill Luc, my sparing him will be the reason Eden dies. I might as well be holding that knife myself.

The doors open, and I step out without thinking about it and find myself inside the condo and in front of the boy I was just thinking about.

He's got on a black sweater and matching ripped jeans whose pockets he's stuck his hands deep into like usual. "You're on time."

"You told me when to come." I force myself not to think of him murdering members of my family. Maybe that's why I'm not in love yet. Because I can't stop thinking about the task.

Luc bobs his head. "You were late for the NuGene Q&A."

"Seriously? I thought we were past this."

"Just wanted to see if you were still annoyed about it." He grips his lower lip in his teeth, and the corners of his mouth tug up a bit. Typical Luc smile.

The same smile he made as he went to cut my sister's throat. "You were an asshole."

He nods and frowns a bit. "I was. I'm sorry about that, honestly."

"Wow, he can apologize."

"Yes, I can. And I did." He lifts his brows. "But you were late. That's just facts."

"I was on time!" Despite myself, my body relaxes in response to the jibe. Now that he's actually apologized, I can appreciate that it was kind of a funny situation, me sprinting to the door.

"Barely." Luc's face shifts from playful to serious, and he says, louder than necessary, "There's something on your collar." Using the excuse to lean forward, he whispers in my ear, "Justin is in the bathroom, and I don't know what he knows, but it's possible that Juras tipped him off to something. Juras is always breathing over my shoulder, hoping that I mess up. Meaning we have two people to convince, and probably Jasmine, too. She and Juras are a package deal." He steps back and gestures to the people at the kitchen island.

I recognize his sponsor siblings from the times I've seen them at NuGene. Juras's springy curls are purple now, and his scarf is so giant and thick it looks like a poncho. Jasmine is in a simple black dress that's a perfect match to her chin-length dark hair.

Sponsor siblings aren't like regular ones. They're not family, they're competition. Sometimes they're the only option to inherit from their sponsor parents, like with Justin, and other times they're an off-putting sort of insurance for CEOs who do have children but aren't sure if they'll take over the business or do it well. I've even heard of business owners who get sponsor kids just for competition to make their own kids work harder.

But Luc's sponsor siblings are especially weird because they act like he's their *only* competition, not each other. It's like they're bonded together just to be against him. He's the odd man out.

Luc glances at me like he didn't look properly before. "Banana print?"

"Is there a problem with that?" I straighten and puff my chest out like I wasn't recently questioning my dress choice.

"It's very you." He pulls his little smile and gestures to his sponsor siblings. "You remember Juras and Jasmine."

I'm going to assume that was a compliment, so I don't get pissed off before dinner even starts. "I remember," I say, nodding at them.

Taking a seat on one of the plush cream stools at the island, I set my sweet bread on the counter and look around the condo. It's enormous, and the space is surrounded by floor-to-ceiling Smart Glass—the NuMoney-level expensive stuff you can control using your phone. Mom nearly collapsed into a fit looking at it on one of the home reno feeds she follows.

As I scan the room, I notice another girl sitting on the couch. Her skin is a warm chestnut color, and her dark hair spills over her shoulders in big loose curls. She keeps her gaze trained on the window.

"Hello . . ." My words slip away as she fails to react.

Luc waves his hands. "That's Maya. Maya, say hello to Voya."

The girl turns with an eerie slowness. "Hello. Pleased to meet you, Voya." Her eyes are almost the exact same shade as her hair. She shifts her gaze and stares at Luc with a sort of vacancy. I squirm in my chair.

"Thank you, Maya," he says.

She smiles in a way that doesn't reach her eyes and turns back to looking out the window.

"A pet project of mine," Luc explains. "I'm afraid I haven't exposed her to much beyond myself. She's having a bit of a time picking up on social cues."

I glance at the other two to see if they know what the hell kind of spam Luc is spouting about this random girl, but their expressions are blank. I glance back at Maya and watch her hand twitch for a second. If I wasn't staring, I wouldn't have noticed. And suddenly it clicks. "She's a NuSap."

"Yes. Officially, it's still suspended, but Justin doesn't mind if I dabble."

He says it casually as if he hasn't talked multiple times about his first love being robotics, and how he can't be on the suspended project. "Her skin . . ."

"It's hard to see if she passes any sort of Turing test if her blueness gives her away before she's opened her mouth, so I gave her a natural tone." The Turing test, a universal standard in whether a robot passes as human, is something every NuSap unit fails. They were designed that way since people weren't comfortable with mistaking machines for people.

"Fair enough."

Juras leans his chin on his fist and stares at Luc. "I don't know why you're wasting time on a shutdown project." I don't think I imagine the sharp edge to his voice.

Luc's fingers flex, and he does an awkward shoulder jerk I suspect is meant to be a casual shrug. "I'm not too deep into it. It's for fun." He won't meet Juras's eyes, which means it's probably a lot more serious than that.

"Maybe you should keep the extracurricular activities to a minimum." Juras glances at me without a hint of shame about doing it.

"Maybe you should worry about yourself and let me handle my business." The harsh spit of Luc's voice is sharp enough to cut. I shift on the stool and glance at Jasmine, who is scrolling through her phone but clearly still listening.

"Like whatever you were handling the other night? You were out late."

"Sometimes I stay out late."

"And yet your logins show you weren't in the office the way you usually are."

Enough of this. I love to see Luc's ego adjusted, but only if he deserves it. Not because his sponsor brother is being a little shit. "He came to dinner with my family on Sunday night."

Juras's and Jasmine's eyes flicker wide.

I clear my throat. "They wanted to meet my match, so he came over. Sorry for keeping him out late."

Luc stares at me.

He didn't ask me to lie for him, but he was at my house. They don't need to know what he was doing there. He wanted my help avoiding suspicion, he's got it.

Jasmine sets her phone on the table. "Two family dinners. Matching must be going well." Unlike Juras, there isn't any derision in her tone.

I don't know what to say back to that. She isn't being snippy, but I also can't tell if she's sincere.

"Everyone's here!" Justin strolls into the room, and I clench my fists in my dress. "Welcome, Voya."

"Thank you for inviting me." I gesture to the tray of sweet bread. "I brought this. It's kind of like a cake?" I glance at Juras to see if he knows what it is. His expression doesn't change.

That's the thing about Black people—there are lots of different kinds. He could be Jamaican, or African, or Afro-Latinx, or Trinidadian but with a family who don't cook much or eat that kind of food. There are a lot of people who assume having the same skin color means you have the same culture, when it's not even close to being that simple.

Justin beams and leans in close. "Smells delicious. Where did you get it?"

"I made it." This is my recipe, not Auntie Elaine's, just in case she ever shared one of her baked goods with him. I didn't want to risk triggering a memory. "It's like banana bread but with coconut. It's called sweet bread. Some people make it like a fruit cake, but my grandma hates fruit pieces, so she would never put it in."

"Did she teach you how to bake?"

"Yes."

His expressions are easy and comfortable. This is a man who can smile even though he tried to blackmail an entire family because one member wouldn't help him discover immortality. "Wonderful. We're not big cooks here. That's why we ordered in." He gestures to Jasmine. "Her mom made us fantastic meals when I visited to offer sponsorship. What was that one with the lamb she made? I absolutely loved it."

"Lamb adobo," Jasmine says, her voice bored as if she's reminded him of this multiple times.

"You're from the Philippines?" I ask. I've heard of adobo from a few of the international cuisine feeds I follow.

She nods.

"Lots of talented kids over there," Justin says with a smile. "Juras is from a small village in the Congo. Great test scores there, too. You can find something special in every corner of the globe, truly." He pauses and examines me. "Where are you from, Voya?"

My lip twitches. There are two answers to this question. The right answer and the answer I know Justin wants. Because the question is less *where* I'm from and more an examination into what type of Black I am. A notch to add to his conversation starters, about how his sponsor son was matched with a Black girl who made this Trinidadian cake whose name he doesn't bother to remember.

"I was born here," I say. "In Toronto."

Justin smiles without saying anything more. He at least knows not to ask the painful follow-up question of *But where are you really from?*

Luc jumps in. "Voya's a great cook. She made me lunch the other day."

My face heats up. Partly I'm grateful to be saved from this uncomfortable back and forth with Justin, but now I'm wondering if he means that. A great cook. I know I am. But does he really think I am?

"I'm sure she is," Justin says with a grin. "It must run in the family."

Sweat breaks out on the back of my neck. He's talking about Granny. Yes. That's definitely it. I said that she was the one who taught me to bake.

The elevator dings open, and the delivery guy steps into the apartment as if on cue. Justin sweeps over to him and takes the food. Juras walks over to a cupboard and pulls out a stack of compostable plates to hand around.

That beautiful smell of pork seasoned with ginger and garlic marinates in my nostrils. There's something addictive about the crunch of fried food.

It's strange to be eating takeout around a breakfast bar. I can't think of the last time our family ordered in or didn't sit around the dining room table. The efficiency with which Luc and his sponsor siblings get everything together makes me suspect this is a regular occurrence. He did say his diet was boxed mac and cheese and instant noodles. Takeout is probably the only time he eats food that was actually cooked.

Juras takes a bite of his pork bun and glances at the watch on his wrist. It's like a timed rhythm. Mouthful. Look at watch. Mouthful. Look at watch.

It's what Keisha used to do at every meal. She used money from her feed modeling to get an upgrade to her implant. On top of the chip behind the ear, she has another one hooked up that calculates calories consumed and burned.

Every single thing she puts in her mouth is recorded via the app, and it matches that data against any exercise she does to burn calories, and the ones she burns based on her metabolism. Granny cussed her out for doing the eat-and-check thing, so she doesn't do it at dinners anymore. But that doesn't mean she's actually stopped.

I've never had to look into the nooks and crannies of our family before this. Now I can't help but be disappointed that Keisha's been struggling like this for years and none of us have done anything. Talking to her about it makes her upset, but ignoring it doesn't help either.

Every day, more and more cracks in our family get exposed.

I look around at my hosts, forcing myself to make conversation. "Do you live here together?" I can't imagine Justin staying here with them. It's weird enough to see him eating takeout from boxes.

Luc jumps in. "Jasmine, Juras, and I live here. Justin stays in Yorkville."

I open my mouth to say that I remember he told me that before but realize I probably shouldn't know about it. "Yorkville is nice." In truth, Yorkville is ritzy. A little north of Toronto, it's the sort of place where, when you announce living there, people know you have money. It's sleek boutique shop outfits and designer electric cars. Regent Park is for tech giants and a lot of NuMoney people, but Yorkville is for families who have had money for so many generations no one can remember what it was like to not have it.

Justin takes a bite out of a bun. "And what about you? Whereabouts do you live?"

"Historic Long Branch." My eyes whip around the room, looking for something to steer the conversation away from me. Again, it's unnecessary. The bionic lenses in Justin's eyes could pull any of my public location tags and estimate my address. When I see the flashing lights of fireworks outside, I almost sag with relief. "Oh! Fireworks." I jump up from my stool.

Luc points at the balcony that wraps around the condo. "We can go out and look."

"I'm fine here," Jasmine says, returning to her phone scrolling. Juras nods. "Same."

"You two can go ahead. We'll stay here." Justin laces his fingers together. "I was wondering about Luc's commitment to the program, but you two seem to get along well. I love to see our programs succeed."

I swallow and don't respond, just shuffle out to the balcony along with Luc.

Once the door shuts, I let out a huge breath. The crack of fireworks booms in the air. "Is he always like that?"

Luc leans on the railing. "Like what? He was normal. I was being paranoid. He hasn't asked about your aunt or anything related to that."

How in the hell is he not feeling the energy that I am? Like Justin is peeling off the layers of what I am to get to a crunchy center he plans to devour. "I feel like he knows. Either he knows you hacked in, or he knows about my aunt, or . . ."

Luc turns toward me. "Justin isn't the type to act normal and then spring a consequence out of nowhere. It's what I admire about him. He's direct. If he knew what we know, he would address it right now."

"Even if it's something as worrying as his dad and my aunt—who was murdered, by the way—dying on the same day?" Technically she was sacrificed, but Luc doesn't need to know that.

"You can't seriously think that Justin . . ." He looks around as if the balcony has CCTV. ". . . murdered her?"

I sigh. "No." I know he didn't kill her. But he may as well have. "Doesn't it make you feel a certain way knowing that something went so wrong with them?"

Luc shakes his head. "They had a falling-out. She died. It's sad, but that's all it is." He stares at me, his eyes focusing in on mine. "My concern is why he didn't credit her with the discovery if they worked on it together. That's not Justin. I'm only an intern and my name is on the NuGene Match program details."

"He's important to you, isn't he?" The more Luc speaks, the

more something deeper than his general fanboy attitude or that simmering annoyance toward Justin comes out. "Juras and Jasmine are competition, but Justin is more than a boss."

He shrugs. "When I was little, we would spend the most time together. It felt like I was with him every moment of every day. I guess that's why Jasmine and Juras ended up sticking together and not liking me very much. But the bigger NuGene got, the less time he had, until one day I realized I was spending more time alone than I was with any of them."

"I'm sorry." I can't even go a day without interacting with at least one person in my family. I wouldn't want to either.

Luc lets out a sigh. "People get busy. Or, I don't know, maybe he just lost faith in me. I'd be shocked if he named me successor."

"Why?" I nearly shout, and have to lower my voice. "You're the lead on the matching program, which is huge. And sure, you're not the most personable, but at least you have a personality. You would be a great successor."

Luc presses his fist to his mouth.

Hack me. Why did I go off spouting that stuff? My entire face feels warm.

"Thank you." He takes his hand away from his mouth but turns away before I can see his expression. "I talked to the guy in the NuGene cafeteria about you. You didn't follow up with him." He turns back with his normal Luc expression.

"I didn't."

"Why?"

Because my future isn't my own. Because I don't get to choose. "It's . . . a family thing."

"How come you can push your cousin toward an internship at NuGene, but you can't do something you love?"

It's my turn to twist away. "The future isn't as simple as doing what you love."

"Isn't it?"

I look back, and Luc is staring straight at me. They may not be genetically related, but he has the same deep probing gaze as Justin. Except I don't feel like my layers are being peeled back. It's more like I'm being seen in a way that no one else can.

He takes a step forward, and my heart decides to do a step routine in my chest. It's loud enough for me to feel the thumping in my ears.

Fireworks explode above us in bright magenta, orange, and ocean blue.

Luc's eyes get that faraway look. He's getting a message on his hijacker chip. "Justin says they're impatient to cut into your dessert. We should go back inside."

My throat is too dry to speak, so I bob my head in confirmation.

Luc walks through the balcony doors. I move to follow him, but stop when something catches my eye. I turn my head, and there she is.

Mama Jova.

In her nude glory, standing and staring out into the city.

"Coming?" Luc says, hand on the balcony door.

I whip my head back toward him. "Sorry . . . I just . . . I got a message, have to make a quick call."

He tilts his head to the side for a moment before nodding. "Sure. We'll be inside."

After he leaves, I pull out my phone to look like I'm doing what I said I am. At the very least, it'll explain why I'm talking to the air.

Mama Jova gives herself a second before looking at me. "Time is running out."

Doesn't she think I know that? "I'm working on it. It isn't Caribana yet."

"And do you think you'll be ready by then?"

I tangle my hands together around my phone. "I—I can do it."

"What confidence."

I bite down on a sudden spark of anger. "*Why* do I have to do this? He could do so much in the world. Why do I have to . . . to destroy him?" My voice sounds weak. Pathetic.

Mama Jova stares at me with her sunken eyes. "What did I say to you about magic in that memory?"

"That it's blood and intent."

"So you do listen."

I swallow and look down. "Listening isn't the problem."

"Yes," Mama Jova snaps, "it is. My task is that you find your first love and destroy them."

"That's what I'm trying to do," I cry.

Mama Jova curls her lip. "What makes a decision hard?"

"I—I don't know. It's just . . . the choices, I guess. Knowing which is right."

"Exactly." For once, my ancestor sounds pleased with me. "You and I, we agonized over our options. Searching for the right one. Because that's the thing, every decision you make has multiple choices."

I stare at her. "I don't understand."

"I can tell," she says with a grumble. "I gave you a task. You control everything else. The choice is yours."

"I control nothing!" I snap back. "There *is* no choice. I have to do this. I can't let Eden die."

Mama Jova is still for a moment, staring at me down her nose, nostrils flaring. "You seem to have trouble understanding the reality of decisions, so I'm going to give you a lesson."

My stomach clenches.

"Give me your hand."

Shit. Heaping trash fire shit. The last time I gave Mama Jova my hand, she assigned me this horrible task. What will happen this time? I glance over my shoulder to make sure the others aren't watching. They're either clearing dishes off the island or looking for more disposable plates.

I give her my hand.

She guides me closer to the balcony and presses the back of my hand to the railing. There must be a loose piece of metal sticking out, because a sharp sting blooms just below my knuckles. Blood slips down the back of my fingers onto hers. I have to bite my lip to keep from crying out as a rush of heat soars up my arm, followed by coolness.

"You need to learn that everything—your task, and your life—is under your control. It's your choice. No matter how much it seems to be otherwise." She gestures out at the others. "Now, touch him."

"Touch him . . . What? What will happen when I do that?"

"What happens is you stop me from cursing your family right here and right now. You need to learn." With that, Mama fades into the wind, leaving only a lingering scent of smoke.

My throat clenches as I stare at my hand. I wish my windpipe would close. That I could pass out and wake up when everything is over.

Except it's not that easy.

Touch him.

Who does she even mean? Luc would be the obvious choice. For all I know, this could mean the end of my task. Touch him and be done with it. But that feels too easy.

As I walk inside from the balcony, wiping the blood from my hand, I swear Maya's eyes are on my back. She's not human, and yet she's somehow aware of how dangerous I am.

Touch him.

I doubt that my touch will bring anything pleasant.

Justin could be another choice, but . . . the way Luc spoke about him. No matter what Justin did to my family in the past, he means something to Luc now, and he's the gatekeeper of Luc's future. Of the sponsorship that seems to drive Luc's entire existence. And more, what if touching Justin makes him remember, and he comes after my family again? But then again, what if I could avenge Auntie Elaine right here, right now, and stop my family from ever having to worry about him?

Touch him.

Juras is the only option left. He's also the person who would make the least sense to go after. Except for the fact that he's Luc's competition.

I can picture Keis raising the most skeptical eyebrow at that thought. It's like I can hear her saying, *What? You're going to take him out for Luc before you kill Luc yourself?*

Even if I open a path for Luc's future, I still have to be the one to take it away. Less competition won't mean much if he's dead.

Luc and his sponsor family sit ready at the table—each of them waiting for me to make the first cut into my sweet bread.

Touch him.

My feet carry me forward, and I keep my eyes on the tray of sweet bread so I can pretend that's what I'm after as I brush my fingers against Juras's bare hand so lightly he doesn't notice, and then I pick up the tray.

The electricity of the spell takes hold, obvious in the way heat rushes from my fingers and leaves my body cold and shivering. My hand shakes as Luc gives me the knife. He frowns at my wrist where the monitor sits. I look at it too, but nothing seems to be out of the ordinary. I plunge the blade into the soft bread.

"Are you all right?" Justin's stare is probing as he holds out his plate. For a moment, I think he looks at the monitor too, but I'm distracted by staring at Juras. He and Jasmine give me their own quizzical stares.

I push out a laugh. "I think I just got a little cold when I was outside."

My hands methodically put the slices onto plates and give them out around the table. Compliments from my hosts slide through my ears.

The more time passes, the more my eyes follow Juras, until the spell takes shape. One half of his face slopes down, his eye droops, and one side of his lips falls. I clench my hands into fists in my lap to stop from covering my eyes.

I don't want to see this happen. But I need to.

"Juras!" Jasmine screams. His head drops against her shoulder as he slurs out incoherent words. "I think he's having a stroke!"

I didn't want this.

But . . . I wasn't ready. I couldn't do it. I try to tell myself it was because there wasn't even a guarantee that it would kill Luc, but I know deep down that I just couldn't.

This was a mistake. I should have tried to refuse giving Mama my hand. This is worse than any vision I've ever seen because this *isn't* me seeing visions.

It's real.

Luc is talking quickly into his phone with a 911 dispatcher while I sit frozen in my seat.

The hair on my arms prickles, and I slide my gaze over.

Justin is staring at me. It's like we're the only two people in the room.

His forearms clench against the counter where he grips it, and his bionics swirl with a speed that makes me dizzy. It's like he's pinned me to the breakfast bar with nothing but his stare.

Sweat coats the back of my neck and turns cold in the same instant.

When my ancestors were being dragged from their homes and hauled onto boats, was that the face they saw right before? A face of discovery and a promise of pain.

CHAPTER TWENTY-FOUR

I've been staring at the same digital poster advertising the importance of regular physicals in the Mount Sinai emergency waiting room for the last fifteen minutes. I shift on the soft yet uncomfortable plastic seats. Despite them, I managed to fall asleep on the cushions long enough for a new day to start. There's no way I could have gone home and faced my family. I don't want to have to talk about what I've done to Juras.

There's a couple huddled together in the corner over a boy whose cough is so bad I cringe every time he starts hacking.

I keep seeing Juras's face in my head as part of it sloped to the side. Calm and collected Jasmine was screaming and clutching onto him. Justin had to physically separate them so he could ride in the ambulance with his sponsor son. The CEO's face is still clear in my mind. He looked furious at *me*, like he knew it was my fault.

The rest of us took an ordered car to the hospital. Jasmine, in her shock and panic, never thought to ask why I was coming. Even Luc accepted my presence as he sat there, staring at nothing. Silent in a way so like himself and yet not like him.

I stare down at my interlaced fingers and the monitor on my wrist. I thought that Justin and Luc had looked at it, but now everything is so jumbled up in Juras's face drooping and Jasmine's screams. And anyway, we checked it. It's not tracking magic.

Maybe they saw I was freaked out and expected some sort of panic response from it. Or maybe I imagined the entire thing.

They all went upstairs when we arrived, and I stayed in the waiting room. Did Luc sleep uncomfortably on one of these seats last night like I did? I can't manage to unroot myself from mine. It's pushing down on me—the gravity of what I've done and what I still have to do. It's so heavy that I don't think I could leave even if I wanted to.

Not until I know Juras is okay.

I may have killed him with a barely-there touch on his arm. Snuffed out his life in seconds the way Mama likely wanted me to do to Luc.

Hack me.

Even though I know I should have touched Luc, after watching it all unfold, I'm happy that I didn't. Even knowing that in the next week and a half, I'll have to kill him with more than a brush against his arm.

I was born in this building, with its crisp white lobbies and rushing nurses and stressed doctors. Every single one of my cousins was too. Even Mom, Auntie, and Uncle Vacu came into the world here.

Now Juras is dead or dying in the same place. Because of me.

My phone vibrates with Mom requesting a video chat. It's usually the time she would be consulting with Brian, one of her private investigator clients. But lately, she's home more often along with Priya, Dad, and Auntie. They're losing work as their magic wanes.

Just more people I'm hurting as this task goes on. I turn on my privacy settings so no one else can hear our conversation, and accept it.

"You better have a damn good reason for why you're not home in bed! I had to drag Maise out to do a spell and see if you came home last night. Which you *didn't*!" Mom is shouting at top volume, and the shrillness of her voice makes me cringe.

"I'm in the hospital."

The anger leaks from her face. "What happened?!"

I grip my hands into fists. "Luc invited me to dinner at his place, and Mama Jova showed up. She put this power in my hand and told me to touch him. The boy I touched, Luc's sponsor brother . . . He's in bad shape. We need to help him somehow."

Mom's face isn't upset, it's confused. "She told you to touch him, and you touched . . . who?"

"Luc's sponsor brother."

"Is that who she told you to touch?"

"Well . . . no, it was vaguer, but I chose to—"

She presses her palms against her eyes and lets out a huge sigh. "She gave you an out, and you didn't take it."

"It wasn't an out! I would have still been killing Luc."

"Yes," Mom says, taking her hands away. "And now you have to do it the hard way."

"That's not fair," I croak, my throat aching from holding back tears.

"*None* of this is fair. *Life* isn't fair." Mom lets out a steups. "You think that I want you to do this? I don't. None of us wants this for you. But you also can't let Mama Jova haunt you forever. You need to finish this."

Finish this. Meaning kill Luc. "I don't want to hurt anyone," I say softly.

"I know you don't."

I have whatever happened to Juras on my hands. A scum covers my body and spreads to everything I touch. "Will you help his sponsor brother or not? There must be something Granny can do. She's a Matriarch."

Mom's eyes dart away from me. "This is one of Justin's sponsor children?"

"Yes. And Justin doesn't act like a guy without any memory of

Auntie or us! He knows I did something to Juras." And I still don't know what he'll do with that knowledge.

"Then why push it? If he thinks we can do anything close to what Elaine could, things will only get worse. We can't risk the exposure."

Get sparked. She's so full of it. "We can use magic to murder, but we can't use it to help people?"

"We aren't supposed to use it to kill, either."

"And yet here you are, encouraging me to finish it!"

Mom's face twists. "Vo—"

"Save it. I get it," I snap. "We can't use magic to help Lauren, and we can't use it to help Juras, but it's okay to murder so we can keep it. Is that right?" I stare at Mom's face. At the perfect curved eyebrows that match mine. The same full set mouth. So similar, yet so different.

"Don't take that tone with me," Mom hisses. Her voice low and dangerous. "This task has made you so mouthy. I am trying to help you. This isn't just about magic, this is about Eden—"

"I know about Eden! I know!" I shake my head. "It's just, we're only ever helping ourselves." I rub my eyes, where tears are threatening to sprout.

It hurt enough to do that to Juras, but to take it further with Luc . . . I imagine his empty eyes staring up at nothing.

Dead and gone.

No more lip-biting smile. No more snappy barbs. No more grateful compliments about my food. Not from him anyway. And no more decomposing Fade Ink tattoos.

My memory sees fit to present the image of Luc with a knife pressed against Eden's throat.

No matter what I *want* to do, I *need* to do this. Mama Jova was wrong. I don't have any control here. "I'm going to go, okay?"

Mom makes a face that says the conversation isn't over, but

lets it drop. "You'd better be home in your bed tonight."

"I will." I end the call and flick a switch to set Mom's number to Do Not Disturb.

I'll get hell for it later, but I can't listen to the hypocrisy.

A message from Luc flashes in front of my eyes: *He's stable.*

I can't get my fingers to move fast enough across my phone: *I'm in the waiting room. Everything's all right?*

Minutes pass without any answer from Luc. I bounce my knee so violently the family with their coughing son gives me the eye, and I have to press down on my thigh to keep it still.

A set of doors off to the side of the waiting room slides open and Luc comes out. He's got his beanie pulled so low that I can't see any of his hair.

I scramble to my feet. "Is everything okay?" Hack me, why did I ask that?

"You didn't have to stay overnight."

I hunch my shoulders. "I didn't want to leave."

Luc gives me a long stare I turn away from. I'm a coward in every sense of the word. He slumps forward. "He's okay. I said I would sit with him until Jasmine gets back from a meeting she has to attend. Justin left a couple of minutes ago."

My brain is struggling to keep up with what's happening while being relieved that Justin is gone. "He's . . . okay?"

"He's going to recover, eventually. You'll see."

I follow Luc out of the waiting room and into the elevator in the main lobby in a haze. Juras isn't dead. I didn't kill him . . . but I hurt him. Which means that even if I had decided to touch Luc, it wouldn't have been the end of my task.

He looks at me and pulls that awkward teeth-biting smile I'm starting to crave. "Glad that I won't have to sit with him alone."

I tangle my fingers together. "I'm glad Juras is okay." I mean it.

We walk out of the elevator onto the fifth floor. Luc makes a left, and I hurry to keep up. Nurses sit at their stations tapping on the computers and chatting with each other.

He pushes open the door on a room marked 5011.

I force myself to move my feet past the threshold.

Juras's dark brown skin looks ashy and pale. There's a massive bandage wrapped around his head and deep black smudges under his eyes. His face is uneven on one side. He's sleeping, and yet it looks deeper than that.

"Did they put him under?" I ask Luc.

There are two chairs pulled up near the bed. He sits in one. "Yes. He got a blood clot and had a stroke. They put him in a coma to give his brain time to recover. We're not sure how affected his speech or understanding of language will be. But that seems to be what they're most worried about."

I sink into the chair next to Luc. His face is stoic as he watches Juras. He probably wouldn't be this calm if he knew he was sitting next to the person who did this. I clench my fists in my lap.

"Have you ever had a thought that made you realize you're not quite who you thought you were?" Luc doesn't turn away from Juras as he speaks.

"What do you mean?"

"I've always thought I was a decent human being. I know I'm not popular, but I felt the essence of who I am is good. Today, I had a thought that I was wrong."

If Luc is looking for some absolution of guilt, he's talking to the worst possible person. Except, I understand what he means. I thought I was good. Then I put Juras in this condition. "I do. Not only thoughts, but actions. Things I felt were wrong, I've still done in the name of something better. The fact that I can do them at all makes me wonder if I was ever a good person."

Luc clasps his hands together. "It makes sense. We are linked together, after all." He turns toward me. "Do you feel like we're a good match?"

"It doesn't matter, does it? Matching is about genetics."

"It matters to me." Luc is close enough for me to smell the hint of coconut from the sweet bread we ate with dinner and a lingering coffee scent. He must have had some in the hospital.

I swallow. "I think that maybe you should have gotten a better match."

"So do I."

I jump to my feet as heat rushes through my face. I turn to leave, but Luc catches my hand. "Sorry."

"You don't have to be sorry that you think you should have a better match." It's exactly what I said to him. And it's true. He deserves better than a girl who's plotting to murder him. Only, I didn't expect him to agree. Not now.

Luc groans and tugs me back. I stumble and end up barely an inch away from being chest-to-chest. Though he doesn't seem uncomfortable with the closeness the way he would usually be. "I'm sorry I wasn't clear. I meant that I feel the same way, that you should have gotten a better match than me."

"What?" When we're this close, I can't tell if it's my heart or his that's thumping loud enough to hear.

"You're a better person than I am. You care about people, about your family, more than you care about yourself. You put their success before yours."

Please don't say those things about me. "I'm not."

"My sponsor brother is lying in a hospital bed, and the first thought I had was that I wouldn't have to compete with him anymore. That I would have a chance. Look me in the eyes and tell me that doesn't make me the worst kind of person."

I stare into his eyes. "I think if you didn't feel bad, you would be. But you do, and that just makes you human."

Luc steps back and collapses into the hospital chair.

I ignore the chill that rushes over my skin in the absence of his body heat and sit next to him. We stay like that, quietly looking at Juras for a bit until Luc gets a message on his phone.

Usually, people stare off into the air while they read messages, or down at their phone if they feel like it, but their eyes move across it, clearly reading. Luc does that for the first bit, but then he just sits there, staring.

"Are you . . . okay?" I ask.

He blinks rapidly, and turns away from me to wipe at his eyes. He lets out a laugh, high-pitched and on the edge of hysteria.

"Luc . . . ?"

"Want to hear something funny?" He turns toward me, his face glistening where he wiped his tears.

"Okay . . ."

"I told you about how I was glad I wouldn't have to compete with Juras again, but it turns out, I wasn't even in the running."

"I'm confused."

Luc has a smile on his face that's nothing like his usual one. It's too wide and strains against his trembling lips. "Juras is Justin's chosen successor."

"*What?*" The NuGene CEO barely acknowledged Juras when I was at their place for dinner. I would have thought Luc was the obvious choice. "How do you know?"

"I was worried about what Justin thought after the dinner. If he was still suspicious about any hacking. I know, I'm terrible. Juras was possibly dying, and on top of shitty thoughts, I was also worried about my sponsorship." He laughs again, the sound hollow and too loud in the room. "I used a backdoor to check on his calls. Not that hard since he needs to give me access to a lot for NuGene anyway. He left the hospital room to make what seemed like a serious call, so I had my AI record and transcribe it for me. The transcription just came in."

"And?"

"It was him checking with his lawyer on what clauses there were if a sponsor was unable to work, 'in regard to my successor plans,' he said. His lawyer confirmed that if that happened, it would automatically apply to the second choice, which he confirmed was Jasmine Cruz."

Hack me. No wonder Justin looked so angry. I threatened the life of not just one of his sponsors but his chosen successor. I swallow. "I'm sorry." It's all I can think to say. If Luc isn't the successor, when he turns eighteen, he'll be cut loose from the sponsorship. Even if Juras can't do it, Luc wasn't even a second choice. Everything that he's built his life around, gone.

Luc shakes his head. "Maybe that's why Justin stopped bothering with me. Because he knew I wasn't worthy enough to take over his company."

"You don't know that."

"But I do! It's right there in the transcript."

I press my lips together. "He can always change his mind."

"Cool, and then I can be second best. Only in charge because who he really wanted is lying in a hospital bed right in front of us." He gestures wildly at Juras's prone body. "Hack me. I'm trash. He's literally in a coma, and I'm here complaining about my sponsorship."

Luc wouldn't be sitting next to me if he could see what's in my head. He wouldn't be able to stand being near me. Because however much of a terrible person Luc thinks he is for his selfish thoughts, I will always be worse.

I'm the one who is planning a murder to save someone close to me.

He was right about one thing: I *do* put the needs of my family above mine.

Luc stands up from his chair, tugs off his beanie, and runs his hands through his hair so hard that the skin on his face gets tugged back too. "I can't stay here. I need to get out. I'll message Jasmine and apologize." He looks at me. "Do you mind being spontaneous with me for a bit? If you can stand being around someone like me, I mean." Luc says the last bit with a laugh, but his eyes are over-bright and feverish. Like if I said no, he might collapse on the spot.

Even with everything, right now, there's no part of me that *could* say no to him.

"Let's go."

CHAPTER TWENTY-FIVE

The streetcar's AC is blasting at Northern Territories–level cold. I press my bare legs together as if that will warm them—the banana print of my dress feeling too cheery now considering everything with Juras. Luc sits next to me in the window seat, staring at the scenery going past. We hopped on at Queen Street West and Spadina Avenue in Chinatown, not far from where Granny and I met Rowen Huang the other day. Though it's like a lifetime has passed since she let her bit of gossip slip. That was the beginning of my task, and now I'm hurtling toward the end.

Outside, clothing stores, boutiques, and small bars and restaurants crowd the streets—all of them closed except for the odd McDonald's or Tim Horton's serving breakfast. My stomach cramps. I would kill for a breakfast sandwich right now.

The instant I think it, the thought makes me cringe. Luc doesn't notice. He's lost in watching everything go by.

I've cheered up my family plenty of times. When Keis got a lower mark on her Poli Sci test than she expected last year, I took her to eat greasy pizza slices and let her rant about how she would do better next time.

When Mom lost one of her big clients, I worked hard to sell extra product so Granny would agree to buy her a special bottle of wine, and we watched cheesy feed movies together while she split it with Auntie.

When Grandad died, I made Granny the first thing she'd taught me to cook: a warm and flaky Caribbean bread called bake, with coconut I shredded myself. Mom had to supervise me while I made the bread, of course—I was only six. She even made me wear garden gloves to use the grater for the coconut so I wouldn't cut myself. But I was so proud because I had done it all myself. Granny and I sat on the back balcony eating the bread together, just the two of us, and she told me how her and Grandad met as we looked out at the lake. Online, but not in the usual way via a dating app. They met on a singing one. Randomly matched in a duet— both of them witches, which in and of itself seemed like ancestral intervention—my grumpy Granny met my almost frustratingly optimistic Grandad, and our family came together.

But cheering up any one of them even for a second would be easier than figuring out how to make Luc feel better. His sponsorship is his entire life. What do you say to someone who's found out they're going to lose everything they've ever worked for?

I point to the theater we pass. "That was the first place I ever saw a movie. I was five, and we went to see *Gobro Babies*."

"When you were five?" Luc says with a raised brow. "Isn't it for, like, two-year-olds?"

"My grandad wasn't one hundred percent understanding of age ranges for movies." I shrug. "I, at least, liked it. My cousins were in agony."

"Why did you go to this theater when there's one in Etobicoke?"

"He wanted to take us somewhere different, on this big fancy downtown trip. He bought us so much popcorn. It was like I was high on butter. And it wasn't modded then, so it was real full-on butter."

Luc gives his signature smile. "Justin specifically orders non-modded butter. We got it the first time he took me there. He says the real thing is worth it. We watched *RoboCop*, you know, that ancient movie they've remade a million times?"

"You *would* go see a robot movie."

"Justin wanted to see it too!"

We pass by the huge Eaton Center mall. I glance at Luc, but he doesn't budge. This isn't where we're getting off. "Just the two of you went?"

"Juras and Jasmine wanted to stay home and study together. Back then, Justin talked about how we should be kids. Have fun. That sort of thing."

"*You* were the adventurous child?" My eyebrows climb to my hairline.

"I was, actually. Justin and I would go to the movies, the museums—we even worked together on a bunch of community science fair projects." He smirks. "We always won."

"Like a family." I mean to think it in my head, but it slips out of my mouth. The way he talks about Justin, the things they did, it sounds like how I would talk about Keis or Granny or Mom. Not a cold mentor. "Why would you worry about him shipping you off? Even if you aren't the successor, he would keep you around, wouldn't he?"

Luc lets out a breath and turns to me. "That's not how sponsorship contracts work. People don't just send kids they don't pick back because they're assholes. To keep me here, he would need to pay to transfer my sponsorship immigration to a regular immigration application. The cost wouldn't be anything to him, but he would still be responsible for me for years. I would become his dependent. And if we put it down to simple cost analysis, it would be more expensive to keep me than to send me back."

"You're also really hacking smart. Doesn't that make it a worthwhile business decision?"

"People don't pick us because we're better than everyone here. They choose us because it's easier to raise someone with complete company loyalty and ensure their devotion with the threat of deportation. Which doesn't exactly work on people from your own country. The leverage isn't the same. Yeah, I'm smart, but at NuGene, intelligence is a dime a dozen. I'm not a lead because I'm a genius, I'm a lead because I'm more trustworthy, and it's likely Justin wanted to test how I would do. A test that I clearly failed. And what else do I have besides being 'really hacking smart'? Most people hate me. The bottom line is that keeping me would be a bad business decision. And I can't be sure that I'm worth that to him. He's not my dad, he's a CEO."

I wring my hands in my lap. This is the first time I've heard Luc say something negative about the sponsor program. It seems too cold even for someone like Justin, to weigh the monetary costs like that and decide that Luc isn't worth it.

"Would it be the worst thing? Couldn't you still do robotics or something in Mexico?"

Luc's lips press into a line. "I came here with the dream of running NuGene one day. I've spent almost my entire life working toward something I now know I haven't achieved. If I don't have that—" He cuts himself off and releases a breath.

If I don't have that, what do I have?

To me, Luc is a genius hacker, geneticist, and artist, with the whole world at his fingertips. He could do or be anything. But to him, everything he is starts and ends with Justin and NuGene. The entirety of his worth as a person is poured into this one thing. I clench my jaw. "How is it that you can walk around with so much ego and think being the NuGene successor is all you're good for?"

Luc whips his gaze away from the window. "Excuse me?"

"You got so pissed at me because I took a spot at that NuGene Q&A away from someone who wanted to work at the company.

You clearly care a lot about it. Why does not being the successor mean you can't make change in the company? That you can't do amazing work there? Okay, you think you're a bad business decision? Then prove to Justin that you're not. Show him that you're worth it!" A couple of people on the streetcar look over, and I duck my head down.

Luc ducks his head too, but his lips are quirked up. "Are you lecturing me?"

I blink. Me? Lecturing? That's something Granny would do, but he's also not wrong. "Maybe! If that's what makes you pay attention."

Luc looks back down at his lap. "Part of me knows that it's useless, but when you say it, suddenly I start to wonder if it's possible."

"Does that mean you'll try?"

He shrugs. "Why not? It can't get any worse, right? I'll do my best at the matching program to show Justin that I'm worth keeping around, and in exchange, you apply for a cooking internship."

"*What?*" I splutter.

"You're always so ready to push everyone else forward. Me and your cousin, and who knows who else. What about you and your future?" He pauses and considers me. "Is that even what you want to do? Cooking? Or is that just what everyone *thinks* you want to do?"

I blink hard and shift my gaze outside the window. We're passing through the Danforth with its street signs in English and Greek, fresh fruit stands, and plethora of restaurants with inviting patios. I can almost taste the honey-covered dough balls I got there earlier this summer at Taste of the Danforth.

Ever since I was little, cooking has been my refuge. As much of a comfort as eating. It's also the only thing I've ever been good at. And not once has anyone, even Keis, ever asked if it's what I actually want for a future. I don't know if they think it's what I want.

But no one bothered to make a guess or question me because I was always meant to do whatever complemented my gift.

And yet, the answer springs to my lips. "No." I pause. "That's not what I want to do."

"What *do* you want?"

"To help my family," I blurt out. It's all I've ever wanted to do.

Luc twists in front of the window so I'm forced to look at him instead of the scenery. "What do you want to do *for you*?"

I let out a little laugh. "Help my family."

I think of summers with the smell of BBQ in the air and kids running around. Of families laughing together. Being surrounded by people who I know would do anything for each other. Family has always been my safe place, and I would do anything to protect it.

My eyes water, and I look away. All I want to do is take care of my family, but I can't even do that much.

I mutter, "No matter what I do, it'll always turn out however it was going to turn out." Dad still left. It wouldn't have mattered if I said I would come with him or not. Both would have had the same result. And no matter what I want to be, my gift will decide my future.

"Okay," Luc says, voice soft. "You want to help your family. How could you do that?"

I could kill you. I swallow. "Take action . . . I guess."

"What's stopping you from doing that?"

Morality. Inability. Though technically, also not being in love with Luc yet. "I'm not ready." I finally turn and look at Luc.

"Why don't you get ready, then? Get ready and try. Trying would be better than nothing. That's basically what you were telling me. You would have a chance to get what you want in life. Isn't that worth it?"

He's giving me a pep talk on killing him and has no idea. My entire life must be a joke to the ancestors. But still, he's so earnest that I can't bring myself to say no. "Okay."

He narrows his eyes. "I'll follow up to check that you're doing it."

"How?"

"I don't know! I'm basically a genius, I'll figure it out."

I laugh despite myself. "A genius who can't even figure out how to return a container."

He turns to look out the window. "If I give it back, what excuse will I have to keep inviting you places to return it?"

I don't deserve to feel the rush of heat that floods my chest. Not with what I've done to Juras. Not when I still have to destroy Luc.

And yet, I can't help it.

Luc jumps to his feet. "This is our stop." We slip out of the seats, and he holds his hand out to me.

Without missing a beat, I slip my hand into his.

It takes Luc approximately thirty seconds to get uncomfortable with the hand-holding and let go. I don't mind because I know reaching out in the first place was probably awkward for him. We get off the streetcar at Queen Street East and Bellefair Avenue, where little gift shops are opening their doors across from a massive park.

The Beaches. The neighborhood synonymous with the sort of people who spend their summers walking along the boardwalk with their strollers and pure-bred dogs to buy locally made, mod-free jams.

"You're making a face," Luc says.

I pull my grimace into a smile. "I'm thinking bitter thoughts about rich people."

"I can understand how this neighborhood would bring that out."

"Then why are we here?"

"Because I like it despite that." He walks across the sidewalk to the stretching grass of the Beaches Park. "Justin grew up here."

"Shock and surprise."

Luc throws a little smile over his shoulder. "It's nice."

"But is there food?"

"Why would I bring you somewhere you couldn't eat?"

I raise my brows. "Excuse me?"

"Your entire feed is either food you make or food you've eaten somewhere." He says it so matter-of-factly, and he's right, but I'm annoyed that he is.

But also, kind of . . . flattered? "You checked out my feed? I mean, since using it to humiliate me?"

Luc cringes. "Sorry again for that. I've glanced at it."

I eye him. "Looked at it once, or twice, or three times, or every day?"

"Glanced!" He points to a food truck in the middle of the park. "This place does amazing Mexican breakfast and lunch."

The truck is a sleek black with red, yellow, and green stripes along one side. It proclaims EL PARQUE, and a woman in a black apron is puttering around inside. The holo board on the outside flashes to life. There are already a few people lined up.

Luc groans. "You can't do anything in this city without waiting in a line."

"A lineup means it's good."

"You should know it's good because I told you it is."

I can't roll my eyes back far enough. I walk ahead of Luc and join the queue. It's late enough in the morning that we've missed the impatient Thursday before-work rush. This line is filled with parents with babies in strollers, young people either on their summer break or doing home studies, and elderly people on their morning rounds.

They're the best kind of people to line up with because they wait calmly while swiping through their phones or chatting with each other. None of that anxious energy that people on their way to work bring.

I glance at Luc, and he's staring at people placing their orders through the truck window. The shadows on his face and pinched tightness of his mouth betray his thoughts. I'm sure he's thinking of Juras.

I turn my gaze to the grass under my feet. A streetcar ride and the promise of food was enough to make me forget what I did for a little bit.

I want to confess. To spill out every secret to Luc like he shared his thoughts about Juras.

To tell him everything about me and my family. About what I did to Juras and what I know about Justin. About this task.

If I could confess every single secret I'm holding in, I feel like somehow he could help. That he could come up with some sort of genius solution. We could work together on it the way we did to find out about Auntie Elaine. When we try, it just works. It's that simple. Like a recipe that comes out perfect every time you make it.

I flex my fingers before pulling them into fists. Only that wouldn't happen.

There's no way he would take knowing any of it well.

I would never see that lip-biting smile again. Never watch that open expression. He wouldn't ever tell me little childhood stories. He would regret ever putting Fade Ink on my body.

He wouldn't even be back to the boy I met at the NuGene Q&A. The one who was annoyed with me.

If Luc knew everything, he would hate me.

My stomach clenches, ripples, and churns all at once. I wince.

"You okay?" Luc's eyebrows push down.

"No, it's fine . . . I'm just hungry. Don't you feel sick if you don't eat at your usual times?"

Luc tucks his hands into his pockets. "No. People just need to eat. Times don't matter."

"How often do you eat?"

"Once a day, usually."

I balk and look him up and down, wondering how his body isn't falling apart with the way he mistreats it.

Luc fidgets. "Can you not examine my body, please?"

"Oh! Sorry." Even after I look away, he keeps fidgeting. "Sorry, I didn't realize it would upset you. I'm just shocked your body isn't in pieces."

"I'm just used to some people being . . . uncomfortably curious about my body. Most people are fine. And I know that's not what you're doing, but it's still not a great feeling."

Heat floods my face. "I'm sorry, I won't do that again." Part of me wants to go on a rant to explain myself and how much I didn't mean that, but I don't. Sometimes you just need to say sorry and stop there.

"Thanks." Luc shuffles forward in line. "And you know those new boxed mac and cheeses have added nutrients."

I roll my eyes and laugh before sobering a bit. "Still, I'm sorry people do that to you. Get invasive about your body."

"Yeah," Luc says. "At the very least, it's more something people do when they first meet me, if they're ever going to. After that, they like to hyperfocus on me for different things."

"Like what?"

"My work and my career accomplishments."

"And your winning personality."

"No one cares about that."

"Your two-star reviews say that a lot of people care."

Luc crosses his arms. "They don't. No matter how shit you are to people, if they think you'll be useful later, they'll still slap a smile on their face." His expression morphs into that version of him that I first met. "You can be nice to people or you can be an asshole. In the end, if they can't use you, you're no good to them anyway. I could be Justin's favorite person in the world, and if I'm not the best professional choice, he can ship me off like anyone else. It's how people are."

I can't even refute it because here I am, with an ulterior motive like everyone else.

"Except for you," Luc says. "I thought maybe you wanted to get your cousin an internship, but she's already being endorsed by someone else, and Justin got her into the tour when I couldn't. And I've already helped you with your aunt. There's no real reason for you to still be around. But you are. And that matters to me."

In this moment, I hate myself. My head drops to my chest to avoid looking into his eyes. I've been disappointed in myself before, of course. Worried if I was good enough more often than I probably should. But I've always generally liked me. Except for right now.

I look up when we get to the woman at the window, whose face lights up when she sees Luc. She says something to him in a rush of Spanish, and he responds back in English. They seem to know each other from the Collective.

"And what can I get for you?" she asks me.

I make my request for huevos rancheros while Luc orders a breakfast burrito with guac and chorizo. I raise my phone to pay, and he presses my hand down. "I can get it."

"I—"

"Please." It's not a plea, just a legitimate request.

I let my arm fall, and he taps his wrist on the pay pad instead. We shuffle over to the other side of the truck to wait for our orders.

"Do you speak any Spanish?" I ask.

Luc shrugs. "Kind of? I can. I'm not very good. Justin put a lot of focus on me getting better at English, and on my robotics and genetics studies."

"You don't speak to your family in Spanish?"

He tucks his hands into his pockets. "Sometimes. But they always want to point out that I have an accent, and it's just easier not to."

The two of us have such different relationships with our families, but some things are the same. We both have pressure from them when it comes to our choices. It makes sense that his family wants him to come home and that mine wants me to murder him to save Eden and our magic. But that doesn't make it fair.

As we wait, I decide on something just for me. For this one afternoon, this small bit of time that Luc and I have together that isn't overshadowed by suspicion about Justin or trying to find out about Auntie Elaine, I won't think about my task. Won't overload my brain by trying to figure out how I'm going to murder this boy.

Just this one hacking time, I want to be a girl spending time with a boy that she maybe-kind-of-sort-of likes.

"If you did want something from me," Luc says with a smile, "what would it be?"

"I want you to live." The words slip out of my mouth like fumbling hot bread out of the oven—too scorching to keep in my hands and tumbling out before I can cool it down.

But it's true. I want him to go forward at NuGene and do something amazing. To keep creating new Fade Ink designs. To, for the hacking love of the ancestors, eat some real food more than once a day.

And I want to be part of it.

"Number forty-four!" the woman at the truck calls.

Luc reaches out for our food and hands mine to me. We find a spot on a picnic bench and eat while we watch the Beaches people with their 1.5 kids and dog stroll along the boardwalk. I sit down, and though he could sit across from me, Luc decides to settle right beside me instead.

"This is amazing food." I lick a bit of salsa from my fingers.

Luc smirks. "Didn't I tell you? My opinion is the best opinion you'll ever get on anything."

"Oh yeah?"

"Scientifically proven. It's in my genes." He takes a bite of his burrito and swallows. "I am sorry, by the way. For how I treated you and Keis at the Q&A." Luc fiddles with the edge of his paper plate. "Even if I thought you were wasting time, it's not an excuse for it."

"I forgive you. Honestly." I tilt my head at him. "What brought this on?"

"I was thinking of the first message you sent me. You apologized straight off for something you didn't even need to be sorry for. That's the sort of person you are. I was thinking that maybe it wouldn't hurt to try to be more like that." His face is open and vulnerable.

"It's not to try to make me raise your rating?"

Luc's lips spread into a smile. "That's a bonus."

And despite myself, I'm proud I did that. I put that smile there.

I always thought falling in love would be this huge spectacle, like touching a hot stovetop—a sharp and stinging burn. But in reality, Luc slipped into my heart like a quality hot sauce. Nothing at first, slowly warming, then a sharp kick that makes you gasp.

I know that I'm not there yet, but it's like I'm on the edge. Heat rises into my cheeks and tugs on a smile that isn't even in response to anything. I'm watching him eat a burrito, for ancestors' sake.

Luc licks his lips and asks, "Is there sauce on my face or something?"

"No," I say with a laugh. "Your perfect face is perfect as always."

He rubs the back of his neck and ducks his head to concentrate on his food. We finish up our breakfast and stay sitting on the bench, watching the people walk by.

It's not like we've never sat in silence before, but this one feels weighty, like the sort of fruitcake April-Mae Davis makes—so full of bits and pieces that you almost needed an electric knife to cut through it.

I like Luc.

Not maybe-kind-of-sort-of like him.

I like him, period.

It's strange to say in my head, and at the same time there's this pushing on my lips to let the words burst out. Like somehow I should declare it to Luc. I swallow with a gulp that sounds ear-splitting in my mind.

"You okay?" he asks.

I bob my head in a nod.

Luc gives his own awkward head shake approximating a nod. He looks up at the tree we're under. "This thing doesn't shed leaves much, does it?"

I stare up with him. "Not really, more of a fall than a summer thing."

Luc says, "Justin told me that if I wanted to kiss a girl, I should say there's a leaf in her hair so I have an excuse to get closer."

My gaze immediately snaps away from the tree to look back at him. He kind of looks back. Mostly, he looks like he's staring at my cheek, eyes stormy. I swallow the tide of saliva sitting in my mouth. "I'm pretty sure there's something in there. It's a lot of hair. Probably a good idea to check." My voice is too high, but Luc doesn't seem to care.

He shuffles closer on the bench, hand reaching to press gently against my curls, and coming close enough that I shut my eyes in anticipation. My legs are shaking, and my stomach is clenched tight enough to hurt.

Finally, he presses his lips against mine. We move together slowly, not from tension, but inexperience. We're finding our rhythm for the first time together. It's a newness that sends the same thrill through my body as when I cook something for the first time—that initial bite, realizing how perfect it came out, creates this ecstasy. I find that same sensation sliding my lips along Luc's. No recipe necessary.

We break apart and stay with our foreheads pressed together.

"Did you find the leaf?" I ask, voice breathy.

"What?"

I snort out a laugh and slap my hands over my mouth, conscious that I did it directly in his face, but he's laughing too. We're both cracking up so hard that people walking by start to look at us.

"I can't believe," I say, "that you draw the line at hugs but are totally okay with kissing."

"It's different!" Luc says indignantly. "Hugs can get so suffocating. You're literally trapping someone in your arms."

"Okay, so we can never hug and kiss?"

Luc shrugs and leans forward again. "Maybe I'll change my mind."

I close the rest of the distance between us, and we kiss for the second time that day. This one is different, not as slow but more comfortable. Tinged with the taste of hot sauce.

For the first time since Mama Jova gave me my task, I have a good day.

CHAPTER TWENTY-SIX

W hen I step off the bus in Port Credit the next day, my foot hits the pavement like an industrial-size slab of concrete. While I lay in bed this morning, reality caught up with me. I was ripped out of the haze that was kissing Luc and sharply reminded that this was a boy I had to kill. For once, the ancestors smiled on me, and Keis was already gone when I got up. No witnesses to the thoughts that swirled in my head.

I let the scanner waft over me and then slip through the gate of the Davises' house. Walking into their home is like entering a circus caravan. There are people in various states of dress, decorated in bright metallic blues and flashy silvers. The Islandz Mas Band has been run by the Davis family for years. Not to mention that every year they clean up at the King and Queen show, where each mas band showcases their massive carnival floats and competes to be crowned. This is their final push to finish their costumes . . .

And the day they do the ritual to protect the carnival.

I've spent this entire task with only one family held up as my example of what murder looks like, wondering how they could do it. How *I* could do it. Now I have an opportunity to get up close and personal with what Mama Jova's asking me to do.

If I can't even stare death in the face, how could I ever hope to bring it myself?

Not to mention, the Davises know how to cover their tracks. Justin may already suspect I have something to do with Juras being in the hospital. If anything happens to Luc, and Justin knows it has any connection to me, there's no way he'll do nothing.

I not only need to be able to kill—I can't get caught, either.

That's the only reason I'm here.

My stomach churns, and my breath comes out faster. Caribana is looming closer every day.

Eight days left.

"Voya? What are you doing here?"

I spin around and come face-to-face with Topaz. His curly hair is tucked under a massive blue-and-silver headpiece, and he's shirtless with extra-tight silver booty shorts as his only clothing. I recognize my beading handiwork on his costume.

He looks around me. "You come here alone? Are you looking for Alex?"

I stick my hands into the pockets of my shorts, but it reminds me of Luc, so I take them out. "I'm looking for Johan."

"Dad? Why?"

"Do you know where he is?"

He must notice me ignore his question but doesn't mention it. That's why I like him the best out of all the Davises. He doesn't need to be in your business. "In the sewing room, hovering over everyone."

"Thanks." I shuffle away from him and try to remember where the sewing room is.

Topaz's eyes burn on my back as I leave.

I find the room on my first try because it's the place where people are sprinting in and out of. The space is enormous. There are three rows of six sewing machines, and each one has someone working at a speed that must be magically enhanced.

To my shock, I spot Alex. After the reveal of everything about Auntie Elaine on Monday, I definitely didn't expect to see my cousin here on Friday, sewing away. She must have a sixth sense because she raises her head the second I glance at her. Her glitter-covered brows go straight into her hairline.

There's a strain at the edge of her eyes. I can't tell if it's from being in this house knowing what Johan did to her mom, or if it's because neither of us has really talked to each other since the beginning of the week. Or a combo of both. Before my task, it would have been strange not to talk to her every day, but now here we are, barely exchanging greetings for a week. I haven't even checked to see if she's been doing all right.

"Are you getting into the rum punch or what? Look at this!" Johan's voice carries across the room as he shakes a bikini top at a woman. He catches my eye as I head toward him and holds up a finger. "In a minute."

Alex's eyes on my back make my skin prickle. It's never been awkward to talk to her, but now I shuffle over with the weight of guilt on my shoulders. I should have told her about Auntie Elaine like I was supposed to before I blurted everything out. But there's also a lingering resentment for how casual she was about not believing in me at her show. I stop in front of her, and her sewing machine comes to a slow halt.

I raise my hands in an awkward ta-da gesture. "You're here."

"So are you."

Neither of us says anything for a moment until I finally choke out. "I should have told you what I knew about Auntie Elaine first before I brought it up to anyone else. She's your mom. I just . . . didn't even think of it, and that's hacked."

"I shouldn't have said what I did at the fashion show," Alex says. "I know this isn't an easy task, and I basically ended up complaining about possibly losing my gift when I know having Eden's life in your hands is probably the most sparked shit you've ever had to deal with."

Both of us stare at each other for a moment, mentally acknowledging what the other said. Then Alex stands from her chair, and I barrel into her arms.

"Okay, okay, too sappy," Alex declares, and I let go of her. "You have glitter on your face now." She laughs and flicks at my cheek.

I laugh along so I don't cry, the tension in my stomach loosening a bit. "I don't mind sparkles." I pause, then ask her, "Are you okay, being here?"

Alex collapses back into her seat. "She asked him. It was her choice." She looks me in the eye. "And I'm learning that when people make hard decisions, they don't do it lightly. If he didn't do it, she would have found someone else. He made sure it got done right."

"Yeah," I say because I don't know what else to say.

"It's not easy to be here, but I am. This is my family too. Even if I'm not blood-related like the twins." She lets out a deep sigh and flicks her chin at Johan. "Why do you need to see him?"

"You're not going to tell anyone that I was here, right?"

That makes Alex's eyebrows climb. "What *are* you doing here?"

"I want to ask Johan about something." I start to walk away, then turn back. "I mean it. Don't say anything to anyone."

"Girl, I heard you." Alex shakes her head. "You're so suspicious right now. I hope you know that."

Get sparked, now she'll go out of her way to figure out what I'm doing. It doesn't matter. No one is changing my mind. Not Granny, not Alex, or anyone else. I need to save Eden. And to do that, I need to be able to kill Luc. If I can't even watch a murder, how could I commit one?

It's like learning a new recipe, I tell myself. Sure, you can read what's on-screen and do it. But it's better to watch it being made on a feed. You can get a better feel for how everything is supposed to come together.

Right now, the idea of murdering a real person is so foreign and impossible. Watching will bring it into sharp focus. And maybe I'll finally understand how the Davises can do it, so that I can too.

I swallow hard as Johan waves me over. "Voya? You want to play mas this year?"

"No." I wring my hands together.

"Then what you want? I'm busy, you know?" His dreads swing as he moves.

I force myself to put my hands at my sides. "I was hoping I could talk to you in private. It'll be quick."

He tosses the scrap of fabric in his hands to the woman he was talking to, then walks to the door.

I hurry to keep up with his long strides.

He takes me to a room straight across the hallway. Emerald is sitting on a couch inside, flipping through feeds.

"We need the room," Johan says.

She bolts up, green-and-black wig swaying, and leaves. It's another reminder of how different our families are.

Johan stretches out on the couch and waves a hand. "Is this about your Mama problems?"

I sink into the seat beside him with hunched shoulders. "I need to learn how to kill someone." There it is. I said it. It's out there. "I know there's a rite tonight. I'd like to watch it. Not join! Just . . . watch."

Johan's dark eyes sharpen. "That would make your granny furious." He tilts his head to the side. "Though that's kind of a pro in and of itself." He frowns. "Either way, this is a big favor. Why would I do that for you?"

"Because we're family."

"Yawn, next."

I cross my arms and draw myself up. "What if I was your intern?"

"Excuse me?"

"Roti Roti. At the block party, all anyone could talk about was my food and dessert. I can cook. You know I can. Don't you want your business to thrive? I thought that was your legacy."

Johan curls his lip. "And my legacy needs you?"

"Caribbean Queen has a fifty-year-old history. We come to you because we're witches and know you. But everyone with any island in their blood or an interest in West Indian food goes to them."

"So you'll give me a three-year internship?"

"One."

Johan steupses. "What you gon' do in that time? Three."

"Two. That's the most."

"Fine."

I blink at him.

"What? You're shocked it worked? I'm about to double back to three."

"No! Just two." This is the best scenario for Johan. He gets me for two years, and since I'm his only intern, the government will pay my salary.

My future is not my own—now more than ever, because for two years it belongs to Johan.

My hands clench into fists.

This is the only opportunity I have to get closer to fulfilling my task. There aren't exactly murder schools out there, and there's a different quality to an impure ritual. The Davises aren't doing this because they enjoy killing people. It doesn't make it right, but at least our intentions align.

Everyone in my family wants me to complete this task to save

Eden, even if they don't like it. But no one has even the first idea about how I'm supposed to do it. Granny would be the only one who might know, and from the conversation I overheard, she seems pretty confident that I won't be able to kill no matter what. Time is running out. If this brings me closer to being able to complete this task, then it's worth two years of my life in the Roti Roti kitchen.

Johan fixes me with a stare. "You were raised with your granny hammering in the importance of staying away from these rites. She thinks her message of purity puts her above us. And yet, here you are." His spits out the word "purity" like a swear. "The ancestors love irony, don't they?"

I don't think I'm meant to say anything, so I don't.

Johan leans toward me. He's so close I can smell the musk of ash that clings to impure witches, with a hint of curry powder. "You make sure you just watch. It is not easy to get bodies in this city, and if anything goes wrong, there aren't any extras conveniently hanging around. This is an important piece of protection for Caribana."

My nails cut into my palm as I squeeze my hands tighter. "I'm just watching. It's not like I'm joining in where you have to worry about me breaking the circle."

He leans back against the couch. "True. Still, it's always good to double-check. Be sure that you're on your best behavior."

Johan doesn't say it, but there's an unspoken warning in his words.

I don't understand what he's worried about. I'm watching, not joining. That's where the real danger is. If you're involved in a ritual, you can ruin everything by breaking the circle. It means you forfeit the rite and the magic that comes with it. That sort of free-flowing power doesn't take well to being left without a host. It lashes back.

I know that because when their last ritual failed, Johan lost his youngest girl. Sapphire. At her funeral, tears rolled down his smooth cheeks as her ashes blew in the wind.

That year at Caribana, a brawl broke out and the police were called. Three people died. Two of them were hit by cars, chased into the street by the authorities. And the last died of his injuries from the fight. Maybe the cops could have cleared the crowds and roads to get him help in time, but it didn't happen. So he lay there and bled out.

I spend the rest of the day tucked away in the room across from the sewing chaos to wait until it's time for the ritual. Will they use sharp blades that make cutting feel easy? Or something blunt so they have to use all their muscle to dig into the victim's skin?

And who is this person they're going to murder? Will their family miss them? I swipe my shaking finger through feeds, picturing every member of my family bleeding out in the name of magic.

A message from Luc flashes across my eyes: *Juras woke up. His speech isn't great, but Justin has the best therapists on it. He'll be okay.*

My chin dips to my chest, and I curl my knees up.

All I can do is hurt.

I send back a message: *I'm glad to hear it. How are you?*

Fine. I'm thinking about things.

Thinking about things?

Wondering if I was wrong. If I missed other people like you who don't just want something from me. Maybe I'll increase my ratings?

You can only try.

My fingers slip away from the phone, and I can't anymore.

Luc is wrong. I *do* want something from him.

I want to trade his life to save my sister's. Even as I wish he could live.

The couch in this room is comfier the more you sit in it. I'm half drowning in brown suede by the time Emerald comes into the room and throws herself down next to me hours later.

"Do you want me to leave?" I ask.

She shakes her head. "Nah. You're fine." Her modded eyes are shining emerald like her namesake. "Daddy says you're coming to the rite tonight. I thought Thomases did pure magic?"

I sink farther into the couch. "They do. Just . . . maybe not me. Not anymore. And I'm only watching." I point at the monitor on her wrist. "How's the matching program been for you?" It's an obvious attempt to change the subject.

She bites. "It's been okay. The guy I got paired with is an intern there."

"What?"

Emerald makes a face like she thinks I'm the densest piece of overcooked black cake she's ever been forced to associate with. "An intern. Apparently, they wanted a few of them in the project."

There's no way two daughters from prominent Black witch families ended up being paired with NuGene interns by chance. Does Luc know about this? No. Justin frequently keeps things from him. This would be another.

But why would he loop the Davises in on this? Justin needed Auntie Elaine's genetic manipulation abilities to help him, but none of us has that gift, and it would take generations for it to cycle through our family. And while the Davises are related to us, it's probably not enough to get her gift. What is his endgame?

Emerald eyes me. "Why are you watching the ritual?"

Looks like I wasn't as good at subject changing as I thought. "I . . . just need to." I almost elaborate, but don't.

"The more you do it, the easier it is."

My vision narrows to the space on the floor just under my feet. I press down on my knees so they don't tremble and clench my teeth together so I don't cry out, *How could something like this ever be easy?*

The door swings open, and Alex walks in. She jerks her head at Emerald. "Can you give us a minute?"

Emerald pushes out a deep sigh at being ejected for the second time today, but leaves.

Alex's makeup has partly run down. Probably from being in that hot sewing room. She hands me a cup. The liquid in it is the yellow orange of a sunset. She has one for her, too.

I take a sip. The sweetness hits, followed by a bitterness that makes me cringe. "What is this?"

"Rum punch. You should drink the whole cup. Help you get through the night."

Hack my feed. I don't know why I thought Alex wouldn't find out. Not after I ran my mouth in the sewing room. "You know?"

"I know."

"And?" I hide behind my cup, taking another sip. I would rather have plain juice. How do Mom and Auntie knock these back?

"Like I said, sometimes people need to make hard decisions," Alex says. "I wasn't spouting spam on Monday. I do think you're the strongest of us."

I don't know if I believe her, but I'm grateful for her words. "I don't want to do it. This task."

"I know."

"But I have to."

"I know that, too." She reaches over and pulls me into a side hug that I melt into.

When I was growing up, I constantly relied on Alex for strength. I would drag Keis out of her room when I had nightmares, and we would both sneak into Alex's for protection. She can't protect me from this task, so all I can rely on is her support.

The door swings open, and I expect Emerald, but it's Topaz standing in the doorway. "It's time to go."

Already? It's eight p.m. Shouldn't a ritual involving murder happen at midnight or something? I tilt my cup and chug the rest of it. When I stand, my head kind of spins for a moment. It's gone by the time I've handed the empty cup to Alex, and instead, a sort of calm fuzziness has set in. I glance at the one in her hand.

She hands it over. "Maybe just take it easy. . . ."

Alex hasn't even finished her sentence, and I've already gulped the whole thing down, cringing from the bitterness. Dimly, I realize this is the first time I've drunk alcohol since Christmas, when Granny let me have a sip of her shandy.

"I'll see you at home later," I say.

She shakes her head. "I'll wait for you. We can go home together."

My throat dries out faster than macaroni pie in an unattended oven, so I don't say anything and follow Topaz out of the room.

We go down a set of stairs to the basement. There's a digital scanner there. The lock on the door clicks, and he opens it for me. "Ladies first."

The stairs are cement, and my steps echo as I make my way down. I have to press my hand against the wall so I don't trip. The door shuts behind me, and I ignore the shiver that works its way along my back. Auntie Elaine came here years ago, knowing she was heading to her death.

I expect the basement to look ceremonial. Stone and bare. It isn't. It's a regular rec room with pool tables and huge L-shaped couches. At the back is a touch screen that spans almost the entire length of the wall. It would look like an ordinary room if not for the plastic sheeting laid down, and the man swinging from the ceiling by his ankles.

They've stripped him naked, blindfolded him, and gagged him. For a second, I think he might be dead, he's so still. Then he makes a muffled cry through his gag.

I slap my hand over my mouth and stumble back. Something touches my shoulder, and I whip around. Topaz pulls his hand away. "Sorry."

"No. I'm sorry. It's okay."

When I turn back, I get a better look at his black springy curls and brown skin. Silent tears stream down the man's face.

I look for a place to spit. I need to get the taste out of my mouth. It's mixing with the rum flavor and threatening to bring everything up as sunrise-colored vomit. Topaz nudges me forward, and I force my legs to move the rest of the way down the stairs.

Johan pushes away from the wall where he was leaning. "Aqua, get them ponchos." He gestures to my feet. "Shoes off. Just in case. Splatter, you know?"

I kick my sandals off and ignore the "splatter" comment. Aqua, Johan's oldest daughter, comes over to Topaz and me with two plastic ponchos. They're the kind they give you when you go to Niagara Falls and ride the *Maid of the Mist*. You feel the cool splashes of water against your face, and if you close your eyes, it's like you're floating through the falls.

Except there's no cool water or floating feeling. There is, however, a sort of fog in my head. The air is heavy with humidity made thicker by the air fresheners meant to cover the stink of sweat. Already, it's like the scent of impurity, the ash, lingers in the air along with it. I sniff the inside of my wrist like it might stick, though I know that's hacked. You have to participate in impurity, in the pain, the suffering, and benefit from the kickback to get that scent. Witnessing wouldn't be enough to transfer it to me.

"You, on the steps," Johan says, pointing to me. "Everyone else, over with me."

I'm cold. Industrial. I cling to Topaz, stopping him from going forward, and whisper, "Is he . . . a bad man?"

"It doesn't matter," he mutters. "We aren't here to pass judgment. We're here to exchange one life for the protection of many." His voice is flat and robotic. These are lines he's been fed many times.

Garnet, sixteen years old, just like me and Emerald, presses a knife into Topaz's hand. The handle is made of ivory, and the blade is a sharp stone. Ceremonial.

The circle is made up of Johan, Topaz, Aquamarine, Emerald, Garnet, and the youngest, Peridot, who's only thirteen.

I sit hard on the cement steps and get rewarded with a sharp shock to my tailbone. Pulling my knees up to my chest, I rest my chin on the plastic-covered surface of the poncho and wrap my arms around myself. My head is too light. The fuzziness brought on by the rum punch is making it hard to concentrate. Hack me, I shouldn't have drunk Alex's, too.

The man shakes in his bonds, and his whimpers screech in my ears, pointed and cutting.

"Voya," Johan barks, and I jerk straight. "Stay there. You can't leave once it starts, and I can't babysit you. This requires a huge amount of focus. Do not distract us."

I've always known Johan is dangerous, but he's never hurt me. I remember being a little girl with Keis at Roti Roti, where he would sneak us pholourie and tamarind balls. He would sit with me for extra hours after class when I struggled with an assignment. Pure or impure, we've always been family. I know what he's capable of, but I've never worried about those claws turning to me.

Until now.

Impure rituals are powerful but fragile. Johan couldn't teach us about them, but of course his kids have whispered about it at the annual backyard party before. Once the rite begins, they need an intense focus on their intent, so much so that they can't pay attention to anything else but the body in front of them. Not to mention it strips them of the ability to cast while it's happening, which is why they need to be in secure places like this locked basement.

"Yes, sir," I say, forcing my voice to be stable.

Johan gives me a curt nod.

The Davis kids have blank expressions on their faces. How many times have they done this? Johan, gay and proud the entire time I've known him, had them made in a petri dish with his love and gives them everything. Their moms are unknowns. In Canada, you can't buy eggs from donors. They can only be given free of charge to families. There are rumors that his kids' moms are witches who asked Johan for favors, and their surrogacy was his price. I asked Emerald once if she wanted to know her birth mom, and she raised an eyebrow and said, "Why? I have Daddy."

This is the only cost of being a Davis. They have to do the dirty work so the rest of us can live safe in this community. Their family takes lives to save lives. It's not as easy to judge them when I'm doing the same thing.

"We come here tonight to honor our ancestors and protect their kin." Johan spreads his arms. "This rite is to bless our sacred day where we celebrate our traditions and welcome our ancestors from their eternal sleep. We will stomp out violence that seeks to harm our people. This carnival is our heritage, and we will protect it."

Johan claps his hands together. "That is the intention of this rite."

They have the intention. Now comes the blood.

Instantly, I want to jerk my head away. To avoid what I came here to do.

But I don't.

Johan lifts his knife high and digs it into the man's stomach. His victim screams in a way that sounds more like a squealing animal than a human. His skin splits away from the blade. Blood gushes and sprays the blue plastic of Johan's poncho. Johan doesn't smile. He doesn't enjoy it. He just *does* it. Crimson coats his victim's hair . . .

Blue-gray hair.

My stomach throbs as if I were the one stabbed.

That hair. Luc?

I jerk up from my spot on the steps, stumbling forward. Wanting—no, *needing*—to get closer.

The others follow Johan, faces grim as they sink their knives into Luc's body. Flesh ripping open and spilling blood like a macabre fountain. And all the while, Luc screams and jerks his body, trying to get free.

Did the adults set this up? Granny, Mom, Auntie . . . Did they bring Luc here so the Davises could kill him for me?

I keep moving closer and closer. Walking in a staggered line.

Peridot's knife gets stuck, and he has to brace his foot against Luc's body to pull it out, Johan coaching him gently all the while.

The magic builds in the room like an extra dose of gravity trying to force me to the floor. Peridot is panting from his struggle with the stuck knife.

"Don't!" Luc's voice is wet—the sobs clogging his throat with spit that gurgles as he screams. "Please stop!"

My legs are as cold and stiff as the concrete floor I'm walking on. His body swings toward me, and blood leaks from his wounds and splashes against my bare feet. I feel it squishing between my toes.

"Stop," I mumble, my voice thundering and thrumming in my ears, but soft out loud. "Stop it."

They're going to kill him.

They're going to kill him!

My fingers press against his face, wet with tears.

"Voya!" Johan screams, suddenly right next to my ear.

The vision snaps, and all at once I become aware that the man in front of me is not Luc.

He never was.

I stumble back, away from his bleeding body.

And it's only once I've done it that I realize my mistake.

I've broken the circle.

The thickening magic in the air changes from a fog to a lightning bolt in a storm. It takes shape and forms a whip of fire.

And it's directed at the circle breaker. At me.

When the first lash of rogue magic hits my chest, a scream shreds my throat. I turn and shrink away from the pain, and the next lash hits my back. The smell of my flesh burning fills the basement. The scent is like charred bacon in a skillet.

I'm sobbing so hard I can't breathe, waiting for the next lash, but it doesn't come.

The loud grunt that sounds behind my ear makes me turn my head.

Behind me, Johan is crouching over my body, his face overcome with agony, every vein in his neck thick and pronounced. Overtop him, the white-hot light of magic strikes down on his back again and again.

Lashes meant for me.

"What are you doing?" I choke out.

Johan's eyebrows knit together, and he lets out a sharp cry as another whip comes down. "I won't let another child die in this house." He bares his teeth. "Even if she's a stupid little girl who brought this on herself."

One final whip echoes in the basement before it dies out, like the calm after a bomb goes off. The scent of ash and decay lingers in the air.

Johan collapses next to me, covered in his blood, my blood, and the blood of the man swinging on the rope.

The man who's no longer crying and jerking.

The man who isn't Luc.

He's gone.

Another sob tears through my throat, and I curl up next to Johan. The pain rushing through my body feels like it will never stop.

The door to the basement slams open, and there's a rush of feet down the stairs. Someone picks me up, and I scream as they jostle my wounds.

"I know it's painful, it's okay," Uncle Cathius whispers by my ear.

I've never been so happy to see him. "It hurts."

Alex comes up beside Uncle and presses her hand to my face. "I'm sorry, I had to tell someone, and he's the only one keyed into the scanner for the basement. It's going to be okay."

She doesn't understand. The pain of the whip stings, but what hurts more is watching Johan bleeding on the ground as his children slice open their fingers to offer blood and heal his wounds. Peridot won't stop shaking.

What cuts into me is the dead man swinging from his rope and knowing that Caribana will not be protected this year or the next. An entire community, vulnerable to anything on the one day we're supposed to feel safe. A life is gone, and it doesn't matter. A man has died for *nothing*.

The pain that thrums in my heart is because, against all odds, I saw them killing Luc and my first instinct was to stop it. This is the second time I've tried to protect him from death when I'm meant to deliver it, even if it wasn't real today.

Alex said she knew fashion was her first love because she couldn't imagine a future without it.

In the back of my mind, I can't picture a world without Luc. I don't want to. Even if he hates me or I never see him again, I would want to know that he's out there living his life.

The realization is as swift as the punishment for breaking the circle.

I can't kill Luc because I'm in love with him.

And my baby sister is going to die for it.

CHAPTER TWENTY-SEVEN

I wake to burning skin and the stink of aloe mixed with medicinal herbs. Around me, the familiar sights of my room come into focus. The huge window beside my bed that overlooks the backyard, the cheap digital board I hung on the far wall that shuffles through food feed photos, and my wardrobe with its mirrored doors.

My reflection shows heavy bags under my eyes, the knotted mess of my hair squished into a bun, and thick patches of a milky green cream creeping up my neck from underneath the blankets.

Uncle sits in a chair beside me, peeling one of his apples. The skin falls away in perfect ringlets under the sharp blade of the paring knife. He slices it into quarters, removes the core, and cuts each quarter into four identical pieces. Skewering a segment on the tip of the knife, he offers it to me.

I shake my head. "How long have I been asleep?" I expect my voice to be as dry as my throat, but it sounds the same as usual.

Uncle retracts his piece of apple and pops it in his mouth. "You shouldn't have been in that ritual."

"I wasn't supposed to be in it." I clench my jaw and curl up off my stomach. "Please don't lecture me right now."

"Keep your back straight! That ointment needs to set." He puts aside the plate and eyes my wounds. "How is your chest?"

My fingers graze the stinging lines that snake from the bottom of my stomach to under my clavicle. I expect gauze and tape, but what I touch is a rubber mesh pressed over the thick green cream. It's the kind that they use in private hospitals for those who can afford the high price. "How did we get these? This is Magic Mesh." Magic Mesh—not actually magic—heals burns and wounds faster with a combo of nano tech and stem cells.

Uncle grunts. "Your boy brought them."

"Luc?"

"Lie down!"

I stop trying to push myself up and collapse back down into the sheets. "Luc is here?" My cheeks warm, and I develop a sudden fear that "I love Luc" is pasted on my body somewhere for everyone to see.

Uncle's crossed arms show his disapproval. "Apparently, that monitor you have gave off some sort of spike, and he was over here pounding on the door and demanding to see you."

My heart is beating too hard and fast. It hurts against my tender chest. "And Granny let him in?"

"He was threatening to get his sponsor dad over here—someone we definitely don't want anywhere near our home, though I doubt he knew that—so she let him in." He clenches and unclenches his fists. "I hate to admit it, but that mesh he brought helped a lot. You were lucky."

"Lucky?" The memory of the magic whipping me burns its way to the surface.

"Sapphire died the last time a circle was broken. And you're alive." Uncle's brows dip, and his entire bald head wrinkles.

"Johan . . . He helped me. Why couldn't he help her?"

He blows out a breath. "My mother stopped him. She's the Matriarch, no matter how he tries to play at it. Her rule is every Davis in that house age twelve and older participates. The same rule her mother and her mother's mother used. If they break the circle, you let the magic decide whether they live or die. You don't interfere. So, he didn't. I guess this time, he wasn't willing to step aside again. Probably helps that she wasn't around too."

His eyes travel over my back. "Ava would never let something like that happen. It's part of the reason I'm proud to assist her. She changed this family for the better. Went against everything she was raised to be and made a difference. My mother would never. She's too invested in power. Your granny has always been willing to put everything on the line to do what's right for her family. If I hadn't married Maise, I would have pledged myself to Ava just to be a part of this family."

I stare slack-jawed at Uncle. I thought he hung around Granny out of some strange wish to be Matriarch, even knowing that he never would. Instead, he only ever wanted to be part of a family that wasn't like his. A family that wouldn't let a child die in their basement for the sake of tradition.

"Sapphire had the most beautiful eyes I've ever seen," he says. "Big and brown. She was too soft a girl born into too hard a family."

"Am I like that?" I've never cared about Uncle's opinions, but somehow, in this moment, I want to know.

"No," he says. "You're a strong girl in a strong family who was given the wrong task."

I think of Alex's words in combination with Uncle's. I was sure everyone in this family thought I was weak. Voya, who can't make decisions no matter how simple. Voya, who already failed her Calling once. Voya, who can't kill a boy to save her sister. But now two people have said the opposite.

Mama Jova said she picked me for a reason. I wonder what she thought of herself before the moment she became a Mama. Did she think of herself as someone strong or as a failure? Could someone like me ever have the sort of strength she has?

My mind goes to the image of crimson whips slicing through bodies, and immediately the screams of that man in the basement fill my ears, shrill and sharp.

That's not the sort of strength that I want.

There's a quick knock on the door, and then Mom and Auntie push their way into the room. I try and use the mirror to see if Keis, Alex, or Keisha is behind them, but no one else enters. No Luc, either.

Uncle stands and clears his throat. "Feel better. And don't do anything like that again." He points to the plate of apples. "Eat something."

I roll my eyes and sink back into my pillows. Classic Uncle. Still, as his hand is on the doorknob, I say, "Thank you. And please thank Johan, too." No matter what Granny or anyone else thinks of him, even if I disagree with some of what he does, Johan helped me last night. He set aside his Matriarch's rules and put his life in danger to save mine.

Uncle nods in acknowledgment before leaving the room.

Auntie settles in the chair while Mom sits on my bed. She tugs out the elastic in my hair and rearranges it into a neater bun.

When I look into her eyes, they're edged with tears. "Mom . . ."

"I shouldn't have told you to finish it," she chokes out. "That day on the phone. You told me you couldn't do it, but I kept pushing you."

"That wasn't why I went. I was trying to save Eden. I thought if I could see them take a life, maybe I would understand how I could too." I let out a breath. "It just went all wrong."

Auntie snorts. "No shit."

"Maise!" Mom shouts.

"What? We know something got sparked because you've got magic lashes on your body taller than you." She shakes her head and brushes my forehead with a trembling hand. "Got you over here looking like Mama Jova."

I press the heels of my hands against my eyes. "My head is messed up. I keep getting confused. And I'm too weak to finish the task sooner and make it stop."

Auntie clucks her tongue. "If weakness is not being able to kill someone you're in love with, we're all weaklings. Mama gave you an impossible task."

"Don't pretend," I snap at her, pulling my hands away from my face. "None of you have ever thought this was something I could do."

Mom stumbles over her words. "It's not because we don't believe in you specifically. Like Maise said, it's an impossible thing to do."

"The ancestors don't give impossible tasks."

Mom grabs my hand. Her eyes are hard and serious. "Do you think I could kill your dad?"

"What?" My ribs press in and make my heart struggle for space.

"Do you think I could kill your dad if I was given that task? If it was for the sake of the family and magic, he may even volunteer to die. But do you think I could murder him in cold blood?"

What kind of question is that? "I . . ." Could she? Mom doesn't like Dad. They fought while together, and now that they're apart, they ignore each other. I don't think she loves him anymore. It should be easier. And yet . . . "No."

"No, I couldn't."

Auntie clears her throat. "Do you think I could kill Cathius?"

My first instinct is to say yes. But that's wrong too. When their relationship went sour, Auntie could have pushed for him to move out. She didn't.

Neither of them could have done this task. Mom and Auntie have always been strong women. I think of them and picture iron will and perseverance. I've never thought of myself that way, and yet it would be as hard for them as it is for me.

Mom grips my fingers. "Your dad and I have had our problems. There have been bad times. There have also been good times. Whether it's your first love, second, third, or fourth, it's not easy to forget about that. It's near impossible to snuff it out."

"Then why would she make me?" It's the question that's been on my mind from the start of this process. Tasks are supposed to help you learn, become better, and prepare for your gift. This . . . What could she possibly be preparing me for?

Auntie sighs. "Who knows why the ancestors do anything? Mom is the only one of us who speaks to them outside of the Coming-of-Age, and she doesn't give anything away."

I clench my fists in my pillow. "Mama said she chose me for a reason. But why? We barely have anything in common."

"You look like her right now," Auntie mutters.

Mom shoots her a look. "It's hard to understand her reasoning. Mama Jova was a different sort of witch. She has always straddled the line. She refused to practice witchcraft for a long time, and so she always ended up in the middle of being pure or impure. She killed those men to save our kin with a method that both used her blood in a pure way and used the blood of others in an impure way."

I nod along to Mom's words, but it's not quite right. Mama told me she couldn't decide which to be, pure or impure. She didn't refuse to practice out of some stance like what Keis does. She just couldn't make up her mind, and when she finally decided to use magic, like Mom says, it ended up in between. "Has anyone in the family ever been able to do what she could? Turn blood into a weapon like that?"

Mom crosses her arms. "You need to get better at remembering your history."

I scowl.

"Other Thomases have tried, but no one could ever do it like she did," Auntie Maise says. "They could do it with their own blood but not someone else's, or the other way around. And never with the power that people say she had. At most they could get the blood to lift up, but it wouldn't form into the deadly whips she made."

"She refuses to explain how to do it, according to the almanac," Mom adds.

As much as I'm not a fan of Mama Jova, I can't help but be amazed. There's a cast that only she can do, which is rare in families. Though her refusal to explain it probably helps with that.

She doesn't like to explain much at all. Like how she keeps saying this is my choice, yet everything comes down to this thing I have to do but don't want to. This thing I *can't* do, if I'm being honest.

Mom clears her throat. "Now, I've had your cousins entertaining him, but there's a boy downstairs who's impatient to see you."

"What does he think happened?"

"We figured we would leave that conversation and decision to you. The question is, do you want to see him?"

I don't need to think about my answer. Even though I got into this mess trying to learn to kill him, I can't say anything but "Yes."

It's only been a few moments of waiting for Luc after Mom and Auntie leave when the sound of something shattering carries up to my room. It's loud enough that I sit up, hissing in pain, expecting to see something fallen in my room, but nothing's out of place.

Someone probably dropped a mug downstairs.

But then, I would expect sounds of Granny telling someone off, or my cousins arguing over the noise, or at least making fun of whoever's butterfingers dropped it.

Instead, there's silence.

Painfully, I push myself up off the bed and stand. Everything hurts, even parts of me untouched by the whip. The soreness and aches punctuate each move I make. I grind my teeth together and hiss out a cry from between them. I make my way to the stairs at the same glacial pace no-bake cheesecake takes to firm up in the fridge. Feel like it too. Jiggly and fragile. Like I was taken out of the springform pan too soon and am collapsing into a giant mess.

Walking down the stairs is even worse. I cling to the banister with shaking arms. I never realized how involved my abs were in every single movement. Everything I do seems to include clenching my stomach and therefore sending a shockwave of pain through my wounds.

The silence below is starting to creep me out. Our house is *never* this quiet in the middle of the afternoon. Even when they're trying to whisper it's still loud.

Suddenly, Keis stumbles out into the hall at the foot of the stairs, clutching her throat.

"What's going on?" I ask, voice trembling.

She shakes her head. Her eyes are so bulged it's like they're trying to come out of their sockets. "You need to run! He . . . I couldn't read it out of his mind. And the adults, their magic is so weak now, they couldn't do anything—"

I forget the pain as I sprint down the stairs, making it to the bottom just as my cousin collapses on the ground.

Foam-tinged russet red spills from her mouth. She gurgles as she shudders and convulses on the ground. It could almost be comical, but it isn't.

This isn't happening. It's another vision. Another way for the magic and Mama Jova to mess with me.

My cousin goes still on the ground. Still like the man in the basement.

It's not real.

Shaking, I crouch onto the floor and reach out. This is a vision. I know it. I'll reach out to touch her and she'll disappear.

Keis's eyes are wide open, and the foam from her mouth has a stink like vomit. I place my hand on her bare shoulder. It's warm.

I cry out and scramble back from her body.

No. This can't be happening. That can't be my cousin lying on the floor with her pineapple bun askew, empty of any life.

I tear myself away from Keis and scream out, "Hello? Where is everyone?"

It's not real.

Wincing, I drag myself to my feet and hobble to the kitchen. Head swiveling, looking around for anyone else. When I get into the entryway, I stop.

The kitchen is a mess of bodies and spilled cups. Limbs splayed, crimson foam leaking from their lips and mixing into pools of brown liquids among shattered porcelain.

Keisha, Granny, Mom, Auntie, Uncle, Priya, and Alex with their teas.

Dad with his coffee.

And little Eden with her hot chocolate.

My family.

Gone.

It's not real.

Luc slips into the room. His face has the same hard expression it did when I first met him. If he's bothered by the bodies on the ground, he doesn't show it.

I can't look at them. Even if they're fake. They *must* be fake.

"You sat there beside me in that hospital bed when you knew what you did to Juras," he says, tone flat. "We spent that entire day together . . . we *kissed*, and the whole time you knew what you were planning to do." He shakes his head. "I can't believe I was so wrapped up in thinking *I* was the terrible one."

I swallow. There's no way Luc would know what happened to Juras, he couldn't.

"You're not going to say anything?"

"You're not real."

"Get sparked," he says, throwing his hands up. "Justin told me everything. He knows you did something to Juras. You did, didn't you?"

Part of me wants to say that I didn't know what would happen. That I never wanted anyone to get hurt.

A wilder part of me wants to shout that I love him, just to see what he does. To see what vision Mama Jova cooks up in response to that.

"Go ahead," I say to the fake Luc. "Say whatever it is you want to say to me." I'm tired of these tricks and visions. This time, I know what's happening. It's better to just let it play out.

Luc runs his hand through his hair and shakes his head again. "You don't even care. You're a liar. You pretended you didn't know what happened to Juras, and you spent that entire day with me knowing it was your fault. You're selfish. Justin told me that your aunt was the same. He wanted to help heal the world, make humans invulnerable to diseases, but she only wanted your people to get stronger magic. She wouldn't help him."

"He wanted to make people immortal," I snap, unable to hold back. "She wanted to help people, but that …" But that went wrong. In the end, she wound up dead and forgotten. I don't understand how this is supposed to help me. I just want this vision to end. To stop living in this place where Luc hates me.

"More lying," he says. "She wanted Justin to help all of you but refused to save his father. You're the same. You'll lie, cheat, and murder anyone for yourselves. Helping your family, just like you've always wanted." He spits the words and advances toward me. "But your family doesn't deserve to be helped."

Auntie Elaine wouldn't have done that. If she could have helped Justin's father, she would have.

She would. Wouldn't she?

It's not real.

I wave my hand at the bodies on the ground that I can't look at. "Is that why you did this? It's not an eye for an eye if I hurt Juras and you murder my entire family."

Luc takes a deep breath and his eyebrows pinch together. "I didn't want to. But it's Justin's orders. He said you and your family would never stop until you had revenge. You told me you wanted me to live, but you've been waiting to kill me. Haven't you?"

I let out a laugh. "Trust me, I can't."

This is just another vision from Mama Jova.

"I know what you want," I say to Luc, but it's meant for her. I'm tired of it. Tired of this task. Tired of these visions. Tired of suffering and surviving.

I rush forward to the block of knives and pull the largest one that I can find from it. A French chef's knife. Mom got it for me for my fourteenth birthday. The same kind professional cooks use. The same one with the partially melted handle that Luc held to Eden's throat in a vision a few days ago. I twirl it in my fingers. "This is what you want, isn't it, Mama?"

Weeks I've spent in agony trying to do her task.

Fine. If it makes this vision end, I'll show her what she wants to see.

"Who are you talking to?" Luc asks, face shifting from fury to confusion and back again.

"You want it, Mama!" I scream, raising the knife. "You got it!" I lunge forward, racing toward Luc, knife raised high above my head, both hands clenched around the handle.

When I bring it down, he jerks out of the way, just in time, and the metal of the blade slams into the island countertop. The sound rings in my ears, and Luc stays still beside me. I turn my head toward him. His chest is heaving, breath coming out in loud gasps, lips trembling in a way I've never seen before. I stare into his stormy eyes, strained at the corners and twitching. It's as if he's struggling to maintain eye contact, but at the same time is afraid to look away. There's something different about him suddenly.

"Are you real?" I ask, because I don't know how to tell anymore.

He shakes his head, dislodges himself from the island, and sprints from the room. The sound of the front door slamming echoes in the house.

"Voya?"

I swing wildly, the knife arcing in my hands, and by the time I realize that it's Dad, it's too late. He raises his right arm up, and I slice a gash across his forearm.

I stumble back and collapse on the floor. The knife falls from my fingers, stained crimson with blood.

The bodies are gone. Instead, my family stands around me, their faces aghast.

"Was he real?" I say again, looking at them. Everyone looks as horrified as Luc did. Priya has Eden's face pressed into her chest, her little body trembling.

Keis rushes over and wraps her arms around me. The tears on my face are drying while hers are beginning. "Did I try to kill him? The *real* him?"

"Yes," my cousin says, her voice heavy and wet.

"I was doing what she w-wanted." My voice catches in my throat.

Keis clutches me harder and shakes.

"I was doing what she wan—"

"Shh! It's okay, it's okay."

I blink against her shoulder. The vision wasn't just a vision.

They were here the whole time. I tried to kill him. "I failed."

Keis doesn't say anything, just tugs me closer. Wetness splashing on my face where our cheeks are squished together.

Fresh tears flood my eyes.

My hands shake as I curl into Keis, and our cries blend into matching sobs.

My earliest memory is sitting with my cousin in the yard, petting a neighbor's beagle puppy. We would run down the halls in matching braids and play any and every game we could think of. She would cheer me up with severely out-of-character funny faces when I was sad. When Grandad died, we both made faces at each other until we were crying together.

I can't bring myself to make any faces now.

From the corner of the room, Mama Jova watches me with empty eyes. "These aren't *my* visions. They're yours. Fears that manifest the longer you take to complete this task," she says. "Don't call out to me to stop them. Only you can. This task has always been in your control. It's your choice."

I can't tell if she's real, so I don't say anything back.

CHAPTER TWENTY-EIGHT

B y the evening, after an entire day of sleeping in my room with Keis curled up next to me, exhausted from crying, I have a better grasp on reality. I slip from the bed without waking her and shuffle down the hall to pee. My arms ache, sore from the force of my stab into the kitchen island. The rest of my body is in even more pain than it was earlier in the day.

On my way out of the bathroom, I glance down the hall where Dad, Priya, and Eden's room is. The last time I really spoke to Dad was when I confronted everyone about Auntie Elaine. Since then, it's been a frosty silence. I keep cooking her recipes, and he keeps refusing to eat them. Now he's likely in his room nursing the slash across his arm that I gave him.

I'm sure it was his touch that got me to sleep. Whenever I closed my eyes, I had dreams of swinging men covered in blood, hot lashes against my skin, and the stench of my burned flesh perfuming the air, stopped only by dreams of my family's and Luc's horrified faces and visions of what I must have looked like, wild eyes, slashing at the air and screaming at Mama Jova. There was a touch on my shoulder, and my muscles relaxed, my mind cleared, and I fell into a dreamless sleep.

I pivot my bare feet in the direction of his bedroom door and walk over. At the sound of furious voices coming from within, I stop.

"Our daughter's life is in the balance! We agreed Voya accepting the task was a good decision. Eden deserves the chance to know her culture and have magic. But none of that is worth anything if she dies!" Gone is Priya's light melodic voice. It's been replaced by this harsh, near-shrieking sound. "We need to go with the backup plan."

"Voya still has a week to complete the task." Dad's voice slips in with a placating tone he developed after he and Mom split up.

"Don't touch me!" There's a shuffle on the floor that I assume is Priya avoiding Dad's hands and his calming gift. "Voya is falling apart! You saw her. Screaming at the air and slashing with that knife. And we just stood there watching. That boy was terrified. I want her to pass as much as anyone, *more* than anyone, but that . . . Alex was right. We're a family. This should be a family effort. You would rather let your first daughter murder someone than do what we need to do!"

I cringe away from her words.

"Mama Jova gave her this task," Dad says. "We can't do anything about that."

"Except we *can*! You just don't want to do it. Voya almost died last night, and Eden is on her way there too. Your purity means more to you than your daughters!"

"Don't you dare say that!" There. That's the Dad voice I remember. Loud and booming.

Silence hangs in the room, and then the door swings open and Priya steps out, slamming it behind her.

I should go back to my room, but I can't make my legs move.

Priya's furious face melts when she sees me.

"Hi," I say, feeling ridiculous as I say it.

"I should have never made you make that promise."

"I'm going to—"

She shakes her head hard, braid whipping across her shoulders. "You're a child. I'm an adult. Holding two lives in your hands is more responsibility than anyone should be given at sixteen."

I swallow. My mouth opens to talk back, but I don't have an argument. It is a lot. Too much.

"I take it back," Priya says. "You are responsible for you. I am responsible for my daughter."

"I won't let Eden die."

Priya gives me a soft smile. "Neither will I." With that, she walks away.

It took long enough to get the adults off the idea that they could fix my task for me and accept that I need to do this. Now Priya's already launched backward.

"Voya?" Dad calls. He's standing in the entryway of his bedroom, maybe finally decided he was levelheaded enough to go after his wife. His forearm is bandaged with thick white gauze. He catches me looking and tucks it behind his back.

"Can I talk to you for a minute?" I ask.

"That's fine, come in."

He opens the door to his room, and I walk inside. We didn't have a bed big enough for the three of them, so Priya sourced some discount mattresses and laid them together on the floor. Once she finished sewing covers and adding floor pillows, it looked better than most of our beds.

I flop onto one of the mattresses.

Dad sits down beside me. "How are you doing?"

One of my ancestors gave me an impossible task I need to complete in the next week or the family will lose magic forever, which, by the way, will also kill my baby sister aka your second daughter. And I have a loose grasp on what's real and what isn't. Oh, and had a freak-out that scared away the boy I have to murder so that it will probably be impossible to get near enough to kill him. That is, if I can even do it. I'm also busy being crushed inside by the way he looked at me, the way you all looked at me.

"All right," I say. "Could be better. How's your arm?"

"All right, could be better," he says with a shrug.

"I'm sorry." It's not often that our family just comes out and says it, but there's no other appropriate way to apologize for attacking someone with a giant knife.

Dad shakes his head. "You didn't know what you were doing."

"I thought it was a test. That if I just killed him, the vision would end." I peer at him. "Did I really try to stab him?"

"The boy is quick. I'll give him that. I thought you were going to get him dead in the chest, but suddenly he moved, just in time. Really hacking fast."

I press the heels of my palms against my eyes.

"Whenever your mom did that, I knew things weren't good."

"What?" I say, pulling my hands away.

He mimes the gesture. "All of you Thomases do that. I caught Eden doing it once too."

"Did Auntie Elaine do it?"

Dad looks away and lets out a sigh. "She did, actually. To poke fun. Whenever she could tell Vacu was getting stressed, she would make this huge dramatic sigh and walk around with her hands pressed to her eyes. He always ended up laughing instead."

My brain can't picture an Uncle Vacu who laughs. I've only known him angry. Sharp words and strong hands. "What was she like, Auntie Elaine?"

"She was . . . bright. Like the stars, not the sun. Exceptional in a quiet way. Always cooking, like you." He focuses his eyes on his lap.

"Did her and Granny cook together?"

He snorts. "I think your granny scared the hell out of her. You two baked together once or twice."

"I don't—" It hits me. Of course I wouldn't remember baking with my aunt.

"You would get so excited, and you'd drag Keis along even though that girl can barely boil water." His lips spread into a small smile.

"Will we ever get them back, the memories?"

Dad turns back to me. "Over time, you should. It'll be harder for you kids. Children's memories are easier to disrupt because they don't stick as well as an adult's do and are harder to get back. But now that you know about her, certain things will start to get them going. That was always the weakness of the cast. Any mentions or significant triggers could bring everything back. It's why we couldn't even mention her to you kids."

"That means that one day, I could know her again."

"Yes."

"Tell me more. About her." Now I'm greedy. How different would things be if my aunt had Called for me instead of Mama Jova? Even in the afterlife, she was desperate to stay a secret to protect us.

"Hmm, what else? Back then, the Thomases were a big power. It was a huge deal to Elaine to be part of the family. Us Jameses aren't as highly regarded."

"It wasn't a big deal to you?"

Dad coughs and clears his throat. "Ava isn't a fan of me, but your mom does whatever she wants. Vacu on the other hand, he was golden child of the family, a doctor, and my sister, a nurse. People loved them as a couple. She fit in with the Thomases better than I ever could."

If Priya hadn't had that issue with her pregnancy, if they hadn't needed Granny's help, would Dad have come back to this house? I try and work up the courage to ask, but I can't. Four years of his absence stretching between us holds my tongue. "You miss her."

"She was my big sister. I loved her. She had a bright future, and it was stolen away."

"She sacrificed herself to stop Justin from coming after the family. To protect us."

Dad's hands grip into fists. "It won't last forever. Just like you kids can remember through emotional triggers, he can too."

"I think he already has," I whisper. I haven't forgotten his face in the kitchen. The way his lips twisted and his bionic eyes swirled. The threat of him looming over the threat of failing my task.

Dad's face doesn't change.

"Shouldn't we be doing something?"

"Her gift is gone. There's no point in him chasing after us because her ability won't be reborn into the family for generations. And it's not like we can pick the gifts we get. They never perfected that bit of genetic manipulation. So he can't threaten us into it." He shakes his head. "You should concentrate on your task." He says it like it's not always on my mind.

"Joy."

He lets out a breath. "What do you think our ancestors want from us?"

"To complete our tasks . . . and become stronger?" Though as of late, it feels more like we're entertainment.

"We call the ancestors Mama, Papa, and Bibi for a reason. They're like our parents. I love your mom's family, but their way of looking at our ancestors is, like, Old Testament. It's pain and suffering for the sake of pain and suffering." He clasps his hands together. "My side of the family, and Priya's as well, we have a different outlook."

My chest puffs out a bit. I know he's not trying to be offensive, but I feel like I have to defend Mom's family against his. Except, his family is mine, too. I deflate. "Okay . . ."

"Your parents are there to nurture you and help you grow."

379

I bite on my tongue. That's what parents are *supposed* to do, and he skipped out on a chunk of it.

Something in my face must sour, because he shifts on the mattress. "Sometimes being a parent means teaching your kids a hard lesson. The aim isn't to hurt you. It's to help. I think if you keep that in mind, this whole process won't feel so painful."

I stare at my toes. "What did you have to do for your Calling? What was it like?"

"I was driving a scooter, went into a trance, and crashed."

"You *crashed*?"

"Yup. Straight into a frozen lake. Came out of it in the water. Had to fight my way to the top and crawl to civilization freezing cold. I guess my choices were swim or drown."

"How have I never heard this story?"

Dad's lips thin. "I wasn't around to tell it to you, I guess."

Oh.

"Papa Dolma watched over me the whole time. I cried out for his help as my toes turned black. I begged him for mercy."

"And he didn't do anything?"

"No. I managed to crawl out and flag down a car. They brought me to a hospital. I lost two toes."

My head jerks to look at Dad's socked feet. How did I miss that? I mean, I must have seen his toes at some point?

He laughs. "I admit I'm self-conscious about it. I wear socks all the time."

Scramble my feed. It's true. I have a vague memory of being at Wasaga Beach with my baby toes wiggling in the sand and his socked feet beside mine. "That's unbelievable."

"I hated Papa Dolma for that. But when I left . . . when I left here, I went to a retreat in Sri Lanka. Fell down a cliff." He lifts up his shirt to reveal a nasty scar running along his side.

Who is this person I've been calling Dad?

"I tapped into the strength I used in my Calling and crawled out of the hole I landed in. At the top, Papa Dolma was waiting for me. He showed me the way to a house, and inside, Priya was there, taking time off to volunteer and research her family history."

"He showed you to *her*."

"Papa knew I would need to get out of that hole. Had he helped me when I was younger, I would have never known that strength, and I wouldn't have tried. Instead, I would have called for him and died there. But I did it, and he rewarded me."

"I'm guessing you don't hate him anymore?"

Dad smiles and tucks a stray dread behind his ear. "Nope. Do you see what I'm getting at?"

I suspect the gist of it is that the ancestors aren't so bad. Which is something I can't bring myself to believe when I'm days away from potentially losing my sister because of Mama Jova's task. "I don't know if that changes how I feel about Mama, but thanks for telling me."

I've learned more about Dad in these five minutes than in my whole life. Still, I'm grateful to have the time at all.

"This task is yours. It's between you and Mama Jova, no one else."

I thought he would have begged me to kill Luc after that fight with Priya. To ask me to save Eden at the cost of my morality. He hasn't.

I've always known that Dad loves me. Even when he left. But it felt obligatory. The sort of love you give because you're supposed to, without truly feeling it inside.

This Dad is so far away from the one who asked me if I would leave with him, a desperation in his voice so plain and raw that it snapped something. That something was my vision of him. He lost his superpowers. He wasn't my amazing daddy anymore.

Instead, he was the man who pushed an impossible decision on a child. The one who left.

Now he's the man who I know will love me no matter what choice I make. Not out of obligation, but because it's how he truly feels.

"Do you not eat my food anymore because it reminds you of Auntie Elaine?" I pick at the nail polish on my toes.

Dad shakes his head. "To be honest, I never liked her cooking that much. Too spicy. Too much butter." He pokes me in the shoulder. "I love *your* recipes. That's what you should enter in that contest."

"It's supposed to be a heritage recipe."

"You're part of that heritage. That's the thing about new generations—they change things in ways that the old ones didn't. They add something new and make it their own."

His words make me think of Johan, who put himself in harm's way and defied his Matriarch's traditions to save me. And yet he'll leave the Carters out in the cold for one favor too many. Auntie Elaine tried to introduce technology to magic, and to combat her failure, she saved our family from Justin, but at the cost of her life and our memories. Granny took our family from years of impure magic and strong gifts into an era of purity and weaker ones.

"I'm confident that you can cook something up that will touch people's hearts," Dad says with a smile. "You're good at that."

Touch him.

Mama Jova's words from that night come back to me in a rush.

Johan *chose* to save me. Auntie Elaine *chose* to protect us. Granny *chose* to be pure.

This task, what *I* choose, won't just alter the future of my first love, it'll change the fate of my family, too.

Mama Jova has been saying from the start that this is my choice. That I have control over my task. She told me to "touch him," and I was the one who decided to pick Juras when obviously I should have chosen Luc.

Again and again, I've chosen to save him.

I don't want to kill anyone. I don't want to murder to save lives the way Mama Jova did in the past. I want to do something new for the future.

Maybe there's a different way to complete my task. To reinterpret it and make it my own. I can shift our family toward a better fate with my decision.

And maybe if I do, I'll finally be able to see my future the way everyone else can see theirs.

CHAPTER TWENTY-NINE

I missed the part where the recipe contest said "live submission" when I signed up. Which is why I'm up at ten a.m. at Trinity Bellwoods Park, hustling my ass over so I have time to make my dish. Hustling in this case means I waddle and wince my way across the expanse of grass and paved sidewalks that mark the park squished between Ossington Avenue and Christie Street along Queen Street West. I've never been more thankful that we always have a stocked kitchen. Uncle and Dad rush behind me, carrying ingredients in EcoOven trays and dodging the masses of cyclists that populate the busy street.

For a park, it's not particularly serene. The city invades the space around it with cafés, bakeries, specialty paper shops, and non-mod health food stores. It's not the kind of place you can relax and picnic unless you're all right with the sounds of car horns, streetcars screeching, and that insectlike buzz of hundreds of people walking and talking. If you're like me and visit for the specialty tarts and ice cream parlors, it's heaven.

"Take it easy," Dad says from behind me.

I grunt through the pain lacing my healing wounds. "We're almost there."

It feels ridiculous to be here doing this when less than a week from now, I could fail, and Eden could die. I even messaged Keis this morning to say as much. But suddenly my door was thrown open, and she was rushing me out as the entire family bustled around getting ready.

I stared at her, confused. "I said I didn't think I should go. My task—"

"Doing this won't change it. And after yesterday . . . I think you need this. You'll have a clearer head after cooking anyway."

And that was that.

There's no line when I reach the two women at a table in front of a roped-off area. My eyes scan the park, and there are a few stalls open. Thank the ancestors that signing up also reserved a table for me. "I'm Voya. I'm supposed to be participating in the contest."

The younger of the two women, with blond hair and the sort of round wire-rimmed glasses that let me know she definitely lives in this area, holds out a clipboard to me. "Welcome! You're number twenty-six. You're allowed one helper—who will it be?"

I look for the rest of the family. Auntie dropped them off behind me, Dad, and Uncle to find parking for the huge minibus. Everyone rearranged their usual work to come and support me. I spot them walking across the park toward us. "My grandma, she'll help."

"That's so sweet. Can you write her name down, and we'll get her a number too?"

I note Granny's name on the sheet. It's strange to write her given name. She's always been Granny, plain and simple. Thinking of how she was in the past, how she must have struggled through a Calling like I am, feels far away and unimaginable. The fact that she was once an impure witch who hurt people, maybe even took lives, feels even more impossible.

The older woman hands me a sheet of paper marked "26" with safety pins. I clip it to my shirt and take the second matching paper she hands me.

Granny, Keis, Keisha, Alex, Priya, Eden, and Mom catch up to us. Eden's hair is covered with a sunhat, and there are streaks of white on her face from her mom slathering sunscreen on her skin.

My chest wound throbs harder as I look at her.

"You made it in time," Granny says.

I hold out the number to her. "I signed you up as my helper."

"Who says I want to cook in this hot sun?"

"Please?"

Granny snatches the number from my hands and pins it to her chest. My lips slip into a smile.

"We'll go sit down for breakfast while you two are cooking." There are lines around Priya's eyes I've never noticed before, and she looks weary just from standing. "It starts at twelve, right?"

"Yep." I turn toward the women for confirmation. "Eleven thirty a.m. judges' tasting, and then twelve p.m. it's open for the public?"

The older woman nods. "We'll announce the winners around twelve thirty." She waves over to the stations. "Your place is marked with your number. There are bain-maries to keep the food hot, mini deep fryers, toaster ovens, coolers, everything you need."

Keis nudges me. "Good luck."

"You mean you don't want to come and watch me and Granny cook? Like old times?"

She rolls her eyes. "No, I want to go eat breakfast."

"And check your messages for the millionth time," Keisha drawls.

"Whatever," Keis snaps.

The NuGene internship applications closed a couple of days ago, and soon they'll be sending messages to people who managed to land positions. "You'll get it," I tell her. Even though her getting that internship will drive her further from me, even if it might be dangerous to work for Justin, this is what she deserves. And more than that, it's what she wants.

She jerks her shoulder in a shrug. "Maybe."

"Not maybe. You will."

A hint of a smile graces my cousin's face. "Go cook! You're running out of time."

"She's not wrong." Granny eyes the other competitors, who are already busy at their stations.

Me, Granny, Dad, and Uncle make our way over to our stall, where, as the woman said, an entire portable kitchen is set up. Dad and Uncle set down the ingredients on the table and leave us to join the rest of the family for breakfast.

Granny squints at what we brought. "What are we making?"

I walk over to the ingredients I packed in a rush this morning. At the time, I felt panicked but focused. Ever since my talk with Dad last night, I've been thinking about what he said about me being a part of our heritage and adding something new.

"Do you remember the first thing you ever taught me to make?" I ask Granny.

She leans against the table. "We're doing my bake recipe?"

"We're doing mine, and yours, and Auntie Elaine's recipe." I pull out a couple of sticks of butter and put them in the freezer of the mini fridge and save one last stick for the fridge. When Auntie Elaine made the soft Caribbean bread, she would use powdered coconut from the store while Granny insisted on a specific brand of canned coconut milk.

When I pull out a whole coconut, her eyebrows shoot up. "You're going to milk that thing?"

"Fresh is better." I never tried it my way because I didn't want to mess up the recipe Granny taught me, but this is a way to add some of myself.

"And how do you plan to split that open?"

I press my hands together and put on my best begging face. "Magic, please?"

Granny rolls her eyes and sneaks the coconut into a corner. She splits her thumb with a tooth in the back of her mouth. It's a retro tradition for witches to have a sharp metal canine installed for easy blood drawing. No one younger than Granny is hard-core enough to do that anymore.

Opening the coconut takes longer than it would usually. With less than a week left until the end of my task, no one is in top operating shape. When Granny brings back the coconut, her forehead is gleaming with sweat from the effort. She grabs a bowl that she places under it.

"It looks whole." There are no cut lines.

"Drop it."

I dump the coconut into the bowl, and it splits it into dozens of small fragments, the fresh milk pouring over them. I grin at Granny, who smiles back. Examining her glistening forehead, I frown. Even Granny is suffering from the effort of using magic this far into my task.

We work quickly together, and I'm taken back to when I was six and sitting on a high stool at the kitchen island, covered in flour and kneading bake dough with her. Some moments, you know that you'll remember forever. That's what it feels like here with Granny. Like, no matter what, we can always come back to this. "Can you make small discs? I'm going to fry them."

Granny wrinkles her nose. "You're going wild today."

I rush over to the back burner to check on the salt fish I set cooking over the fire. There's also a second pot with a mix of sorrel flowers, cloves, orange juice and peels, and a generous amount of sugar. Exactly like how I've always made it for the holidays. A drink from my heritage to go along with the meal. I turn it off and set it to the side to cool.

I take the salt fish off the hot plate and drop it into one of the trays over a heated bain-marie. Grabbing the stick of refrigerated butter, I mix it with a combination of herbs and mashed sweet mango.

Granny's eyebrows look like they're about to disappear into her hairline forever.

"It's gonna be good!" I assure her.

"If you say so."

I use a piece of Iron Film to wrap the butter into a small roll and stick it in the freezer.

Granny finishes prepping the last of the dough and puts it in the fridge. I spot the judges on their rounds and drop three portions of bake dough in the fryer. By the time they come around, we'll be ready.

Granny pulls over a plastic chair and sinks into it. "I'm too old for this."

"You're young."

"Don't flatter, girl. I'm not going to be here forever."

My hands twist themselves into a knot. I can't imagine what life would be like without her. She's the Matriarch. She holds our family together. "You can't go anywhere. Who else is gonna be Matriarch?"

"Maybe you'll take over."

I snort out a laugh, but Granny doesn't join in.

"How are you doing?" she asks.

"It's all ready. I think they'll like it. I mean, I hope they will."

"Not what I meant."

Ah. She means how am I doing after yesterday when I almost impaled Luc with a kitchen knife. I haven't told anyone about how I've been rethinking Mama Jova's task. I've even been keeping my thoughts elsewhere when Keis is around, her gift dull enough that I actually have the ability to hide thoughts. "I'm . . . all right, I guess."

I'm not, really. I didn't realize how often Luc and I sent messages back and forth until I woke up to none. How empty the day would feel looking at my phone without his name popping up. And that's without even getting into the stress of looking at Eden and wondering how I'm going to save her. I can't picture her not here. My bright and happy baby sister.

Granny blows out a breath. "Tell me this. When you realized your knife had missed its mark, that you hadn't stabbed him, how did you feel?"

I open my mouth.

She cuts me off. "Don't you dare lie to me either."

I press my lips together and wait a moment before responding, "I was relieved." I thought I was going to kill a fake Luc to stop the vision. If I had really stabbed him through the heart . . . Even thinking about it makes my stomach clench and burn.

Granny gives me a slow nod and leans back in her chair. "In our family, you only participated in rituals if you were a witch. I had just passed my Calling. Got my gift in the Pass, alone, as we did back then. No Amplifying ceremonies either. Mom felt they were for weak families. And it was customary back then that right after, you perform your first ritual and take a life, to start you off with a high bandwidth. Alone, like everything else."

"Alone? You had to do a ritual by yourself?!"

Granny pulls a grim smile. "There were ten of us in the house, not much less than we have now, but I constantly felt as though I were living by myself. Especially because I was the oldest. That was tradition too. The oldest would become Matriarch. My siblings didn't like me very much because of it."

This is the most I've ever heard her talk about her childhood or her family. I'm ashamed to realize that I never asked. I assumed that everything I knew about her was what was important, and anything else was just her past. She never volunteered the information, so I assumed she didn't want to discuss it. "And you did it? The ritual?"

"I did." She shakes her head. "I left the woman blindfolded and sliced across her neck as fast as I could. Magic filled me and I got stronger. And in the afterglow, I cried. I kept my voice as quiet as I could so no one else would know."

I don't know what to say to her. I come closer until I'm standing right in front of Granny.

She gazes up at me. "Every day since, I've regretted it. I tried to find out about her, but there wasn't any information. Those are the sorts of people we tried to find. Folks without records. At first, I ran. From my family, from that woman, from everything. Packed up in that van with your grandad and Vacu, and hit the road as soon as I could. Because I knew that one day, he would have to stay in a room, alone, and cry over a dead body, a person he would never know.

"When I got pregnant with your mom, I realized that she would become the Matriarch after me. Or at least that's how it would have been under my mom's rule. It's different now. But at the time, the idea of her taking on that horrible legacy was too much. I wouldn't let my children suffer like that."

She licks her lips. "I came back home and pretended to be everything Mom wanted up until the day she died, to be sure I would be made Matriarch. It was my right as the oldest, but I had been away for a while, and was worried she would take it away from me. The day I was crowned, I told my family we were going to switch to purity. If they didn't want to, they would have to leave."

My jaw drops open. I knew Granny's family cut ties with her, but I thought they just left. I didn't realize that she kicked them out.

Granny smiles. "They all renounced me as their Matriarch. Some stayed Thomases and lived without connection to a leader or our family here, but most married into other families or pledged to new Matriarchs. For a time, I was the only Thomas-born witch in the house. But I had your grandad, Vacu, and your mom growing inside me. For once, I wasn't alone." She points behind me. "Take the bake out of the fryer."

Blinking, I rush over to my station, pull out three plates, and lift the fried bake out. The judges are nearly here, and I didn't even notice. I pat the pieces dry and assemble them on the plates. A piece of fried bake with a slice of the compound mango-and-herb butter and a spoonful of salt fish on top. To finish, I ladle out a portion of the sorrel into cups filled with ice, garnish with orange peel, and arrange them next to the plates. All the while, Granny's story plays on a loop in my head.

The judges stop in front as I finish. I recognize them from my food feeds. The Black woman with a pixie cut, Irae, blogs about Jamaican Chinese fusion meals; the man, Stephen, is a Japanese Canadian blogger who does traditional meals; and the last judge, Chaturi, is a woman who emigrated from Sri Lanka for a sponsorship and is one of the top food bloggers and reviewers in Toronto.

Irae smiles as she steps up to my booth. "What do we have here?"

I straighten my back and suck in a wince as it irritates my wounds. "This is fried bake; it's a flour and coconut milk–based dough, with a mango-and-herb compound butter, and salt fish with mixed peppers." My fingers shake as I hand them their plates and cutlery. "I've paired it with sorrel, a traditional spiced drink made from the sorrel flower."

There's a drone hovering beside us to film them making their rounds, and I try not to look at it.

Stephen glances at Granny in her chair. She has no reaction except to scroll through her feeds. "Who's helping you today?"

"My grandma," I squeak, and wave a hand in her direction. She puts down her phone to squeeze out a tight smile. "She's the one who taught me to make bake when I was little. It's a recipe she learned from her mother, and I've made some adjustments based on her recipe and some changes my aunt made."

Stephen looks around the space. "Is your aunt here today too?"

"She's . . . She passed away."

His eyes go wide. "I'm sorry to hear that."

"It's okay. She left a lot of recipes behind I've tried." I wish now, more than ever, that I could remember her. Dad said we used to bake together. At least I know now that the memories aren't gone forever. It may be harder for me to find them than it would be for an adult like Justin, but I can try.

The judges finish everything on their plates and their cups of sorrel, but the portions are small, so I'm not sure whether I should be reading into it. I search Chaturi's face, as she's the only one who's been silent this entire time.

She says nothing, only smiles, and they thank me and move on.

Granny clears her throat. "Are you going to fix me a plate, or what?"

I hustle to set up the dish for Granny and hand her a serving. Knowing what I know about her now, she looks different somehow. This entire time, I didn't realize there could be overlap in what I was struggling with and what she had already worked through. Granny put everything on the line to do what she thought was right.

She chews with small, measured bites and eyes me. "You came up with this recipe?"

"Yeah . . . I thought it would be good."

Granny finishes off her bake and sets down the empty plate. "I never asked what you wanted to do with your life."

"What?"

"When I was younger, a witch's gift was everything. Your entire life depended on what it was." She grits her teeth. "I hated that."

"What *is* your gift?"

"It doesn't matter," Granny scoffs. "What matters is I didn't want it to be my whole life, but I didn't raise any of you like that. Discouraged it, even. Keis is the only one who didn't listen to me."

"It's okay, I don't know what I want to do with my life."

Granny's eyes narrow. "That's the problem." She stands abruptly. "I need to go to the bathroom." She pauses for a moment, and with her voice just above a whisper, she says, "It was delicious." Before I can respond, she walks off.

"Can I try some?" Luc's voice slaps against my back as hard as the magic whip in the dark ritual.

I spin around. He's standing in front of the stall in a sleeveless black hoodie and ripped jeans. Typical Luc attire. His face has the same set to it as when we first met, that pinched expression, but it's lacking heat. I haven't seen him since I came at him with a knife.

This is also the first time I've properly interacted with him since realizing my feelings. Suddenly, I'm embarrassed. Like he can tell just by looking at me. I'm just an ordinary teenage girl with a serious love-level crush on a boy I almost killed. "Sure." I drop some bake in the fryer.

He looks around the stall. "Has Keis heard back? About the internship?"

Our shit is so sparked. Standing here. Making small talk like nothing happened yesterday.

"Not yet . . ." I swallow. Luc himself said he can't affect the positions, so whatever is going on with us shouldn't mess up her chances. And, even after yesterday, I don't think he would do that to her, to me. "What brings you here?"

"You."

Heat surges through my chest, and my hand shakes as I check the fryer basket.

Luc lets out a deep breath. "Justin is letting me reopen the NuSap program. I'll be moving away from NuGene Match and leading the research into the NuSaps. It'll take a lot of PR work, but he's giving me the chance to revive it."

"That's amazing!" I gasp. "That's what you wanted to do this whole time, isn't it?"

"It is."

"What changed?" Why did Justin decide to let him on board?

"I spoke with Justin about what happened."

My hands tremble as I lift the bake out of the fryer and top it with the compound butter and salt fish. I slide the plate over to him. "Oh yeah?"

He shakes his head. "When you came at me, there was no hesitation. Like you were really trying to kill me. Why would you do that?"

"Seemed like the only choice at the time." They're the only words that I can come up with.

"Are you still going to?"

"I don't know."

Luc lets out a sound that's somewhere between a scoff and a laugh. "You really would have done it. I could tell. The only reason I'm here is because something saved me."

"What?" I blink at him.

"Right before the blade was supposed to go in, I got jerked to the side. By something I couldn't see. I didn't move. Something moved me."

I don't even know how to begin explaining that to him because I have no idea what he's talking about.

"I told Justin that, too. I wouldn't have normally because it sounds so improbable, but my match had just tried to kill me, and I was reasonably shook up and rambling. He showed me the readings from your monitor. Special spikes in a specific sequence of neurotransmitter activity, the flashing I was wondering about." Luc stares at the plate in front of him with a wrinkled brow and lets out a forced laugh. "He seems to think they're indicators of magical activity. The sequence fires when the user performs magic. Actual *magic*. Can you believe that?"

I don't move my face. Not even to blink. Justin *was* tracking the sequence for magic. But in the Electronics Den . . . no magic was happening. No magic was ever happening because I don't have any. That's probably why the girl didn't notice it. A cool sweat breaks out on the back of my neck. What is Justin doing with that information? Why would he want to track that with someone who hasn't even passed a Calling? But then I guess he wouldn't know that.

"Did you hurt Juras?" Luc lifts his head to look at me. "You were talking about him yesterday. Justin said the only spike in your neurotransmitters, the *only* one, happened at the same moment Juras had his stroke. I saw the monitor flash myself. He seems to think that you did something to Juras with magic. I just . . . That's not a real thing. Right?"

Mama's spell. Of course. Passing it on could have registered as me doing it. I did, technically. I could deny it. Even if they can tell when magic is used, even if he saw the flash, it proves nothing. Luc doesn't even seem to believe in magic. He's looking for me to tell him it's not true.

But I'm tired. I'm exhausted from trying to figure out how to kill Luc and failing at every turn. From deciding that I don't want to but having no idea where to go next. I'm worn out from watching my family struggle. I'm sick of seeing visions of blood. And I'm finished with lying. "Yes. I did do something. With magic."

Luc's lip trembles the slightest bit. "Assuming you *could* do that, why *would* you?"

"Seemed like the best choice at the time," I say, almost exactly echoing my reason for why I tried to kill him.

Luc lets out a long breath. "Two attempts. One on Juras's life, and one on mine. Do I have to spend every waking moment worrying about you trying to murder us?"

"No, just until next Saturday. I have until then to figure it out. I would rather not if I can."

To his credit, he doesn't run. Even though I've basically said I might still give killing him another try. He stands his ground and cuts into the fried bake, eating a mouthful. It's the longest few seconds of chewing of my life.

I point to the plate. "How is it?"

Luc shakes his head, blue and gray strands blowing in the heated summer wind. "Perfect. Like everything else you make. Meals, magic, and murder, I guess that's your thing, eh?"

"I don't want to hurt anyone."

"Then why are you?"

Now that I've started, the desire to spill everything is overflowing. "I'm meant to destroy my first love. If I don't, my little sister will die." I want to look away but end up staring straight into his eyes. This isn't the best time or place for a confession, and yet here I am.

Luc laughs. This one is genuine. There's mirth in his face because this situation is that comical to him. "Unbelievable. This is ridiculous. I know magic doesn't exist, but something stopped you from killing me, and I couldn't see it. There are countless scientific explanations for phenomena that, before they were fully understood, people called magic. Did you know that?"

"If that makes it easier for you to understand, sure."

"It doesn't! Nothing about this is easy to understand." He runs his hands through his hair. "Least of all the fact that, by your admission, you are trying to kill me to save your family, but somehow you think that *I'm* the first person you've ever loved?" He shakes his head again. "You're smarter than that."

"Who do you think it is?" I snap back.

"Excuse me if I'm not jumping at the chance to help you pick a murder victim." He turns, and something he sees changes his expression. His eyes flare wide, and the color drains from his face.

I follow his gaze and land on who else but the Carters. Rena is done up as usual and winding through the stalls with her son. But Luc shouldn't know her, and yet he's acting like he does. "What else have you and Justin bonded about?"

"I was wrong."

"About what?"

Luc swallows, his throat bobbing with the movement. "I am the successor. Justin's call was about his second choice all along. Juras. With Jasmine as third choice." He crosses his arms. "He thought it was funny. He said if he knew I was worried about it, he would have just told me. He never did because he thought it was obvious."

I can only stare at him. It makes sense that Luc would be the real successor. He and Justin spent so much time together. Both his siblings bonded together and kept him out, probably because they were jealous. Even they could tell. It was obvious until Luc insisted that he wasn't. Now, more than ever, I understand why his sponsor trusted him with the truth about magic. They're bonded even more now.

Luc has everything he's ever wanted. And yet, he's here.

"Why did you come?" I ask.

He points to my monitor. "You need to take that off."

"I need to keep it on for the next week to get paid for being in the beta. And chances are, if Justin wants to find me, he will." I press myself closer to him. "You recognized Rena over there. Her daughter, Lauren, has been missing for more than a month. Does Justin know anything about that?"

He avoids my eyes and says nothing, staring out at the expanse of the park with all the other contestants handing out samples of their dishes.

The more I think about it, the more sense it makes. That's

why Justin didn't want to help look for her. And she *did* get the custom curl pattern, which meant he had access to her genes in a way he didn't have mine until I agreed to be in the beta program.

"Luc!" I snap out, voice shaking. "Does he know where Lauren is?"

"Justin . . ." Luc tears his eyes away from gazing out at the park and instead looks down at his plate. "He wants something from you, and I don't know how he plans to get it."

"Where is Lauren?"

"I don't know!" Luc shouts. "I saw a family genetics file on his computer with that woman." He flings his hand toward Rena. "He had some location data on her. It's nothing."

"Nothing doesn't make you look at her like that."

Luc gets in my face. "I don't know anything anymore. I can't trust my mentor, or my sponsor siblings, or you. I am floating on an island by myself. All I know is I can't confirm Justin has hurt anyone, but you have."

"Then you don't know him as well as you think you do."

"Just . . . watch yourself."

"Why help me? I tried to kill you. I still might." I don't want to take any lives. I still believe there may be a way around Mama Jova's task the same way I got around her "touch him" command, but I don't know for sure yet.

Luc tucks his hands in his pockets, his stare penetrating. "I wasn't aware that you were in love with me."

I gape at him because I don't know what else to do. I wasn't expecting to accidentally confess my love today, and I'm not prepared for it.

"I think it's best if you stop sending me messages. I'm putting a block on, so I won't see them anyway. Justin has agreed that he won't hold my seriousness regarding the matching program to being around you."

Are you breaking up with me?

The words rush to my lips, and I bite them to keep them in. We weren't even anything in the first place. Just matched up by a series of genes that a company decided means you're compatible.

My throat aches, and I don't trust myself to speak, so I don't. Tears spring to the corners of my eyes, so I turn away from Luc, ending the conversation. As if he hadn't already made things final enough.

There's nothing but the sounds of the park around us and the gentle sizzle of the fryers for a moment. Then the grass crunches in a sound that means Luc is leaving.

Blocked.

I won't have access to his feed or anything he's tagged in. Any messages I send to him will be deleted before they even hit his phone. He'll get alerts to any public location tags I use to make it easier to avoid me. Even if I didn't use them, I'm sure he could use his skills to manage to never see me again.

The boy with stormy eyes, gone from my life forever.

I turn around, just to watch him walk away, but he's still there. Staring at me. Only one foot stepped away. The rest of him very much here.

His eyes flare wide, and he stalks away from the park before I can say anything else.

My first love, come and gone.

The contest drone swoops in, and the judges materialize in front of my stall.

"Congratulations, Voya Thomas, you're our grand prize winner!" Stephen shouts, and they usher me out from behind the stall.

"That's my baby!" Mom screeches. She's sprinting over with the rest of the family and taking photos with her phone at the same time.

I look at the drone as the judges crowd around me for a photo.

This is what I've been working toward for weeks. I should be happy, not so miserable that I have to fake a smile.

As my family huddles around to cheer, I watch their bright faces, and my heart swells and clenches all at once. They set aside whatever it is they had planned for the day to come here and support me. So I could have a day to cook and recover from the mess that's been the last couple of days. With dwindling clients, they can't afford to avoid any chance to earn money, but they did anyway.

Hack me.

Luc is right.

He isn't the first person I've ever loved and was never going to be, not when I've always been willing to do whatever it takes to protect my family.

I'm not destroying a boy with blue-gray eyes and lip-biting smiles.

I'm snuffing out one member of my family to save the rest.

As the camera flashes, they become a cavalcade of corpses, each standing with hollow eyes and multiple knife wounds—blood oozing from their bodies and collecting on the ground.

Blood I'll be the one to spill.

CHAPTER THIRTY

N early a week later, we join the hundreds of people flooding into Lamport Stadium—the imposing field in Liberty Village that's been the site of the King and Queen show for more than a hundred years. I wouldn't call it a *nice* venue, but it is a venue. The rough concrete seats have been a staple for more than a hundred years, and it's played host to the showcase of the Caribana parade floats for nearly as long.

It's dark outside, but the flood of stadium lights makes it feel earlier than it is as we walk to the entrance. Auntie drove ridiculous again, worse because we're downtown, but she managed to get everyone here alive.

For once, Keisha and Keis flank her on either side. The former asking if she can hang out with the groups of kids lounging near the entrance, smoking flavored O2, and the latter asking if Auntie's sure that she filled out the NuGene parental forms properly. Some kids have started to get acceptances, but Keis hasn't yet. I'm sure she will.

Looking at the three of them together makes me think of when we were little, and they would pester Auntie Maise to say which twin she preferred. Auntie always replied that she most loved whatever unborn child wouldn't bother her. Of course, parents aren't supposed to pick favorites.

But I have to.

This is the first time I've been out of the house since the recipe contest and the revelation brought on by Luc. Nearly a week since I realized that my first love wasn't him but someone in my family. The whole "deciding who in my family to kill" thing in combination with the "how to destroy someone without murdering them" thing hasn't been going well. I've been both trying to avoid it and obsessing over it in equal measure.

Mom has been checking on me but hasn't mentioned Luc or the task. She still radiates a nervous energy but refuses to bring it up. After the scene in the kitchen, it's like everyone is too afraid to ask me what I'm going to do.

Instead, the adults have started having little secret meetings in Granny's room. Keis's gift is too weak now to overhear them, though she brushes it off by saying it's obvious they're talking about me, so why push it? It's still my task.

And yet she hasn't asked about the way my interpretation of the task has changed. I've been careful to not think too loudly about it around her, and she's been too preoccupied to bother digging in my head.

To everyone else, my task hasn't changed.

For me, *everything* has changed.

Tomorrow is my task deadline, and I'm no closer to a solution than I was a week ago.

I need to figure out who my real first love is now if I don't want to fail. Assuming that I can do what needs to be done.

Across from me, Dad and Priya walk hand in hand with Eden in the middle. Tonight, my stepmom seems different. Instead of looking tired, there's something bright about her face, almost determined. I guess her and Dad made up. They've been spending the entire week skirting around each other. Once, I even caught Dad sleeping outside on the porch swing instead of inside their room. Now they look like an ordinary happy family.

Alex slides up next to me in her sparkling red gown, spare headpiece feathers artfully glued to the corners of her eyes and blended into her makeup. "What are you going to wish for at Caribana this year?"

"What are *you* gonna wish for?" I throw back.

Keis comes up behind us and says, "The ancestors never grant anything you ask for."

"Ancestors help me, who invited the realist?" Alex groans.

Keisha comes up on her other side and they link arms. "Don't you know, there can only be one fun twin."

My best friend crosses her arms. "It's good to be realistic."

During Caribana, when the ancestors appear, you can ask any of those from your family for a favor. Every year, Auntie and Mom ask for the same $1,000 bottle of wine and never get it.

I shake my head. "They listen to Granny." Last year, she whispered something into Bibi Olivae's ear, and the next day we had a freezer full of salt fish. I cooked it for breakfast that morning and just used up the last of it at the recipe contest.

Keisha rolls her eyes. "She's the Matriarch—of course they'll listen to her."

"Granny also makes worthy requests. It's supposed to be something that benefits your descendants. You ask for stuff for yourselves, and that's why it never gets granted." Keis nods sagely.

"If she ever asks for us to have better gifts, the ancestors don't give it to her. Not often enough anyway."

Keisha's not wrong. I say, "Maybe there are limits to what you can ask for? Gifts excluded, that sort of thing."

"She could have used her Matriarch wish for it, but I guess she didn't know things would go to shit gift-wise back then."

I always forget that you get a wish when you're crowned Matriarch. Not anything as big as solving world hunger or erasing racism. Things within the means. I think it's to soothe the fact that a new Matriarch can only ascend when the former dies. Or is killed. That's the bit that Auntie and Mom don't like to talk about when they go back and forth about who's going to be Matriarch.

It's not exactly a happy occasion.

I don't even know what Granny asked for.

I'm never going to be Matriarch, so there's no chance of me getting that wish to fix my task.

An ancestor request is more realistic.

I wonder if that's even something you can ask them? Can you make me pass my Calling? Probably not. It would be too easy.

What would I ask for otherwise?

For Luc not to hate me. To go back to that moment at the Beaches where we had something close to happiness. When all I had to think about was his lips moving against mine.

Keis nudges me with her shoulder. "Are you okay?"

It's not something my cousin has had to ask me since she got her gift. She's always known. I stare around at my family. Alex and Keisha, who are chattering about which of the people smoking against the stadium walls are cute, the latter focusing on the girls and the former on the boys. Mom and Auntie, now with linked arms, laughing. Priya and Dad, who are swinging my baby sister between them. Even Granny and Uncle Cathius are having some sort of light, casual conversation.

"No, I'm not okay," I say finally. "And I don't understand why everyone else seems to be."

"They aren't."

"What are you talking about? Look at them."

Keis shakes her head. "Eden could die tomorrow. They're not fine, Vo. They're pretending to be fine."

I'm hearing her words, but I can't see what she can in our family's faces.

"Maybe it's because I've been in their minds, but there's a way people look when they're actually happy and when they're pretending to be. It's subtle." She shrugs. "You've had the last month to work out what you're going to do. Either you kill Luc tomorrow, or you don't. What is obsessing over it tonight going to do for you? If everyone else is pretending, you may as well too."

Would she be saying the same thing if she knew the truth? That someone in our family is on the chopping block and not Luc? Probably not. But she's also right. It's not like dwelling on it is going to make me finish any faster. What difference will it make to pretend that things are okay for the next couple of hours?

Alex and Keisha look over at us. "What are you gonna eat?" my older cousin asks.

"Am I the expert?" I say back.

"Yes!"

"Fried plantains, for sure. Pholourie."

"No doubles?"

I wrinkle my nose. "It's too messy, and they make them watery here."

"They're not that watery."

"They are! And the spices taste off. The plantains and pholourie are safe. Can't go wrong with fried foods."

Alex smiles, rouge lipstick and white teeth. "I'll trust you."

Somehow those words, even though they're about stadium snack foods, make me relax.

We scan the ticket codes on our phones at the turnstile and walk into the concourse full of food vendors. I shuffle after my cousins to get my food, plus a bottle of cream soda. We make our way up the steps and find our assigned seats near the bottom rows. The benches are hard slabs of concrete.

Uncle Cathius, ever the dutiful son-in-law, has brought cushions for Granny to sit on. The rest of us are too lazy to bother, so every year we end up with cold, sore butts by the end of the night.

Out on the stadium field, there's a huge black screen meant to obscure the waiting performers, except the floats are so giant that their multicolored feathers and metallic sheeting peek over the top. Soca music pumps through the speakers, and the air is full of curry smells and smoke from the fog machine the performers use.

I end up with Keis on my right side and Eden on my left. My little sister has tamarind sauce on her face from the pholourie she's been eating. I hand her a napkin, and she smiles as she wipes the mess off.

I know I love Eden, but she isn't the first family member I've ever loved. And my failing would ruin her future by default, so that can't be right. Mom or Granny would be the obvious choices. They raised me, after all.

But my first *love*, out of the two of them? I don't know.

"Welcome to the King and Queen show!" the MC yells into the mic as if he doesn't have a mic. "Tonight, as in tradition, we'll open with last year's winners, starting with the females. Put your hands together for the Islandz Mas Band."

We burst into applause and scream for the Davises' mas camp.

The soca music cuts and the field lights dim. A single woman runs out onto the field. Her hair and skin are caked in black ash, and she's clad in booty shorts and a tankini top. Under the makeup, I recognize her as Aqua, Johan's oldest.

She opens her mouth and lets out a scream, followed by a stepping combo of foot stomping and hand slapping.

"We came from the ash," the MC booms. "We came with our songs, passion, and traditions."

Three more women run out into the stadium and stand behind Aqua. They do another stomping-and-clapping combination before letting out their own screams.

"We grew and made plenty."

An army of twenty women covered in soot stomp onto the

field. The powerful sound of their feet and claps combine with the rhythm of their shouts. Once seeming like incoherent screams, they blend together into something like a chant.

"We were taken from our homes. We were chained. We were made subservient."

Their chant rises to a crescendo. The heat of magic swells in the air. Even the regular patrons will feel it but won't understand what it is.

The women do one final stomp, and the stadium erupts into a cloud of black smoke and ash. It doesn't touch us in the stands, but it obscures everything on the field.

"Now we are our own people. We spring from the ash and make the world vibrant with our color."

The words drum into my brain and stick there, firing like lightning in neuron flashes. I'm chained by Mama's task. After I complete it, like how the ancestors rose from ash, I'll become someone new too. I won't ever again be the same Voya I am now.

The dust settles, and the speakers blare out with the sounds of an electronic soca beat. A wind machine blows the last of the ash away, and from it comes a sparkling blue-and-silver float. Ten-foot-tall plumes fan out into the air and shimmer like a flight of glitter in the now full-blast stadium lights. The plumage surrounds the semirealistic face of a woman painted with black streaks. Mama Ublea. She's an ancestor of the Davises and is said to be invulnerable to lava. She was known for being covered with a thin film of ash, which helped heighten her gift.

Emerald is strapped into a human-powered float—the whole apparatus is attached to her body and outfitted with wheels on the bottom to make sure it follows her movements. She's wearing a giant matching headpiece, bikini top, booty shorts, and a body covered with so much glitter she'll need at least three showers to get it off.

She's also changed out her green-dyed-ends wig for one with silver tips. She dances a circle around the field with the float moving in response and stops for the most aggressive minute of wining and booty shaking I've seen in a long time. Finally, the song ends, and she makes her way off the stage. The crowd erupts, and we join in the clapping and screaming.

In the midst of the chaos, Keis is staring down at her phone. Slowly, a smile spreads across her face, and she immediately seeks out my eyes. I know, even without Keis's mind-reading gift, that she did it. She got the internship.

My brilliant cousin. I'm watching this huge leap in what will be her amazing life.

She'll move out of the house into university dorms and split her time studying and working. I won't be dragging her downtown for restaurant visits because she won't have the time.

She'll graduate and move from dorms into the NuGene apartments and become a shining star in their PR department, probably even discovering a way to put a new spin on the NuSap's reputation as the program is relaunched.

She'll come home maybe for Christmas Eve and Day. Sometimes she might even stop by for the odd birthday or anniversary.

And I'll always be there. At home, waiting for her to have time for me.

She turns to shout the news to the rest of the family, half of whom can't hear her and the other half who are celebrating. Finally, everyone catches on, and we're all jumping up and screaming. Even Uncle Cathius. The adults never wanted this for Keis, but now that she's got it, now that she's this happy, none of them can deny it.

My eyes linger on Keis's face. I try and memorize the perfectly drawn arch of her eyebrows I know she spends at least fifteen minutes on, the deep brown of her eyes that ignite when she gets into debates, the patches of dry skin we would stay up late making homemade coconut oil face masks to treat because Granny didn't want us "wasting" the high-end product.

I remember Keis with twists in her hair running up and down the stairs with me to see who was fastest.

Keis helping boost me up on the counter so we could sneak sweet tamarind balls out of the cupboard.

Keis sitting with me when I cried that it was my fault Dad left because I couldn't give him the right answer.

Keis with a huge smile on her face when she got her gift. Before she started to worry about it being the only important thing about her.

My thoughts were the first she ever read. The glowing emotion of pride reached out to her from my mind.

Eden tugs my shirt. "Why are you crying?"

"I'm going to the bathroom." I don't wait to hear Eden respond before I slip away from my family and out of the stadium.

I break out into the cool night outside, and a sob tears from my throat. Loving Mom and Granny feels like something automatic that happens in the background. I didn't think about it, it was always just there. Not to mention, I've always known that they wouldn't be around forever. That at some point in my life, I would be without both of them.

But Keis, I've never pictured any aspect of my life without her. One of the earliest memories I have is running down the hall of the house with her, Granny shouting at us to slow down. I expected my last would be us in rocking chairs as old ladies. How I felt about Keis was never how you tend to naturally love people in your family. It was deliberate. It was my choice. And it shone brighter than any other love in my life for it.

Keis is my first love.

And now, on the day her entire future has changed and that

spark I helped build is bright and new, I know that's what I have to destroy.

Keis's future is wrapped up in this dream I've helped her achieve. This internship is the catalyst that changes her life. To take that away from her, to resign her to the type of life meant for me, an empty future, would be as good as destruction in her mind.

And I don't know that she won't hate me for this. Even if it's to save Eden.

But at the same time, Luc is still a first love. Not my first love ever, but my first romantic one. The same way that I could choose which "him" to touch at the dinner, why can't I choose which first love the task applies to?

A platonic first love: Keis, my best friend and cousin.

And a romantic first love: Luc, the boy with blue-gray eyes and an awkward smile.

Both of them with futures at NuGene brighter than anything I could ever achieve.

Taking that away would destroy either one of them. And it would save Eden.

I just have to choose.

A chill settles over the back of my neck. I turn around, preparing myself for what new vision might be there.

Mama Jova stands, illuminated in stadium lights, naked and strong. "Your choice," she says, her voice a wisp on the wind. She frowns at something behind me, and I turn.

Keis looks beautiful in the night. Her curls float around her face, and her eyes sparkle with light. She has her left arm hooked around Luc's neck while her right hand presses a blade against his neck.

"You would destroy him for me, wouldn't you, Vo?" she asks. "Aren't I worth more to you?"

Luc says nothing in his defense. Only slumps against my cousin's hold. Resigned.

Keis shakes him. "He has everything! The internship, the money, the education, and he's an asshole to everyone he meets. He's ungrateful!" Her eyes water. "You know I would never waste that opportunity. I would do better there than he would in his entire life." Keis takes the knife away from his neck and holds it out to me. "Destroy him for me. What's the alternative? Ruining *my* life?"

I rub the tears from my eyes and squeeze them closed. Luc will be the successor of the company, and he's been given the chance to run the program he's always dreamed of. But is that worth more than what NuGene could potentially give Keis? She hasn't had the chance to enjoy a crumb of the privilege he's had since he was a child.

This is my cousin's dream. My best friend's future up against a boy who I've just met.

But what will Luc do without the sponsorship? Without Justin? He doesn't get along with his family and hasn't lived in the country he was born in for half his life. And NuGene is *everything* to him.

But am I willing to take away from Keis to let him keep what he has? Could I manage to complete my task without shedding any blood? Or am I wrong, and I still have to kill to do it?

When I open my eyes, Keis stretches out her hand farther, the blade glinting in the moonlight.

"What are you doing out here?" Granny's voice is soft but has the impact of a sharp hiss of steam from a pressure cooker. I flinch and turn to face her.

She lingers near the entrance to the stadium, the gray hairs in her little afro even more illuminated in the lights. Every day she seems to get older. Tired.

"I don't know what to do," I choke out. "Tomorrow is the deadline, and I have no plans for how I'm going to complete this task. How I'm supposed to save Eden. I can't let her die."

I'm tired of pretending like I have any idea what I'm doing. I don't even care that I just admitted to Granny that she and the adults were right. I can't do this. But I have to. I need to make a choice.

Granny doesn't do anything but press her lips together.

"You talk to the ancestors," I say. "Why would Mama do this to me? What does she want me to do? How am I supposed to fix this?"

"The ancestors haven't spoken to me in years."

My mouth is halfway open to beg for more help when I stop. "What?"

"I call, but none of them come. Alex was right. I let her mom face the consequences of something we all agreed to by herself. The ancestors couldn't forgive me for it." She pauses and lets out a soft sigh.

I want to ask if she forgave herself, but her face, the sort of vacancy of it, tells me she hasn't either.

Granny walks closer to me and looks back at the stadium, where strobe lights flash and soca blares. "Mama Jova was the last to visit me, eleven years ago, on the day that Elaine died. She let me know that your aunt had been named a Mama, and she had some other choice words as well." She scoffs. "I never realized how important a role Mama Jova would come to play in our lives."

It shakes me. The idea that all these years, Granny had been cut off. It made sense now, why she didn't have any answers from Mama Jova about the task in the beginning when everyone was telling her to. She couldn't. "But wait, that one Caribana, you asked for the freezer full of salt fish. Bibi Olivae gave it to us. The ancestors have never granted anyone else's wishes."

Granny laughs. "Girl, why would I ask for a freezer of salt fish? I went over there to try and get an ancestor to talk to me. The salt fish was *your* wish."

"That wasn't—" I pause.

That day, Bibi Olivae had glanced over at me when I followed Granny to speak to them. I hadn't met them before and was curious. Bibi asked me if there was anything that I would like. I was thinking about how it would be nice to do a big bake and salt fish breakfast the next day, so I blurted out that I wanted a freezer full of it, like I was fully sparked or something.

Granny rolled her eyes at me and whispered something to Bibi Olivae. I assumed that she had asked for it on my behalf. It never crossed my mind that Bibi was granting the wish for *me*.

Suddenly, the last piece of the puzzle clicks into place.

I know how I complete this task.

I thought Mama Jova made Caribana the deadline because of how much it means to us. But what if she knew all along that I would need help? She has been obsessed with *choice* this entire time, not method.

Hack me. What if that was my chance, when she put the power into my hand? It seemed too easy, for the task to just end like that. And I didn't think I was in love with Luc yet, but maybe I was. Maybe the moment I decided to risk gaining Justin's attention to help Luc, it was love. But if all Mama Jova's ever cared about is my choice, that could have been it. It wouldn't have killed Luc, but it may have destroyed his chance to be successor of the company if Justin decided that, given his injury, it would be better to go with Juras.

And just like Juras did, Luc would have recovered. He would have lived, even if his future was destroyed. Mama Jova gave me an out. One that let me have everything without requiring that I suffer as much as I would now.

I was right. I never had to kill anyone.

Everything has always been my choice. Exactly like Mama has been saying since this task started.

All I have to do is choose.

But no matter what decision I make, Eden will live. I know that now.

I slap my hands over my mouth, and tears brim in my eyes. My chest heaves as adrenaline courses through my body. I think about voicing my plan aloud but can't. How do I explain to Granny why I'm struggling to choose between Luc and Keis? Family is always first. She wouldn't understand why that decision would be hard.

Granny frowns at the tears in my eyes and the rapid rise and fall of my chest. "I failed Elaine, but I won't fail you. I promise." She lets out a soft breath. "I've been sitting on a decision for the night, but I finally know what choice I'm going to make."

"What decision?" I croak out.

She grins at me. "Should we go for ice cream after this or frozen yogurt?"

I break into a laugh that's intermixed with sobs.

"Everything is going to turn out all right. Eden will be fine. She's not dying tomorrow." Granny's voice is strong and resolute. Like it's obvious that I won't fail this task.

Almost like she actually believes in me.

This time, she has a reason to.

I know how I'm going to save my baby sister.

All that's left is to make the hardest decision of my life.

CHAPTER THIRTY-ONE

By the time I clue in to the fact that I'm being shaken awake, I suspect it's been happening for a while. I open my eyes blearily, my room still cast in darkness. We got back from the King and Queen show close to one a.m., and it feels like barely any time has passed since.

"What?" I groan, squinting as Mom's face goes from a blurry smudge to a slightly more recognizable one.

Her fingers tremble against my bedsheet where she clutches me. "I'm gonna go out for a bit, okay?"

"Okay." Did she seriously wake me up to tell me she's going out?

She pets the silk bonnet on my head, put on every night to protect my hair from getting too messy or having the strands ripped out. "I know this has been a hard time for you, but everything is going to be all right."

I'm too groggy to put together what she's saying to me.

"Don't go to Caribana without us. Be sure to wait until we get back home." Mom grasps my shoulders. "Do you hear me?"

"Yeah, don't leave without you."

"Just . . . wait. It's very important that you wait."

I give a firmer jerk of my head, but my eyelids are already closing again. Mom presses a long kiss to my forehead and leaves the room.

. . .

I wake up to the sounds of my cousins walking outside my door and talking loudly to each other. Or it feels loud anyway, but it may be normal volume for them. I stretch out, and a vague memory itches at my brain. As I lie there, staring at the ceiling, whatever the thought was is obliterated by the realization that it's my task deadline day.

My only saving grace is that I at least know that Eden won't die today.

But I have to choose, destroy Keis's or Luc's future.

I press the heels of my hands against my eyes.

This should be easy, but it's not.

Family first. I should save Keis's future. She's my cousin and my best friend. She's worked so hard to get to this point in her life.

I pull out my phone. Luc blocked me so I can't see his feed anymore. But still, I look up his name just so I can stare at the lack of results. I've looked him up enough that I can almost picture what I would see. Mostly NuGene articles with barely anything of what makes Luc *Luc*.

I look up his sponsor sibling, Jasmine, who hasn't blocked me. Probably because Justin and Luc haven't shared anything with her. I'm too ashamed to look up Juras. Not that it matters; her feed is full of him anyway. The two of them really do spend all their time together. They feel like a proper family. A real brother and sister duo. It's like Luc doesn't even exist in their lives. Them against the favorite—the sibling they knew would be successor, right from the start. Alienated from his sponsor siblings and biological family.

All Luc has is Justin and NuGene.

There's one day left in the matching program. I have enough money from the recipe contest to cover the cost of the oven. If I wanted to, I could take off the monitor.

I don't.

Taking it off feels final. Like shutting the door on something I've only glimpsed.

And if Justin wants to come for us, he will. Monitor or no monitor.

I scroll through Keis's feed next. It's filled with photos of our family. Mostly of the two of us together. She posts about impassioned political stances and shares the odd hair tutorial video. Her latest post exclaims in large block letters how she'll be starting as a PR intern at NuGene in the fall. My stomach clenches.

There's a knock on my door, and I jerk up in bed. I fill my head with thoughts of worrying about my task, of wondering about Luc, of stressing over Justin, anything but my cousin.

Keis doesn't wait for me to answer before slipping into my bedroom. Despite the firm set of her mouth, the happy energy from last night is still pouring off her in waves. It's just suffocated by the anxiety of the day.

I cover my thoughts loudly with a pop song annoying enough to stick.

"You're supposed to be dressed," she says. "Everyone is ready."

I slink out of bed and drag myself to the closet to yank out an outfit. "The adults are up?" The memory starts to come back to me, Mom at the edge of my bed. "My mom said not to leave without them."

Keis shrugs. "The adults have been gone all morning, but it's already ten a.m. Keisha and Alex have their costumes on, and they're ready to go. If we wait any longer for them, the crowds are going to be ridiculous." She stares at me for a moment. "It'll be good, I think. To just get out. Today is going to be . . . a lot. I know you. If we stay here, you'll spend the entire time in your head. I've been in it. It's not always the nicest place to be. Better if you're out there with us."

Because it's deadline day. Because I could fail. Because Eden could die.

Keis thinks so anyway.

In my head, I sing over the thoughts and mumble, "Mom seemed pretty serious about us not leaving without them."

"None of them are answering any of our messages. They're probably just worried that if we don't go together, we won't be able to find each other later."

I bob my head in a nod, pulling off my silk bonnet and tossing it on the sheets. I tug on the same jean shorts and off-shoulder shirt I wore last night and douse my hair with a spray bottle to help fluff it back up. Better that Keis is distracted by the adults than concentrating on my mind. I sing the song louder in my head just in case.

Keis glares at me. "That song is scrambling my feed."

"Sorry. It's stuck."

"If you sing the entire song instead of the chorus over and over, it'll go away."

"I can't remember."

"AI search it! Or at least try not to sing so loud, damn." Keis stalks out of the room and I follow after. We make a brief stop in the bathroom so I can brush my teeth and use the toilet.

When we make our way down the staircase to the entryway, Keisha and Alex are already there, decked out in their mas costumes, sparkling blue and silver just like the float we saw last night. Their feather headpieces are at least a foot and a half tall, and both of them opted for the bikini-bra style top but have to wear shorts for Granny to allow them to play mas at all. Their bodies are covered in silver glitter, and their sneakers and small backpacks are similarly bedazzled. My cousins also took the time to get matching silver-and-blue makeup with ash streaks like Emerald had last night.

"Wow," I say, coming up in front of them. "You really are ready."

They both smush their mouths into something like smiles, but they don't quite work. Usually, they would lap up the compliments. Keis stands beside me with the same sort of expression.

It's like we're going to an extremely colorful funeral, not carnival. I guess it's hard to be pumped up when the life of the smallest member of your family is in danger.

I swallow hard and look around at them. "Eden isn't going to die today. I have a plan. Don't worry."

"But that means . . ." Keisha trails off, and my cousins exchange looks. Probably thinking about me in the kitchen, coming at Luc with a knife.

I shake my head. "I . . . don't have to kill anyone either. I figured it out. No one is going to die."

Keis stares at me. I sing the same song in my head as loud as I can. Her eyes narrow.

"I don't really want to talk about it," I say, throwing a desperate look at my best friend.

My shoulders slump as Keis leans back and nods. Her own nonverbal promise that she won't pry. The last thing I need today is to have her know that I'm still waffling between destroying her future or Luc's.

"Well, hack me." Keisha sighs dramatically. "Now that Eden's not going to die and Voya's not going to be a murderer, we *have* to celebrate. This is the earliest I've ever been ready, and the adults just expect us to sit around here for ancestors know how long for them? Nah. We gotta go now."

"Voya hasn't already passed," Keis says, crossing her arms over her chest.

"Urg, not-fun twin strikes again. Vo says she's got it, so she's got it. Aren't you the one who's always saying to trust her?"

Keis hunches her shoulders up. "I do trust her!"

"Great," Alex chimes in. "So do we. Let's go."

For a moment, tears rush to my eyes, and I have to suck in a breath to stop them from coming out. Trust is a bond that goes both ways. I spent so much time reaching out for it, hoping that it was there without truly knowing, that I wasn't prepared for them to reach back. I've always believed in and trusted my family, and I hoped they felt the same way, but it's only now that I realize a big part of me had never expected it to happen.

Alex's eyes soften. "You good?" she asks.

"Yeah," I say, my voice more choked up than I want it to be. "Where are the adults?"

"They went to Johan's to help with mas stuff," Alex says. "That's what Granny told me before she left."

My eyes bug out. "Granny went too?!" There's no way. She is not a fan of Johan and usually would rather take the GO train in with us.

"She said she wanted to have 'a talk' with him about you."

"Ohhhh," Keisha says. "She's pissed that he corrupted you."

I scowl. "He didn't corrupt me. I asked to watch, and it wasn't his fault." I cross my arms over my chest, not exactly overjoyed to be reminded of the scene in the basement. The man still appears in my dreams, hanging from the ceiling, bleeding out and morphing between himself and Luc. "What about Eden?"

"They took her with them." Alex shrugs. "Probably going to make one of Johan's kids look after her."

I'm about to say that we could have looked after her when I pause. The adults don't know that I've figured out how to save Eden yet. Dad and Priya probably wanted to stick close to her just in case. I don't blame them.

"Can we go?" Keis interrupts. "The train leaves in like fifteen minutes." She blazes the trail by heading for the front door, and my cousins follow along behind her.

Mom's words burn in my ears. She told us to wait like it was important. I hover in the entryway.

"Voya, come on!" Keis shouts.

I follow them out, lock the door behind us, and start to send a message to Mom to let her know we're going ahead.

"Oh my God, Vo, you better not be telling on us!" Keisha says, staring at my phone.

"I'm just letting her know!"

"Let her know once we're already there, 'cause then we can say it's too late to go back. If you tell her now, we won't have an excuse for why we can't wait when she messages you back."

"Can I at least message them to say I figured out my task? They might be worried about Eden."

"Fine! But nothing about us going. They're not answering their messages anyway, so they probably won't see until later."

"Then why can't I just say we're leaving now?"

"Voya!"

"Fine," I say, and send a quick message to the adults to let them know that they don't have to worry, that I know how I'm going to save Eden. Like with everyone else, I avoid mentioning that I still have to choose between which first love to destroy. They wouldn't understand. It wouldn't even be a choice to them, but it's not that simple for me.

The four of us make our way to the train station. On Caribana parade day, the hassle of getting downtown in the van is too much for even Auntie to handle. We tried it one year, and she got so furious that she melted the steering wheel down.

Granny gave her hell for that.

Now, we take the GO train a couple of stops over to Exhibition Station, where the parade will come through at its fullest force. It would usually be a happy occasion, all of us gathering with other people in a celebration of our culture. This year is different.

Alex and Keisha are delighted, stopping to take photos with people in their costumes like feed celebrities. Completely unburdened by trusting in me knowing how to complete my task without shedding any blood.

Keis is more reserved. She knows that I'm hiding something, and it's got her on edge. Her shoulders are stiff even as she hums the pop song I got stuck in her head under her breath. It's like the atmosphere in the crowd. There's a nervous energy rippling through them. Like even they know how important today is.

"What's up with everyone?" I mutter. The feeling going around is making me paranoid, and I'm searching for more visions of blood and death, but none have come so far. Maybe now that the deadline is here, there's no more point to them. No reason to rush me into my decision because I'll have to make it today, no matter what.

Alex looks around at the crowds as we get onto the train platform. "We don't have the Davises' protection this year. Even non-witches can get used to the feeling of magic in the air. It isn't here now. They can sense the difference even if they don't consciously know. Didn't you notice that it's been like this for a couple of years? Since the last time things went wrong with the rite."

I guess I hadn't noticed. Maybe because I had never been this on-edge before. I wring my hands until my knuckles crack. The ritual to protect Caribana. The one the Davises have been doing for years that I ruined when I broke the circle. I had been thinking of my failure and its direct consequences for me and Johan. I forgot about the intention of the ritual.

The last time the circle was broken, three people died.

I swallow so hard that it hurts my throat going down.

Keis nudges me in the shoulder. "It'll be okay."

"If something does happen, that's life," Keisha drawls. "We can't protect each other from everything."

If something *does* happen, it'll be my fault.

During the train ride, I let everyone's conversations rush over me, staring out at the scenery as it goes by. The familiar train yards and back views of neighborhood homes and kids playing in parks. For some of us, this is a special day of celebration, and for others, it's just an ordinary Saturday. For me, it's the day that everything changes.

The train reaches Exhibition Station, and we flood off it. As we walk toward the entrance, the pumping beat of soca music thrums through my body. At Caribana, you don't just hear the music; it spreads through your limbs and warms your blood and spikes your adrenaline. I'm bobbing my head before I realize it, and Keis is bouncing on her toes. Keisha and Alex are carrying on—outright wining up on each other and laughing, rushing ahead of me and Keis.

I dig out my phone and send a quick message to Mom to let her know we're at the parade. The crowd we walk with is awash in color. Even though not everyone is participating in the parade, there's still the odd person with glitter on their face. Some of them have flags worn as bandannas or tucked into their back pockets. I spy Trinidadian, Jamaican, Montserratian, and Canadian flags, and a whole lot more I don't recognize.

"We forgot our flags," I say. We have a few Trini ones packed away somewhere.

"There will be a million people selling them once we get inside," Keis says.

And of course, when we get through the ticket booth, the first thing we see is a lineup of three vendors set up with huge flag displays from cloth flags to giant portable holos.

"You want a holo belt buckle that says 'Trini Pride'?" Keis points to the offensive object.

I grimace.

She laughs. It's an open and free sound.

I've heard her laugh so many times. If I destroy her future, would that happen anymore?

Something must show in my expression because she stares at me. "What's going on? You said you know how to save Eden, and you're not going to kill anyone. How?"

"I would rather not talk about—"

"Cut the spam, Vo. Alex and Keisha are happy as hell with the news, but you look like someone is still going to die today."

I crack my fingers, one knuckle at a time.

Keis's eyes narrow, and she stops dead on the sidewalk. "What are you going to do?"

"I just have to make a choice. That's all."

Her expression clears because she must know that me and choices don't go together well. "You still don't know what you're going to choose."

She doesn't need to read my mind to know that. My cousin briefly presses her palms to her eyes before pulling them away and nodding sharply. "You can do it."

I laugh. "That would be great if I knew what I was going to do."

"I know you. You'll get through this." She pulls a grim smile. "As cheesy as it is, we have each other. You have the entire family behind you. What you're doing is going to save Eden without taking any lives. That's what matters."

I try to fill myself up with the warm feeling from her words, but it falls flat. Would she be saying the same thing if she knew the choice that I had to make?

I swallow and jerk my head in the direction of Keisha and Alex. "We should catch up."

Keis leads the way and I shuffle along behind her. When we catch up with my cousins, the air is thick with the smell of spices and pepper. Vendors drop fresh dough into fryers to make pho-lourie and roll thick paratha roti skins around chunks of curried chicken and potato. Most of them have bottles of bright-colored sodas imported from the Caribbean, and there are people shouting their orders with accented English.

The King and Queen show was only a taste of what the parade brings. The soca music is so loud that my body vibrates as giant floats roll down the street. A full steel pan band on wheels passes by, playing while they dance along to the music. The mas camp bands follow along behind them. Feather headpieces more than a foot tall are perched on the heads of people dancing down the street in sequined bikinis and shorts, covered in body glitter. Whistles scream in the air as people blow them to the music, and my nose is full of the smell of vaporizer clouds and island spices.

"There they are!" Keisha screams, and points.

I follow her finger, and sure enough, there's Emerald leading the charge in their now award-winning human-powered float. She's in her shiny blue-and-silver outfit with an overdramatic smoky eye. My chest lifts to see the sequin work on her costume that I helped with.

You'd think she would be tired from the booty shaking she did last night, but she charges down the street with renewed energy. A few paces behind her, Johan is wining up, sparkling and dewy as if he never took the whipping he did a couple days ago, in the King version of the float. He's bare-chested, dancing away in booty shorts that might be shorter than his daughter's. When he turns to the other side of the crowd, he reveals the thick crisscrossing scars across his back.

I grimace and clutch at my chest. A flash of heat goes through my scars as I look at his.

"Let's take a picture fast," Alex shouts. "Before we jump in!"

My cousins and I squish together under Alex's phone while the AI takes dozens of photos of us. I force myself to smile and mean it. I don't want to look back on them and see a version of myself too preoccupied to enjoy a moment with my family.

"Okay, let's go!" Keisha drags Alex toward the metal barrier so they can run out into the parade and join up with the mas band.

Keis scans the parade. "Shouldn't the adults be with them? Maybe they're at the house?"

I mean to respond to Keis, but the scent of smoke and sugarcane shoots through my nostrils. I turn my head and there they are. The ancestors. Those in the crowd with magic in their blood bow their heads to them. The others are oblivious to their presence.

The ancestors walk sure-footed in the outfits of their time. There are some in dashikis and others in the outfits of tribes so old most others have forgotten them.

Auntie Elaine isn't here. Not every ancestor appears at Caribana.

But Mama Jova is.

She's obvious for her nakedness, the thinness of her frame, and the scars that mark her body. And she's the only ancestor not smiling and dancing along with her descendants. Alone in a crowd.

The moment I see her, I know the choice that I'll make. In some ways, I've known since last night. And the entire day since has just been me convincing myself that I didn't know because I didn't want to make it.

It's time.

"I have to go," I say to Keis.

She's distracted—someone is calling her, but she can't seem to hear over the noise of the parade. "Wait, hold on!" she says to them.

I leave her and walk over to Mama Jova, slipping between the parade barricades, and making my way across to her. She stands tall and proud as always, her eyes meeting mine.

"I'm here to make a request." I try to pull myself up straight.

"Make it." She appraises me with critical eyes, as if she knows what I've come to ask but doesn't think I'll actually do it.

From the start of this, Mama Jova has wanted me to take control of my future and choices. And this whole time I've believed that I would make the wrong choice. That's how it's been with everything in my life. Every decision was another chance to mess up.

I don't know if this is the right one either. But it doesn't matter.

It's my choice, and I have to make it.

So I do.

Today is Caribana, the one day of the year we can see the ancestors . . . and the one day of the year we can ask them for a wish.

I speak that wish with tears in my eyes and a trembling voice.

Mama doesn't smile. She only stares at me. "You're sure?"

"Yes," I say, and this time, it's without any hesitation.

"Then it's done."

I don't feel relief. There's no joy in this. "Does this mean I pass? I did what you wanted. I destroyed my first love."

"You pass." Mama turns her head to look over my shoulder in the direction of the train station. There, far back from the parade, are the adults with Mom and Granny leading the pack, trying to push through the crowd. I squint at them through tear-soaked eyes.

"Ava interfered," Mama Jova says. "She and the rest of your brood."

"What do you mean they interfered?" I say, turning back to her.

She tilts her head to the side and examines me. I let her. After everything, this probing stare is simple to bear. "You keep changing. Each day, you become a different sort of girl than I thought you were."

"What sort of girl did you think I was?"

"One so afraid to fail that she would never make a choice. You didn't seem to be one who could take charge of her future."

"And that's why you gave me this task?"

"That's part of it." Mama presses her lips into a firm line. "There are still hard choices to be made, and the next time, you won't have a month to decide. Do you remember what I said about magic?"

"That it's blood and intent?"

"Why do you think I keep saying that to you?"

My first instinct is to say that I don't know, but really, I just haven't had time to think about it because I've been so preoccupied with my task.

"I have faith that you'll come to understand. It isn't complicated to be a witch, Voya. That was my mistake. It's actually incredibly simple when you understand what magic is. And that understanding is the difference between what makes a witch good, and what makes a witch great." She reaches out and caresses my cheek. "You could be a great witch."

Everything rushes out of me. I thought Mama Jova must hate me. For my weakness, if anything. But here she is now, saying that she thinks I could be great. Like her.

She rolls her shoulders back and frowns. "It's only too bad your family couldn't see your potential in time."

I frown. "What does that mea—"

A series of gunshots slice through the air and whistle through my eardrums. Screams ring out, and the crowd rushes forward, bodies shoving around me until I fall to my knees. My wounds burn as people keep running past me, stomping on my hands and knocking into me as soca music blares overtop.

I search for Mama in the mass of people, but she's gone.

Someone gets ahold of my top and yanks me off the ground

and out of the crowd. It's only when he drops me on my feet that I can look up and identify my savior as Johan.

"What's happening?" I splutter. "Where is everyone?"

"Cops got a call about someone here having a gun. Of course, he didn't. Not that the cop listened to that." Johan's eyes are hard and dig into me. "You see what happens when you break a circle, girl? There are consequences! I told you that."

"I don't—but who—the shots . . ." My words run over each other, and I can't get anything out straight.

"There are people bleeding in the street because you messed with my ritual. Remember that!" Johan stands and shakes his head at me.

I won't let him shame me. Keisha's words spill from my mouth. "We can't protect each other from everything."

"Whatever helps you sleep at night," he hisses. "Go home." He stalks away from me into the crowd.

I pull myself up and do as he says, not because he said it, but because there's no way I'll be able to find anyone in this mess. And I already know exactly where to find Keis, and it isn't here.

Searching for the rest of my family ends up being impossible. It's chaos. People are running everywhere, and police are flooding into the space. My mouth dries out, and sweat drips down my back.

Home.

Granny always told us that if anything dangerous happened, we should do everything in our power to get back to the house, where we would be safe. It'll be okay. Everyone will be at home.

The GO trains have been stopped, so I order a car instead. Thank the ancestors for that contest money. During the ride, I pull out my phone to fire off messages to my cousins and check on them, but instead stop at the dozen messages from Mom sent in the past five minutes:

Don't finish your task! Don't do it!

Each one is a variation of that message over and over. I frown and message her back to ask what she means. Why would she not want me to complete my task? I even call, but she doesn't pick up. I try Granny and the rest of the adults, but none of them answer their phones or messages.

I gnaw on my lip. Maybe they're just caught up in the crowds. They have to be okay. They're going to be at home. They might already be there. Though a voice in the back of my head asks, if they're home safe, why wouldn't they message me? I jiggle my leg and will the car to go faster than its law-abiding programming.

When I step up to the front door of the house, there are no sounds from within. No loud conversations about what happened. And no Mom anxiously pacing in front of the house, looking for me. I check my phone again, and there are no alerts. Not a single message. I swore I saw them running through the crowd. There's no way Mom or Granny wouldn't have sent a message to make sure that I'm okay.

Something is wrong.

I push open the door and stand there.

On the steps leading upstairs, Keis sits with her phone in her hand. She looks up when I enter. Her eyes are puffy and strained. She tilts the phone toward me. "I tried to send you a message. It won't let me."

I expect a reaction from Keis, but nothing. With the task completed, she should have her magic back and be able to read my mind. She's choosing not to.

"Mom sent me messages, but she hasn't been responding otherwise. None of the adults have." I look around. "Where is everyone?"

"Gone."

"Gone?"

Keis swallows. "Some men showed up. Tried to drag me out of

the house. Every time they reached the door, I disappeared from their arms and reappeared in the house, so they gave up." She widens her eyes at me. "Disappearing, Voya. There one moment and gone the next. That's not normal. That's not just something that happens to me every day."

The heat of her gaze feels as intense as her mom's flames.

"They left this, by the way. The men who came." She flicks a card across the floor to me.

I pick it up.

You are cordially invited to join Mr. Justin Tremblay for a family gathering at NuGene headquarters at your earliest convenience. The earlier, he advises, the better.

"He took them." The gunshots. Johan said that someone called the cops. Justin could have done it and used the diversion to grab my family.

"Voya," Keis says. "Why did I suddenly appear in the house when seconds before I was at the parade? I was on the phone with your mom, who I couldn't even hacking hear, then suddenly I was in the house and the call was cut off. Why can't I leave? Why can't I send messages?" She stands from the stairs and walks toward me.

I swallow. "You can read it out of my head."

"I don't want to read it out of your head!" she snaps. I flinch from the sound. "I want you to tell me."

"We need to figure out what to do about Justin and everyone. It'll be faster if you just read it out of my h—"

"Tell me!"

My request to Mama Jova comes flooding back to me.

"I ask you to bind my cousin Keis Thomas to our ancestral home so that she may never be able to leave. Never step outside those doors. Block her from communication with anyone and anything beyond our home." The words leave a thick gunk on my tongue.

My cousin, my best friend, my first love—the girl whose dreams revolve around being out in the world and making change, who can't stand to stay in the house for an entire day, who just got the internship of her dreams, whose future is set out in front of her and infinite with possibility in a way mine has never been—will lose it all.

She'll be bound to a house she wants to leave. Those memories of us running through the halls in braids will become the suffocating pain of halls she can never escape. Our kitchen where we sat with Granny and spent time together will become a cloistering space she can't leave.

Everything Keis and I share will be forever tainted by this choice.

And still, I have to make it.

My voice is a small, pathetic thing. "I had to destroy my first love."

"Luc."

"No. He's my first romantic love, but you . . . you're my first love ever. I just . . . needed to pick one of you."

Keis's eyes are dry. Somehow, that's worse than if she were crying because I know the only reason she isn't is because she can't. She's already cried too much. There's nothing left. "That was the choice? The one you were struggling over? And you picked *me*? What does that even mean?"

"You can't leave the house. Or communicate with anyone outside it." The words come out harsh from my constricted throat.

"I can't leave . . . or talk to or message anyone outside this house?"

"I need to go to NuGene and do something about this. I'm sorry. I just . . . need to go. We can talk about this when I get back, I promise."

Keis's nostrils flare, and her breathing becomes labored and noisy. Her fingers flex, and she grinds her teeth. "You wanted this."

Of all the things she could say, that wasn't what I was expected. "I never wanted this task!"

"You wanted me here! You knew the internship would mean

that I would leave this house to have my own life. That I wouldn't be able to spend every waking moment with you!" She screams the hateful words with a shaking voice. "You did this so I could be like you. Stuck in this house without a future."

I clutch my arms to my body, and my throat burns with pain from holding in tears. She's wrong. I was afraid of losing her, but I wanted that future for her. I would never ruin it if I didn't have any choice. "I did this to save Eden! You said that one life was worth saving hers. You said that saving her and not shedding blood was all that mattered."

"Save it! Don't throw my words back at me." Keis turns away from me, shaking her head and tapping her foot. "You chose the future of someone who's already lived a perfect life over mine, and now his sponsor daddy has our family. You chose him over *me*! Your cousin! Your best friend!"

"That's exactly why!"

She spins back to face me. "What?"

"If I took away his sponsorship and he had to go back to where he was born, away from Justin, he wouldn't have *anything*. He doesn't get along with his family. He doesn't even get along with the family that he has here aside from Justin."

"Boo hacking hoo," Keis hisses.

"I know you! You can come back from this. I've destroyed the future you have now, but you can make a new one. You've always been like that. And you have the entire family to support you. I don't know Luc. Not the same way. He lives like NuGene, this sponsorship, and Justin are all he has. Like it's the only thing about him that's worth anything. If he loses that, I don't know that he can make something new the way you can. I couldn't do that to him."

Even with his art, if he was sent back to Mexico, back to the parents who wanted him home to pursue that, would he even still love it? Or would he stop drawing, too? The long and short of it is that I don't know. Destroying Luc's future might be just the same as murdering him.

But I know that my amazing, talented cousin could carve out a new future for herself. Even out of a tragedy like this.

Keis snarls at me, "I will *never* forgive you for this."

The feeling that hits me is like Dad leaving multiplied by a number so large I can't comprehend it. And I can't blame her for it either.

She throws up her hands. "Our entire family has been kidnapped, and I can't go anywhere! I just have to wait here!" Keis shakes her head and lets out a scream. There's no point to it. It's pure frustration. She glares at me. "What are you going to do about this?" She points at Justin's invitation.

My stomach rolls and cramps. "I'm going to go get them."

I know I'm not a Matriarch, and the chance of the ancestors listening to me is slim to none, but as I leave my cousin behind in a house she can never escape, I ask Auntie Elaine for the strength to face Justin as she did.

I'm not coming home to Keis empty-handed.

CHAPTER THIRTY-TWO

W hen I arrive at NuGene HQ, Luc has to unlock the door for me. According to the hours posted out front, it's usually open on Sundays, but not today. He doesn't meet my eyes as he beckons me inside and pushes a button to lock the doors again. His all-black outfit, considering the situation, feels grimmer than it should. Even if it's just jeans and a long-sleeved shirt.

"It's empty today," I say.

"Justin declared a spontaneous mental health afternoon and sent everyone home." Luc shakes his head at me. "You shouldn't have come."

"It's my family."

"I know. That doesn't mean I'll stop wishing you hadn't."

"Then do something about it! He's kidnapping people." My fingers clench and unclench as I step close to Luc.

"And you wouldn't do as much as that, maybe more, if you thought it was right?" he snaps. "Justin is doing what Justin does. He innovates and pushes into the future. To him, that's worth this. Just like to you, whatever you did to Juras, whatever you planned to do to me, was worth it for your family."

"You're both alive. Can you say the same for Lauren?" I haven't forgotten the way that Luc looked at her mom in the park. He saw her mentioned in Justin's files. Maybe he doesn't know what happened to Lauren exactly, but his expression didn't make whatever he *does* know seem like it was anything good. Was Lauren here in this all-white building, scared and alone? Is she still here? Is that what will happen to my family? Pronounced missing without any leads?

Luc's face crumples, and he turns and strides away. "Come if you're coming."

I pick up the pace and follow.

Together we step into the elevator. Luc's eyes follow me as I move.

The doors close, and we start to rise.

After we leave this elevator, everything will change again. The future will shift, and our lives will be different.

"I did like you, you know." I wind my hands around each other. Staring at the way my fingers link up. "Love" is too hard to say. "Like" dampens it. Makes it less than it is. Just like using the past tense when the present still applies.

Luc doesn't say anything.

"When I met you, I thought, here's a person whose entire life is open to possibility. He could be anything or anyone he wants and is choosing to be this rude, industrial asshole." I let out a little laugh. "But in some ways, we're alike. We both grew up hinging our entire futures on one thing. You with your sponsorship and me with becoming a witch."

He scowls at the mention of witches, clearly still not totally on board with the idea.

"I realized that I've always admired my cousin because she wasn't like that. Keis wants to be a part of NuGene so badly, but I knew that if she didn't get in, she would find something else amazing. With you, I'm not so sure. It's unfair to her. I gave her the short end of the stick because she can do more than you can." My throat goes dry, and my voice shakes. "Maybe you don't care, but through this entire thing, I've learned that your future is what you make it. And I hope that one day you can see yourself as more than a sponsorship."

"She got the internship, though," Luc says. "Keis is going to be a part of NuGene."

"Yeah. She did. But no, she won't."

He narrows his eyes. "What did you do?"

"I made a choice."

The elevator dings, and the doors open.

It's brought us to a room that must be Justin's office. I recognize the white walls and screens from when he announced the matching program's release. In the corner, there are two large glass cases, and as Luc said, one contains the first genetic manipulation machine, and the other has the first NuSap prototype. The android in the case doesn't have an obvious sex, only smooth cornflower-blue skin, a slight build, and closed eyes, waiting for a command that won't ever come.

Justin is there to greet us with his swirling bionic eyes. He sits behind his nearly wall-to-wall desk in front of giant floor-to-ceiling windows that shimmer with the effects of a strong tint I suspect will block out anything that happens in this room. The CN Tower stands tall in the distance.

It's not the view I'm interested in.

Eden is sitting on a chair inside a third glass-encased box next to Justin's display of the NuSap prototype like she's a part of his gallery. The box gives her about two feet of space in all directions, and she's hooked up to some sort of machine. "Voya!" She leaps off the chair and bangs on the glass. She's got tears running down her face, and the redness in her eyes means she's been crying for a while.

"What's she doing here in that box? What do you want with

her?" I snap my head to Justin. "Where's the rest of my family?"

"Safe and out of sight for now. Eden is here to make sure you behave." Justin straightens his cuffs. "But don't worry too much—I'm not in the business of murdering children."

"Lauren is a child. Does that mean she's alive?" A spark of hope dashes through my chest.

Justin releases a breath. "I'm sorry about her. I thought if I could shift her genes enough, maybe I could recreate Elaine's gift, but it didn't work. That's how I learned that you can't do anything after someone's had their Calling. Not all experimental trials are successful."

I step away from him. A *trial*. Lauren was a girl with her own hopes and dreams. With a family. She was my friend. "She's . . ."

"She didn't make it." He delivers the news with a tone that's both regretful and flippant. Like a news reporter listing casualties.

Lauren. My energetic and bright friend. Her family is never going to find her. None of us will ever get to see her alive again. No more rushing into a room with curls bouncing. No more whispered stories about her latest escapades. She'll never come to another backyard BBQ and twirl around her baby brother.

Gone.

Just a failed experiment.

Tears choke me, and I swallow them down. "Is that why we're here? Another experiment? Is that why you have that thing on my sister?"

Luc shakes his head. "It's just a device that monitors her genes and vitals on an ongoing basis. At Trinity Bellwoods, you were worried about her dying if you failed your task. We want to make sure she's okay. It won't hurt her."

My eyes go wide. "You told him about that?" Not to mention, they haven't realized that I've already passed my task.

"I was trying to look out for her," he says back.

I bite down on my lip but don't say anything else.

"See? Totally safe." Justin grabs an instrument off his desk and walks toward me.

I try to step back again and hit the cool door of the elevator.

"Don't worry, I just need to check your DNA." He holds out a portable DNA reader to me, and I press my finger to it. I don't wince as the metal prong pokes the tip of my finger for blood.

I look at Luc, who stares at his sponsor dad even as he speaks to me. "It's fine, Voya. He just wants to test everyone's DNA. No one is going to get hurt."

"You kidnapped my family, you *murdered* Lauren, but no one is going to get hurt?" I say, incredulous.

"Yes," Luc insists. "It was impossible to get all of you to agree to let us sequence your DNA. This was our only choice. Even you can't argue against that. Neither of us wanted it to be this extreme, but everyone will be let go after testing."

I frown. It's true. There's no way my family would give their DNA away again. But deep inside, Luc must still be worried. Otherwise, why would he say that he wished I hadn't come?

"Just some tests, no one gets hurt, and this ends," Luc says, partly to me, partly to Justin, and partly to himself.

Justin busies himself at the computer with my DNA sequence. He says to Luc, "Can you please go check Eden's machine? The readings aren't transmitting properly."

"Sure," Luc says, and walks over to the glass enclosure where Eden sits. Justin pushes a button to let him inside. The doors slide closed behind him automatically, too fast for me to run over to my sister.

Meanwhile, Justin pulls up my DNA. One of the screens lights up with my genetic code. The screen splits, and another code comes up.

They're different. I'm looking at my DNA before I completed

the task and after. Now that it's done, my genome is changing to accommodate whatever gift I'll get.

Justin lets out an exasperated sigh and shoots a look at Luc. "You said she had until today, and last time that I looked, you're still alive."

Luc shrinks in on himself.

"It's fine, don't get upset," Justin says to him. "We'll figure it out."

I draw myself up. "What?"

"Such a mess. I only started properly remembering things in the last couple of months. One of our interns noticed an NT sequence anomaly in a girl getting a curl pattern modification, Lauren. I recognized it but had no idea why. I won't bore you with details. Eventually, I came to understand that you or your sister would be ideal candidates. But I didn't particularly feel like waiting ten more years for her to be Called. You would be the best choice, as someone who was related to Elaine, in a family powerful enough to inherit a strong gift, but young enough to not have had a chance yet, I assumed. I couldn't be sure if you'd had your Calling or not. Though the monitor showed you weren't doing any magic, I was curious to observe you myself. It's why I had Luc invite you for dinner. Not that Luc knew, of course. After what happened with Juras, I was positive that you had passed your Calling, that I was too late and would have to find a way to get to Eden. The monitor even confirmed that you had used magic. I was a little miffed, I'll admit."

The face he'd made at me that night. That furious expression that he's calling "a little miffed." I thought he could be angry that I hurt his sponsor son. But he wasn't. He was upset thinking that he missed his chance at whatever experiment he has going on. Juras was having a stroke right in front of him, and that's what he cared about most.

Justin continues, "But then you tried to stab Luc, and when I sent him to see you at Trinity Bellwoods and get some real details, you said you had until Saturday to decide to kill him or not. Extreme enough that it must be a Calling task. And a piece of information he only felt compelled to share this afternoon."

He looks at Luc with pursed lips. "I assumed you hadn't finished your Calling or he would be dead. And when I tracked you and saw that you were headed to that carnival, I realized that was the best time to grab your family, given the short notice."

I snap my eyes to Luc, who, to his credit, meets my gaze head-on. In the end, I gave away the most valuable bit of information myself: the timeline.

Still, he tried to keep it from Justin until the last possible moment. To stop him from getting whatever it is he wanted from us, which Luc *must* know will involve more than just genetic testing.

He set his mentor up to fail. And he did it to protect me.

I swallow. "That means you're done, then? You've tested me. You've tested Eden. If you have my family, I assume you've tested them."

The NuGene CEO says nothing, only considers the screen with my DNA.

"Justin?" Luc says. He walks forward to leave the glass enclosure, but the door won't open for him. "Justin?!" He bangs on the glass, but his sponsor refuses to push the button to open it.

Justin crosses his arms and shakes his head. "We're too far gone now. The issue with Lauren is she never would have been a proper genetic match." He jerks his head at Eden. "I thought she would be the next best option, but I tested her genes as soon as I got her here. They're strange. The expressive ones are in line with her lineage, but the underlying ones that connect to magic are more Thomas, barely a hint of anything from Elaine's family. As bad a match as Lauren was."

Of course. As far as magic is concerned, Eden is a Thomas. And Auntie Elaine was only one by marriage, not by blood.

"You were the closest I was going to get. That was the whole point of risking a mass kidnapping to grab you *before* your Calling ended and the genes shifted."

Luc only told Justin about the deadline this afternoon, maybe at the same time I was meeting Mama Jova at Caribana.

If I had gone with the original interpretation of the task and murdered Luc, none of this would be happening.

Mama Jova stares at me from the back of the room. She closes her eyes in a pained expression.

She knew.

She knew how the future would look with him in it. She even gave me an out. If I had touched Luc that night at dinner, I would have completed my task *without* killing him, and he would have been out of commission and unable to pass that information to his sponsor. He wouldn't even have any information to pass because he wouldn't have been in the right condition to come see me at all. Justin would have left us alone.

But it was my choice.

I chose *not* to choose Luc. Not once. But twice.

I chose to destroy Keis's future instead of his.

I chose *this*.

"What are you doing? Let me out!" Luc shouts, banging on the glass over and over.

I swallow. "You said you were just testing our genes. That you wouldn't hurt anyone." But if that were the truth, he wouldn't be locking up his sponsor son to keep him out of the way.

Justin's tone is sharp. "That was when I expected to get the results that I wanted to get. When I thought you hadn't passed your Calling, and we could neatly proceed with shifting your genes to make sure you got the right gift once you did. Theoretically, of course. Unfortunately, now I'll have to resort to other, more drastic measures." He looks over at Luc. "Why do you think I had you get into that box just a moment ago? I knew that you were overly attached. Now you can't interfere more than you already have. But you *can* watch me secure your future. You're welcome." He claps his hands together in a single loud motion. "This is why we have backup plans." His bionics swivel as if he's viewing said alternatives.

My body goes still. "Backup plans?"

"The Matriarch ceremony should do the trick. It always seemed an extreme option, but we're far enough into the extremes now, don't you think?"

No.

Crowning another Matriarch kills the current one. I shake my head. "My grandma will die in that ceremony! I can think of something else." Except, I don't have any other ideas.

This isn't Caribana. There are no ancestors to hand out requests.

"I'm afraid I'm not in the mood for alternative hypotheses right now," Justin says, brushing it aside. "You will complete the ceremony and use your Matriarch wish to have Elaine's gift of genetic manipulation. She told me a story once about an ancestor who did the same thing, so don't act like it isn't possible. It's the less scientific method, but we're working with what we've got."

I turn desperate eyes to Luc, who's banging on the glass in earnest with Eden joining in, smashing her tiny fists against the door, though neither of their efforts matter.

I'm alone.

I can't lose Granny.

"I could wish for you to be dead!" I shout.

Justin rolls his eyes. "You think I don't have a failsafe for that?" He gestures to Eden. "The machine she's hooked up to, which can be harmless in theory, can also do a little extra. A special program by me that I didn't share with my sponsor son, who I suspected wouldn't like it very much." He directs a little shrug at Luc. "If the computers sense that my neural network has died during the casting, it will activate and attempt to change little Eden's genome to that of Elaine's. And we know what happened when I tried that with an imperfect match."

Lauren. That machine killed her when he tried it. She was past her Calling then, so it may not do the same to Eden, but what if it does?

Luc reaches for the cords connected to Eden, but Justin makes a little tutting noise. "Don't touch them, Luc. Unhook anything, and I'll manually trigger it myself."

Luc's fingers still.

My hands shake, and I cross them to hide it from him. "How do I know this isn't all a bluff?"

"You don't, but would you risk it?" He gestures to Luc. "And if he didn't know it was possible, why would he look so afraid?"

He's right. If Luc thought that was bullshit, I 100 percent believe he would have just yanked the cords out of my sister, but he hasn't.

"I thought you were above murdering children?" I say, hating the begging tone in my voice.

Justin shoots me a cool look. "This isn't murder. It's science." He turns back to his computers and pulls up a screen that shows my family encased in a glass box not unlike the one Eden and Luc are in. He presses a button and speaks. "Hello, Thomas family. Would Ava, Keisha, and Alex please join us? Better to avoid any adults who might think to cause trouble. I'm going to open the doors for them. Simply follow the hallways to the elevator, and they'll bring you to us. And remember, those monitors you have on mean I can tell when you use magic, and there will be consequences for doing so. I do have Voya and Eden up here with me." The threat in his words is obvious.

On-screen, my family exchanges tearful hugs as the doors open. Only Granny, Keisha, and Alex leave. The cameras follow them as they make their journey toward us through a series of glass hallways.

Justin sits in his desk chair and watches the progression of my family. After a moment, he notices me standing and waves toward Eden and Luc. "You can go be with them if you like. It'll take everyone a bit to make it over to us."

I rush over to the glass case, pressing myself close to a tearful Eden and shaking Luc.

"I'm sorry," he whispers, shaking his head. "I shouldn't have believed him. I just . . . wanted to. I wanted to believe that he was better than this. Part of me still thinks he can be."

I don't have the same optimism that Luc does about his sponsor dad. "I don't think he's going to change his mind."

"I'm sorry," Luc says again, his voice on the edge of a sob.

I stare into his stormy eyes but can't force myself to smile to make him feel better. It's too dire right now. "I know." I look at Justin, who's slowly moving his chair back and forth as he pushes buttons to open doors for my family. "Seeing the NT sequence for magic in Lauren's data. That's all it took to remember what you were meant to forget?" I ask him.

Justin waves his hand. "I always had a sort of memory after Elaine was gone. Dinners in a house by the lake, late nights in the hospital . . ." He trails off for a moment, casting an empty stare out the window before returning to his button pushing. "Eventually, names started to stand out to me. I ended up noting them down: Thomas, Davis, Bailey-Huang, and Carter. Though I couldn't remember Elaine's maiden name. Or even her first." He leans his head on his chin. "I sent everyone with those last names messages for free genetic modification. Just to see what might happen. That's how I found Lauren." He shrugs. "I hadn't paid that much attention to Lauren's genetics, honestly, but after the intern pointed out her strange NT sequence, I went back through the data to compare the sequence anomaly to other genetic data we've collected over the years. Not everyone had the anomaly—only a few, in fact—but it was enough to run some hypotheses. Lauren was the only unfortunate casualty."

Unfortunate casualty.

That's what my friend was to him.

My nostrils flare, and I grind my teeth.

Those countless "free genetic modification" messages I thought were spam were Justin trying to lure in witches. Now I remember Lauren laughing and saying she got the curl pattern for free. I was sure that it was a joke. Hadn't even thought about that until now.

I press the heels of my hands against my eyes. "Was the matching program part of it?" I haven't forgotten about Emerald also being matched with a NuGene intern.

"Not exactly. It's a legitimate program, though it was also a good way to get access to your genetic data and get the monitors on you all. I just made some adjustments by pairing everyone with those surnames with an intern for easy access. For additional qualitative data."

I look at Luc, whose jaw drops the slightest bit.

My toes curl in my flip-flops. "So Luc and I aren't a legitimate match?"

"Not genetically, no. I think you're about seventy-six percent. Not bad. It didn't matter anyway, did it?" He turns toward Luc and me, perched on either side of the glass. Justin's eyes penetrate my skin and make it feel like insects are crawling on top of it.

I toss him my own scathing gaze. "Auntie Elaine died because of you."

Justin's lip pulls back in a snarl as his shoulders hunch. It's an unfamiliar expression on his smooth and calm face. "She died because of *her*. We were supposed to be a team. Partners. She was willing to let my father *die* because of her belief about what was pure or impure. So I put her in a position where her family was on the line so she could feel an ounce of the desperation that I felt. And if she cared about me the way I cared about her, she would have understood. But she didn't." By the time Justin finishes, he's near shouting.

I knew there was something extra going on with Justin and Auntie Elaine, but the way he talks about it is so hacked. He expected her to just do whatever he wanted. Like that's what love is. I'm not an expert, but I'm pretty sure that's *not* what it is. "Then he died," I say.

"Yes, sorry for yelling," Justin says, voice terse. "Then she was gone too. And I was alone with something missing in my life, and I couldn't remember what it was. Do you know how frustrating that is? To feel this never-ending grief and not know why?"

I shift on the spot. I don't want to hear him talk about her this way. Like he misses her. Like he actually cared about her the way he says he did.

"She wiped my surface files, but there were hidden layers. That's the beautiful thing about data. It's reliable. Once I started remembering more, I was able to find backup videos of our trials." Justin lets out a sigh. "I made the mistake of thinking she would always be here to help, so I never put my full effort into discovering how to modify a witch's gift without an existing genetic relationship. After my memories began to return, I waited, hoping Elaine's ability would cycle through, but decided it was better to create what I wanted. Find the closest genetic match and make an attempt."

"Lauren."

"Yes. Not a great match, but easier to access since she was in the system already and had frequent runaway attempts to cover a disappearance if things went badly."

From the start, he knew that what he was doing could kill Lauren. Had prepared for it. And had done it anyway.

An up arrow pops onto the screen above the elevator. Justin smiles, all white teeth. "That will be them." He stands up from his chair and plants his hands on his hips.

"Don't do this," Luc begs. "Please."

The elevator dings, and Justin glances over at me. "I appreciate your cooperation."

How the hell am I going to get us out of this?

CHAPTER THIRTY-THREE

The elevator door opens to reveal Keisha, Alex, and Granny. My cousins are still in their Caribana outfits, headpieces and everything. Their eye makeup is smudged, and the sequined outfits are too joyful for the occasion. Granny stands straight and proud as always.

Justin clears his throat. "You're here to help with a Matriarch ceremony since I've missed catching Voya before her Calling. She will take the title from Ava and be granted a wish, which she will use to attain her late aunt's gift. Any interference will result in nasty consequences for Eden."

His explanation is neat and tidy. It hides the ugly bit about Granny needing to die for me to take on the title but leaves in the twisted threat against my baby sister.

But Granny is a Matriarch. She must have dozens of alternative ways for Justin to get what he wants. "I'm sure my grandma has other spells we could do to achieve the same effect."

Granny's voice is flat when she says, "No."

"There *must* be some other ceremony or spell," I push.

"There are two ways to acquire a past gift: through the natural passage of time or by an ancestor granting a request. If we had other ways to get strong gifts, we would have never needed his help in the first place," Granny says, striding over to me. "Why is my granddaughter in here hooked up to that thing?" She gestures toward Eden, still locked in the glass case with Luc.

I've never heard Granny call Eden that.

My baby sister presses herself to the glass, crying out for Granny. Tears spring to my eyes.

"To ensure your cooperation," Justin says to my grandma.

This isn't happening. It can't. There must be something that can help us. "What about your gift?" I hiss just loud enough for Granny to hear.

She lets out a soft laugh and offers nothing else.

Justin clears his throat and taps on his wrist where our monitors sit. "Just in case you're thinking about doing anything untoward."

I stare at the monitor. My brain hadn't gotten that far, but of course, if I didn't have it on, I could try and cast something on the sly. Bite the inside of my cheeks for blood or something. After all, I'm a witch now. But even if I had taken mine off before, Justin would have just had another one waiting for me. He had enough to outfit our entire family with them.

Both of Luc's arms are shaking with the force of his clenched fingers. "You lied about *everything*," he hisses at his mentor.

"Sometimes lies are just the little bit of sugar you need to get a bitter medicine down. You were never going to accept what we need to do here for scientific advancement. You're too empathetic for that. Not a bad trait, just not useful right now." Justin waves a hand at me. "Now, why don't you get in a circle and begin? I'll give you lots of time to say your goodbyes, no rush on that. But rest assured that you won't leave here today without having completed this ritual."

No.

I snap my eyes to Granny. She must have a way out of this. Something.

Alex and Keisha are looking at her in the same way.

451

"Granny . . . ," Alex says.

Keisha looks between the two of us. "You have a plan, right? To get out of this?"

I don't want Granny to die.

Who will pester me about getting my deliveries done on time?

Who will stand in the kitchen and boss us around during our morning routine?

Who will make bake and salt fish for breakfast with me on Christmas Day?

Who will be my grandma if she's gone?

My eyes must be shining because Granny's soften in return. She gestures to me, Keisha, and Alex. "Are we doing this, or not? Let's get in the circle," she says in her usual bossy voice.

"*Please* stop this," Luc says to Justin. "We can figure out a way to replicate the gift without doing the ceremony."

His sponsor lets out a loud sigh. "This is what I was never able to teach you. There are costs to scientific advances. Not everything can be ethical. The idea that it can is a fallacy." He gestures at Luc. "Was it ethical to take you from your home and parents and bring you here? Maybe not. But if one day you change the future of genetic manipulation with what you learned here, won't it be worth it? That's the part of the picture you're missing."

"Does it also not matter that I can't even have a conversation with my parents without arguing? That I've forgotten how to speak my own language because you told me it wasn't important? If the outcome is good, are the consequences irrelevant?"

"You've always been such an idealist."

"You want her grandmother to *die* so she can get some sort of magic gift, and *I'm* the idealist?"

Justin laughs, loud and booming, so hard that he clutches at his stomach. "That's why I chose you as my successor. You've never been afraid to call me out on my bullshit."

Hope rises in my chest, and I swivel wide eyes between Luc and Justin. Hack me, did he actually manage to convince him?

"But I disagree," Justin says with a shrug. "I am helping us evolve as a species. This is how scientific discoveries are made. I can't yet explain magic to you with science in a way you'll believe, but you'll see it firsthand when this happens. That's how I learned."

"You can't kill her!" Luc cries.

"I am not killing her," Justin says back, exasperated. "This is a sacrifice. You know, I picked you up as a child playing with robots, and I treated you like I thought you should a child. It was a mistake. You never grew out of it. You have childish thoughts and ideas about the world. We are going to have to work on that before you take over."

Luc gnashes his lip between his teeth. "I thought you were a visionary."

Justin, his face impassive, stares at him. "And now?"

"I think you're a murderer who happens to be a genius and who is so scared of death that he's prepared to stomp out anyone in his way to achieve immortality."

His sponsor smiles. "I didn't like my dad much either until I understood him. You'll grow out of it." He gestures to us. "Go ahead, say your goodbyes and then complete the ceremony."

Luc and I look at each other, but then Luc looks away. He can talk all he wants, but he can't change this any more than I can. Justin has the power here.

Granny taps on the glass case before turning to Justin. "Let me in so I can say goodbye to my granddaughter."

"Say it through the glass," he says back, voice firm.

She huffs and presses her hand against the glass, where Eden lines up her little fingers. "Be a strong girl. And behave for your parents, okay?"

My little sister nods her head, tears and snot sliding down her face.

"Good girl."

Granny walks over to the middle of the room. Me, Keisha, and Alex follow her. Keisha chokes out a sob and throws herself at Granny. Alex follows, and they curl against her. I mean to stand apart from them, to punish myself for not killing Luc and bringing this upon us, but I can't. If this is my last chance to hug my grandmother, I'm not going to miss it.

Granny squeezes us back. There's a strange scent on her collar like smoke. Probably from the vendors cooking at Caribana. It seems like years have passed since the parade.

I catch a shine in her eyes that disappears when I look too long. "Okay, get back, let's do this." Her voice switches to her usual Granny-in-charge tone. "Organize your intention. We'll need something to draw blood." She directs the last bit to Justin.

He comes forward with a penknife and slices a shallow cut on the palms of everyone in the circle. It's the sort of thing someone who didn't grow up in a magical community would do. In rituals where we need to hold hands, we slice across our fingertips and let the blood drip onto our palms. Cutting in the middle of the hand just guarantees a lengthy and painful healing. It makes everything sting that much more.

Justin doesn't know or care about magic. What it means to our family. Nothing about the culture or history. He only cares about power.

"Granny!" Eden cries, her little voice carrying across the room. Tiny fists banging on the glass.

Luc shakes his head at Justin, tears spilling that he wipes away furiously. "Let her in! You're seriously not going to let her hug her granddaughter goodbye?"

"Why? So you can run out and interfere?"

"I won't do anything!" Luc screams. "I promise. I won't do anything—just let her say goodbye."

Justin presses his lips into a line.

"Please!"

The CEO turns toward his computers, and my heart sinks.

Until the glass doors slide open.

Me and my cousins hop away from Granny so that she can shuffle into the glass case. She tugs Eden up into her arms and squeezes her into a huge bear hug.

"That's enough," Justin says. "Get out of the box."

Granny puts Eden back down on the chair and pauses to stare at Luc. "Thank you."

"Please don't," Luc croaks.

"Too bad. I already thanked you."

She walks back out of the glass case, and Justin has the door shut soundly behind her. Luc lets out a shaky exhale. Eden is still crying, but not as hard as before her hug.

I was only a year older than her when we lost Grandad.

This can't be happening.

We gather in a circle and join hands. Me, Granny, Keisha, and Alex.

"I'm sorry. I thought I was making the right choice," I whisper to Granny. From the start, I had it right, but I didn't do it.

She lets out a breath. "You never wanted to kill him. Remember what you said to me at that cooking competition? You were relieved."

A sob releases from my throat.

"That's why I stopped you that day in the kitchen."

My eyes flare wide, and my cousins blink at Granny. "What?" I choke.

"I borrowed Cathius's gift. He can give people a little push." She laughs a little. "He's not the biggest fan of it, but it's useful."

Luc said that something moved him so I couldn't land the killing blow. In the vision, he seemed to dodge on his own, but he didn't do that in real life. Granny did. "You borrowed Uncle's gift?" Borrowing gifts is not a Matriarch power I've ever heard of, but maybe it's been her own gift all along.

"I stopped you from doing something I knew you didn't want to. I kept trying to protect you from that stain I put on myself when I killed that woman. It's why we did that ritual to save Eden."

"Ritual to save Eden?" I look around at my cousins, who seem as confused as I am. "What does that mean?"

"We sacrificed a life to tie our magic to the house and counteract your task. As long as our home stands, we'll have magic, and Eden will live. If you failed, you would have never been a witch, and magic in our lineage would have died out, but Eden would live, and we would keep what we had. You were supposed to wait for us before going to Caribana so we could tell you everything. You hadn't even talked about the boy for a week, and we were sure you just weren't going to do it."

The scent on Granny. It's not smoke from food cooking. It's ash. The smell of the impure. Only the people who participate in the ritual and benefit from the kickback magic have that stench. It's why us kids don't stink of it. Why none of us realized what they had done.

That was why Mom was so adamant that we not leave without them. She didn't want to tell me what they were doing when she woke me up in case I tried to stop it. They assumed that I would fail, and they would come home and be the heroes who saved the day. They went behind my back and took a life to get around my task.

My family went to Johan's basement and drove knives into the body of someone's parent, friend, or partner. The blood drained out of their victim while they claimed their intention.

I grind my teeth together. "And if the house falls?"

A shadow looms over Granny's face. If our magic is tied to the house and a disaster destroys it, then everyone in the family loses magic and Eden will die. They didn't fix anything. They put shitty Band-Aid gel over it.

And that also means that I trapped Keis in the house for *nothing*. I destroyed her future to save Eden, but her life wasn't even in danger anymore. It was only once Mom and Granny had time to read my message that they realized their mistake. That's why Mom sent me those frantic messages. But it was too late.

I suck in a harsh sob. My chest throbs. "Why would you tell me this now? Why would you make me sparked as shit with you right as you're about to die?"

Granny gives me a sad smile. "Because I regret that I didn't believe in you when Mama Jova did. She knew you would find a way to complete your task. I don't know what you did, but she made sure to come tell me that you passed. I was too scared to let you make your own choices. I didn't trust you. And I'm sorry."

I swallow. Granny apologizing to me is not something I ever predicted. I don't want it. Not like this. Not because she's going to die. She may know that I passed, but I'm sure she doesn't know what it cost to do it. Otherwise, she would have mentioned it. Now things are even worse. Because not only did I have to lock Keis in the house, but now that house makes us all vulnerable. "You didn't trust me!" I snap back, hands trembling as they grip hers. "That means you can't die. You have to make it up to me. Borrow someone else's gift. Fix this."

"That's not how it works." She lets out a breath. "I trust you this time. Do a better job at being Matriarch than I did."

"How can I? I'll mess everything up."

"You won't. I would have chosen you, even outside of these circumstances."

My eyes go wide. "*What?* But Mom. Or Auntie? Or Keis?"

"No." Granny smiles at me. "I knew it would be you since you were six years old."

"I don't understand."

"Your dad had just left. You were crushed. I could see you hurting, but you pushed through. You were there to cheer up your mom by helping with her hair obsession, you would mediate fights between your cousins, and you kept Alex company after that mess with Vacu. You even comforted me when I lost your grandad. You have always lived for the family more than you lived for yourself." She squeezes my hand. "Being a Matriarch means understanding how you lead us into the future."

"I don't know how to do that."

Granny snorts. "You know it better than me. Because when it came down to it, I folded under the possibility of you and Eden hurting. I didn't trust in the ancestors the way I'm supposed to. I haven't since Elaine." She screws up her eyes. "I am no longer the Matriarch that I said I would be when I took the title and pledged purity." She presses her lips into a grim smile. "Eleven years ago, when Mama Jova came to see me, she said, 'I believe in your choice and I'll help her.' It didn't make any sense at the time. I didn't settle on you until a year later, after all. Then she gave you a task that I thought was impossible, and once again I couldn't trust her and believe in you. When she came to tell me you had passed, I understood where I went wrong. You proved you could do better than I ever could."

My cheeks burn from the heat of tears sliding down them. "I don't care what kind of Matriarch you said you were going to be. You are the best grandma I could have had."

Alex and Keisha nod their heads furiously. Keisha tries to speak but can't through her tears.

Granny smiles. "Good to go out on top."

We begin.

I try to memorize the feel of Granny's hand wrapped around mine. Our intention rises, and the magic follows. I keep squeezing her fingers. Desperate to hold on to her.

How many times have I held her hand? When she used to walk me to Johan's school when I was little. When we praised the ancestors at Christmastime. When she cried at Grandad's funeral.

The light that surrounds us hurts to watch, and through it, tears slide down Granny's face.

"You're afraid," I whisper.

She shakes her head. "No, I'm angry."

"At me?"

I get a glare for that. "I'm mad because I never did enough to be a Mama. I won't be able to guide you as a Matriarch. I'll miss the beautiful moments of your life."

"You can imagine them. I'm going to be a famous astronaut."

Granny lets out a bark of a laugh. "Is that so?"

"Yup!" I force mirth into my voice for her.

Her eyes slide shut and the lines of her face smooth out. "I don't care what you do, only that you do it for you. Not just the family." She squeezes my hand. "Promise me that."

"I promise."

"For real, girl! Don't just say shit because I'm dying."

I grip Granny's hand as hard as she holds mine. "I *promise*."

A smile spreads across her lips.

I keep squeezing her fingers even after her hand goes slack in mine.

I clench my eyes shut. I want to believe that this is just another terrible vision. A trick.

But I know it's not.

I open my eyes, not to Justin's office but to a hospital room. The walls are a stark white, and there's an old Black man sitting in his bed with a tray of food pulled toward him. He looks at me. "Are you my nurse?"

I blink and turn around, searching the small space for someone. The door opens and Auntie Elaine bustles in wearing scrubs the exact teal shade of the NuGene logo.

She knocks the door closed with her hip and smiles at the man. "Hello, Mr. Grant."

"I'm ready for my bath now."

"Can you finish your lunch first?"

He narrows his eyes at the green peas left on his tray. From the dregs of brown on there, I figure there was potato and meat with some sort of gravy. "Not a huge fan of peas."

Auntie looks around the room, then lifts the tray and dumps the peas into the garbage, covering the evidence with a couple of tissues. Mr. Grant smiles at her.

"We won't tell anyone. Our secret," she says.

He squints at me. "What about her?"

"She won't say anything either. Right, Voya?"

"I won't!" I blurt out.

"Do you mind if I take a minute to talk to my niece?" Auntie says to Mr. Grant. "Then we'll do your bath?"

He bobs his head and digs a tablet out from the drawer next to him. "Take your time."

Auntie straightens and walks over to me.

"What is this?" I look around at the huge glass windows and white sheets. "This place . . ."

"It's my space. When you communicate with the ancestors, we choose somewhere to meet. Often a memory. Mr. Grant was my favorite patient when I worked at Bridgepoint Health."

The same hospital where Justin's dad died. They did meet here.

She tilts her head and regards me. "You've grown into such a lovely young woman. Granny must be proud."

My face warms at the same time that tears spring to my eyes. "Can you bring her back?"

"I can't change the past." Her eyes soften. "But that's not what you came to ask me for, is it?"

"Justin wants me to inherit your gift. It's the only way to protect the family."

"Is it? If you want my gift, I'll give it to you, but is that truly what you want?"

What *do* I want?

I do this for Justin and then what? I've never been able to envision my future, but now I imagine it. I picture being forced to do his research while he holds my family over my head. I look into Auntie's eyes and see the future she tried to avoid, now made mine. But I need to do something, or Granny died for nothing.

"Think about it, Vo. Really," Auntie says, her voice earnest. "What do you want for *you*?"

I'm taken back to that streetcar ride with Luc where he asked me the same thing. Back then, I told him that I wanted to help my family.

My broken family.

But it was always more.

Because Mom, Dad, Granny, Keis, Auntie Elaine, and everyone in the house aren't the only family that I've ever had. Once, I had more. I had Lauren. I had all the Carters in her little family unit. And the Davises. I had birthday parties where Baileys held me up to chocolate cakes to blow out candles. I went to BBQs where Jameses pinched my cheeks and snuck me extra dessert. I used to know Lee as more than just a woman abandoned by her family, working in the basement of Dixie Mall.

My family used to be an entire community.

I want exactly what Auntie Elaine wanted. To make our community, our bigger family, better.

I stare at Auntie Elaine, whose gaze softens. "I always knew that we had the same dream. I just had to wait for you to give yourself permission to dream it."

"If you couldn't do it, how can I?" I whisper. "I—I could barely complete my task, I—"

"But you did complete it, didn't you?"

I swallow.

"I didn't want you kids to remember me because I didn't want what I did to ever hold you back. I didn't want my failure to stop you." She shakes her head. "But I didn't count on how much it would hurt you. And you, Voya, have felt the changes that my death brought more keenly than anyone else in this family. You see the cracks that everyone wants to look away from. And more, you want to fix them. And you can start with right here and right now. Don't make this decision based on what Justin wants. Make it based on what *you* want."

For the first time, I let myself feel the dream that I'd hidden inside.

Granny is gone. Keis is trapped. Our house is tied to our magic. Lauren is dead. I can't fix any of those things because they're in the past.

And just like the recipe contest, I can't use what Auntie or Granny did. Their time is gone. Granny said that being a Matriarch means understanding how I lead the family into the future.

I don't think she ever imagined that I would want to change the future of a family so much larger than our own. To bring our community back together and make it something that any Black witch family could be proud of. And it starts right here, with Justin Tremblay.

He has his own dreams that he's fighting for the same way that I am.

What does he want? The genetic modification gift? No. He

wants to change our genetics to live longer. To avoid the sort of death his father had.

He wants to be immortal.

I won't kill him. I don't want to shed any blood, even without his threat to Eden. There must be a way he can get what he wants without having the ability to come after us anymore.

We just need to be able to contain him. Which is easier said than done. We can't just command him like he's a . . .

My eyes flare wide and jerk up to meet Auntie Elaine's. "The NuSap unit," I breathe. "In Justin's office, there's a prototype. Could you transfer his mind into it?"

"Is that your wish?"

He would live, and without his physical body, his mind could go on forever. Justin's neural networks would remain intact so the genetic modification machine wouldn't trigger and harm Eden, because what is a neural network if not electricity? And we would have control over him. I could limit his programming to keep him from doing anything harmful to the family and shut off the remote capabilities so he couldn't connect to his own computers and escape. I would keep him on the local network. As secure as our family almanac.

In my future, I see us free of his influence. The witch community in this city that I love coming together to support each other. And I'm there to help lead the way.

"Voya?" Auntie tilts her head to the side.

"I need it to look like I killed him. Luc can't know he's alive. No one outside our family can know." If they did, they would come after him and maybe help him continue his quest to abuse our magic.

Auntie gives a solemn nod. "When you strike a killing blow, his mind will travel not to the place where the dead go but will instead join with the circuits of the prototype. He will live on through it." She presses her hand against my cheek. Her expression is something between joy and grief. "Please tell my brother to think of me with happiness. His anger hurts, even this far away."

"I will."

She beams at me with a smile so like Dad's that it brings tears to my eyes. "I cannot wait to see the Matriarch you become."

No sooner are the words out of her mouth than the world goes dark.

When I open my eyes next, I'm back in Justin's office, and Granny's body is slumped on the floor with a slight smile still on her lips. I press my hands to my mouth to keep from crying out.

It's so much like how it was in my vision in the kitchen.

Except this is real.

Justin's eyes are alight, the brilliant red bionics pulsing with his excitement as he stalks toward me. He holds the portable DNA machine tight in his hands, ready to check that I have Auntie Elaine's gift. Just behind him, Mama Jova stands in her usual naked glory.

She isn't here for nothing. This is my first moment as Matriarch of this family, and the decision that will mark how we move forward.

I know what I have to do, but not how to do it. This is my one opportunity to force Justin's mind from his body to the NuSap prototype.

I stare at my bloody palm, back up at him, and over to Mama Jova in the corner.

She gave the people on her plantation a new life when she used blood to slay those men. A skill that no one else in the family has ever been able to use. The pure ones could only cast with their blood, and the impure ones could only manage to do it with the blood of others. Neither of them could command enough power to do what Mama Jova did. That's what Mom said. It wasn't a pure or impure ability. It was something in between.

All magic is.

Finally, I understand what Mama Jova meant. She used to get caught up in decisions and choices. Afraid to make the wrong one, the same way I was. Except there aren't always good or bad decisions. Only options, and the ability to choose them.

What Mama Jova did to save those people wasn't about being pure or impure. Neither was my choice not to kill Luc. Things don't fall into neat categories like that. And being one or the other doesn't preclude you from being morally right or wrong otherwise.

Like Mama Jova said, I don't have two weeks to make a decision this time. I only have one moment.

In that split second, I make my choice.

Magic isn't complicated. It has always been and always will be nothing more than blood and intent. Pure and impure are just restrictions that we've put on ourselves. It's not about being *bad* or being *good*. *We* decide who we are, not the magic we practice. And I need to trust myself enough to know, however I choose to use my power, it'll be for the right reasons.

To reunite our community, I need to go beyond the labels of pure and impure that we've used to stay apart. I need to honor the past while forging a different future.

I need to be something new.

I raise my hand in Justin's direction and slice my arm down with a scream that rips my throat raw.

Blood gathers from my palm, from Keisha's and Alex's hands, and Granny's limp hand on the ground. In a single crimson rope, the blood shoots out and snakes around Justin's neck. It squeezes tight, and layer by layer, faster than my eyes can follow, slices straight through. Like the plumes of a sorrel flower, blood blooms and splatters across the white floor. Eden's screams pierce through my skull.

Justin's eyes empty, and his knees hit the floor. As if in slow motion, he slumps to the ground with blood pooling around the clean slice in his neck. His head rolls to a stop less than a foot away.

A sound invades my ears over the shrill screech of Eden's screams. A low whimper like a dog dying alone in a gutter. I turn my head toward it, and Luc is there, unmoving, staring at his sponsor father's broken body.

"I'm sorry," I whisper. "I needed to choose."

Luc isn't paying attention to me, gaze glued to Justin. Tears stream from his eyes as he mumbles, "Why couldn't you listen to me? Why couldn't you find another way?"

I didn't know it would look like this. That it would be this real. He's not actually dead, I know that. He's in the body of the prototype. I haven't taken a life, but it's hard to feel that when I'm staring at his corpse.

I swallow down vomit and shuffle over to Justin's computer. I push the button to open the glass case and put a paperweight from his desk on top of it so the door can't close after. Entering the box, I go to unhook Eden from the machine, only to find that she's already disconnected. My neck snaps toward Luc, who's still looking at Justin's body.

"I took them out when he was distracted with going to check your DNA after the ritual," he mumbles. "I just . . . hadn't figured out how to let you know."

I swallow and reach out my hand to Eden. Right up until the end, he was still trying to help us. My little sister's fingers wrap around mine, and we leave the glass box.

With blood still leaking from my hands, I imagine both Granny's and Justin's bodies burning and dissolving into ashes. I then pull the iron from Granny's bones to make her a metal urn.

I can't give the same courtesy to Justin's body. There can be no evidence. I force a hole into one of the windows and siphon his ashes through it. Letting them disappear into the wind. I couldn't break down his bionic lenses. They lie on the floor. All that's left of him.

Alex picks up Granny's urn with shaking fingers while Keisha gapes at me. We don't have this kind of spell bandwidth.

Mama Jova said things changed when she understood what magic really was. That without the restrictions of what was pure or impure, a good witch could become great. I wonder if this is what she meant.

I stumble as I move toward the NuSap prototype. Raising my hand, I try to slice open the glass case, but nothing happens.

My legs give out. Alex and Keisha catch me before I hit the ground. Even Eden is doing her best to help hoist me up. "We need to bring the prototype with us."

"Why?" Keisha's eyes are wide and strained.

I don't say anything. All I do is stare at her. Somehow, she gets it, even though she doesn't.

"Alex, help me break the glass." Keisha raises her bloody hand and Alex follows. Both of them manage to slice open the dome holding the NuSap. The two halves thump with a hollow thud as they hit the floor.

Alex lets go of me to grab the NuSap unit and controller, handing Granny's urn to Eden, who clutches it in her tiny hands. I lean my weight fully on Keisha and turn to Luc. "How do I get the rest of my family out?"

He whips his head toward me and there, that's the Luc I first met. But more. It's the Luc I imagined once he knew the truth. That hateful twist to his mouth and narrowing of his eyes.

He finally leaves the box and goes to Justin's array of screens, typing rapidly. Footage of my family appears on one of them, and the glass door keeping them in the cell opens. Luc snatches a wireless mic from Justin's desk and speaks into it. "Your family is coming. Meet them outside." I admire the strength in his voice. He wipes the tears on his face with the back of his hand.

On-screen, Mom and Auntie lead the charge out of their glass prison.

There's no hesitation as Luc sinks onto the floor on the spot where Justin's body used to be. He picks up the bionics that once belonged to his mentor and cradles them in his palm.

"Let's go." In front of the elevator, I pause and gaze at the boy I fell in love with. "For what it's worth, I'm sorry. But don't forget that we both lost someone today."

Luc shakes his head. "You lost someone. I lost everyone."

I step into the elevator, but Luc doesn't look up again. He stays in the same spot, growing smaller as the doors slide shut. I'm left staring at stainless steel.

It's the end of Luc and me.

It's the beginning of something else.

That night, I set up the app on my phone and turn on the NuSap prototype. Its eyes flicker open, and they're an unexpected blue-gray shade that makes my chest ache.

When it catches me in its gaze, the eyes narrow, and it snarls, "What did you do to me?" The voice is stilted and machinelike, but the tone is familiar.

"I made your dream come true."

CHAPTER THIRTY-FOUR

I'm floating in a tank with no end and no beginning. Except we don't have the money for a bath that big. My toes tap against the foot of the tub, and I keep my hands crossed over my chest, so my arms don't bump into the sides.

In my mind, I see the blood from my palm racing around Justin's neck and squeezing. This wasn't a faceless man who I watched die in a basement. I knew him. And even though I didn't kill him, I ruined him.

It's been a couple of weeks since we rushed from that white office with the NuSap unit and Granny's ashes in tow, leaving Luc behind. I've never heard Mom bawl like that. Auntie stormed away, and in the distance, flames shot into the sky. Uncle didn't speak for days.

And Keis ...

She stays in her room, mostly. She's not even able to send NuGene the message that she's turning down the internship.

Justin was declared missing, and they announced Luc as the successor in his sponsor dad's absence. Sixteen years old and he's the CEO of a billion-dollar company. He's not alone, either. He's keeping his siblings by his side, funding their immigration processes and helping them stay in the country. He's blocked everyone in the family, but I've seen him in public feeds and on billboards downtown. Now the three sponsor siblings stand together as a unit instead of Luc on his own, bonded by the loss of their mentor.

I tried asking around to see if anyone had a gift that might help with Juras's recovery, but it didn't matter in the end. His symptoms cleared shortly after Luc was named CEO, and he's business as usual now. Whatever power Mama Jova put in my hands wasn't meant to last. Sometimes I think about what it would have been like if I had believed in her and myself that night on the balcony. But it hurts too much to dwell on, so I try not to.

Already, Luc's been making changes at NuGene. Alex said that now her ID brings up XX the way it should.

Luc is going to be a very different leader than Justin was.

He hasn't contacted me. But we haven't suffered any threats from him in the fallout. Maybe because he's scared that the same thing that happened to his mentor could happen to him.

I like to think it's because he's better than that.

When I stare down at my chest, the scars from the Davises' rite still stand out on my skin. I don't know that they'll ever fade enough to not be noticeable. Even if they did, I would never forget.

Two Black people died at Caribana. One, a man, the one who the cop shot. Lucas Pumb. The other was an older woman who got trampled when everyone ran. Henrietta Lewis. The courts quietly charged the officer with first-degree murder and said nothing more about it. He'll probably get convicted on second. That's usually how it goes. There are consequences to killing us now that there haven't always been, but they still can't stop themselves from taking that shot. It happens less than it ever has. To the point where some people want to claim it doesn't happen at all anymore. But it does. It did. It makes me think of Mama Bess's words: "It was better, but it was not good."

When news feeds do talk about Caribana, they show videos of drunk people at carnival, fighting. Like it's our fault. Us and our inherent violence that's apparently ingrained in the color of our skin. Some were called out on it and deleted their feed posts. Once news of Justin's disappearance hit, they stopped reporting on it altogether.

I know it isn't, but it feels like it's my fault. The Davises tried to protect us, and I ruined it. I mourn for Lucas and Henrietta along with Granny. The family does too. People in the community hang their heads lower. We all feel it. And we won't forget as easily.

Meanwhile, Justin spends his days doing a mix of pacing and writing in the basement where he's programmed to stay, his electronic activity regulated to a small corner of our local network far away from the almanac. I don't trust him with a tablet, so I got him a roll of paper and a pen.

Dad asked, his voice a vicious and spiteful thing, why we don't shut him off and leave it at that.

But that's no better than if I killed him, and I won't. Even after all the pain he's caused. We can be better. Justin is free to be Justin, but he isn't able to manipulate my family. I like to think that maybe these limitations will mean he uses his genius for good. That has yet to be proven.

I press the heating button, and the jets warm my cooling bathwater.

The door to the bathroom bangs open, and Keisha stomps inside. The white dress she wears is strapless and skintight. "Get out of the damn tub."

My stomach twists. I push myself up on my elbows, stand, and reach out for a towel.

"That easy?" she says, blinking. "I thought I would have to drag you out."

"Better to be done with it."

She holds out a long white gown, lace, with a low back. My Calling dress. It's tradition to wear it a second time for the Pass at the end of your Coming-of-Age.

I slip it over my head and accept the crumpled underwear she hands me. Touching my thumb to the metal tooth in my mouth, I bite down. The three or so drops of blood that fall are enough. I dump a wad of Thomas Brand All-in-One Perfect Curls in my hair, and let the magic do the rest, moisturizing, stretching, defining, and drying the strands in one go. Perfect in seconds.

It's the same metal that was in Granny's tooth. I fished it out of her ashes and used magic to fit it overtop an existing canine. It's a way to carry her wherever I go. Mom thinks it's macabre.

I smile at Keisha. It's real, the smile. Nothing is perfect. But we're safe and together. That's more than I gave Luc. "Let's go."

We walk into the hallway and down the steps into the entryway. I make a quick pit stop into the kitchen to check on the food keeping warm for dinner after the ceremony. The scent of slow-cooked curried goat wafts through the room as I peek into the new chrome oven. Bones float naked in the sauce. The meat's dropped right off. There's some macaroni pie staying warm alongside it and a tray of pone. I even got a little deep fryer, ready with sliced plantains to drop down and fry fresh right before we're ready to eat.

I'm not ready to make bake again. I keep thinking of that day when Granny and I were in the cooking stall making it together, and before that, way back to the two of us with Keis, with Granny teaching us how to knead dough for the first time. The Voya then had no real idea how her future would turn out.

Now I'm a different sort of girl.

The family is gathered in the backyard around a rent-a-pool— one of those smart storage boxes they dump at your house filled with treated water for pool parties. Around the side of the pool, there's a landing that everyone is standing on. It brings the edge of the pool to their waists.

I wanted to get a little one inside the house so Keis could join in. She let me know that she wouldn't be coming either way. But apparently, it has to be done outdoors anyway. For tradition.

Priya smiles at me from the pool landing. Granny would have never allowed her to be here. As far as I'm concerned, she's my family, blood or not. Priya and Dad's pledge even transferred to me when Granny died. I feel the threads of their magic along with everyone else like extra fingers and toes. It's a sensation that I haven't gotten used to yet.

Dad stands next to Priya with a small smile and Eden on his hip. She's too big to be carried, but he does it anyway. Since I told him Auntie Elaine's message, I've noticed more of a lift to his shoulders. He's done well at pretending that the man who's to blame for her death isn't now living in our basement.

There's a bit of a shift among my family. I notice that now. When I come into the room, everyone stands straighter. I've heard the muffled conversations and arguments the adults have when they think I'm not around. None of them ever predicted a future where I would be Matriarch at sixteen years old. The power to tug at their magic or affect their abilities with my mood aren't things they want a teenager to have control over. And yet they can't do anything about it.

Mom pulls me into a hug and presses a kiss against my forehead. "I'm proud of you. You've worked hard."

"You've done well." Dad shuffles over and waits until Mom is done for his turn.

Hugging Mom is natural. Hugging Dad is like breathing in water. Awkward and hard at first. Then that moment of zen in the middle, where you feel almost comfortable. But the longer it goes on, the more strained it becomes. I break from his arms.

I look at Keis's bedroom window, not expecting her to be there. But she is. She stands with her hair in its signature pineapple bun. I give her a little wave that she doesn't return.

My shoulders relax. At least she came. That's progress.

Uncle gives me a boost into the pool.

I don't know why I bothered to do my hair.

I push my stomach up and spread my arms and legs out to keep afloat.

Around me, my family slices across the tips of their fingers and lets the blood drip onto their palms before they join hands. They begin a chant of the words "Blood to blood." Their voices glide over me as the magic rises to bring my gift to the surface.

At the same time that Mama Jova gives me my gift under the water, she'll announce it to my family above me. We'll learn what my power will be together.

I close my eyes and enjoy the sensation of being in water that truly feels endless. A hand brushes against mine, and my eyes snap open. Floating in the water next to me is Mama Jova. For a moment, I just look at her. She looks younger up close. I'm sixteen now, and she'll be sixteen forever. Mama Jova never got to grow beyond the moment that changed her life. I have a chance that she never did.

She reaches out and holds my hand. "I knew you were a strong girl." Her eyes drift to the surface of the water. "You've suffered for your family. I wish you didn't have to hurt more. I'm weary of suffering and surviving. But there's still more pain in your future. Will you go through it to help those beyond your family, despite knowing that the path will be hard?"

"Yes."

I don't need to think about this choice. My future is to lead the family into something new, something better. I owe it not just to Granny or Auntie, but to myself. Whatever gift I get, it can only help.

She smiles and grips my fingers tight. "Here are your gifts."

Gifts? Plural?

Mama Jova fades from my sight, and I sink to the bottom of the pool. I get no warning as my eyes roll back into my head.

Hospitals feel like they should be silent. Especially on a floor like this. Instead, there's the persistent beeping of a heart rate monitor coupled with the sounds of nurses speed-walking down the halls in sneakers and scrubs in colors too bright for the occasion.

The window next to the bed takes up the entire far wall and shimmers in a way that hints at touch-screen capabilities. You're supposed to change the view to anything you want. Imagine that you're in Peru on a group hike, or in the Maldives above a waterfall, or maybe you're on a trip to your childhood cottage in the Muskokas.

You can imagine yourself anywhere except Bridgepoint Health Rehabilitation Hospital, in the Palliative Care unit, waiting to die.

I step forward, and my feet make no sound. The chart at the foot of the bed says "Tremblay, Peter."

Justin's father is hooked up to an IV drip with morphine pumping through it. His joints and bones are visible with his tight skin stretched over them. He looks like one wrong touch could crumble bone.

Justin sits in a chair next to the bed. Not a single bionic lens in sight. He's hunched over and staring at the floor, dressed in white chino pants and a matching plush sweater.

"I'm ready." I expect Mr. Tremblay's voice to be a croak, dry and brittle the way his body looks. Instead it's hard, confident, and strong. The voice he must have used for years in his business.

Justin hunches more. "What does that mean?"

"Don't play this game. Not with me. Not now."

"I can fix it. I'm working with this woman, and we're so close to cracking the genetic code. She's being a little . . . She has an ethical concern, but I can convince her. And—"

Mr. Tremblay curls his lip, and the disgust is so plain on his face that even I shrink back from it. "Genetics are not a code to be cracked. Your research is as fruitless as searching for the philosopher's stone."

"You don't understand. If you could see the things she does . . . Dad, people could live forever. You would never die."

"I'm ready. I've had a good life." He pins his eyes on his son. "Do you know what true immortality is? Not what you're trying to do with your genetics. *Real* immortality?"

Justin looks uncertain. "What?"

"When death comes and you're ready. It's the only forever there is."

"You're wrong! You'll be gone. It's not the same!" Justin is up on his feet, shaking his head. "You haven't seen what we could do. What I could do! What I could *be*!"

Mr. Tremblay's face crumples like a piece of paper. "I've seen enough."

Justin sinks back into his seat and stops talking.

Mama Jova appears beside me.

"What is this?" I whisper. "Why am I seeing this? Feeling this?"

"I give you the gifts of the past and the future." She gestures to Justin. "This is the past."

"But why Justin's?"

"Our past creates our future. And you are at a point in the present that can pivot and change a life. This man had a future set out in front of him, and your actions have changed it forever."

I feel like I've jumped into an ice bath instead of a lukewarm rent-a-pool. "I'm seeing this because I ruined Justin's future?"

"You changed it significantly, in a way where it can't get back on the path that it was on. The value you put on it, ruining or improving, is subjective." Mama Jova crosses her arms. "This will be a difficult journey. I needed to know you could reshape the past

476

and create a new future. That you could see them both in your mind and wield them to your benefit."

The task was more than a task. It was more than preparation for my future. More than a way I could have stopped Justin. It's a promise of the actions that will fuel my gift.

Mama Jova laces her fingers together. "When you destroy something, you also have the opportunity to create something new in its place."

I took away Keis's future, tainted our past together, but only because I know she has the strength to create another one. If she'll let me, I want to help her. To help us all. To lead the family, the entire Black witch community, into something new.

I am definitely that now. Already, I've moved beyond magic that's pure or impure. I've begun the first steps of the journey into a different world than the one I lived in before. I'll have to learn how to keep that momentum with these gifts. And maybe one day, surviving won't have to mean suffering first.

Mr. Tremblay starts to cough from his bed. A red splatter shoots from his mouth and sprays onto Justin's white sweater. Nurses run in. Justin is pushed aside. Auntie Elaine stands in the doorway with her hand over her mouth.

When Justin sees her, he snarls, "This is your fault! You could have stopped this!"

She shakes her head at him and draws herself up. "Saving him wouldn't have made him love you the way you wanted."

"Get out!" he screams.

With one last long look, she leaves.

The heart monitor stops beeping. Instead, it rings out a single, final note.

Justin yanks the plug out of the wall.

And finally.

Silence.

My eyes snap open, and I wake in the pool with a gasp. My chest heaves, and I kick out with my feet to stay afloat. Everyone in my family stares at me with wide eyes. Mom is on her knees with her hands over her mouth.

I've become the first Thomas in our entire history to be given two gifts. If I change the present enough, I can see the past that led us there, and the new future that I created when I took our old one away.

I used to be a girl whose past made it impossible to live in my present without fearing the future.

Now I'll be able to see my choices laid bare, in multiple timelines.

The ancestors must love irony.

CHAPTER THIRTY-FIVE

I keep thinking the curry scent is going to sink into the cakes. It's September, and it's still sweltering and desertlike in the Roti Roti kitchen. Johan has the air conditioning on a money-saving schedule. Every hour it creates an icy blast that cools the sweat on the back of my neck in blissful relief. After fifteen minutes it stops, then it's another hour of suffering.

During regular hours, there would be at least three other people in here moaning about it. That's one of the reasons I wake up early when I have wedding dessert platter orders—one of the new services Johan's added since I came on board.

I pull open the industrial-size oven and take out two black cakes in rectangular pans. It's sweet and soft perfection. I grab two more pans from the oven and stack them on a cart before wheeling the finished cakes over to the blast chiller.

Johan may be cheap with the air con, but he pulled out all the stops with the kitchen. I shuffled in on my first day, a month after the Pass, expecting the worst, only to stop and stare in awe at the collection of high-quality kitchen appliances.

I take a stainless-steel pot from where they hang and whip up some simple syrup—my special weapon for making moist cakes. Once the sugar and water melt together, I take it off the fire and add a couple shots of Trini-imported rum. Not as much as Auntie

Elaine would have put in hers. I'll pour it over the cooled cakes, where it'll soak in and make for a somewhat boozy dessert, as per Illenia's request. She made a point of mentioning it so many times I started to wonder if she wanted black cake or a bottle of liquor in the shape of one.

A message from Keisha flashes in front of my eyes: *Let us in.*

I set the pot of syrup onto the metal prep table in the middle of the room.

I've tasked her and Alex with doing the runs for the beauty business. With both of them doing the deliveries I used to do alone, they finish faster and have more time for their own stuff.

Grabbing a backpack full of product from under a prep table, I make my way to the front of the shop. Keisha is in jean shorts and a tube top that says, "Get Retro." Alex is in a pair of high-waisted white pants and a sheer top with enough glitter to make me squint.

I unlock the front door and let them in. Keisha lets out a huge sigh and dumps an empty backpack on the closest table.

"All done for that batch?" I exchange the empty bag for the full one.

Keisha lets out a groan as she looks at it. "Hacking Dory Bailey gave me the evil eye, and her family isn't exactly the picture of squeaky-clean purity."

I chew on my lip. Technically, I didn't kill Justin, but my avoidance of it didn't matter in the end. The adults did what they did to latch our magic to the house. None of them will talk about it, but we know the cost of impure rituals.

It took Trudy James getting one sniff of Mom at the grocery store for word to get out to the other pure families, and since then, they've been tittering over our so-called "tainted" product. Dad's attempts to smooth things over with his cousin failed too. There's no mistaking that ash scent. Everyone still buys, but we've lost those relationships Granny cultivated. No one recommends us anymore or gives our products as gifts.

That's not even the worst of the problems. There was only so much product Granny had left, and no one in the family knows what she was doing to make it so special. If she was using her gift-borrowing trick, no one knows whose gift she was borrowing or how she was using it. None of the adults even knew that was something she could do. We can sell what we have, but eventually people are going to notice that the next one is off.

I blow out a slow breath through my nose. "I'll go visit the Huangs and see if I can talk to Rowen and patch things up. If she gets on board, the others will follow."

"That's a Band-Aid solution," Alex says. "We need something more permanent. Stop bothering with pushing sales on the pure witch families and stick to non-magic folk maybe?"

"Or Voya can start putting her gifts to work and bring in some real money." Johan strolls out from the back with his hands on his hips. His face is dewy perfection even in the shitty restaurant lighting.

I pull myself up. Johan has more of an interest in my gifts than I would like. I suspect he hasn't decided how he wants to take advantage of them yet. But every time he mentions it, the hair on the back of my neck rises. "I didn't realize you were coming in early."

"I know you didn't because you got your girls here hanging out like it's social hour." He waves a hand at my cousins.

Alex crosses her arms. "You're not happy to see us?"

"We're family," Keisha insists.

Johan rolls his eyes and pokes the empty backpack. "Sales look good. If you need some new customers, I know a few people who would be interested."

Keisha's eyes go wide and she opens her mouth to respond, but stops as I hit her with a look.

She shrugs, suddenly nonchalant. "Nah, I got a bunch of feed fans clamoring for product. We've been backed up on their orders for a while."

Johan swivels his skeptical gaze between the two of us. He ends up distracted by a woman knocking on the window. "Hack me, again?"

Rena is at the window with a slick weave long enough to reach her ankles. She stares long and hard at Johan. Her face looks vicious, but the wetness of her eyes gives away her desperation.

Johan shakes his head. "I don't know what that woman thinks I can give her. Her child is dead, end of. Ain't nothing going to bring her back." He cuts his eyes to me. "That platter needs to be ready by the afternoon. You gonna have it?"

I nod.

"You go on, then. Vo's gotta work," he says to Alex and Keisha.

My cousins paste smiles on their faces. Alex grabs the backpack. "We'll see you at home later."

"I'll walk you out," I respond.

Johan disappears into the back of the shop. Rena moves away from the door as I let my cousins through it.

I avoid eye contact with her. "I'll walk to the end of the block with you."

Keisha throws a look at Rena, then turns back to me. I ignore it. Alex doesn't even bother looking at me or Rena.

We walk next to each other down the block and stop at an alley. I would rather Johan not know that I'm helping someone who he refused. I continue into the alley, but my cousins don't. They keep walking toward the bus stop to finish their deliveries.

I come face-to-face with Rena. Lauren is evident in the shape of her eyes and plump set of her mouth. My throat dries. I still miss her.

Rena sweeps her hair away from her face and swallows. "I've heard that you can help if Johan won't."

"I'll do my best. I promise I'll always try, even if I don't succeed."

She wrings her hands together. They're painted with fresh polish and pointed tips. There's pride in her, even as she's begging for help. "What do you want from me?"

I hold my hands out, and she puts hers in mine. "All I want is to help you."

All I've ever wanted is to help my family.

"I need to see what happened to my baby girl." Her voice is a firm whisper. It's like she knows what she wants and fears it.

I try not to let the relief show on my face. Glad that she craves the past, to see Lauren, instead of the future of a world where she doesn't exist. Part of me thought she might want to know if her daughter's killer is punished someday too. But maybe that's just not something that matters to her right now. Or maybe once she realizes it's the missing NuGene CEO, she'll assume that he got what was coming to him.

I haven't seen the future I created when I trapped Justin in the NuSap body. I've been too afraid to look. And a selfish part of me wants to see my friend one last time before I say goodbye forever. "The past it is."

I've been waiting for this moment.

I can't force Luc to acknowledge Auntie Elaine as the co-creator of genetic manipulation. It would cast his former sponsor in a light that I don't think he's willing to shed. That's assuming that I could get him to talk to me. I can't give my aunt the recognition that she deserves.

But right now, I can give to Lauren in death what I couldn't do when she was alive. Someone will witness what she went through. "It won't be pretty," I say.

Rena closes her eyes and squeezes my fingers. "I don't need pretty. I need the truth."

I shut my eyes and reach out for the link that bonds me to Justin. I think of Lauren as she was at her Coming-of-Age celebration—hopeful and happy. I travel down into a glass basement at NuGene where she breathed her last breath.

Impure magic has a scent. The ash of the dead. My magic doesn't smell like that. It doesn't have the scentless air of pure spells either. It's something different. So light it would be easy to miss. But sometimes I catch it, and when I inhale, I think of rows of sugarcane fresh from a burn.

Rena gasps.

I open my eyes, and two single teardrops of blood leak from hers.

I bring the intent. They bring the blood.

We both pay for the gift of magic.

ACKNOWLEDGMENTS

Thank you so much for being on this journey with me and Voya. This story was born out of a yearning for the city where I grew up, and a desire to tell the story of magic Black girls. I'm so thankful for all the support that I've gotten, from the first draft of this book to the final version.

Thank you to my mom, who has always believed in me. I was raised with the privilege of knowing that no matter what I did, she would be proud. She has always been an example of what it means to put your best foot forward, and I appreciate how hard she worked so that I could have the best life possible. Her creative pursuits inspired me and gave me the courage to pursue my own. I don't think I would be anywhere near the person I am today without her.

I also want to acknowledge all the amazing support and hype from all of my family members who got excited for the book despite not always knowing what it was about and being very confused about when it was coming out. An extra thank-you to Grandma Jo for letting me know what rotting sugarcane smells like. Since then, I have had the unfortunate experience of not only smelling but tasting this flavor, and your description was spot-on. Thank you also to my partner's family, who have been just as hype and supportive as my own.

On that note, I would like to thank my wonderful partner, who has always encouraged my writing and who has been subject to my many confusing book- and writing-related rants. And thanks to our little beagle, Beau, aka Bobo, who, of course, cannot read but kept me company during many writing sessions, and to Princess, who isn't with us anymore, but was my OG beagle writing buddy.

A huge thank-you to my agent, Kristy Hunter, who has been such a gift to know and work with. Kristy was integral in helping bring this book to the caliber that it is today, and I will be forever thankful to her for believing in my story and being willing to put in the time to make it better. I won't pretend that I'm not prone to moments of author panic, and she has always been such a positive and encouraging force on that front. She is, in every sense of the word, a dream agent.

And another momentous thank-you to my editor, Sarah McCabe, whose on-point edits constantly have me in awe, and whose support of the story has meant the world to me. She really understands the essence of Voya's journey and has worked so hard to help bring that to the world. I am so appreciative of all the love, time, and passion she put into this book.

Thank you to the entire Margaret K. McElderry and Simon & Schuster team for all their hard work and help with the book: Justin Chanda, Karen Wojtyla, Anne Zafian, Rebecca Syracuse, Katherine Devendorf, Rebecca Vitkus, Elizabeth Blake-Linn, Jen Strada, Mandy Veloso, Lauren Hoffman, Chrissy Noh, Devin MacDonald, Karen Masnica, Cassandra Fernandez, Brian Murray, Anna Jarzab, Emily Ritter, Annika Voss, Christina Pecorale and the rest of the Simon & Schuster sales team, Michele Leo and her education/library team, Lisa Morelada, Mackenzie Croft, Athena Reekers, and Jenny Lu. Thank you also to Thea Harvey for the beautiful illustration of Voya on the cover—those curls are popping and I love it.

I would also like to acknowledge my fantastic sensitivity readers, Gabe Cole Novoa and Mey Rude. Another thank you to Ava Mortier for being such a helpful early reader.

And of course, I need to mention the amazing critique partners, betas, and mentors who helped me with *Blood Like Magic* in all of its iterations. Thank you to Sione Aeschliman, who took me on as a mentee in #RevPit and made such a huge difference in the quality of my story, and was a fantastic mentor and editor. Thank you to Cassie Spires, who, in addition to being a wonderful friend, continues to read all of my manuscripts in all of their various forms, and gives me amazing and helpful critiques even when I'm grumpy about it. Thank you to Jess Creaden, who has never been afraid to tell me what I need to hear and has been cheering for this book from the start. Thank you to Kate Havas, ZR Ellor, and Emily Thiede, whose early feedback was an enormous help in shaping this story. And thank you to Fallon DeMornay, who is not only a fantastic CP and all-around human but was also a huge early supporter of Voya and this story, which I appreciate so much. On that note, an extra thank-you to the Toronto Writers Crew, who are always such an incredible source of community and support—shout-out to Louisa Onomé, Kess Costales, Ashley Shuttleworth, June Hur, Sasha and Sarena Nanua, Elora Cook, Deborah Savoy, Kelly Powell, Joanna Hathaway, Maggie Horne, Daniel Aleman, Elizabeth Urso, Sarah Rana, and Terese Mason Pierre.

Though it may seem strange, I would also like to thank the city that raised me. Toronto hasn't always been the place that I've lived, but it has always been home. As much as this book is a love letter to Black girl magic, it is also one to my hometown.

Finally, thank you to everyone who came before me that made it possible for me to be here today. My family history, like that of many Black people born in the western world, is not easy to track. There are huge chunks that are lost, maybe forever. Writing *Blood Like Magic* gave me a chance to explore what it might be like to learn from and connect to them directly in a way I never can. Just like Voya, I hope they would be proud of who I've become.

ABOUT THE AUTHOR

Liselle Sambury is a Trinidadian-Canadian author who grew up in Toronto. Her brand of writing can be described as "messy Black girls in fantasy situations." She is a social media professional and spends her free time embroiled in reality TV, because when you write messy characters, you tend to enjoy that sort of drama. She also shares helpful tips for upcoming writers as well as details of her publishing journey through a YouTube channel dedicated to demystifying the sometimes complicated business of being an author.